THE
BOOMSDAY
VERDICT

JOE PURKEY

AN ACE SLEUTH NOVEL
THE DETECTIVE WITH AN ATTITUDE

PublishAmerica
Baltimore

Hardcover 978-1-4560-7906-2
Softcover 978-1-4560-7905-5
PUBLISHED BY PUBLISHAMERICA, LLLP
www.publishamerica.com
Baltimore

Printed in the United States of America

I would like to give credit for the cover photo to
The 'Knoxville Tourism and Sports Corp.'

"LIFE IS LIKE A ROLLER COASTER; THE FIRST HALF OF YOUR LIFE IS SPENT GOING UP AND THE SECOND HALF COMING DOWN."

"WHICH IS WORSE; A COMPANY THAT IS TOO BIG TO FAIL OR A GOVERNMENT THAT IS TOO BIG TO EXCEL?"
THE AUTHOR

FOREWORD

This is a book of fiction and all the characters are figments of my imagination and any resemblance to actual persons living or dead is purely coincidental.

The greater part of this novel takes place in Knoxville, Tennessee and most of the places there are real but the events that take place at these establishments and places are not.

The report on nuclear power by the newspaper reporter Al Jameson in this book did not actually occur but is only my idea of what would have taken place if it really happened. I have, however, tried to be as factual as possible with all the data used in this fictitious report; I got much of the data from the Tennessee Valley Authority's (TVA) web site and used some of my knowledge that I learned and absorbed while designing nuclear power plants at TVA. All the characters in the report working for TVA are figments of my imagination as is, Al Jameson, the Newspaper Reporter.

I titled this book "The Boomsday Verdict" because it starts out on Boomsday in 2010 and concludes just after Boomsday in 2011. A brief description of Boomsday is given in Chapter 1.

In this book, A University of Tennessee (UT) coed was raped, brutally beaten and left for dead and a young UT (University of Tennessee) engineering student was charged with the crime. Brad Adams knew the young man personally and did not believe that he was capable of such a dastardly deed and agreed to defend him against the advice of his wife, Elizabeth, who herself is a Judge in Knox County. Brad had never tried a criminal case in his life.

Brad would go to almost any lengths to get an acquittal for someone he believed to be innocent. As a result of one of his courtroom maneuvers in the rape case, he became in danger of being disbarred.

I have taken a few liberties with our legal system I am sure, so don't use the courtroom scenes in this book to arrive at any legal conclusions.

Following this foreword is a list of central characters to enable the reader to better understand who the characters are. Many times I have been reading a book and have come upon a character whose name escapes me; causing me then to have to leaf back through dozens of pages to find out just where this character fits into scheme of things. I don't want my readers to have to do that.

LIST OF CENTRAL CHARACTERS

1. Ace Sleuth- A former struggling private detective who now works for Brad Adams
2. Paula Sleuth- Ace's wife
3. Lisa Sleuth- Paula's daughter and Ace's adopted daughter
4. Brad Adams- a very successful Knoxville Attorney
5. David Adams- Brad's son
6. Jennifer Adams — David's wife
7. David Bradford Adams —David and Jennifer's three-year old son and Brad's grandson
8. Little Ace the Second- Ace and Paula's three-year old son who was born the same day as David Bradford Adams who now goes by the name of Freddy
9. Denise Hart - Brad's Secretary-Receptionist
10. Doug Hart - Denise's husband
11. Rupert Cooper — A shady Tort Lawyer whom Brad turned the tables on and embarrassed in court by winning a $500,000 judgment against him for the very lawsuit he brought against Brad's client.
12. Alex Parker — A Financial Advisor who has an office on the same floor of The BB&T Bank Building as Brad Adams
13. Trisha Parker — daughter of Alex whose wife, Amanda was killed by a drunken driver three years ago
14. Mel Crosby — Knox County Attorney General (AG)
15. Mason Young — Knoxville Police Chief
16. Jim Satterfield- Assistant to the AG
17. Kristen Smith- University of Tennessee student who was a rape victim

PROLOGUE

Brad Adams was a wealthy former corporate attorney until he was sued by a former classmate of his at the University of Tennessee College of Law School. The former classmate, Luther Spenser, wasn't the sharpest knife in the drawer and his elevator didn't go all the way to the top floor. He practically had to cheat his way through law school in addition to riding on the coattails of what few friends he had in college. He had always been jealous of Brad in law school because Brad got such good grades without a lot if apparent effort while he himself had to struggle and cheat. In 2006, he and a former movie stunt man by the name of Bret Martin faked an accident in the parking garage beneath the BB&T bank building in which Brad has his office. Bret stepped out in front of Brad's car and fell to the cement floor; he was taken to the Baptist Hospital, given a pain killer, and placed in a room. Not long afterwards Luther filed a five million dollar lawsuit against Brad. That was when Brad, who had never tried a court case in his life, decided to act as his own attorney and hire a private detective to assist him in getting to the bottom of the scam. He found 'Ace Sleuth, Private Eye' listed first in the yellow pages and walked the eight blocks to his office on Gay Street and hired him on the spot.

Due to the diligence of Ace's undercover work, and Brad's excellent courtroom maneuvers, both Luther Spenser and Bret Martin were found guilty of perjury, and in addition, the jury awarded a two million dollar judgment against Spenser and his client payable to Brad

Adams. Neither of them had a penny to their name but both of them were found guilty of conspiracy and were given prison sentences; ten years for Spenser and five years for Martin. Martin has already been paroled for good behavior and Spenser will come before the Parole Board early in 2011. As a result of the scam lawsuit brought against him, Brad decided to give up his lucrative corporate work and devote full time to defending clients in what he considered to be unjust or frivolous lawsuits. He was on a mission to change the way tort lawsuits in this country where conducted, where just about anyone can sue anyone else for any reason and escape with impunity even if they lose their case. Brad has since defended several tort cases where the opposing attorney had to pay the defendant damages when he proved in court that his client had been damaged by the lawsuit.

Brad is fifty five years old standing six-foot-two and weighing around 220 pounds; just ten pounds over his playing weight when he played fullback for the University of Tennessee Volunteers in the mid seventies. He graduated from the University of Tennessee Law School in 1979 and went on to become a very successful corporate attorney. This all changed in 2006 because of the scam lawsuit. After his success in the courtroom in this case, Brad decided to dedicate all of his energies defending what he considered to be unfair, unjust, frivolous, or just phony lawsuits. He hired Ace sleuth to be his full time investigator and Ace's wife, Paula to serve as a jury evaluator. The three of them became a top notch team until Paula gave birth to their son, Ace Sleuth the second in 2007.

Brad's office comprises one quarter of the top floor (24th) of the beautiful BB&T Bank Building in downtown Knoxville, Tennessee on Gay Street and a couple of blocks north of the Tennessee River.

Ace Sleuth is 48 years old standing six feet tall and weighing 200 pounds; he bears a striking resemblance to Tom Selleck of ten years ago. Paula, his wife of three years whom he met while working for Brad on the scam lawsuit case, is a very attractive woman about five foot six inches tall with beautiful brown eyes and brunette hair is ten years younger than Ace. She was working as the Secretary-Receptionist for Luther Spenser; the man who was suing Brad when they first met and they hit it off from the Start. They were married about three months after they met and Ace adopted Paula's fifteen year old daughter, Lisa, and Paula gave birth to little Ace on October 12, 2007. Lisa is now enrolled at Vanderbilt in Nashville studying premed; there is no doubt in her mind that she is going to become a doctor.

Chapter 1

Friday September 3, 2010

The work day was almost over for Brad Adams and his right hand man and investigator, Ace Sleuth and his secretary-receptionist, Denise Hart.

"I want us all to have a great weekend and enjoy the Labor Day holiday. Elizabeth and I along with David, Jennifer, and my three-year-old grandson, David Bradford plan to ply the waters of the Tennessee River in my boat and just relax and take it easy. It's too bad that neither of you could come with us but I guess I asked you too late."

"I can tell you what I am going to do," said Ace; our entire family, Paula, Lisa and Sean, and Little Ace are all going to Boomsday on Labor Day night. (Boomsday is a free day of family fun which takes place every Labor Day weekend in downtown Knoxville, Tennessee on and about the beautifully arched concrete Henley Street Bridge that spans the Tennessee River impounded by Fort Loudon Lake. Up to 400,000 people from in and around Knoxville and from all of the eight surrounding states and possibly from many other states as well attend the Labor Day event. There are twenty breathtaking minutes of continuous fireworks choreographed to music as ten thousand pounds of explosives fireworks are ignited. One of the highlights is when the fireworks are directed down to the water from the road level of the bridge and give the length of the bridge a waterfall effect. Boomsday has become known as the nation's largest Labor Day weekend fireworks show. This year Dignitaries from Europe and the

Far East will visit the event and National Geographic will film it for a special. This year's festival will feature new additions never seen in previous years- including a petting zoo, pony rides, a community stage featuring some of the region's best athletes, and Allegiant Air Fly-Bys which features selected air craft in action. These spectacular flight formations will be demonstrated by the Air National guard, the Knox County's Sheriff's Office Aviation Unit, and the Tennessee Museum of Aviation.)

'With 400,000 people attending you won't be able to get within a mile of the Henley Street Bridge," said Brad.

"You know, Brad that we could have a pretty good view of the fireworks from right here in your office. We're only two blocks away from the bridge but we're not going to be observing from here; we have ringside seats. In fact you could also have a ringside seat from your boat if you could find a nearby place to tie up or anchor."

"I never thought about that; we may just do that. Where are your wonderful seats located, Ace?" asked Brad.

"For ten dollars per person we get a meal of barbeque sandwiches, slaw, drinks, and chips along with the ringside seats."

"Where does this take place, Ace?"

"It's in the parking lot of Church Street United Methodist Church about a couple of hundred yards from the banks of the Tennessee River adjoining Henley Street that crosses the bridge. There is room for about a hundred or more cars and vans and people get there three or four hours before the fireworks start so that they can find a good parking place for the tailgate parties prior to the fireworks displays. People bring all types of food and drink along with cakes and home made ice cream. It's similar to a tail gate party at the Tennessee Vols football game a mile west on Neyland Drive. The fireworks don't start until nine thirty which gives you plenty of time to visit the Worlds Fair site across the street. Last year we went over there and took the Sunsphere elevator to the observation deck." (The Sunsphere was the focal point of the 1982 World's Fair hosted by Knoxville. The structure is a gold tinted sphere sitting like a golf ball on a tee rising 266 feet up in the air. It is seventy five feet in diameter with eight levels, of which, the center level housed a rotating restaurant during the World's Fair. Since the fair the Sunsphere has served several functions. It has been rented out in the past for hosting wedding receptions. Today the elevator still runs to the observation deck and is free to the public.)

"It sounds like a lot of fun," said Denise who had been silent up to his point. "I haven't told anyone else about this yet, Brad, but I would like for you and Ace to be the first to hear; I'm engaged to be married."

"Who's the lucky man?" asked Brad and Ace simultaneously?"

"You're not going to believe this but his name is Doug Hart."

"You won't even have to change your name," said Ace.

"And you will also be saving me a lot of paperwork," spoke up Brad; "let me restate that; you'll be saving yourself a lot of paperwork."

"When are you getting married?" asked Brad.

"We are getting married on Thursday November 11, Veterans Day. Doug is very patriotic. He served off and on in Afghanistan and Iraq for three years and has only been out of service for six months."

"I think I like him already." said Ace; what type of work does he do?"

"He works as a stocker at Kroger's Supermarket in Bearden four hours each night and goes to UT (University of Tennessee) during the day."

"What's he studying?" asked Ace.

"He's in engineering and plans to become a Mechanical Engineer."

"That's a tough row to hoe," said Ace; I did that for two years until I got married and dropped out."

"I'm sure that he will make it," replied Denise; he said that this was a piece of cake compared to fighting the terrorists."

"The wedding is only about two months away, Denise," said Brad; how long have you known Doug?"

"I've known him for about a year: he was stationed in Afghanistan with a mutual friend of mine who gave Doug my name and we corresponded by letters and email for six months before he was discharged."

"Where is he from?" asked Brad.

"He's from Nashville."

"Is there any chance that he will be called back into service like so many others have been?" asked Brad.

"He got his discharge free and clear, and unless the US declares war, he's free and clear."

"Why don't you bring him around," said Brad; "I'd like to meet him."

"So would I," said Ace.

"Do you think that you and Doug would be agreeable to your wedding reception taking place in the Sunsphere at my expense?" asked Brad? "However there is one catch, you would have to limit the number of people to around 100. Would that be a problem?"

"No, we didn't plan on more than that anyway and I believe that I could talk Doug into it, Brad; thanks a lot for the offer."

"How do you plan to pull that off Brad?" asked Ace; "there hasn't been a wedding reception in the Sunsphere in ten years?"

"If I told you how I was going to do it, Ace, I would have to kill you. Just suffice it to say that I can pull it off."

Chapter 2

Monday, Sept 6

Monday was Labor Day and almost all businesses were closed as Brad got into his car at his home on Cherokee Blvd in Sequoyah Hills Subdivision and drove the three miles or so to the Post Office branch on Sutherland Avenue with the zip code of 37919; the branch office was closed but the doors to access the lobby, the post office boxes, and the letter drop were always open. He took the key to his personal Box, 10085, and retrieved several letters; most appeared to be junk mail but one letter in particular caught his attention. It was addressed to Bradford Adams and was stamped, "PERSONAL." It bore no return address but it was mailed from somewhere in Knoxville because it bore that postmark.

Brad was so interested in the letter that he took out his pocket knife and sliced it open. He was bewildered when he saw the contents of the letter; it appeared to be written in some sort of code; it read:

HKT JXYF X RMLZ UKKQMLI IEXLOAK ML OXCMO SWXORKWO; EJXN MA JZ, NJWZZ?

Brad had no idea what the jumbled letters meant or what type of code it was. He couldn't understand why someone would send him a message that he didn't understand; he thought perhaps it was some kind of joke. He decided to have Ace take a look at it the first thing in the morning.

Chapter 3

Tuesday, Sept 7

Brad got to his office at 9:00 a.m. as usual and Ace and Denise were already there eating their donuts and enjoying their morning cup of coffee.

"The two of you said that you would like to meet my Fiancée; well he's dropping by around noon today," said Denise.

"I'm really looking forward to meeting him," said Brad.

"So am I," spoke up Ace.

"I'll let you know as soon as he comes in," said Denise, as she walked back to her desk.

"How did you and Paula find the fireworks, Ace?"

"We enjoyed it tremendously, but Little Ace enjoyed it more than anybody; we wore him out. After we had eaten we took him to the top of the Sunsphere in the elevator and then we took him to the spouting geysers. (The spouting geysers consist of several dozen nozzles that are recessed in a circular disc around fifty feet in diameter; these nozzles spray water upward at various heights and the children run through not knowing which one will suddenly come on and squirt them. The up and down motion of the geysers seem to be choreographed.) I think little Ace enjoyed this as much as the fireworks if that is possible; he was held spellbound for the twenty minute show,"

"I took your advice, Ace, and we took the boat up early enough to find a nice anchor point and David Bradford behaved the same way as Little Ace."

"I would have liked for both of them to have seen the fireworks together, Brad."

"I think that I would have enjoyed that also. Ace, I have a letter that I found in my post office box yesterday and it appears to be in some kind of code; I was wondering if you would take a look at it and give me your comments?"

"I would be glad to," said Ace, as Brad handed him the letter. Ace looked at it.

HKT JXYF RMLZ UKKQMLI IWXLOAK, ML OXCMO XWXORKWO; EJXN MA JZ LKE, NJWZZ?

"What do you make of it, Ace?"

"I believe that it is nothing more than a cryptogram, Brad; I should be able to decipher it in about thirty minutes; this one is rather short and the shorter a cryptogram is the harder it is to decipher; the longer ones are much easier."

Ace took the letter back to his desk and it didn't take very long for him to figure out what it said; it read:

YOU HAVE A FINE LOOKING GRANDSON IN DAVID BRADFORD; WHAT IS HE NOW, THREE?"

Ace showed the solution to Brad.

"What do you think it means, Ace?"

"I don't want to alarm you, Brad, but it looks like a threat."

"Who would want to threaten me, Ace?"

"Two people come to mind," said Ace; Luther Spenser and Rupert Cooper, and Luther is still in prison as far as I know."

"What do you think I should do about it, Ace?"

"I suggest that you show the letter to your son David so that he could make sure that the boy is always closely supervised, but I would not tell Jennifer under any circumstances at this time; I believe that she would panic. If you receive another letter like this one you should remove it from your post office box with a pair of tweezers so that we can check the envelope for prints."

"There's bound to be other prints on the letter besides mine; the postal employees would leave prints, Ace."

"That's true, Brad, we could rule them out but the less prints we have to work with is all the better."

"You have a point there, Ace, and I agree with you; I think that it might be Rupert Cooper who is behind this. I understand that he has been in some financial difficulties recently and he probably blames it all on me."

"He has never forgiven you for embarrassing him and winning a half million dollar lawsuit against him when he was the one expecting to walk out of the courtroom with the money. I understand that Rupert isn't doing too well financially; he had to move out of his $500,000 condo into a modest three bedroom bungalow in a somewhat undesirable part of the city and he probably blames everything on you and possibly me. About the only work he is getting these days is defense attorney work for the AG (Attorney General, Mel Crosby) and from what I hear from the grapevine is that there is no love lost between the two of them and the AG only hires him when he can't get anyone else."

It was almost noon when Brad picked up his ringing phone.

"Doug is here," said, Denise.

"Bring him on back," replied Brad.

"Brad and Ace; I would like for you to meet my future husband, Doug Hart. Doug, this is Brad Adams and Ace Sleuth."

"I am certainly glad to meet you Doug," said Brad.

"I am honored to meet you, Sir."

"You don't have to call me Sir," replied Brad.

"I am calling you Sir because that is what the Marines instilled in me and I really respect what you are doing to help clean up our horrible tort system which is surely destroying our country as much as some of our worst enemies."

"In that case, I will be honored to be addressed in that form," replied Brad.

"If you call me Sir, Doug; I will have to kill you," spoke up Ace.

"Denise has already told me all about you, Ace, and I also have a lot of respect for you also, but don't worry about me calling you Sir; she has already warned me about that."

"I have an idea," said Brad; why don't we close up shop here and all go over to the Marriott Hotel and get some lunch and get to know one another a little better?"

They all agreed and took the elevator down to the parking garage, got into Brad's S550 Mercedes, and drove the short distance to the hotel.

Chapter 4

The four of them found a table where they had a view of the lobby and all the passing people. After they had ordered, Brad suggested that they get to know each other a little better.

"Brad, I think I know quite a lot about you and Ace. Besides what Denise has told me, I have read about both of you in the newspapers."

"I guess you know that you are getting one fine girl in Denise, don't you Doug?"

"You don't have to tell me that, Ace; I am one lucky Dude."

"I understand that you are from Nashville, Doug; why don't you tell us a little about yourself?"

"There is not a lot to tell, Ace; when I got out of high school I had planned to go to Vanderbilt but our country had just gone into Afghanistan so I decided to join the Marines and do what little I could to fight the terrorists who were trying to destroy our great country; I served two four year terms until I was just recently discharged."

"I think that is absolutely a gallant and patriotic thing you did, Doug; you have my admiration," said Brad.

"I know that Doug is too modest to tell you this himself, but he was an Eagle Scout in Nashville," spoke up Denise.

"I'm really impressed," said Ace.

"How about your family, Doug; Do they live in Nashville?" asked Brad.

"My mother does, but my dad passed away recently and that's one of the reasons that I left the military; I wanted to be there for my Mother."

"Do you have any brothers and sisters," asked Brad.

"No, my mother and father couldn't have any natural children so they adopted me when I was two months old. I was very fortunate to have been adopted by them; I couldn't have gotten better parents if I had chosen them myself."

"Have you two found a place to live when you get married?"

"Right now I am living with two other guys who are also UT students; Denise and I will live in her apartment when we get married."

"Where are you going on your honeymoon," asked Ace.

"We really can't afford a long and expensive honeymoon," said Denise; "we will just drive up to Gatlinburg and stay in a motel for a couple of days"

"That's really all the time I can spare," said Doug, unless we postpone the honeymoon until the Christmas holidays."

"Would the two of you be terribly upset if I could arrange a one week honeymoon cruise to the Caribbean during the holiday period as a courtesy of my company?" asked Brad.

"That would be asking too much of you Brad," said Doug; could we just consider it a loan?"

"Only on one condition, Doug," said Brad.

"What is the condition?" asked Denise.

"That you never pay it back; I'll just set it up at a negative interest rate and that will wipe out the loan in a few years.

"I've heard of cooking the books, Brad, said Ace; "but this takes the cake."

"What do you say, Denise and Doug; I'm going to be awfully hurt if you don't say yes."

"How can we refuse," said Doug; we will never forget what you are doing for us; first the reception and now the honeymoon."

Doug had to go back to a two o'clock class, and Brad, Ace, and Denise, went back to work.

Chapter 5

Saturday, September 11

Ace was home sitting in his easy chair watching a college football game and eagerly awaiting the televised Tennessee-Oregon game which would come on at 7:00 p.m., when the phone rang.

"City morgue," he answered; "there's no one available to come to the phone right now."

"I just want to talk to you, Mister Ace; nine year old Trisha Parker replied; I don't like talking to dead people anyway." (Today was the third year to the day on which Ace rescued her from the home of a pedophile that had kidnapped her in 2007 from the play ground at the Sequoyah Elementary School. It was Trisha's testimony at the pervert's trial that had sent him to prison for life. Trisha had never forgotten and she always called him every year at this time; she also calls him each June 15th to wish him a happy birthday.

"I just want to thank you for saving my life, Mr. Ace; I will never forget what you did for me."

"I will never forget you Trisha," said Ace; "Little Ace really enjoyed your birthday party on July fourth and so did Paula and I; can you believe that he is now three years old?"

"I just love Little Ace and David Bradford; they are both so cute and smart." (Little Ace and David Bradford Parker were both born the same day, on October 7, 2007.)

"How is school this year, Trisha?"

"I just love it; I am in the fourth grade and my favorite subject is math."

"Do you like to work problems, Trisha?"

"I like written problems better because they make me think."

"Would you like for me to give you a math problem?"

"I'm ready with my pad; I will write it down."

"Here goes: suppose that you have a ten volume set of encyclopedias, each with 100 pages, sitting on a book shelf with books ends on each end. A bookworm starts eating through the ten volumes; he starts and eats his way through page one of volume one and eats all the way through the next eight volumes and through page 100 of volume ten. How many pages did the book worm eat through; the covers of the volumes don't count."

"You're trying to trick me, Mr. Ace; I don't think that the answer is 1000 because that would be too simple; I'm going to have to work on this. I'll get back to you when I get the answer."

"You are one smart cookie, Trisha."

"I never did thank you, Mister Ace for getting my Daddy and Brittany together after my mother was killed by that drunk driver; I just love Brittany. Daddy has become a different person after he and Brittany were married. I didn't think that he would ever get over my Mother's death."

"I knew that they would hit it off but I did have to do a little 'behind the scenes' maneuvering to pull it off."

"I should have the answer to your math problem by tomorrow, Mister Ace"

"I have the utmost confidence in you Trisha; tell your Dad and Brittany that I said hello."

"I will, Mr. Ace; bye."

Chapter 6

Sunday, September, 12

It was Sunday afternoon and Ace and Paula were sitting in their den and Ace was watching the Tennessee Titans' Sunday football game while Paula was reading the Sunday paper when the phone rang and Ace answered.

"This is the Vatican; Pope speaking."

"I must have the wrong number; I was trying to get the City Morgue."

"We work hand-in-hand with the morgue; is there anything that I can help you with?"

"I think I got your bookworm problem worked, Mr. Ace."

"Like I always say; it takes one to know one."

"Are you calling me a bookworm?"

"What else do you call a nine year old as smart as you are; tell me how you worked the problem, Trisha?"

"I just looked at our set of encyclopedias on the shelf with the titles and volumes facing me and I saw that page one of volume one was on the right hand side of the book; that means that the bookworm would only eat through the last page of volume one which happened to be page one, I looked at volume ten and noticed that page 100 was the first page so the bookworm just ate through one page of volume ten. So he ate through one page in volume one, one page in volume ten and 800 pages through volumes two through nine, for a total number of 802 pages."

"You are one smart cookie, Trisha; I think that you are smart enough to be on the TV Show: 'Are you smarter than a fifth grader'."

"I bet that you could win the million dollar prize on the show, Mr. Ace."

"I sure would like to try, Trisha."

"How's Little Ace doing?"

"He's as sharp as a tack; he watches 'Sesame Street' every day and he already knows his ABC's.

"Is he a chip off the old block?"

"I certainly hope not for his sake. Do you know what a prime number is, Trisha?"

"No I don't; we haven't had that in school yet."

"Have you had your multiplication tables yet?"

"Yes; I know them all the way through my twelve's."

"A prime number is a number that is divisible only by the number one and by itself; two, three, and five are prime numbers, but four is not."

"That's because four can be divided by one, two, and by itself," said Trisha.

"You catch on real fast, Trisha; I would like for you to make me a list of all the prime numbers from one through one hundred. Do you think that you can do that?"

"I would like to try."

"I want you to promise me that you won't look up the answer on Google; I want you to do this on your own."

"I promise, Mr. Ace; I don't know how long it will take me, but I'll call you as soon as I get the answer."

"Thanks for calling me, Trisha; I will breathlessly awaiting your answer."

"Bye, Mr. Ace."

Ace continued to watch the football game when the Quarterback for the Titans was speared in the head by a defensive tackle's helmet. He lay on the ground for several minutes and there was a hush in the stadium; you could have heard a pin drop. After about five minutes he was helped up and taken into the locker room to let the trainer give him a closer inspection. It turned out that he was not seriously injured and he later returned to the game. Paula had laid down the paper she was reading and seemed quite concerned about the Quarterback as he was lying on the ground.

"Isn't there anything that can be done to protect the players from getting hit by those hard helmets, Ace?"

"I think that they should require that all football helmets have at least a half inch of padding on the outside of the helmets. Helmets were originally made to protect the wearer but they have become more of a weapon lately. The padding would not only help protect the player who is hit but it would also lessen the impact to the tackler," replied Ace.

"Speaking of padding, the dash in your old Mustang could use a little padding, Ace."

"I seldom have a passenger in my car, and padding wouldn't help me at all when I'm sitting behind the steering wheel."

"I worry about you in that old car, Ace; you don't even have an airbag."

"No, but I've got the safest and best driver in Knoxville sitting behind the steering wheel."

"Touché, Ace."

Chapter 7

Monday September, 13

Brad stopped by his PO Box as he usually did every morning and when he opened it up he noticed an envelope similar to the one he found in there last week; he carefully removed it with his fingernails to avoid adding his prints to those already on the letter. He decided to take it to the office with him and open it there in the presence of Ace.

When Brad arrived at the office he joined Ace and Denise at the small conference table and had some coffee and donuts with them while they discussed the day's work. They got that out of the way and Brad excused Denise and she went back to her desk.

"I got another one of those letters in my PO Box again this morning, Ace, and I wanted to open it in your presence; take a look at this."

"Do you have a pair of tweezers and a letter opener?" asked Ace.

Brad passed the items to him.

"There is no return address on this letter either," said Ace, "and it also has a Knoxville postmark."

Ace slit the envelope with the letter opener as he held it with the tweezers.

"Take a look at this," said Ace as he handed the letter to Brad.

Brad looked at the letter which had been put together by clipping letters from the newspaper. They both looked at it closely.

If I WERE yoU
I woulLd WaTch

hIM very

CLoseLY

"What do you make of this, Ace; first I get a coded message and then this one made up from cuttings from a newspaper. Why would someone go to all the trouble to send me these kinds of messages?"

"I think someone is trying to mess with your mind, Brad. I don't believe that there is any danger to your grandson; I think whoever is doing this is just trying to make you miserable like he is."

"I still haven't shown the first letter to David, Ace; do you think I should say anything to him?"

"If I were you, Brad, I don't believe that I would say anything to him just yet, but it might be a good idea to mention to him and Jennifer to keep a close eye on David Bradford with all the perverts running around today."

"I'll do that, Ace; do you think we need to let the police in on this?"

"I don't think that would be a good idea, Brad; neither of these letters constitutes a threat and I don't think the police would put very much effort on something like this with all the crime going on in this city."

"What do you think we can do, Ace; we need to do something?"

"Let me take this letter and dust it for prints and see what shakes out; I haven't used my fingerprint kit since I started working for you four years ago."

"Thanks, Ace. Just let me know what you find; let's get back to our regular routine now."

Chapter 8

Saturday

As usual Ace was sitting in his easy chair watching college football. Lisa had come home from Vanderbilt for the weekend; she is now a junior in Premed along with her boyfriend Sean Davis. Paula was in the kitchen and Little Ace was playing with his Lego's.

"How is school?" asked Ace

"It is very hard but I have managed to make the Deans' list every semester so far."

"That's because of all the difficult problems I have given you over the years, Lisa."

"You are not very far wrong on that, Ace; I have actually run into problems at school that were very similar to some of the ones that you have given me, but I think the biggest help that you gave me was to make me think for myself; I used to get so annoyed when you would ask me to derive problems such as the quadratic equation and the Pythagorean theorem, but I think working them has been an asset to me in my studies."

"Would you like for me to give you anymore problems, Lisa?"

"Heavens no," replied Lisa; I have enough in college to keep me busy."

"Since Lisa doesn't have time to work my problems, I'll just have to find someone else to give my problems to" thought Ace

Ace had no sooner gotten the words out of his mouth when the phone rang; he picked it up and answered:

"Hello, Trisha."

"How did you know it was me, Mr. Ace?'

"If I told you; I would have to kill you."

"I think that I have heard that somewhere before."

"Lisa is here with us this weekend, Trisha."

"Tell her I said hi; I think I got all the prime numbers from one to a hundred with number 101 thrown in for good measure; I knew that all the even numbers except for the number two were not prime numbers because they are all divisible by two; I didn't look any of them on Google but I did use my calculator to see which of them were divisible by other numbers and themselves."

"You used the term, 'good measure'; do you know where that term came from?"

"No, I have just heard it a few times."

"I believe that it comes from England several hundred years ago. When a customer would go to the market to buy things such as flour, milk, or eggs, the seller would place the flour or milk in a container and add a little extra to each. If it were eggs, he would throw in an extra egg; if it were a dozen doughnuts, he would throw in an extra doughnut which became known as a Baker's Dozen; but I'm getting too far off the subject matter. What numbers did you come up with?"

"I came up with the following numbers, Mr. Ace"

1

2

3

5

7

11

13

17

19

23

29

37

41

43

47
59
73
79
83
89
97
101

"I forgot to tell you, Trisha; that the number one fits the definition of a prime number; but it is not considered a prime number. Other than that you got them all right and it's my fault that you got number one wrong."

"Thank you Mr. Ace; if you have any more problems for me, just give me a call."

"I'll talk to you later, Trisha."

"Trisha must be a pretty smart little girl, Ace," said Lisa, who had overheard the conversation.

"I believe that she is as smart as you were at that age, Lisa."

"That smart, huh?"

"What are you and Sean planning to do tonight?"

"We don't have any definite plans; as long as we're together we're happy."

"Paula and I plan on eating out at Ruby Tuesday's at the West Town Mall; would you and Sean like to go with us?" (Ruby Tuesday restaurant was formed in 1972 by five University of Tennessee students and the first restaurant was located on the Strip (Cumberland Avenue) adjacent to the UT campus. The chain now consists of several hundred restaurants with locations in forty four states and The District of Columbia. In addition there are also Ruby Tuesday restaurants in Hawaii, Mexico, India, and the Philippines. The chain is headquartered a few miles from Knoxville in neighboring Blount County.)

"I think I can talk him into it; what time?"

"We will leave about seven."

"Thanks Big Daddy."

Chapter 9

Monday, September, 20

As usual, Brad stopped by his PO Box and there was another letter which looked exactly like the other two he had removed from the box. He decided to take it to the office and let Ace see it before he opened it. He got to the office at 9:00 a.m. and Ace was already there along with Denise. He handed the letter to Ace and he slit it open with a letter opener and handed it to Brad; it read:

"He must be a great joy to you; Keep him safe at all costs"

"It looks like more of the same, Ace; what is your take on this?"

"I dusted the other envelopes for prints and found a few, and I bet they belong to The PO employees. I did not find any prints on the contents but I didn't expect to."

"What do you think we should do, Ace; I don't want to keep getting these things for the rest of my life?"

"I would bet my bottom dollar that Rupert Cooper is behind this and I think I know how to put a stop to all these letters, but it will probably take about three weeks."

"What do you plan to do, Ace.

"I would rather you didn't Know, Brad; because I would hate to have to kill you."

"Just keep it as legal as you can."

"I'll do my best."

"Let's get back to work now, Ace; keep me informed."

"Will do," replied Ace. (Ace was contemplating what he was going to do and it required a little after hours work)

Chapter 10

Monday evening, 9:00 p.m.

Ace was in the bedroom donning some old used clothes that he had purchased at the Goodwill Store; Little Ace was in bed asleep.

"What are you doing putting on those old clothes?" asked Paula.

Ace filled her in on the letters that Brad had been receiving and told her that he was going to pay a little visit to Rupert Cooper's garbage can.

"You be careful, Ace; I don't know what I would if anything happened to you,"

"You don't have to worry about me, Paula; I don't want anything to happen to me either."

Ace got in his 76 Mustang and headed to 238 Moon Beam Place; it was now almost 9:30 p.m. He parked his car about a block away and walked to the house. He located Rupert's garbage can in the alley behind his house with no nearby street lights. He had brought along a couple of tall white kitchen trash bags and one large black garbage bag along with a small flashlight. He donned a pair of gloves and transferred all the contents of Rupert's garbage can into his own bags; most of the trash in the can was already in bags. He was out of there in three minutes and he decided to take the trash home and lay it out on the garage floor and see just what he had. He was back home by 10:00 p.m. and he opened the garage door with his remote. He parked the Mustang in the driveway, grabbed the trash from the car, walked into the garage, and closed the door behind him. He could hardly wait to see what he had in those bags.

He noticed that Rupert had done a good job in sorting out the different types of garbage; he even had all his old mail and other paperwork in the same white plastic bag. He opened up that bag first and was relived to find that Rupert evidently didn't use a shedder. Ace had hit the jackpot when he dumped the contents on the garage floor and saw some credit card bills in the mix. He stuffed those in his pockets and looked at the rest of the trash; the only thing that he thought that looked promising was a wadded up Kleenex which Ace thought might be handy if ever he wanted to get a DNA analysis of Rupert. Ace dumped the rest of the garbage into his own garbage can. He could hardly wait until tomorrow to make a phone call.

Chapter 11

September, 21, Tuesday morning

Ace called Denise and told her that he wouldn't be in until around ten. He then called the Green Valley Nursery; a female voice answered the phone.

"This is Rupert Cooper calling and I was wondering if you have any loose cow manure?"

"Yes we do sir; how much do you need?"

"I'm not sure; how much does it cost?"

"Its $175 per ton and we don't sell it in less than one ton lots; how much do you need?"

"I think five tons would be enough; I have a fairly large yard."

"Do you want us to spread it for you?"

"No, I have a spreader; just dump it under the large elm tree in my front yard."

"How would you like to pay for this, Mr. Cooper?"

"I would like to pay with my Visa and just give you my card number over the phone; if that's okay?"

"That's no problem; we do that all the time; let me have your card number, please."

"Its Visa card number: 2269 4437 2876 4498."

"What is the three digit number?"

"That's on the back of the card; isn't it? Let me turn the card over; here it is." Ace had no idea what the three digit number was since he didn't have the card but he blurted out 671 and kept his fingers crossed.

"What is your address, Mr. Cooper?"

"238 Moon Beam Place in the City."

"Thank you for you business, Mr. Cooper; your order will be delivered by 2:00 p.m. this afternoon."

"Thank you for you fast response," replied Ace, as he hung up and reflected: *"This should give Rupert something to stink about,"* thought Ace.

Chapter 12

Wednesday morning

Ace got to work at nine and Denise and Brad were already there; he got his usual coffee and doughnuts when Brad walked over with the morning paper.

"Ace, did you see the article in the paper about Rupert Cooper?"

"I haven't had the chance to look at the paper yet," replied Ace, as he looked at the article; it read:

A HUGH HUNK OF DUNG

Local Attorney, Rupert Cooper, arrived home from work yesterday evening to find a huge pile of cow manure dumped on his front lawn; his neighbors weren't too happy about the odor; they said the pile of manure was actually steaming in the hot sun.

Mr. Cooper was rather philosophical about the matter; he stated that if someone wanted to give him several hundred dollars worth of manure that he would just hire someone to spread it over his lawn. He said that he had just been thinking about having it done anyway. It is a mystery how the mess ended up in his yard, he said; the driver may have mistakenly delivered the manure to the wrong address, he added.

"Isn't that just like Rupert, Ace; he would never admit that maybe one of the people he has maligned over the years did it to get back at him."

"I bet whoever did it also charged it on Rupert's credit card," replied Ace.

"I think that would be rather hard to do, Ace."

"I was wondering, Brad, if we should run a DNA on the letters that we have been receiving and see if it matches Rupert's."

"I think that we would have a problem with that, Ace. We couldn't even find prints on the letters; I don't see how in the world that we could come up with a DNA sample."

"I thought that we might be able to get a DNA sample in case the sender licked the envelope. I also thought about checking the stamp but most stamps these days come already pre-licked; we could send a couple of the envelopes to a lab and find out."

"I hadn't thought about that, Ace; but what would we match it against if we found anything?"

"We could match it against a Kleenex that I found in Rupert's garbage can a couple of nights ago."

"You sly devil, you; you didn't just happen to find a credit card number in his garbage can, did you?"

"I refuse to answer that question due to Client confidentially, Brad."

"But I'm your client, Ace."

"I don't play favorites, Brad."

"That's OK; I really don't want to know; but I think I will give the AG a call and see if he can recommend a local lab that does DNA testing; I would like to find out once and for all if it's Rupert who has been sending me these letters, or at least rule him out. I'll get back to you after I call the AG."

"I'll get back to work now, Brad."

As soon as Ace left his office, Brad had Denise get Mel Crosby, the Attorney General, on the line.

"Mel, this is Brad Adams, and I have a small problem that I am trying to clear up." Brad filled the AG in on the letters he had been receiving and about a DNA analysis. The AG agreed that the letters did not constitute a definite threat and there was nothing his office could unless the letters did become more threatening in the future.

"There is a local lab that we use to do our DNA analysis, but I'm not sure if they do work for private individuals, but I will give you their number and you can call them. The firm is Knoxville Biological Testing Laboratories and their number is 545-2993. Be sure and contact me if the letters become more serious."

"I will, Mel; and thanks a heap for you help."

Brad dialed the lab number and asked to speak to someone about doing some DNA testing; the receptionist transferred him to a Dr. Harvey. Brad introduced himself and explained his situation.

"We don't normally do DNA testing for individuals, Brad, but that's because there is not much demand for the service."

"Do you think that you could get a DNA sample from an envelope that still has the sealed portion intact; the envelope was slit open with a letter opener?"

"We can do the analysis, and if the envelope was licked by the sender, there is a strong possibility that we can lift the sample; do you have anything to compare it to?"

"I have a used Kleenex that should contain a specimen that would render a DNA sample."

"Why don't you give us what you have and let us see what we come up with."

"What is the cost of this?"

"It is $600 per sample and your cost will be $1200 regardless of what we find."

"That sounds fair enough; I'll have someone drop the samples off this afternoon if that's OK with you."

"That's fine with me, It will probably take a couple of days to get the results; I will call you when we're finished."

"Thanks, Dr., Harvey."

"You're welcome, Brad."

Chapter 13

Friday afternoon

Ace was sitting in Brad's office when the phone rang.

"Dr. Harvey is on line one, Brad," said Denise.

"Good afternoon, Dr. Harvey."

"I just wanted to call and tell you that we have a positive match on the two DNA tests we ran on the specimens you sent us."

"Just how positive is the test, Dr. Harvey?"

"It is 100%, Brad; you can send someone by to pick up the paperwork or I can mail it to you."

"I'll have someone pick it up before the end of the day."

"That will be fine, Brad; your total cost is $1200; we'll absorb the sales tax; make sure your pick up person gets here before five."

"I will; thanks a lot, Dr. Harvey."

"You're welcome, Brad."

"I guess that you overheard enough to know that Rupert Cooper is the one behind the Monday morning letters, Ace; what do you think should be our next step?"

"I think that Rupert needs at least one more treatment before we get the letters stopped; I don't think he sees any connection between the pile of dung in his front yard and the letters, but that may change when he gets his next Visa statement."

"When do you think that will be, Ace?"

"It's just a guess, but I would say he will get it right around the 8th of October, but I don't think we ought to wait that long to find out. You will probably still be getting those letters up until that time;

I think he ought to have another treatment right away; what do you think, Brad?"

"I don't even want to know, Ace; do what you think is best, but keep it as legal as possible."

"You know I will, Brad."

"Have a nice weekend, Ace; oops; I almost forgot that tomorrow is Tennessee's big game with Florida and it's a home game to boot; I assume that you and Paula still want to go and sit in my skybox. I have plenty of room tomorrow so why don't you bring Lisa, Sean, and Little Ace along with you and Paula if you like?"

"I think that I would like that a lot, Brad."

"Fine; we'll all meet here at the office around 11:00 a.m. for the one o'clock kickoff and I'll have a limo pick us up."

"That will be great, Brad."

Chapter 14

Friday evening

Ace and Paula and Little Ace had arrived at Regas Restaurant a little before six to get the early bird special and to ensure they could get Little Ace back home for his 8:00 p.m. bedtime; as soon they put him to bed he fell fast asleep.

Ace was putting on his Goodwill homeless outfit when Paula walked into the bedroom.

"Are you going to the prom, Ace; I've never seen you so dressed up?"

"Flattery will get you nowhere, Paula."

"I can see that you have on your best garbage can browsing togs, Ace: I thought you would stay here tonight and see your TV show that you like so well."

"Paula; I would love to stay home and watch one of my favorite TV programs but I have something that I must do concerning Brad; I probably won't be home until around ten."

"I understand, Ace; I'll tape the show and we can watch it together when you get home; I think I like watching 'Are you smarter than a fifth grader?' almost as much as you do."

"You are an angel, Paula."

"I know, Lovebird."

Ace got into his 76 Mustang and drove to 238 Moon Beam Place hoping that Rupert had gone out on the town for the evening; he had no such luck; Rupert's car was parked in his driveway. Ace didn't mind waiting; he had done a lot of that in his many years as a private detective. He decided to wait until nine thirty to see if Rupert had any plans to leave; the time was now eight thirty. Ace didn't have to wait very long; at nine, Rupert emerged from his front door, got into his car, and left.

Ace drove his car about a block from the house and walked through the alley behind Rupert's house; it was very dark and the coast looked clear, so he donned his white gloves, picked the lock on the back door, and walked in. He walked over to the computer desk and found what he was looking for Rupert's portable phone. He dialed a five dollar a minute 1-900 toll number and when a female voiced answered, Ace told her that he would like for her to read to him.

"The only reading material that I have is the book, 'War and Peace' by Leo Tolstoy," she replied."

"That would be perfect," Ace answered. "You just read the entire book to me and I will listen and not say a word."

The female voice started to read: "*Well, Prince, Genoa, and Lucca are now no more than private estates of the Bonaparte* family."

Ace listened to the first line and then he stuffed the phone down into the sofa cushions as far as it would go and hoped the Rupert would never find it.

He got into his car feeling more relaxed and satisfied than he had felt in years; he was looking forward to going home and watching one of his favorite television shows with the woman he loved.

Chapter 15

Ace got home about nine thirty and he and Paula watched the television show, 'Are you smarter than a fifth grader' that she had taped. After watching the show and fast forwarding through the commercials it was ten twenty.

"Paula, I sure miss having Lisa around to pick her brain; have you ever played twenty questions?"

"No, I haven't, but I would like try; how do you play it?"

"One person thinks of a subject and secretly writes it down on a piece of paper so that there can be no cheating."

"That's no problem, Ace; I trust you."

"I wasn't worried about me, Paula."

"You sure know how to hurt a girl, Ace; explain the game further to me."

"Suppose that you pick an object, such as the Eiffel Tower and write it down; I have up to twenty questions to ask you to find out what it is."

"I don't see how you could ever find out what it is unless you just ask me outright."

"You have to tell me if it's animal, vegetable, or mineral; the tower in this case would be mineral. Vegetable can be anything that grows like a tree or fruit. Animal is any kind of animal including humans. Suppose that you go first and tell me the category and then I can start asking questions that you only answer with a yes or no; if I don't solve it in twenty questions I lose. Do you think that you understand it well enough to start? I'll let you go first just to level the playing field."

"You're all heart, Ace; I'll give it a try."

"OK, is it animal, vegetable, or mineral?"

"It's mineral."

"Is it man made?"

"No."

"Does it have a definite location?"

"Yes."

"Is it in the Western Hemisphere?"

"No."

"Is it in Europe?"

"No.'

"Is it in Asia?"

"No."

"Is it in Australia?"

"No."

"Is it north of the equator?"

"No."

"Then it must be south of the equator; is it in Africa?"

"No."

"Is it in New Zealand?"

"No."

"Is it at the South Pole?"

"No."

"Is it in New Guinea?"

"No."

"Is it in Indonesia?"

"No."

"Is it in Madagascar?"

"No."

"Is it in Borneo?"

"No."

"Is it the Pacific Ocean?"

"No."

"Is it the Indian Ocean?"

"No."

"Is it Tasmania?"

"No."

"Is it in the Cook Islands?"

"No."

"Is it French Polynesia?

"No.

"You have really got me stumped, Paula; you did say that it was in the Southern Hemisphere; didn't you?"

"No; I said it wasn't in the Northern Hemisphere."

"Well; it's got to be one or the other; is it in the Southern Hemisphere?"

"No."

"Is anywhere on the earth?"

"No, and your twenty questions are up."

"Well what in the world is it?"

"It's not anywhere in the world; it is the moon."

"You really surprised me, Paula; just for that I'm going to give you a real duzzie."

"Fire away; I'm beginning to like this game."

"OK; it's mineral."

"Is it manmade?"

"Yes."

"Is it in the Western Hemisphere?"

"Yes."

"Is it the Statue of Liberty?"

"No,"

"Is it the Mall of America in Minnesota?"

"No. Look, Paula. You need to narrow the answer down more or you will never get it; you need a system."

"You didn't do too well with your system, did you?"

"Touché, Paula."

"Is it the 'Gateway to the West Arch' in Saint Louis?"

"No."

"Is it the Space Needle in Seattle?"

"No."

"Is it the Sunsphere here in Knoxville?"

"No."

"Is it the Golden Gate Bridge in San Francisco?"

"No."

"Is it the Sears Tower in Chicago?"

"No.

"Is it the New Yankee stadium in New York?"

"No. Paula the way you're going you're never going to get the answer."

"Is it Mount Rushmore in South Dakota?" There was silence from Ace.

"Let me see what you wrote down on that piece of paper, Ace."

"Paula, you have got to be the luckiest person on the face of the earth. First you had that beginner's luck on our cruise two years ago and caused them to shut down the crap table and now you just luck into the right answer."

"You are right about one thing, Ace. I am the luckiest person in the world; I married you, didn't I?"

"I think I was the lucky one in that deal, Paula; do you want to play another round?"

"I Think I'll quit while I'm ahead."

"That's what the winners say; the losers cry: 'deal' and it's your deal."

"I was only kidding; I love this game, Ace. The category is mineral."

"Is it real?"

"Yes."

"Is it manmade?"

"Yes."

"Is it in a fixed location?"

"Yes."

"Is it in the Western Hemisphere?"

"Yes."

"Is it in the United States?"

"Yes."

"Is it east of The Mississippi River?"

"No."

"Does it border the Pacific?"

"No."

"Is it in a state that borders Canada?"

"No."

"I'm going to take a wild guess; is it in Arizona?"

"Yes."

"Is it in Phoenix?"

"No."

"Is it the London Bridge that was moved from London to Lake Havasu City in Arizona?"

"No."

"Is it Sheriff Joe Arpaio's tent prison in Maricopa County?"

"No."

"Is it in Tucson?"

"No."

"Is it in Yuma?"

"No."

"Is it in Flagstaff?"

"No."

"I have tried everything that I can think of in Arizona; could this thing be shared by two states?"

"Yes."

"Is a Four-Corner State one of the shared bordering states?"

"Yes."

"Is it New Mexico?"

"No."

"Is it Colorado?"

"No."

"Is it Utah?"

"No."

"What's going on here, Paula? You said it was one of the four corner states; which one is it?"

"It's Arizona."

"I already knew that. Paula."

"I know that, Ace, but the way that you worded the question gave me no choice but to answer it with a yes. You asked if a Four-Corner State was one of bordering states. You should have asked if the bordering state was also a Four-Corner State; I couldn't answer your question with a 'no'."

"You are right Paula; let's get on with the game."

"I'm sorry, Ace, but your twenty questions are all used up."

"What is the answer, Paula?"

"It is Hoover Dam that straddles the Colorado River between Arizona and Nevada."

"You really got me good on that one, Paula: I'm tired; let's go to bed."

Chapter 16

Saturday- The Tennessee Florida Football Game

Paula had dressed Little Ace up in orange and white so that he wouldn't feel out of place with the other 100,000 plus football fans at Neyland Stadium. Lisa and Sean were all decked out for the ride to Brad's office parking garage. Nobody was more excited than Little Ace; it was his first football game and he was going to make the most of it;

"We going to football game, Daddy, and see the Vols'" said Little Ace."

"We sure are son and you're going to have the time of your life."

The five of them got into Paula's crossover with Ace driving and headed to the parking garage of the BB&T Bank Building; it would be about an hour until the limo showed up and Brad wanted them all to go up to his office for refreshments before they left for the game. Several people were already there; Brad's wife, Elizabeth, his son, David, and his wife Jennifer, along with their son, David Bradford, who was born the same day as little Ace. They have been friends since they were old enough to recognize each other and they wasted no time in getting together. They walked over to the southwest corner of the office where they had a view of the stadium and watched as the hordes of people came to the game. It was exciting to see hundred's of boats of which many had been anchored for several days; many of the boaters made a vacation out of the game. There were small boats, large boats, and yachts all tied to one another so that to get to shore the boater's had to walk across the other boats which could be as many as twenty deep.

Many of them stopped and partied along the way. If you looked west toward the stadium you could see the chartered train and coaches that were parked on the rails just outside the stadium. About two miles to the southeast you could see all the airplanes that had flown to the game parked at the Island Home Airport across the Tennessee River. Neyland Drive which runs parallel on the north shore of the river and beside the stadium had been made one-way East before the game and would be made one-way West after the game. There were more cars, vans, and motor homes parked along the road and anywhere else they could find a place; some people parked as far as two miles away and walked to the stadium while others parked many miles away and were bused to the game.

A few minutes after Ace and Paula had arrived, Denise and her new boyfriend, Doug Hart, arrived at the same time as Alex Parker and his beautiful wife, Brittany, a former Miss Nebraska. (Ace and Paula had met Brittany and her four-flusher husband, Roger Bridges on a Mediterranean cruise in 2008 where Roger had faked his own death in order for Brittany to cash in on a $10,000,000 double indemnity life insurance policy, however he had one problem, Brittany wasn't in on the scam and she thought that he might have actually been murdered or fallen overboard. Ace was skeptical from the start and brought the whole thing to a head and exposed Roger along with the sleazy ship doctor who was hiding Roger in his suite. Brittany decided to go back to Knoxville with Ace and Paula where she got a job as a nurse. After her divorce from Roger, Ace did some conniving so that she could meet Alex Parker whose wife had been killed by a drunken driver a year before. Alex's daughter, Trisha, was in on the deal with Ace because she loved Brittany and wanted her to become her mother and also to give her father a new life since he had not been the same since his wife Amanda was killed.

Brad got a call that the limo was ready on Gay Street in front of the BB&T Bank Building where he had his office and they all loaded into the elevator and rode down to the lobby level. Ace had never seen a limo quite so big; it was a stretch limo with four bench seats behind the driver's seat. Ace had no way of knowing that Brad had paid a thousand dollars to rent the limo for the rest of the day and evening. He planned to take everyone to the Copper Cellar for dinner after the game. They all climbed into the limo and Little Ace climbed on Ace's lap and stuck his head out of the sun roof. Ace hoped he didn't get a seat belt ticket; the three-year-old was having the time of his life along with three-year-old playmate, David Bradford.

Chapter 17

The limo let them off at gate 16 and they only had to wait for about five minutes for the elevator ride to Brad's sky box which straddled the fifty yard line on the west side of the Stadium.

In the concourse outside the Skyboxes was a spread of the best food and drinks that money could buy which was included in the Skybox's cost. In addition Brad had provided several bottles of champagne with a brand that Ace had never heard of, but he knew one thing, it was an expensive one. Brad always liked to go first class and that also included his friends.

Trisha was chaperoning the two three year olds before the game got ready to start. The highlight of the pre-game ceremony was when Lee Greenwood sang his signature song which he wrote: "I'm Proud to be an American"; the audience stood for the song and continued standing for the National Anthem.

At the north end of the stadium the 300 plus Tennessee Marching band formed a giant tee with the base of the tee open to the tunnel from which the Vol players would emerge in just a few minutes and come running through the tee to their respective side of the field.

"Look Trisha." spoke up little Ace: "Look at the big tee."

"You sure know your alphabet, Little Ace; do you also know your numbers?"

"I know them to a hundred."

Denise and Doug were seated next to Ace and Paula.

"These seats are a lot better than the student bleacher seats," remarked Doug."

"I know all too well, Doug; I sat in those same seats many years ago," replied Ace.

The officials and the team Captains met in the middle of the field for the coin toss; UT won the toss and elected to defer their decision until the start of the second half. Ace hoped that his Vols would fare better against Florida than they had the past dozen years. Brad had told the limo driver not to pick them up until almost all the traffic had cleared out; the driver arrived at six thirty and drove them to the Copper Cellar in the 7000 block of Kingston Pike in West Knoxville where they arrived at seven p.m.

Chapter 18

Saturday evening

The Copper Cellar Restaurant was started in 1975 by two University of Tennessee Students, Michael Chase and Curt Gibson in a basement near the UT campus. Since the space had a copper bar and was downstairs they decided to call it The Copper Cellar. The business grossed $42,000,000 in 2005.

The Copper Cellar Restaurant like Ruby Tuesday's is a Knoxville home grown one, but unlike Ruby Tuesday's hundreds of restaurants, Copper Cellar only has two Restaurants that go by the name Of Copper Cellar The second one is located in the 1800 hundred block of Cumberland Avenue near the University of Tennessee Campus. The one in which they are dining tonight is a little more upscale and pricy than the other one; this location near Bearden on Kingston Pike actually has two restaurants in the same building. In addition to the Copper Cellar there is an adjoining Italian restaurant called 'Cappuccino's; however Brad's gang will be dining in the Copper Cellar side. In addition the Copper Cellar Family of Restaurants has a total of fifteen restaurants with locations in Knoxville, Nashville, Gatlinburg, Pigeon Forge, and Lenoir City that go by different names and some of them have more than one location. They are:

1. Calhoun's
2. Chesapeake's
3. Cherokee Grill and Steak House
4. Smoky Mountain Brewery

Brad had already made reservations and their table was ready as soon as they arrived; the fifteen of them were taken to the left side of the restaurant and seated at three tables pushed together to form one long table with seven chairs on either side and a large arm chair at the head of the table that the restaurant had reserved for Brad.

A lovely waitress with blond hair who looked to be in her early twenties presently showed up and announced that her name was Jenny and that she would be their waitress.

"My name is Ace and I along with the rest of our horde will be your customers. Around the table left to right are: Paula, my wife and my three-year-old son, Little Ace." *(Paula felt like crawling under the table.)* "To the left of them is our daughter, Lisa and her boyfriend, Sean; to the right of Sean are David Adams, his wife Jennifer, and their son, David Bradford. Next are Alex Parker, his wife, Brittany, and their nine-year-old daughter, Trisha; next is Doug and Denise Hart, however they are not man and wife, but they intend to remedy that situation in a month or so. Last but not least, is the man who is paying for all this, Brad Adams, and his wife, Elizabeth. So be especially nice to him; he's the man with all the money."

"I'm certainly glad to meet all of you," said a befuddled, Jenny.

"Just to make sure that you got all the people's names right, Jenny; it might be a good idea if you repeated them all back to me in the order in which I gave them to you," said Ace.

"We're ready to order now," spoke up Brad; "you may order anything you want from the menu," he said.

A relieved Jenny took out a pad and pen to take their orders.

Ace ordered a twelve ounce prime rib. Paula had the Maine Lobster and Brad ordered four bottles of their best wine along with his food order. When the food was served Ace looked at his prime rib and took a bite of it; he then called Jenny over and told her he had a complaint with his food.

"What's wrong with it, Ace, does it taste bad or is it tough?"

"No, it's delicious and tender, but I ordered a twelve ounce prime rib and this one must weigh at least 18 ounces."

"We always like to make them a little bigger rather than a little smaller, Ace; that way we have fewer complaints. You are the first one to complain that it was too big; is every thing else OK?"

"I hate to complain, Jenny, but I believe that my coffee has been warmed over."

"That coffee was just brewed and I got the first cup of it; what makes you think that it was warmed over?"

"I just don't see how they could get it that hot all at one time." said Ace. Jenny laughed and Paula was ready to crawl under the table again, but she said: "Don't pay any attention to him, Jenny, we just checked him out of Lakeshore a few hours ago and we have to return him before midnight; just humor him."

Jenny, getting in the last word, looked at a completely worn out Little Ace asleep in Lisa's lap and remarked to Ace: "You sure have a fine looking grandson there, Ace,"

"Touché, Jenny," replied Ace. (Paula had a sly grin on her face.)

Around eleven they had all eaten and were getting up from the table and Ace lifted his plate and placed a twenty dollar bill beneath it with just enough of it showing so that Jenny would see it and get it rather than the Bus Boy; with the $150 tip which was included on the bill along with what Brad added, Jenny would have a very profitable evening.

"You don't have to tip, Ace," said Paula; at tables of eight or more, almost all restaurants add eighteen percent to the tabs."

"I know that all too well Paula. When I was a junior in High School I worked after school in a nice little upscale restaurant from about five in the afternoon until closing time which was normally about ten p.m. One night as we were getting ready to close thirty men showed up and wanted to know if we would serve them. There were three of us waiters and the manager asked us if we would mind working only for tips. We all agreed and we shoved several tables together to make one big one and brought them all water and took their orders. Almost all of them ordered our specialty, which was a small filet mignon steak with French fried potatoes and salad thrown in. It took about an hour to get them all served and another fifteen minutes to get the tables cleared. When we started clearing the tables we found that not a one of the thirty cheapskates had left a single penny."

"Why do you think that they didn't tip, Ace; was your service bad?"

"Our service was excellent, but the result of what I just told you is the reason that eighteen percent is added to the tabs.

"Explain, Ace."

"It's simple, Paula, most people only tip because it's expected of them; if they had their druthers, they would prefer not to tip at all. When you have a large table such as we have tonight everyone feels that they are anonymous and the server won't remember if they forget to tip; they don't realize that everyone at the table will do the same thing; like stiff the server."

"That makes a lot of sense to me, Ace, but I still believe I would tip whether anyone else did or not; however, you still haven't explained why you left our server a twenty in addition her eighteen percent."

"I gave her such a hard time having fun at her expense that I just wanted to show her that it was nothing personal."

"You're all heart, Ace."

"I know, Love Bird."

The limo had been waiting and took them all back to the BB&T Bank Building where a tired bunch got into their cars and headed home. It was cheaper for the limo company to pay the driver to wait than it was to drive the gas guzzler back to the garage and back again to the Copper Cellar.

Chapter 19

Monday Morning

When Ace got to work at nine Monday morning, Brad and Denise were already there drinking their coffee along with the usual donuts; Ace joined them.

"I would like to talk to you, Ace, as soon as we finish our coffee." The two of them walked over to the small conference room and Brad tossed another Monday morning letter on the table.

"Tell me what you think of this one, Ace."

Ace took a look at it and it seemed to be in some kind of code; it read as follows:

"semit lla ta drofdarb divad no eye na peek dna erus eb esaelp."

"What do you think it means, Ace?"

"I think that Rupert is trying to play with your mind, Brad. He has written this message in reverse; if you start at the end of the message and read backwards you can see what it says:

"Please be sure and keep an eye on David Bradford at all times."

"What do you think we ought to do about it, Ace?"

"I still don't believe that Rupert has connected his treatments with the letters he has been sending you, but that's probably because he hasn't had time for the other two treatments to show up on his credit card."

"What two treatments are those, Ace? On second thought, don't tell me; I don't want to know."

"I am going to give him one more treatment that he will know about immediately. If that doesn't work we will send him a letter that he will immediately know came from you."

"You're not going to sign my name to it, are you, Ace?"

"No, we don't need to do that; we'll just send him a letter in the same format as one of those he sent you."

"Which letter is that?"

"That's the letter he sent you that was made up of letters that he had clipped out of the newspaper and pasted on a sheet of white paper."

"What are you going to write in the letter, Ace?"

"I'm going to keep it simple; it will read something like this: 'Tell me when you've had enough, Rupert.' When he gets this letter there will be no doubt where his treatments are coming from."

"Just keep it a legal as possible, Ace."

"I will, Brad. I almost forget to tell you what a great time we all had at the football game Saturday and the wonderful food at the Copper Cellar afterwards. Little Ace had the time of his life and slept until twelve noon Sunday causing us to miss Church."

"David Bradford acted the same way. Those two boys have more in common than most siblings. They were both born on the same day in the same hospital and their mothers had adjoining rooms."

"You're quite right, Brad, but in addition, both mothers were married on the same day in a double wedding ceremony."

"I remember quite well, Ace, since the wedding ceremony between you and Paula and David and Jennifer was performed by my wife, Elizabeth."

"Touché, Brad."

"I'll let you get back to work now, Ace. I also have a lot of work to catch up on; keep me informed."

"I will, Brad."

Chapter 20

When Ace got home from work Monday and looked in his mail box, he found the package that he had been waiting for. It was what he was going to use for Rupert Cooper's next and final treatment. Ace was browsing on eBay a few nights ago when he ran across an item that caught his attention. He had never heard of this substance and didn't know if it was natural or man-made but he ordered a ten gram dose that came in a hypodermic injection kit. All he had to do was attach the needle that came with the kit and he could inject a substance called 'Essence of Skunk' anywhere he wanted and he knew exactly where he was going to do the injecting.

He opened the package in his garage and found several layers of leak proof paper so that none of the potent stuff could escape from the packing. He finally got down to the vial and opened it just enough to get a whiff of the contents; it smelled just like the real thing to him. He walked into his house where Paula was playing with Little Ace, who was watching Sesame Street out of the corner of his eye. He ran up to Ace and with Ace's help jumped into his arms yelling Daddy, Daddy.

"That's my boy," said Ace to Paula.

"If I'm not mistaken it was me that gave birth to him," said Paula.

"I will never forget it," said Ace.

"Supper will be ready at six and then we can watch the News and then Wheel of Fortune at seven," said Paula. Do you plan to watch Monday Night Football after that?"

"Yes I do, but first I have a small chore to do; I should be home before nine,"

"Are you going to be wearing your scrounging clothes tonight?"

"That is my plan."

After they had eaten and he and Paula had played with Little Ace until he became sleepy, she put him to bed.

"Where are you going, Ace; I worry about you when I don't know where you are?"

Ace decided to tell Paula all about the letters that Brad had been receiving after she swore not to tell anyone; especially Jennifer.

"I think that this will be my last night trip for quite awhile, Paula."

"Just be careful, Ace; a million dollar life insurance is comforting but not as much as your loving arms."

"I promise that I will, Lovebird; I love you too."

Ace donned his garbage can clothes, kissed Paula goodbye, got in his Mustang and headed to Moon Beam Place.

It was around eight when he arrived at Rupert's home and complete darkness had set in. The street lights in this part of town were weak and sparsely placed. Ace saw no sign of activity as he got out of his car and retrieved his tool kit from the trunk. He walked to the rear of the house and found the air conditioning unit he was looking for. It was called a gas pack which provided the cooling and gas heating for the entire house. The only connections with the house were the air supply and return air ducts. Ace was looking for the supply duct; he found it and took out his screwdriver and removed the access panel and went to work. He put on his white gloves and took out his portable drill and drilled a one eighth diameter inch hole in the side of the supply duct. He then took out piece of duct tape and taped it over the hole. He then punched the hypodermic injector needle through the strip of duct tape already on the duct and injected the entire ten gram contents into the supply duct through the small hole. He quickly retracted the needle and placed another piece of duct tape on top of the first piece and placed the needle into a leak proof zip lock bag as quickly as possible. He then replaced the access panel, and made sure that he had gathered up everything that he brought with him. He then got into his Mustang and drove off hoping that he had not missed very much of the football game between his two favorite teams, The Tennessee Titans and The Indianapolis Colts.

"I don't think that Brad will be receiving anymore letters from Rupert in the very near future," thought, Ace.

Chapter 21

Later Monday evening

Ace got home from doing his dastardly deed around nine and sat down with Paula to watch the Titans and Colts football game on TV. Paula wasn't very interested in football so she decided to catch up on her reading. She read for about an hour until she became so sleepy that she could hardly keep her eyes open.

"I'm going to leave it with you, Ace; I'm going to bed," said Paula as she kissed him on the cheek.

"Good night, Love Bird."

As Ace was watching the rest of the Game, he recalled years ago when he was a teenager and Howard Cosell and Don Meredith were the play-by-play announcers for Monday Night Football. He recalled two separate amusing incidents. San Francisco was one of the teams playing and Cosell went into one of his spills that only he could pull off. He was talking about what a great tight end that Ted Kwalick was for the Giants; he remarked: "Kwalick has such good hands that he could catch a bucket of water if you threw it to him." It wasn't more than two plays later that a perfectly thrown pass hit Kwalick in the hands and he dropped it. "They should have thrown him a bucket of water," spoke up Meredith.

The second incident also involved Cosell and Meredith in another Monday night game. A player for one of the teams had caught a pass around the twenty yard line of the opposing team and there was no opposing player in sight; it appeared that he could just about walk into the end zone; Cosell remarked: "The wide receiver has just caught a pass on the twenty yard line and he is heading for the goal line. Nobody, and I mean nobody, is going to catch him." Just as Cosell got the words out of his mouth, a defensive player for the other team appeared from out of nowhere and tackled the receiver on the two yard line. Meredith remarked: "Old Nobody just tackled the receiver on the two yard line." Cosell, who was not shy about speaking, was silent in both incidents. It seemed to Ace that Don was a burr in the saddle of Howard.

The Colts won the game that Ace was watching and he was still wide awake from the adrenaline flow from his earlier escapade. He looked at the TV menu and saw that there was a world Championship Pool Tournament on ESPN and switched to channel thirty two. Ace was a very good pool player himself, having won the University Of Tennessee Pool Tournament Championship more than twenty five years ago; he loved to watch good players in one on one competition.

The world tournament format consisted of nine ball games where the nine balls, one through nine, had to be shot at in consecutive order starting with the one ball and ending with the nine ball. The player who made the nine ball was declared the winner. The players had to shoot the balls in numerical order, but if they happened to pocket another ball after they had hit the ball at which they shooting, that ball was counted as a pocketed ball. If that ball happened to be the nine ball, it was a game winner. That meant that it was possible to luck in the nine ball for a win. You could also hit the nine ball with the object ball you were shooting; this was called this a combination shot and they would sometimes make the nine ball this way and win the game. Another way to make the nine ball and win the game was to bounce the cue ball off the object ball and into the nine and pocket it. The game was also won if the player made the nine ball on the initial break of the game. The break is when the player shoots the cue ball into the nine object balls which are racked into a parallelogram shape touching each other.

Ace sat back expecting to see some great pool shooting. It didn't take him very long to realize that he would get to see very little great pool shooting.

70

He had never seen a nine ball game of pool played in this format before. It seemed that every time a player had a difficult shot that he would play safe rather than attempt the shot. What the player would do is shoot the cue ball into the object ball so that the cue ball would roll behind another ball where his opponent did not have a shot on the object ball. Ace considered this sissy pool; sort of like playing touch football, he thought. This was very boring to him; *"I would just as well watch a good game of curling,"* he thought. Under the format in which they were playing he never saw any difficult shots; the players would even pass up a simple across the table bank shot to play safe. It seemed to Ace that the player would play safe unless there was almost a 100% chance of making the shot.

Ace really became concerned when one of the players scratched (inadvertently pocketing the white cue ball). The penalty for this mistake was giving the other player 'the ball in hand'. This means that the player can place the cue ball anywhere on the table he pleases and shoot from there. This results in a sure winner ninety nine times out of a hundred for the player. Ace compared this rule to giving the football with a first and ten to the opposing team on your own one yard line after you fumbled anywhere else on the field.

The way that Ace had always played the game was quite different. After a scratch the cue ball had to be placed behind the imaginary lines between the second pair of white dots at the break end of the table. This was referred to as placing the ball in Tennessee when Ace used to play. He had always thought that pocket pool was a game that was supposed to be played in one plane, that being the surface of the table. He was shocked when he saw one of the players jump a ball so that he could hit the object ball; this was an illegal shot back when Ace played and was always used by some of the less talented players. These jump players were asked to leave the pool room if they were caught jumping a ball.

Ace knew that the players playing the game were excellent world class players and he would really love to see them in a nine ball game played like he used to play; that was where each player had to make an honest effort to make the object ball which resulted in some remarkable and innovative shots being made. He decided that he would never watch a nine ball game again on TV. He did, however, enjoy watching the trick shot artists when he discovered them on ESPN later.

Chapter 22

Tuesday

Doug Hart had stopped by the office to take his future wife, Denise out to lunch and he was waiting for her to finish typing a letter for Brad. Since he had a little time to kill he walked back to Ace's desk.

"Why aren't you in school, Doug?" asked Ace.

"I don't have another class until three this afternoon so I came by to take Denise to lunch."

"Where are you taking her?"

"She has always wanted to eat at the 'Tomato Head' on the Market Square Mall."

"Paula likes that also, Doug. How are you doing in Engineering?"

"I'm doing pretty well, but I wish now that I had taken more math and physics in high school,"

"I made the same mistake as you, Doug. When I entered the university we had to take a math test to determine if we needed to take an algebra course with no credit. I felt real proud of myself because I passed the test, but I realized later that I would have been better off if I had flunked it."

"Why is that, Ace?"

"I didn't know a lot of the little math tricks that could be used that would have saved me considerable time on my homework and tests."

"They still have that test, Ace and you've made me feel a lot better about flunking it."

"Do you realize, Doug that you are going into one of the most honorable professions in the world and I think engineers are the most honest of all? I think that Herbert Hoover, a civil engineer before he became president, said it best when he summed it up in a short paper he wrote about the engineering profession over seventy five Years ago."

"What did he say in the paper?' asked Doug.

"I made a copy for you and I intended to give it to you framed as a wedding gift, however I have a copy here that you can read now; I'll give you the framed copy at your reception. Take a look."

ENGINEERING
By Herbert Hoover

Engineering…it is a great profession. There is the fascination of watching a figment of the imagination emerge through the aid of science to a plan on paper. Then it moves to realization in stone or metal or energy. Then it brings jobs and homes to men. Then it elevates the standards of living and adds to the comforts of life. That is the engineer's high privilege.

The great liability of the engineer compared to men of other professions is that his works are out in the open where all can see them. His acts, step by step, are in hard substance. He cannot bury his mistakes in the grave like the doctors. He cannot argue them into thin air or blame the judge like the lawyers. He cannot, like the architects, cover his failures with trees and vines. He cannot, like the politicians, screen his shortcomings by blaming his opponents and hope the people will forget. The engineer simply cannot deny he did it. If his works do not work, he is damned….

On the other hand, unlike the doctor his is not a life among the weak. Unlike the soldier, destruction is not his purpose. Unlike the lawyer, quarrels are not his daily bread. To the engineer falls the job of clothing the

bare bones of science with life, comfort, and hope. No doubt as years go by the people forget which engineer did it, even if they ever knew. Or some politician puts his name on it. Or credit it to some promoter who used other people's money...but the engineer himself looks back at the unending stream of goodness which flows from his successes with satisfactions that few professionals may know. And the verdict of his fellow professionals is all the accolades he wants.

Chapter 23

Tuesday Evening

Ace was sitting in the den reading when Paula came in from the kitchen after doing the dishes; Little Ace was watching cartoons on TV.

"What are you reading, Ace?" she asked."

"I was looking in my almanac to see where the Florida International University is located."

"Why did you want to know that?"

"I had never heard of it before I saw one of their football games on TV and I was just curious. I was surprised by its size; it's a large University with over a 35,000 enrollment."

"Did you find it in your Almanac?" (Ace kept an Almanac beside his recliner at arms length and he used it almost every day to look up all sorts of information)

"I finally did after the Almanac gave me the run around."

"I don't understand how a simple Almanac could give you the run around."

"I looked in the table of contents under 'Universities' to see what page the information was on and do you know what it said?"

"No."

"It said See 'Colleges and Universities.'"

"What's wrong with that?"

"I had to thumb through several pages to find where the page numbers of the information I wanted were located when all the Almanac Editors had to do was put the page numbers also under

'Universities' instead of typing in the page number they used more ink and letters by referring me to another heading. It seems to me that Almanac people have an abnormal fear of double indexing a subject."

"It does seem rather odd, Ace."

"This single indexing practice occurs in several other places in the Almanac and this is one of my pet peeves."

"Do you mean to tell me that you have others, Ace?"

"One of my big pet peeves is the way the local food markets do their weekly colored ads which are inserted into Sunday's newspapers. For some unknown reason some of the pages have about a two column width of the ad paper folded over so that you have to lift it up to see what's on the other side. I don't understand why they would do this; I usually just ignore what's on those two column fold-overs.

Another of my pet peeves is when the cover of a magazine highlights a story inside the magazine without giving the page number. When you go to the table of contents which could be as many as twenty pages from the cover of the magazine you can find nothing there that bears any resemblance to the description on the cover. Sometimes it takes as much time to find the table of contents as it does to find the featured article. As you are looking for the featured article you will soon discover that all the pages are not numbered. I'm not talking about the ad pages which are not numbered. I'm talking about the magazine article pages. When you finally find the featured article and start reading you will come to about ten pages of ads that you must thumb through to find where the article continues."

"Why do you think they do this, Ace?"

"I think it is quite obvious; they want you to see all the ads."

"That makes sense to me," said Paula. What time do you have, Ace?"

"According to my trusty watch it's almost seven thirty. Have you ever taken a close look at the watch on my wrist, Paula?"

"It looks just like any other wrist watch to me, Ace."

"That is what concerns me; did you ever see anyone wear a wrist watch on their right wrist?"

"I don't recall ever seeing anyone doing that, but I'm sure that left handed people do."

"Place my watch on your right wrist, Paula, and tell me what you think about it."

"Its backwards, Ace; when I turn it so that I can read the time the watch stem is on the opposite side from my hand. I can't set the time or date without taking the watch off my arm."

"That's the reason no wears them on their right arm," replied Ace. My watch is made for right handed people so that they can set the time and date without taking the watch off their wrists. I have never seen a watch made for left-handed people. About one of every ten people in this country (30,000,000) is left handed and I believe that there is a market for watches for south paws. If I only made a dollar a watch; that's thirty million dollars I could make."

"How do you dream up with all this stuff, Ace?"

"Just lucky, I guess."

Chapter 24

Wednesday

Ace got to his office around nine in the morning and walked over to see Brad.

"Have you seen the morning paper, Ace?"

"No, I'm too cheap to buy one: I always read yours."

"Take a look at the lead story on page two."

It read:

> **"BIG STINK ON MOON BEAM PLACE"**
> **Several neighbors of local Attorney Rupert Cooper called the police department yesterday to complain about a skunk odor emanating from the Cooper residence. It was thought that perhaps a skunk had crawled under the house but no sign of a skunk could be detected. A pest control company was called in to try to locate the source of the odor and found that is was coming into the house through the air conditioning system. The pest control man said that this was highly unusual because the air conditioning system is a closed system and that there is no way an animal could possibly get in it. He also said that the A/C filters will have to be changed out and it might be necessary to replace all the ductwork in the system.**
>
> **"This is the second time within the past few weeks that Mr. Cooper has been faced with a smelly situation.**

**A few weeks back five tons of cow manure was dumped
in his front yard. Is this a coincidence? Who knows?**

"You wouldn't just happen to know anything about this would you, Ace?"

"I am going to have to plead the fifth on that question." replied Ace, "but suffice it to say that I don't believe that you will be receiving anymore letters from Rupert."

"Well that's a relief, Ace; good work."

Chapter 25

Thursday

Ace was working in his office when he got a call from Al Jameson of the local newspaper.

"What's going on, Al?" asked Ace.

Things are going a little slow here right now and I was wondering if you might be able to put me on to something news worthy. There hasn't been much news in Knoxville since the trials of the kidnappers for the murder, torture, and rape of Channon Christian and her boy friend Christopher Newman. (Channon Christian and Christopher Newman, who were both white, were carjacked on the morning of January 7, 2007. Five black suspects were arrested in the case and four of them charged with murder and another as accessory after the fact. Channon was repeatedly raped, front and back, and forced to drink liquid bleach while she was held in the home of one of the suspects. When they were tired of her after a few days, they tied her up in garbage bag and threw her, still alive, in a garbage can where she suffocated. Her boy friend didn't fare any better. He was also raped, shot in the back of the head and thrown into a ditch and set on fire. Knoxvillians were outraged when the National News Media didn't pay much attention to the crime or give it much news coverage. Some of the local people stated that if the complexion of the kidnappers had been reversed that the National News Media would have converged on Knoxville like a chicken on a june bug and given the crime more coverage than the Rodney King beating at the hands of the Los Angeles Police. One resident remarked, however, that he didn't believe that was possible.

The costs of the trials of the five suspects was estimated to cost, more by far, than any other case in the history of the state of Tennessee)

"Let me ask you a question, Al," said Ace

"Fire away, Ace."

"How do you feel about nuclear power?"

"I don't know a whole lot about it but from what I've read I think that it must be unsafe."

"If the news media was the only place I got my information I would probably feel the same way," said Ace. Why don't you undertake an investigative report about nuclear power? Go into it with an open mind and visit some of the plants and talk to the engineers and see what they say. Check and see if you can find out how many deaths and excess doses of radiation have occurred in nuclear power plants operating in this country since the first plant went to operation over fifty years ago."

"That sounds interesting, Ace but I don't think my paper will want to foot the bill for this."

"If they won't, why don't you do it on your own time? Take a couple of week's vacation and visit some of TVA's (Tennessee Valley Authority) nuclear plants. I'm sure that they would be glad to show you around if you tell them what you are doing. You might even be able to sell your story to the Associated Press or one of the other national news services. I know some people at TVA and I could open the door for you."

"I think I'll do it, Ace; it sounds exciting."

"While you're at it, Al, find out all you can about the cooling towers at the nuclear plants. See if you can find out the exact purpose of the towers and by what authority was TVA forced to install them. Find out exactly how the towers affect the cost of producing electricity."

"I will, Ace and I promise that I will go into this venture with an open mind and let the chips fall where they may."

"I couldn't ask for anything more, Al, but remember that I get ten percent of everything you make off this report," joked Ace, "and if I can be of any help, feel free to call me."

"I may have to take you up on that offer, Ace. Thanks."

Chapter 26

Monday, Oct 6

Ace got to work at 9:00 a.m. and walked over to Brad's desk.

"I didn't have another letter from Rupert in my P0 box this morning, Ace; do you think that Rupert has gotten the message yet?"

"I think that he has gotten the message but I'm not sure if he's connected the messages to us. I think we ought to send him a short message so that there will be no doubt in his mind who he's dealing with."

"I'm going to leave that entirely up to you, Ace."

"I'll handle it, Brad."

Ace grabbed the morning newspaper and took it back to his desk where he donned a pair of rubber gloves, pulled out a pair of scissors and a roll of scotch tape, and started to work. When he had finished he walked back to Brad's office and showed him the finished product.

"That ought to do it," said Brad as he looked it over. "There should be no doubt in his mind from whom the letter came."

Still wearing the rubber gloves, Ace stuffed the message in an envelope for mailing making sure that there were no fingerprints on the message, the envelope, or the stamp. He knew that Rupert Cooper would know who sent it but he wouldn't have any proof. The message read:

Let us know

when you have

had 'enough

Chapter 27

Thursday, October 14th

Today was the day that Little Ace and David Bradford had been waiting for; it was their third birthday and a joint birthday party was awaiting them. Brad had rented the Star of Knoxville paddle wheel boat along with its pilot for the hours of one to five p.m. It had to be back in dock to allow time to clean up the boat for the six thirty dinner cruise.

Little Ace and David had become inseparable since they had so much in common. Their parents Ace and Paula Sleuth, and David and Jennifer Adams, had been married in a joint wedding ceremony performed by Elizabeth Adams, David's Step Mother. They had both been born the same day in the same hospital in which their mothers unknowingly had adjacent rooms. Brad had gone all out to make this one of best birthday parties ever seen in Knoxville. Almost two hundred people made up mostly of kids were invited. He made sure that there were plenty of adults to keep their eye on the children. He had assigned each adult five children to watch but not to interfere unnecessarily in their activities. He didn't want any kid to get injured or fall overboard.

He had hired a Ventriloquist who had all sorts of puppets and dummies that the kids adored. The kids could communicate with the puppets by asking questions of them and the puppets would talk back to them and answer their questions. This was the highlight of the party.

There were all sorts of food and ice cream for the kids as well as the adults. There were hot dogs and hamburgers on the grill with plenty of potato chips. There would be a gift bag for each child to be picked up as they left the boat. Ace and Paula were sitting with Jennifer and David watching the children and enjoying each other's company when Ace spoke up.

"We are very fortunate to live in this world today where all we have to do is sit back and enjoy our boat ride while one man controls the speed and direction of the boat. Its not at all like the olden days when boats of this size would have more than a hundred men in the belly of the ship using all their strength to propel the boat."

"Where are you going with this, Ace? I know you all too well and I know that you are setting us up for something." said Paula.

"I'm glad that you asked me that question, Paula. Back a long time ago in the days of yore, the King was on his ship and a hundred and twelve oarsmen where pulling their oars along with sweating and swearing down in the galley when the Coxswain stopped them for a minute to relay the following message:

"I have some good news and bad news for all of you; which do you want first?"

They all agreed that they wanted to hear the good news first.

"The good news is that there will be double portions at dinner today."

"What is the bad news?" they asked.

"The bad news is that the King wants to go water skiing after dinner."

Chapter 28

The wedding day of November 11 for Denise and Doug was fast approaching and preparations were well under way. Brad had been able to rent the Sunsphere for the reception for a thousand dollars. He had invited Doug's mother, Martha Hart to stay in the small guest house behind his home where Brad's mother-in-law lived for a few years before she moved into the Echo Ridge Retirement facility. She had arrived two days early to see the sights and to rehearse the wedding. The couple had decided to get married at the Second Presbyterian Church on Kingston Pike. Brad's wife, Elizabeth, a Knox County Judge had been chosen to perform the wedding ceremony.

The day of the wedding had arrived and about a hundred people showed up. Brad had spared no expense on the reception which took place in the Sunsphere, and he had employed the most expensive caterer to provide the best in the way of food and drink. Endless crystal clear Champaign was flowing freely from a beautiful fountain. Approximately 100 invited guests showed up for the reception; about half from Knoxville and half from Nashville.

Toward the end of the reception Denise and Doug, along with her parents and his mother, approached Elizabeth and Brad to thank them for the beautiful wedding. Most of the attendees had left and the eight of them took the elevator to the street level where Denise and Doug found that Brad had hired a horse and buggy to drive them down the length of Gay Street and then to the Hilton Hotel where he had arranged for them to spend their honeymoon night plus a couple more. It would be about six more weeks, December, 19 to be exact, before they would catch a plane from McGhee-Tyson Airport to Fort Lauderdale, Florida to depart for their one week cruise on the Caribbean Sea which Brad had given them as a wedding present. That was when the college Christmas and News Years break would allow Doug the free time.

"We will always be indebted to you, Brad for all you have done for us," said Doug. There is no way that we can possibly repay you but we will never forget your gracious generosity. You and Elizabeth will always be dear to our Hearts."

"We are glad that we were able to make your wedding more unforgettable; I can't think of a more deserving couple," replied Brad. "Have a great honeymoon."

Chapter 29

Monday, November 16

Denise was back at work after the honeymoon weekend and her husband, Doug was back in school. She took some fresh doughnuts and coffee back to the small conference room where Brad and Ace were sitting.

"How did you like the article in Sunday's paper about your wedding, Denise?" asked Brad.

"I haven't seen it, Brad. I didn't know they still did the weddings."

"I bet Brad pulled a few strings, Denise," said Ace

"I don't think that was what did it, Ace; I think they did it because they could come up with such a catchy heading. Take a look, Denise." said Brad.

HART TO HART

A most beautiful wedding ceremony took place Wednesday November, 11 at the Second Presbyterian Church on Kingston Pike as Denise Hart and Douglas Hart exchanged their vows. The beautiful bride wore an exquisite white wedding dress with a ten foot train. Beautiful flowers were in abundance as the Bride and Groom and their eloquently dressed entourage walked down the aisle. Denise's parents from Knoxville were in attendance along with Doug's mother from Nashville.

After the wedding the happy couple were driven down Gay Street in a horse-drawn carriage and then

to the Hilton Hotel where they spent the weekend. The Harts will go on a Caribbean cruise as soon as Doug gets out of the University of Tennessee for the Christmas-New Year Holliday break. The couple will reside in Knoxville where Denise works for the Brad Adams firm and Doug is enrolled in Engineering at the University of Tennessee.

"You can have this paper for a keepsake if you wish, Denise," said Brad.

"Thanks, Brad; I have one at home so we will send this one to Doug's mother in Nashville. I can't imagine how I missed this article or why you were the first person to point it out. My mother reads the Sunday paper with a passion but both she and Dad were out of town for the past few days after the wedding."

Chapter 30

Sunday, December, 12

Ace, Paula and little Ace were home from church and the Red Lobster Restaurant where they had eaten lunch. Ace was almost asleep while watching the Tennessee Titans and The Dallas Cowboys Football Game. Little Ace was taking a nap when Paula walked into the den with the Sunday paper; she looked saddened.

"You look like you have just lost your best friend, Paula; what's going on?"

"I just read in the paper that Regas Restaurant is closing after more than eighty years."

"That is sad news, Paula; that's where we went on our first date."

"I remember that quite well, Ace; that was when you told the waiter it was my birthday and it wasn't. I never told you this before, but that was one of the most enjoyable days of my life."

"When is it closing?" asked Ace.

"December the thirty first is their last day."

"Then we need to make a New Year's Eve reservation ASAP, Paula."

"I'll go do that right now before they fill up' I hope it's not too late."

It was not too late but if Paula had waited another ten minutes it would have been. Ace and Paula left Little Ace with his friend David where he spent the night and they both happily ushered in the New Year at Regas.

Chapter 31

Monday January, 3

The year end holidays were over and everyone at Brad's office was back at work including Brad, Ace, and Denise, and they were all enjoying their traditional coffee and doughnuts,

"How was the Cruise, Denise?" asked Brad?"

"It was just wonderful, Brad; we can never thank you enough for giving us that cruise; it will always be in our hearts and memory. We really enjoyed Puerto Rico with all of its old historical forts and buildings. I think Doug and I both must have gained ten pounds each from eating all of that wonderful food on our cruise ship."

"Is Doug back in school?" asked Ace.

"Yes, and he found his grades in the mail when we got home; he had a 3.5 GPA for his freshman semester but he deserved it; he really studied hard to get those grades."

"Those grades are really great to get in Engineering, Denise, I'm proud of him," said Ace. "I'm not going to tell you what my grades were the first semester."

"I think we all need to get back to work now," said Brad, "and make me some money."

As soon as Ace sat down at his desk his phone rang.

"Joe's pool room," answered Ace, after he noticed who was calling on his 'state of the art phone'.

"You're not going to believe this, Ace, but my paper has agreed to fund my investigative report on the Nuclear Power Industry," said Al Jameson.

"That is great, Al; just let me know if I can be of help. I think you have a rare opportunity to provide the American People the truth about nuclear power. There has been way too much misinformation put out by the national news media and Hollywood movies such as the 'China Syndrome', and other half-cocked movies concerning nuclear power, that I'm surprised that we even have any operating plants at all. It may take blackouts, brownouts, and rationing of electricity before the people of this country wake up and start demanding electricity from nuclear plants. You may well be the first newspaper reporter in his country to undertake an investigative report on this subject. Good luck to you on this controversial venture. You will probably get a lot of grief from your fellow newspaper employees but hang tough and go with the truth as you find it. It won't be easy for you as you, Al; you will be coming under fire from the environmentalists and the far left, but hang in here and don't give in. Sometimes the truth is hard to handle for some people when it goes against their belief system. The American People have been spoon fed propaganda regarding nuclear power for the last half century and the news media has been a willing accomplice in this farce. Most Americans probably believe this nonsense, but just remember, many years ago most people thought the earth was flat, and believe it or not, some still do. Did you know that there are some people in this country who do not believe that a man has walked on the moon?"

"No I didn't, but if you find one of them let me know. I've got some prime beach front property in Arizona that I would like to sell them."

"I thought I had cornered the market on all that good property, Al."

"I will take your advice regarding my report, Ace and I promise to publish nothing but the facts."

"I know that you will do a good job, Al; break a leg."

Chapter 32

Friday January, 14

Ace and Paula had dined at the Copper Cellar on Kingston Pike and had taken Little Ace along with them; it was almost 7:30 p.m. when they got home. Little Ace had gone to sleep in the car so they put him straight to bed when they got home. Ace's favorite show, "Are You Smarter than a Fifth Grader' would come on at eight. As he and Paula had settled in their comfortable TV watching furniture, he in his recliner and Paula on the Sofa; she told Ace that there was something that they needed to talk about.

"Fire away, Paula."

"We can't keep calling our son, Little Ace, for the rest of his life. He will be four his next birthday and pretty soon he is not going to like being called 'Little.' He is now insisting on wearing long pants like the big boys. What do you think we should call him?"

"His name is Ace the second which means his name is the same as mine with a two added onto it. Since my name is Fred Ulysses; why don't we just call him Freddy?"

"There's one problem with that, Ace; his birth certificate reads Ace sleuth 11. Nowhere on the document does it say Fred Ulysses."

"I won't tell him if you won't, Paula."

"What's he going to think, when all at once out of the blue, we start calling him Freddy?"

"We will give him a choice of whether he wants to go on being called Little Ace or Freddy, and I bet you a dollar to a donut that he will prefer Freddy."

"You may be right; I'm sure he won't want to be called Little Ace by his friends when he goes to kindergarten. Let's talk to him about it real soon."

"I don't think that calling him Freddy will be a problem for him, Paula when I point out to him that one of the most respected golfers goes by the name of Freddy."

"What golfer is that, Ace?"

"His name is Freddy Couples and he is a macho man."

"Lets start calling him Freddy tomorrow so that he will get used to it, Ace."

"I think that's a good idea, Paula; I had a friend who had a son named George Patrick Smith but they always called him Pat; he didn't know any other name. On his first day of school the teacher was calling the roll and when she called out the name, George Smith, Pat was silent; he didn't know that she was calling his name."

"That's funny, Ace."

Ace and Paula watched their favorite game show and then watched a movie on The Turner Classic Movie Channel; 'The Return of The Pink Panther' with Peter Sellers. As soon as the movie was over they switched to the local Knoxville news on Channel 3 where they were covering a breaking story.

A University of Tennessee Coed Student was discovered in her apartment near the UT campus earlier tonight in a near-death condition and was rushed to nearby Fort Sanders Hospital emergency room. We are not able to get any information on her condition at this time.

We did talk to her roommate who discovered her when she arrived at her apartment around 9:00 p.m. As she took out her key to unlock the door, the front door flew open and a young man came out the door and almost ran over her. This alarmed her greatly and made her very suspicious so she called out her roommate's name, and when there was no answer,

she opened the door and walked in. She found her roommate lying on the floor and she didn't know whether she was alive or dead. She was in such a state of shock at what she saw that she had to be taken to the same hospital for sedation, however she did have the presence of mind to call 911. Our reporter who just happened on the scene was able to talk to her for a few minutes before the ambulance took her to the hospital along with the victim, her roommate. He was able to get a little more information from the shaken girl. She did manage to relate a little of what she found before she was taken to emergency. She stated that her girl friend's clothes had been ripped off, her face was all bloody, and she was unconscious and unable to speak when she discovered her. "At first I thought that she was dead," she said, "until I saw a slight movement of her chest; she was barely breathing. I dialed 911 as soon as I could and the police and an ambulance arrived in about five minutes."

We cannot give you the name of the victim or her roommate at this time but we do know that they are both students at the University Of Tennessee. We will continue to pursue this matter to its conclusion. We are always on top of the news and we are the first News channel to report this crime; keep your TV tuned to Channel 3.

"It sounds like the news reporter beat the police and ambulance to the scene, Ace.

"The News Business is highly competitive, Paula; they have ways of getting on top of things."

"I sure hope the poor girl lives," said Paula.

"So do I, Paula. If she does, I hope and pray that she is not disfigured."

"What type of animal would do something like this, Ace?"

"I can't imagine anyone doing this; I just hope they catch the pervert before he does it again. I bet you a dollar to a donut that this is not the first time for this scum bag. We need to lock people like this up for life for their first offense because a leopard never changes his spots. Do you remember last year when a pervert named Phillip Garrido, who had abducted eleven year old Jaycee Lee Dugard eighteen years earlier, was discovered and captured when the now 29 year old woman called her family to tell them that she was finally coming home? He had held her captive for 17 years and forced her to live in his back yard where she bore two children by him. He had been convicted and sentenced in California to fifty years for rape in 1977 but was paroled in 1988 after serving a little less than eleven years. I think the parole board that turned him loose should have to serve his remaining time."

"I agree with you, Ace; I think that the criminals in this country have more rights than the victims and the victim's families."

"I don't understand the thinking and the mind set of some of these people who sit on these parole boards, Paula; don't they realize that these scum bags are incurable? It would solve a lot of our problems if just castrated the vermin and put them back on the street."

"But that would be cruel and unusual punishment, Ace; we wouldn't want to violate their constitutional rights" said Paula half jokingly.

"I have a better idea, Paula; let's just put the perverts in with the general prison population and let nature take its course."

"Amen to that, Ace; I'm ready for bed but I doubt that I'll get very much sleep."

Chapter 33

Saturday, January 15

After Ace and Paula had eaten breakfast Ace went to his mail box and got the morning paper. (The only Paper) Ace could remember when Knoxville had two thriving competitive daily papers. He looked at the headlines.

UT FRESHMAN STUDENT RAPED

An eighteen year old University of Tennessee freshman was raped, brutally beaten, and left for dead last night in the Fort Sanders area near UT where she lived in an apartment with another girl. She was discovered by her roommate when she returned to the apartment around 9:00: p.m.

The victim was rushed to Fort Sanders Hospital emergency room where she is now being treated. We are not able to release the name of the victim at this time, but this reporter was able to get some information on her condition. One of the ER attendants told this reporter that the young woman was brought in looking more dead than alive. She was barely breathing and her face was black and blue and it appeared that she had been choked. She said that the victim's face was badly beaten and it appeared that a few of her teeth had been knocked out and it was obvious that the she had been raped. The attendant also stated that

it appeared to her that her attacker had intended to kill her and would have probably succeeded if her room mate had not returned home when she did and frightened the attacker off.

We don't have any official word from the hospital on this young woman's condition but this newspaper intends to stay on top of this story and keep the public informed. We recommend that the University's female students never walk alone on the streets at night near the university but pair up with someone; the rapist may still be in the area.

When Ace and Paula watched the six o'clock Saturday evening news they learned that all the news media, ABC, CBS, NBC, CNN, and Fox News had picked up the story and were running with it; it appeared that this crime was going to be big news across the country. Ace did not understand exactly how the news media decided which stories they wanted to pursue. They seemed to ignore the case in Knoxville in 2007 where a black gang high jacked a young white couple whom they raped and tortured for days before they were both brutally murdered. "I guess they know what the public wants," thought Ace.

Chapter 34

Sunday January, 16

Sunday's paper had a half page story covering the rape and brutal beating of the University of Tennessee Coed that took place the previous Friday night. According to the paper there was no change in her condition; it was still touch and go whether she would live or die. There was some additional information about the young woman. She is eighteen years old and is from Dixon, Tennessee and her parents flew in Saturday to be at her side. They are withholding the names of the Coed and her roommate at the request of the parents of both girls. Ace also realized that usually was the case with most rape victims.

The story was all over the national news media. For some reason Ace believed that this case was going to be as big as the one about this time last year when a Yale graduate student, Annie Le, was murdered and her body hidden in a wall recess and not discovered until five days later. His observations would not be far wrong. He would be right about how big the case would become but he had no idea the role that he, Paula, and Brad would play in the outcome of this case.

Sunday's paper also had another feature in which Ace was very interested; it read:

Our Reporter Al Jameson has been assigned to perform an independent investigative report on the nuclear power industry in this country. He has been instructed to enter this venture with a blank sheet of paper and an open mind to try to get a true picture of the safety and the effects that these plants have on our

environment. We have received several 'Letters to the Editor' over the years that have taken us to task for articles in our paper which the readers thought were not fair to the nuclear power industry. We may have been at fault but it is common practice for newspapers to pick up stories from the various news agencies and run with them. We don't have the personnel to check out the accuracy of all of them; that is why we have assigned our most senior reporter to this very important task. We will be publishing his findings in weekly installments in the 'Features Section' of our Sunday paper; we expect the first installment in the January 30 edition of our paper.

Chapter 35

Sunday January, 30

There was a short article on the inside page of Section 'A' of Sunday's paper regarding the rape and beating of the eighteen year old University of Tennessee coed. Ace thought that he must have been wrong on his theory that this was going to be a big story nationally. The article read:

> **It has now been a little over two weeks since the brutal rape and beating of the eighteen year University of Tennessee coed and we are happy to report that she is much improved and is sitting up and talking to her family. We have learned that her attacker was a white male around twenty five years of age. She told the police that he forced his way into her apartment when she opened the door to enter and threw her to the floor. She said the man had evidently been following her. She stated that her attacker was wearing a ski mask which she ripped off his face as she fell to the floor. It is believed that the attacker tried to kill her because she could recognize him without the mask. The girl said that she had never seen her attacker before but that she would never forget his evil face and would recognize him if she ever saw him again. The young woman's roommate said that she also got a good look**

at the rapist and could recognize him if she ever saw him again.

The young woman will have to undergo some minor plastic surgery on her face but the Plastic Surgeon believes that she will not have any visible facial scars; she will however, have to have two of her teeth capped. We have learned that both the Plastic Surgeon and the Dentist have offered their services free of charge. Neither of them would allow us to publish their names. We will keep our readers up to date on this heart warming change in this young woman's condition.

The Knoxville Police Department reported that they have no suspects at this time but they are putting all their available detectives on the case to try to find the attacker. They have given us a phone number that can be reached twenty four hours a day by anyone who may have some information concerning this case; even anonymous calls will be appreciated. The number to call is: 865-555-0695.

There was another story in the Sunday paper that caught Ace's eye; it was the first installation of Al Jameson's investigative report on nuclear power. Ace could hardly wait to read it.

THE TRUE STORY OF NUCLEAR POWER IN AMERICA
Story by Al Jameson

I am going into this endeavor because of a challenge from a friend of mine who is a strong proponent of nuclear power. He asked me what I thought about nuclear power and I told him that I had an uneasy feeling about the safety of it due to the radioactivity associated with it. He challenged me to do an unbiased investigative report and go into it with an open mind. I told him that would not be a problem since my mind is blank most of the time anyway. He said that he had never seen a fair story concerning the nuclear industry in any of the news media. I am going into to this report as if I had never heard of nuclear power and let the chips fall where they may.

I intend to limit my investigation to The Tennessee Valley Authority (TVA), since they have all types of electrical generating stations imaginable, and I need to learn more about the different generating systems so that I can compare them to the nuclear system. TVA produces electricity from various types of facilities. They include wind turbines, hydro units, fossil fuel plants (including coal and gas), nuclear plants, and a pumped storage facility. (pumped storage is a system whereby TVA can generate a large amount of electricity when their system is at peak power with all available units operating. Pumped storage is a cheaper alternative than purchasing expensive electricity from outside the TVA area. The pumped storage works by TVA pumping large quantities of water to a large man-made reservoir high on a mountain top above the lake from which it is pumped. They pump the water late at night when electricity demands are very low and they have excess power available. They can fill the huge reservoir in a few hours and when they release the large volume of water to the turbines and electrical generators hundreds of feet below they can generate electricity at a rate greater than from one of their largest nuclear units for several hours.

I plan to publish a weekly report for the Sunday edition of my paper. The reports will be in this same section every Sunday for the next four weeks or so.

Chapter 36

Sunday, February, 6

Ace was in his den when Paula brought him the Sunday paper and told him to look on the front page; he read:

> **We are pleased to tell our readers that there is good news concerning the condition of the eighteen year old University of Tennessee coed who was raped, brutally beaten, and left for dead, just a little over four weeks ago. She got to go home yesterday and will be able to go back to school and get back in her classes that she was taking prior to her attack. She plans to go back tomorrow, February, 7 after missing four weeks of class. She did not want to get out of sync and have to go to summer school to catch up. She also wanted to be in the same sequence as her friends. All of her instructors have agreed to give her past homework assignments so that she can catch up with the rest of her class. She has one week in which to prepare and she has already been going over and boning up on what she has missed the past four weeks and feels that she can catch up with her class mates. She feels that starting a normal life again will help her emotionally and keep her from dwelling on her horrible ordeal. She was able to get back in all of her classes that she was taking before her ordeal except for English 102.**

That class is now full but she will be able to take this course by the same instructor at a different hour than the previous one.

She has already received the plastic surgery on her face and has had her two missing teeth capped. We are still unable to give out the coed's name but it will be hard to keep it a secret when she gets back in class with a few bandages still on her face. She stated that she doesn't mind her classmates knowing that she was the coed who was raped and realizes that it is almost impossible to keep secrets on a college campus anyway.

We really would like to congratulate the young lady for her attitude and her determination to get on with her life. She did say, however, that there was one thing that she was going to change; she was moving into a dorm on the campus where she would feel safer. We wish her luck.

Chapter 37

Also in the Sunday paper of February, 6 was the first installment of Al Jameson's investigative report on nuclear power; it read:

Investigative report on Nuclear Power
Report by Al Jameson

My first visit was to the TVA Headquarters here in Knoxville to get their permission to do this investigative report on nuclear power generation; they could not have been more cooperative. They seemed more than eager to get their story before the public. Their public relations manager, John Gilbert, was most helpful. He called the Watts Bar Nuclear Plant and Kingston Steam Plant managers and made arrangements with them for me to visit the plant sites. He instructed them to give me the red carpet treatment and to give me any information for which I asked. He informed me that if I had any problems to call him.

I first drove down I-40 about forty miles to the nine unit fossil coal-burning Kingston Steam Plant on the Clinch River. I was informed by the plant manager, Dan Rivers, that the combined output rating of the nine units was around 1.5 megawatts or about thirty percent more than the unit one of the Watts Bar Nuclear plant. Our conservation follows which I have transcribed from my voice recorder.

"Do you mind, Dan, if I record our conversation?"

"I don't mind at all, Al."

"Thanks. I have no idea of what 1500 megawatts means, Dan; could you put it in laymen terms for me?"

"I would be more that happy to; 1500 megawatts is the total rating for all of our nine units. A megawatt is a million watts or 1000 kilowatts which you are probably more familiar with. So our plant rating in kilowatts would be 1.5 million. If all of our nine units were operating at full capacity we could generate 1.5 million kilowatt hours of electricity (KWH) per hour or roughly 1100 million KWH per month; that equates to 13.2 billion KWH per year. However not all of our units operate continuously, so we generate around ten billion KWH per year. That is enough electricity to supply 700,000 average homes." If TVA sold power at five cents per kilowatt hour (KWH), these Kingston units would generate about $75,000 per hour; almost a billion dollars a year if it ran continuously."

"Those figures boggle my mind, Dan; how much coal do you have to use to generate all of those KWH's?"

"We use about 14,000 tons of coal per day."

"How does burning the coal end up producing the electricity?"

"It's a pretty involved process, Al, first we grind up the coal to the consistency of baby powder and send it to our powerful blowers that blow into our extremely hot furnaces, where instantly it almost explodes as it heats the water filled tubes above. The water in these boiler tubes is converted to superheated steam with a temperature of one thousand degrees Fahrenheit and a pressure of eighteen hundred pounds per square inch. The high pressure forces the steam out of the tubes and is piped to the turbines in the Turbine Building.

The superheated steam is directed to a series of steam driven turbines that are on the same shaft as the electrical generator. The power that the condensing steam imparts to the turbines on the shaft, which we refer to as the rotor, causes the generator to spin and make electricity."

"I think that I understand a little of what you have told and I realize that you have probably simplified it somewhat for my benefit and I appreciate it, but how do you condense all the steam that goes back to the boiler?"

"About a third of all the energy in the steam is used up in the various stages of the turbines. After we get all of the energy out of the steam that is possible, the remaining low energy steam and water falls onto the condenser tubes and is condensed back into water. The heat is removed by water that is pumped from the Clinch River; the temperature of this water rises about ten degrees and goes back to the river farther down stream. Almost two thirds of all the energy that is generated in the boiler is removed by the condenser, but this is low temperature energy. I believe that the temperature of the condensate in the condenser is, on the average, one or two degrees above 100 degrees Fahrenheit and the water going back to the river from the condenser has to be lower than that; probably about 90 degrees maximum in the summer and much less in the winter."

"How much river water is pumped to the condenser, Dan?"

"If I remember correctly; the total capacity of the pumps down at the river is around 300,000 gallons per minute."

"That's a lot of water Dan, I don't use any more than that in a year at my house; is there any problem sending all that hot water back to the river, Dan?"

"I don't consider it to be hot water; it is not even lukewarm, it's tepid. Some people seem to think that it harms the fish but I have never seen any dead fish floating downstream from the plant and I drive by there every working day. I fail to see how water that is only ten degrees above the temperature of the river water could have an impact on the fish. If the fish don't like it they can swim around it. Two or three miles down the river the temperature is practically back to normal. In fact, I think the fish like the tepid water which is evidenced by all the fishermen who prefer to do their fishing there."

"I think you are right, Dan; I saw two fishing boats out there when I drove across the I-40 bridge over the Clinch River,"

"The only dead fish I have ever seen in the Clinch or the nearby Emory River were due to our big ash spill in December of 2008," replied Dan. (The coal fly ash that is removed by the electrostatic precipitators from the smoke of the coal that has been burned in the furnace had been stored in huge ponds on the Kingston Steam Plant site. Due to heavy rains the pond gave way in December of 2008 causing the largest fly ash spill in the United States. It cost TVA around a billion dollars to clean up and there are still lawsuits pending as a result of the spill.)

"I have just one more question, Dan; what do you do about all the gases that are caused by the burning the coal?"

"We have made great strides in that area, Al. To reduce sulfur dioxide (SO2) emissions, all nine units use a blend of low sulfur coal. Limestone scrubbers have also been added to further reduce this gas. To reduce nitrogen oxides (NOx), all nine units operate with selective catalytic reduction systems which reduce these gases by 90%. In addition, Units one through four and Unit nine use combustion controls and boiler optimization. Units five through eight utilize low NOx burners."

"You have been most helpful to me Dan; do you mind if I quote you in my articles?'

"Not at all, Al; I am more than glad if I have been able to answer your questions and help to educate the public on how we operate our plants. I get sick to my stomach when I see so much propaganda and half truths in today's media regarding the power industry."

"My report will be in the Knoxville Sunday edition, Dan; I will send you a copy if you wish."

"Here's my address. I would like that very much; thanks."

This concludes my first report; my next report will be in this same section of next Sunday's newspaper.

Al Jameson

Chapter 38

Monday evening, February 7

Ace had arrived at home from work around 5:00 p.m. and was Playing with Freddy (The kid formerly known as Little Ace) while trying to watch TV at the same time when Paula came in from the kitchen.

"Did you have a busy day, Ace?

"Not too busy right now but Brad is considering taking on a case in Chattanooga. We have never gone to trial in another city before but we did have a case in Nashville a few years ago that we settled out of court so I don't know how that is going to play out."

"How far from Knoxville is Chattanooga, Ace?"

"It's right at one hundred miles, Paula."

"Thanks, Ace; supper will be ready at six."

"What are we having?"

"Spaghetti and meat balls along with a Caesar salad."

"Goody Goody," said Freddy; I just love getti."

They let Freddy watch the PBS (Public Broadcasting System) channel until the local Channel 3 Nightly News came on at six p.m. There was breaking news to start the program.

We have a breaking news story here at Channel 3 to lead off our news tonight. We have just learned that a suspect has been arrested in the January 14 rape and brutal beating of the eighteen year old coed at The University of Tennessee. We understand that the

coed entered her English 102 class at the last period of the day and recognized one of the students as her attacker. Upon seeing him she ran screaming from the room and University Security was called to find out what was wrong with her. They got her calmed down long enough for her to explain to the security officers that her attacker was still in the classroom. They immediately called the Knoxville Police Department (KPD) and they took the suspect into custody and transported him to the police headquarters for questioning. The KPD would not release the name of the suspect at this time; however the police are going to let the coed's roommate see if she can identify the suspect from a line up sometime tomorrow at police headquarters. We should be able to supply the suspect's name at that time.

We will keep our listeners informed here at Channel 3; stay tuned to this channel for all the latest news.

Just as the newscast ended the phone rang and Ace picked it up from the small table beside his Lazyboy recliner.

"Ace here" he said. He had been tempted to answer in his usual humorous voice with "City Morgue" but he was relieved that he hadn't when he heard the hysterical voice on the other end.

"Ace, screamed Denise at the top of her voice; do you know where Brad is? I must talk to him immediately; I have tried to call him on his home phone and cell phone but he doesn't answer."

"Today is his and Elizabeth's anniversary and they are dining at the Copper Cellar on Kingston pike and he did not want anything to interfere with their celebration. If it's important I can have him paged."

"It's extremely important, Ace; Doug has been arrested for the rape of that coed at UT (University of Tennessee).

"This is unbelievable, Denise; where are you?"

"I'm at the police station and they won't even let me see or talk to Doug; there's no way that he could have raped that girl. He just remarked to me the day when we first heard about the crime that he hoped that they caught the pervert and threw him under the jail."

"I know that Doug is innocent Denise; I am going to call Brad right now and have him meet us at the police station. Stay where you are and I will be there in thirty minutes."

Ace immediately had Brad paged at the restaurant and Brad said that he would leave at once and he and Elizabeth would meet him and Denise at Police Headquarters.

After Ace explained the situation to Paula, she remarked:

"I know that Doug did not commit this heinous crime, Ace; I wish that I could go with you to comfort Denise, but I have to be here with Freddy."

"I know, Paula; I'll let you know what I find out. I love you Love Bird, but I still can't get used to calling our son Freddy."

"He has already starting to answer to Freddy, because I think, it makes him feel big. Be careful, Ace, and if I can do anything from here let me know; I can make any needed phone calls."

"I don't know what time I'll be home but I'll call and let you know as soon as I can."

Ace jumped into his Mustang and probably broke a half dozen traffic laws getting to police headquarters and parked in one of the spaces reserved for detectives; at the moment he didn't give a hoot.

Chapter 39

It was about six thirty when Ace arrived at the police station; Denise was waiting for him and ran up to him and hugged his neck; she just needed someone's shoulder to cry on."

"Tell me exactly what happened, Denise."

"It must have been around five this afternoon when they walked into the classroom and arrested Doug. It was the last period of the day in English 102. They brought him here to police headquarters and allowed him to make one phone call and he called me. I had just walked into the house after I got home from work, and after I called you, I just turned around and got back in my car and drove here. I asked them to let me see Doug when I got here but they wouldn't allow me."

Just at that moment Brad and Elizabeth walked into the station.

Denise ran up to them and hugged them both and related to them what she had just told Ace.

"Can you point out to me the person who refused to let you see Doug?" asked Brad.

She led him around the corner and pointed to the man sitting in a room with a nameplate that read: "**CHIEF JAILOR**"

Brad knocked on the door and walked in without an invitation.

"The police arrested a young man named Doug Hart a few hours ago and His wife Denise has not been allowed to see or speak to him. I just want to know if he has been charged with a crime. His poor wife is at her wits end. They have only been married for about two months and out of the blue she finds her husband in jail and can't even talk to him. What is going on here, Mr., Chief Jailer?"

"Just who might you be, Sir?"

"My name is Brad Adams and Mr. Hart's wife works for me and I am here to protect her and her husband's rights; just what is your name and in what capacity do you serve here?"

The jailer recognized Brads name immediately and seemed to ease up a bit when he said; "my name is William Howell and I am the Chief Jailer."

"Is your last name spelled with one or two ells," said Brad as he took out a small pad and wrote the name on it.

"Wh wh why do you want to know that," replied the nervous Jailer.

"I just want to get the name right of the person I am going to sue for violating the constitutional rights of Denise and her husband if she doesn't get to talk to him."

"Let me see what I can do Mr. Adams; I have to make a phone call."

"Well make it fast; I don't think Denise can take much more of this."

Brad walked back to Ace, Elizabeth, and Denise.

"I think that you will be able to talk to Doug in a few minutes, Denise. Would you like for me to be Doug's Attorney?"

"That would be wonderful, Brad; I would rather have you than anyone else in the world."

"I don't think that would be a good idea Brad," said his wife and judge, Elizabeth; you have never tried a criminal case before." (Elizabeth was the presiding judge when Brad was sued in a scam lawsuit in 2007; they fell in love and were married a few months later)

"I am not signing on for the entire case, Elizabeth; I am just trying to get Denise to see Doug right now. I don't know whether there will even be a trial at this point in time." He turned to Denise and asked her if she had a dollar.

"No I don't, Brad. When Doug called me I was in such a state of shock that I left my purse lying on the kitchen table."

"Would you give her a dollar, Ace?"

"Sure," he said as he handed it to her.

"I want you to write the following on this sheet of paper, Denise and hand it to me with the dollar Ace just gave you."

"I hereby am engaging Brad Adams as my attorney for my husband, Doug Hart, on this the seventeenth day of February, 2011 in consideration for a one dollar retainer."

After she had written the document and signed it, Brad said: "Now let's go talk to Doug Hart. I don't know how long it will be before we get to see Doug or how long we will talk to him so it might be a good idea if Ace took you home, Elizabeth; I will be home as soon as I can."

"I will be glad to take her home," replied Ace, but call me if you need me; I don't think I'll be getting much sleep tonight anyway."

Chapter 40

It was around seven p.m. before Brad and Denise got in to see Doug. Brad had insisted that they be given a private room where they would not be overheard. They had to pass through a security check point to ensure that they had no weapons or drugs. They were cleared and taken back to a small room where they waited for the jailer to bring Doug out from his cell. A couple of minutes later a dejected and bewildered looking Doug was allowed to join them.

The minute Doug entered the room, Denise ran up and hugged him; they were both in tears. After they had calmed down, Brad began to question Doug.

"Tell me exactly what happened, Doug?" asked Brad.

"It was the last class period of the day and I had just sat down in English class 102 when this girl walked in and looked around and became hysterical and starting screaming and ran out of the room. We were all trying to figure out what was wrong with her because we saw nothing unusual or out of place in the room. Our instructor seemed also puzzled by this outburst and he left the room to see exactly what was going on. About five minutes later a University security guard came into the room and asked me to step out in the hall with him; I had no idea what he wanted with me. Two of them took me down to the security office without explaining to me what it was all about. I sat there for about ten minutes until a Knoxville police officer walked in and sat down next to me and said:"

"My name is detective Lt. Mize of the KPD (Knoxville Police Department) and you have been pointed out as the man who raped the coed on January 14 of this year. I need to see your driver's license and your University ID card."

"I handed him the cards and asked him if it was the girl that ran out of English Class 102 screaming that was accusing me of the rape charge."

"She is the one," he said

"I have never seen that girl before in my life, I said. Don't you think I would have fled from the classroom if I were the one who raped her?"

"That is not for me to decide, Mr. Hart; that will be up to a jury if you are charged. She is bringing charges against you and I am going to take you downtown for questioning,"

"I need to call my wife, Denise; she'll be worried sick if I don't come home on time."

"You'll get to make one phone call when we get to Headquarters, Mr. Hart."

"That's all I know, Mr. Adams."

"Did they read you your Miranda Rights, Doug?" (Brad believed that everyone should be aware of their legal rights although most criminals violate every right in the world of their victims but he did not believe that a criminal should be allowed to pass 'GO' and get off Scot Free just because a police officer forgot to read him his rights in the heat of an arrest. He felt that anytime within forty eight hours after the arrest would be ample time to mirandize them.)

"Yes; that was the first thing they did when they arrested me."

"Do you have an alibi for the time of the rape?" asked Brad.

"I think so; I don't know the exact time of the rape, but I was studying in the Technical Library at UT (University of Tennessee) until it closed at 10: p.m."

"Do you have any witnesses that you were there in the library, Doug?"

"There were about fifteen people in there but I didn't know any of them. May I ask you a question, Brad?"

"Fire away, Doug; I think I know pretty well just what that question is."

"How is it possible that in a free country the police can arrest and handcuff an innocent citizen in the presence of his fellow students and take him to jail without letting him talk to his wife?"

"Doug, you and I both know that you are innocent, but suppose that it was the real rapist that they arrested? Wouldn't you want him arrested and taken off the street? Based on what information the police had, they were just doing their job."

"I see your point, Brad; I guess it was just a roll of the dice."

"That's correct, Doug; we have to put all that behind us and work to clear your name right now. We have no control over what has happened to you in the past few hours."

"Will you be my attorney, Brad?"

"I'm not sure that is a good idea, Doug; I have never tried a criminal case before. I have signed on as your temporary attorney just so that I could get them to let you talk to Denise and me. I am going to call Mel Crosby, the Knox County AG, the first thing in the Morning and find out a few things. We need to know when your initial arraignment is to be held and I also want to know what public defender he may assign to your case."

"What is an arraignment, Brad?"

"It is where the AG or his appointed prosecutor takes you before a judge or a Magistrate who will set your bail and advise you that you are entitled to a lawyer in every upcoming step of your case. A date will be set at the arraignment for the preliminary hearing that is acceptable to all parties; the prosecution, the defense, and the accuser. The appearance bond is usually set high enough to ensure that the defendant will show up for trial, but I have to warn you that in some criminal cases the bail may be denied and the suspect will be held in jail until the trial."

"When do you think the arraignment will take place, Brad?"

"I am going to push for the earliest date I can get, hopefully this week sometime. I think that there are a maximum number of days that a suspect can be held before he is charged, but I am not sure just how long that is, somehow forty eight hours sticks in my mind but I'm just not sure."

"How long is it after the arraignment until the preliminary hearing?"

"It all depends on the availability of a criminal judge and the readiness of the prosecutor. I will do my best to get it speeded up; I hope it will be no longer that a month."

"What happens in the preliminary hearing, Brad?"

"You will appear before a judge without a jury and he will decide, based on the evidence presented to him by the prosecutor and whoever your lawyer may happen to be, if there is enough evidence to send the case on to a Grand Jury. In most cases the Grand Jury is nothing more than a rubber stamp for the preliminary hearing because you won't have your lawyer there to represent you."

"How long after it is decided to have a trial for me will it be before the trial takes place?"

"That is hard to say, Doug; sometimes it takes a year or more but you are entitled to a speedy trial by the US Constitution. I am going to brush up on that and see if we can get things speeded up."

"What am I supposed to be doing all this time, Brad; I don't have any money for bail?"

"You don't have to worry about bail, Doug; I'll take care of that. I want to get you out of jail ASAP so that you can go back to school without losing a semester and getting out of sync with the rest of your class. I plan to have you out of jail as soon as the arraignment is over."

"I don't believe that I could go back to UT (University of Tennessee) and face my classmates after what happened."

"That would be the best thing that you could do," said Denise. "I want you to go back with your head held high; you are innocent and I want you to act that way."

"I think you are right, Denise. I think that it will keep my mind off my problem and I know the studying will keep me occupied. However I don't believe that I could go back in my 102 English Class and have to face that girl again, whoever she is; I don't even know her name."

"I don't either, Doug, but we'll find out at the initial appearance and so will everyone else in Knoxville. I don't want either you or Denise to have any hard feelings toward the young women; she has been through hell and she really believes that you are the culprit. If you go to trial and show any animosity toward her the Jury will assume you are guilty. I want you to treat her with the utmost respect."

"I will do my best in that regard Brad and I have just one more question. If the judge at the preliminary hearing rules that I am to be tried what do I do about getting a lawyer?"

"In that case, the AG will assign a public defender to your case before the trial and he will work with you to come up with a defense."

"Do you have any idea who the AG might assign to me, Brad?"

"No I don't, but I am going to talk to the AG and see if he might give me a clue. He is a personal friend and I know he will be fair and try to appoint his best public defender to this case as a favor to me. Do you have anymore questions, Doug?"

"Not at this time, Brad. I just want to thank you for you help; I don't know what I would have done without you."

"I don't like to see an innocent man sent to prison for something he didn't do, Doug; I'll be in touch with you. I think it would be a good idea if Denise brought you your text books so that you can keep up with your assignments and stay occupied at the same time. I'll see if Ace can get the assignments from your instructors if you can give Denise their names."

"I can do that right now, Brad, and you can take it with you."

"That's good, Doug; write down the names and times of the courses, the name of the instructor, and the building and room number of each class."

After a couple of minutes Doug handed Brad the list. Brad would get Ace working on it the first thing Tuesday morning.

"Denise, would you bring me a good close up picture of Doug's face so that Ace can check to see if anyone remembers seeing him in the library the night of the rape?"

"I'll bring it in first thing tomorrow morning, Brad; thanks for all you've done for us."

"You're quite welcome, Denise; I'll see you tomorrow morning."

Chapter 41

Brad, Denise, and Ace all got to the office at seven a.m. so that they could get a heads up on helping Doug. Denise brought in a good close-up picture of Doug's face for Ace to use in his investigative work he was going to do at UT. Brad was going to call both the AG and the Knoxville Police Chief.

"Did either of you see this morning's paper?" asked Brad. Neither of them had seen it and were both shocked when they saw the headline; it read:

FORMER MARINE BEING HELD IN COED RAPE

Former Marine Sergeant, and now a UT student, Douglas Hart, is being held by the KPD (Knoxville Police Department) for the rape of the eighteen year coed on January 14 of this year. Police are waiting until sometime today when they will place Hart in a police lineup to see if the rape victim's roommate also recognizes him as the man whom she saw running from their apartment the night of the rape. He has already been fingered as the rapist by the victim when she walked into her English 102 class, the last class period Monday, and freaked out when she spotted him in the class room. We still don't have the identity

of the victim or her roommate, but we will keep our readers up to date.

"The law states that a person is innocent until proven guilty, Brad; so why do you suppose the newspaper used the term 'Former Marine in the headline? It looks like they are trying him in the paper?"

"What you just said is a common misconception, Ace; the law states that a person is 'presumed innocent' until proven guilty. In fact a person is guilty the moment he or she commits the crime. I'm more interested in how the newspaper came up with Doug's name and his service information; that information has not been officially released to the public. The news media and newspapers in particular want to sell newspapers," replied Brad, "and they do what they can to catch their readers eye. I remember a few years ago when there was a headline that read something like this:

CHURCH DEACON AND LOVER
PLOT TO KILL HER HUSBAND

"In a letter to the editor a few days later the writer pointed out that the Deacon was actually a reporter for a nearby city newspaper. He was stating that the paper should have identified the man as a reporter, his primary profession, instead of referring to him as a Deacon. To their credit, the newspaper published the writer's letter."

"I am and going over to the UT Technical Library and see if I can find anyone who remembers seeing Doug there the night of the rape." said, Ace.

"You go ahead Ace; I'm going to call the AG and the Police Chief to see what time the lineup is going to be for the raped girl's roommate to see if she picks Doug out of the lineup as the rapist. I want to make sure the lineup is made up of young men who are similar to Doug in height, age, weight, build, appearance, and hair color. I trust Mason Young, the Police Chief, but it would be real easy for someone to throw two or three local prisoners into the lineup who would skew the whole thing. I'll be there to protect Doug's interests. Let's try to meet back here some time this afternoon," said Brad.

"I'll try to make it back before quitting time," replied Ace, "but I will have to go back over there later this evening to visit the Technical Library to see if I can catch the same Librarian who was working there the night of the rape."

Chapter 42

Ace took a cab to the University of Tennessee campus because he knew it was almost impossible to find a parking space there during the weekdays. Doug's first class was math and it met at eight a.m. in the top floor of Ayres Hall Tower and there was no elevator; you had to walk the stairs. Ace remembered when he was at UT thirty years ago and lived on a fifth floor dorm room underneath the football stadium. Back then there were dorm rooms in the East and South Stadium halls. The football players lived in the East Hall and the basketball players lived in the South Hall along with ordinary students such as Ace. He also remembered that he had a math class in exactly the same room as Doug on the top floor of Ayres Hall. To get to his math class, in addition to having to walk down four flights of stairs, he had to walk up 99 steps from the ground level of the stadium to the top floor of Ayres Hall which was situated on top of the largest hill on campus.

It took Ace almost all day because he had to contact all of Doug's instructors and explain to them the situation and convince them to give him the lesson plans for Doug's classes. Most of them were sympathetic when Ace explained it to them. They all agreed to take Doug back in class if he showed up Monday of the coming week. They said he would be too far behind to catch up if he came back later than that because in engineering you learn as you go and each following class instruction depends on what one has learned in the previous class.

When he had gathered all the class lesson plans he called a cab to pick him up and take him back to his office. He arrived around 4:30 p.m. and Denise and Brad were still there. He greeted Denise and walked back to Brad's office.

"How did it go at UT, Ace," asked Brad.

"It went pretty well; I got all the class assignments but it took me all day. I am going back over there around eight this evening and see if I can get an alibi for Doug from the Librarian or some of the students who may have been there the night of the rape. How did it go with you, Brad?"

"Not so good I'm afraid. The lineup was scheduled for ten this morning but when I saw the lineup I was furious. There were only two out of the six who looked anything close to what Doug looked like and I believe that they might have been prisoners just taken from their cells. At least two of them looked to be in their early thirties. I threw such a fit that the Police Chief pulled out four young men from the Police Academy to come to the station and replace the four men that I had objected to."

"How did it turn out with the new lineup?"

"It didn't help at all, Ace; the young student picked Doug out of the lineup right away and she acted scared of him as well. It appears that he is going to be charged."

"Do they have any other evidence, Brad?"

"Not to my knowledge but they have the mask that Kristen pulled off the Perp's face. I don't think it will be too much longer before they test Doug's DNA against a hair from that mask."

"Is Kristen the name of the girl that was raped?"

"Yes, her name is Kristen Smith and her roommate is named Julie Brown. Both girls are from Dixon, Tennessee, a small town about forty or fifty miles west of Nashville."

"What if they don't find a match with Doug's DNA," asked Ace; "will he still be charged?"

"With the two strong ID's by the two girls, I believe that they will go on with the case without the DNA evidence, but if they do make a

DNA match, the ballgame is over and we will have to take our balls and gloves and go home."

"Mel Crosby will be coming up for reelection for AG next year, Brad; do you think that will affect his decision about charging Doug with rape and attempted murder?"

"I would like to think not, Ace; Mel has always been honest and up front with me. I don't believe he has any other choice."

"If that happens, Brad, Doug is going to need a good defense lawyer and I can't think of a better one than you. I think we owe it to Denise to provide Doug that defense. We could probably find a psychiatrist to testify that he is suffering from post traumatic stress (PTS) and is innocent due to his war experiences in Afghanistan."

"I am sure that we could find one, Ace, and I am also sure that the prosecution could find one who would who would testify exactly opposite to ours. I have seen that happen in court cases before and I can only draw two conclusions from those testimonies."

"What are they, Brad?"

"I can only conclude that one of them has no idea of what he is talking about or that one of them is lying."

"I totally agree with that, Brad, but we have to do something. Maybe we could use the Zoo Man's defense that was used back in February 1999." (On February 13, 1999, in the jury trial of Thomas 'Zoo Man' Huskey, the twelve panel jury deadlocked at 6-6 and a mistrial was declared by the judge. Huskey, a former zoo elephant trainer, had been charged with the killing of two prostitutes and leaving their bodies in nearby woods in East Knox County. At the time of the trial he was already serving a sixty six year term in a Tennessee prison for raping several women in 1991 and 1992 and had already confessed to the killing the women and explained in detail exactly what he did to them and also gave them details of the crime that only the killer would know. The defense claimed that Zoo Man possessed multiple personalities that he couldn't control. One personality in particular, an evil alter ego named "Kyle", who according the Zoo Man, confessed to him the 1992 murders that claimed the lives of four prostitutes. After the 6-6 jury deadlock, the AG decided not to try him again because they had already spent more on his trial than any case in Tennessee history; they reasoned that he would probably die in prison during his sixty six year interment.)

"I don't believe we could come up with a jury that would render a verdict like that again, Ace."

"You are probably right, Brad, but if we could find the right jury, we might be able to convince them that Doug received improper potty training as a child."

"I don't believe we could be that lucky, Ace."

"Don't rule it out, Brad; Paula can do wonders in jury evaluation as she proved in your case when you were sued in that scam car injury that occurred in the parking garage beneath the BB&T Bank Building.

"She's the best I've seen, Ace, but she not a magician."

"Do you know how I would have voted if I were on that jury in the 6-6 tie, Brad?"

"You would probably have voted to convict the Zoo Man Ace."

"No; I would have voted not guilty for the Zoo Man, but I would have voted to send Alter Ego 'Kyle' to the gas chamber."

"Touché, Ace."

"What is our next step, Brad?"

"None of what we just talked about is going to happen; Doug is innocent. I am going to call in a favor to the AG and see if I can get him to speed up the arraignment; hopefully before the end of the week. If Doug is charged with the rape based solely on the two girls' ID's, I don't see how they can deny him bail. If they do allow him bail, he can start back to class Monday morning."

"How will he come up with the bail money, Brad?"

"He has no bail money; I am going to try to get him released to my custody, but if they do set his bail I am going to fight to keep it as low as possible, hopefully around $100,000. I have enough money in Treasury Bills to cover almost any bail figure they arrive at, and I won't be out one red cent when I turn the bills over to them; they will continue to draw what meager interest they are drawing now. If you have nothing to add, Ace; I need to call Mel Crosby, the AG, before he goes home."

"I have nothing further right now, Brad; I'll keep you informed about what I find out at the UT Technical Library."

As soon as Ace left, Brad had Denise get The AG on the phone.

"What can I do for you, Brad," answered The AG, Mel Crosby.

"As you probably know, Mel, the wife of Doug Hart works for me and you probably also know that her husband, Doug, has been identified in a lineup by the victim's roommate as the man she saw running from the apartment. I would like to ask you to set the date for the arraignment as soon as possible so that he can get back in school by next week. I know that Doug is innocent of this crime and I am going to help him as much as I can."

"I will do everything within power to get it concluded before the end of the week, Brad."

"Can you tell me what evidence you have against Doug other that the two eye witnesses?"

"We have the ski mast which yielded a few hairs which we plan to send to the lab for DNA analysis."

"What about the semen sample?"

"We don't have a semen sample, Brad. According to the victim, the perpetrator used a prophylactic."

"Did you find the prophylactic?"

"No, he must have taken it with him."

"I have never heard of a rapist using a prophylactic, Mel; why do you think he did it?"

"I think the reason is simple, Brad; he didn't want to leave a DNA sample as evidence."

"That sounds to me like the rapist knew that the police already had a sample of his DNA on file with which to match it, Mel. I know that you don't have a DNA sample from Doug unless they have already taken it since his arrest."

"We don't plan to take a DNA sample from him unless we get a good DNA specimen from the hairs we found in the ski mask. Is there anything else that I can help you with, Brad?"

"You have been a great help, Mel; I couldn't ask for anything more at this time. I would appreciate it if you would keep me in the loop on everything that happens in this case."

"I will, Brad, and I'll also let you know as soon as the date is set for the arraignment. Are you going to be his attorney in this case?"

"I plan to represent him at the arraignment, but I have no plans at this time to further represent him."

"I'll see you then, Brad."

"There is one more thing, Mel; if this case does go to trial, I am going to request a speedy trial as is his constitutional right; he needs to get this injustice straightened up so that he and Denise can get on with their lives."

"Exactly what does the Constitution say about a speedy trial, Brad?"

"I have it right here in front of me, Mel; I was just reading it. I will read it to you; it reads:"

AMENDMENT V1
Right to speedy trial, witnesses, etc.
In all criminal prosecutions, the accused shall enjoy the right to a speedy and public trial by an impartial jury of the State and district wherein the trial shall have been committed, which district shall have been previously ascertained by law, and to be informed of the nature and cause of the accusation to be confronted with the witnesses against him; to have compulsory process for obtaining witnesses in his favor, and to have the Assistance of Counsel for his defense.

I go along with everything in the amendment except for the part of 'enjoying a speedy trial', Brad; I have never known a defendant to enjoy his trial."

"That was probably a poor choice of words; written in a different time," replied Brad.

"What is the maximum amount of time between the time the defendant was charged and the start of the trial do you consider to constitute a speedy trial, Brad?"

"No more than three months, Mel; I am going to insist that it be no longer than that."

"If you give me no longer than that, its really going to limit me in assigning one of my top defense lawyers to the case; you may end up with Rupert Cooper as the defense attorney."

"If that happens, Mel; I will take the case myself. I think that Cooper would intentionally lose the case just to get back at me." (Brad had embarrassed Cooper in a bogus lawsuit brought by him two or three years back when the jury found in Brad's client's favor and brought in a verdict finding Cooper at fault and assessed a $500,000 judgment against him payable to Brad's client.)

"I will let you know if and when we charge Doug Hart, Brad."

"Thanks, Mel."

Chapter 43

Tuesday evening

Ace got to UT around eight p.m. and had no trouble finding a parking place near the Technical Library. There were about twenty students in the library sitting around the tables. Ace walked up to the Librarian and apprised her of why he was here.

"My name is Ace Sleuth and I work for Brad Adams who is representing Doug Hart who is accused of the rape of The UT coed. I am trying to confirm an alibi for him because he has been mistakenly identified as the man who raped her on January 14, this year. He claims that he was studying here in the library until it closed at ten p.m. the night of the rape. The time of the rape was around nine p.m. If I can confirm that he was here it will clear him of this horrible crime. He had only been married for about two months when this accusation came from out of the blue and just about devastated Doug and his wife, Denise, with whom I have worked for over three years."

"My name is Judy Mullins; how can I help?"

"I would like for you to take a look at this picture of Doug, and see if you recognize him."

"Yes, I have seen him in here before and it is hard to believe that a nice young man such as he could be guilty of rape. He is one of the most polite students who studies in here."

"Do you remember if he was in here the night of the rape on January 14?"

"It would be hard for me to say exactly whether he was here, and if he was, at what time he left. I have seen him in here several times, but I couldn't swear in court one way or the other whether he was here during that time period. "

"Thanks a lot, Judy, for your kind words concerning Doug; his name will be cleared but right now he and his wife are at their wits end, not to mention his mother and Denise's mother and father. I also know that the raped girl and her family are also going through some terrible times, but it's simply a case of mistaken identity."

"I hope you can prove him not guilty, Ace; I will be praying for him."

"I appreciate that very much, Judy; do you mind if I pass this picture around to the students here in the library?"

"No, go right ahead; I hope you find someone who saw him here during that period."

Ace showed the picture to the twenty or so students in the library, but he didn't receive much help. A few remembered seeing his face somewhere but they didn't know where or when they had seen him since there are more than 30,000 students on campus; it could have been almost anywhere including classes, nearby restaurants, the Student Center, or even on the sidewalks. Ace walked back to his car feeling dejected; he drove home and went to sleep in his easy chair. Paula had already retired for the night.

Chapter 44

Wednesday afternoon

Brad had just returned from lunch when Denise informed him that, Mel Crosby, the Knox County AG was on line one.

"What's up Mel," answered Brad.

"I just wanted to tell you that I have assigned my assistant, Jim Satterfield to the Doug Hart case."

"I have a lot of respect for Jim, Mel. I appreciate you naming him; he will be fair.

"Yes he will, Brad; I consider him to be my best Assistant."

"Isn't it true that you have nothing on Doug except for the recognition by the two eighteen year-olds, Mel?"

"Yes; that is all we have."

"Do you still plan to go ahead with the arraignment, Mel?"

"I believe we have to, Brad; the recognition by them is very strong. I agree with you that Doug is probably innocent, but don't you think it would be better to have him cleared in a court of law than have everybody in Knoxville thinking he is guilty and the only reason he is walking the streets is because of your and my friendship?"

"I would sure like to see him cleared, Mel, but its going to be extremely hard on everyone involved. Look at all the people who will be going through sheer agony; there is Doug's mother, Denise's parents, and the two girls and their families.

I must warn you, Mel, that if I end up representing Doug I will do everything that's legal to defend him. I will conduct a rigorous search of the two girl's background and anything I find will be aired in court;

you might want to inform both of them and see if they still want to proceed. There is no doubt that Doug is innocent and I am going do everything in my power to prove it and let the chips fall where they may."

"We have to proceed, Brad; I have already made arrangements for the arraignment which will be held in courtroom 204 in the City-County Building (CCB) this Friday morning at nine; you are welcome to attend."

"I wouldn't miss it, Mel; are you going to request that a bail be posted?"

"I think in a case such as this, where the charge is rape and attempted murder that I have no choice, but I will keep the bail as low as I can."

"I have never been to an arraignment, Mel, just how does it play out?"

"It's really very simple, Brad; the judge or magistrate will inform Doug Hart of the offense for which he has been charged and also inform him that he has a right to a lawyer at every stage of the proceedings. The amount of any bail will be determined and a date set for the preliminary hearing which is the next step in the legal process. All the parties involved in the case including the witnesses and the accused must be present and agree to the date set for the preliminary hearing. A lawyer for the accused must represent the accused at the preliminary hearing; do you plan to represent Hart at the arraignment?"

"I will probably represent him at the arraignment but I'm not sure about the preliminary hearing at this time. Will I be able to speak out for Doug at the arraignment?"

"Of course you will, Brad, but we will not be debating his guilt or innocence at this stage of the proceedings. You will be able to discuss the bail issue and the date for the preliminary hearing only. You may try to get him released on his own recognizance or to lessen the bail amount. We will not be discussing the evidence or the lack of it at the arraignment."

"Speaking of evidence, Mel; it seems very strange to me that there was no hair from Doug in the ski mask if he was the one wearing it."

"That is a good point, Brad, but it is not uncommon for someone to wear something that covers their head and not leave a hair in it."

"Well someone wore it and someone left two hairs in it, and I believe that someone was the real rapist."

"You will have your say at the preliminary hearing, Brad, if you are Doug's attorney; I'll see you Friday morning."

"Thanks, Mel; I'll see you there."

Chapter 45

Friday morning. 9:00 a.m.

Brad, Denise, and Ace met outside the CCB courtroom 204 for the arraignment. Both the young coeds were present along with Mel Crosby the AG and his right hand prosecutor, Jim Satterfield. Presiding was Magistrate, Michael Strange.

Brad had never met or heard of Michael Strange, the Magistrate, but he was sure that he was not a judge or he would have heard of him through his wife, Elizabeth who is a judge. He wasn't exactly sure of the protocol to use in addressing the Magistrate so he decided to play it safe and address him as "Your Honor"; he decided that would be the safest way to go. It never hurts to bolster another person's ego, especially when that person was in a position to render decisions that could affect his client's life. This was the first time that Brad had seen the victim, Kristen Smith and her roommate, Julie Brown. Kristen was about five feet three inches tall with beautiful brown eyes and matching hair with a cute figure to go along with them. She was a clean-cut looking young girl with no apparent tattoos that some young girls like to exhibit. The plastic surgeon and dentist who volunteered their services to Kristen after her face was mutilated had evidently performed expert jobs on it because the scars were almost invisible and probably would be completely gone in a few months, and her teeth showed no signs of damage. Kristen's roommate, Julie was a couple of inches taller than Kristen and sported long blond hair that Brad guessed, came mostly from a bottle; but he had to admit that it looked good on her. Both girls were quite attractive.

138

After everyone was seated and settled in, the Magistrate made his opening statement:

"Are all the necessary parties here from both sides of the case?"

"The prosecution is ready, Mr. Strange," replied the AG.

"Who is representing the accused?"

"I am You Honor," spoke up Brad.

"Very well; let's get started. Mr. Hart, would you please stand?" Doug stood up.

"Mr. Hart, you have been charged with rape and attempted murder of Kristen Smith. I want to inform you of your right to be represented by a lawyer in every stage of this case. The next stage is the preliminary hearing for which the date will be set here today at a time which all parties must agree on. If bail is required we will also set that amount today; do you understand all of this?"

"Yes, Your Honor," replied Doug. (Brad had instructed Doug to also to refer to the magistrate as 'Your Honor.' It couldn't hurt and might just help.)

"I would now like to hear from the AG's office before we look at the bail issue," said the Magistrate.

"My assistant, Jim Satterfield will address the issue, Your Honor," said the AG, who had picked up Brad's method of addressing the Magistrate.

"We have looked at all the evidence presented to us by the KPD (Knoxville Police Department) and we believe that we have sufficient evidence to proceed in this case and we recommend that a bail be set at $200,000, Your Honor."

"What is your input on this, Mr. Adams?"

"I would like to see Mr. Hart released on his own recognizance Your Honor."

"What assurance can you give me that he will show up for the preliminary hearing?"

"There are several reasons, Your Honor. His wife, Denise has been my Secretary-receptionist for the past several years and still works for me. Mr. Hart plans to start back to the University of Tennessee in engineering this coming Monday and pick up where he left of if he is released on bond or otherwise here today. I will keep in contact with him every day and I will personally guarantee his appearance at the preliminary hearing and at his trial, if it comes to that"

"To help you along with your guarantee, Mr. Adams, I am going to set his bond at $50,000."

"Thank you, Your Honor; I will personally post the bond myself to show how much faith I have in this young man."

"Very well, Mr. Adams; see the court clerk concerning the bail bond. Now we need to set the date for the preliminary hearing. I have some dates for which judges will be available."

"I would like to make it the first available date, Your Honor," spoke up Brad, "so that all these young people can get on with their lives."

"I concur, Your Honor," replied the AG; both of these young ladies are also in school and need to get on with their lives and put this horrible ordeal behind them."

"Very well; the first available date for the hearing is on Monday, February, 28, 2011. Is this agreeable to everyone? OK, since we all agree, the hearing will be held in Criminal Courtroom 308 of the City-County Building (CCB) at 9:00 a.m.; the presiding judge will be the Honorable James Watson. This hearing is now concluded."

Brad met with the clerk to post the bond and gave him a $50,000 treasury bill and got a receipt. He and his entourage, including Doug, then returned to Brad's office.

"I thought that went rather well for us, Ace," said Brad.

"So did I," replied Ace.

"I am going over to UT (University of Tennessee) and see about picking up my classes where I left off a week ago," said Doug."

"What are you going do about English 102 where you and Kristen were in the same class?" asked Ace.

"To prevent further embarrassment to her I am going to ask to be transferred to another English 102 class."

"You don't sound like a rapist to me, Doug; you sound more like a gentleman," said Brad.

"I appreciate those kind words, Brad; I can never repay you and Ace and everyone else for sticking by me in my unfortunate situation.

I promise that I will not let you down. I will uphold my end of this case."

"I have no doubt of that Doug," replied Brad. You and I will have to get together before the preliminary hearing, would Saturday February, 26 be Ok with you?"

"That would be perfect, Brad; "do you want to meet here in your office?"

"Yes; let's meet here at 9:00 a.m."

"I'll be here, Brad, thanks again. I must be going now to arrange my classes."

Chapter 46

Saturday

Ace was home in his den with the Saturday local newspaper when he noticed the headlines:

ACCUSED RAPIST RELEASED ON $50,000 BOND
Former Marine Doug Hart was released in his arraignment hearing with a bail bond of only $50,000. This is an unusually low bail for the crimes for which he was charged, rape and attempted murder. His attorney, Brad Adams, apparently convinced the Magistrate, Michael Strange that he would personally vouch for Mr. Hart which he backed up by posting the bond for him.

The preliminary hearing has been set in criminal court for Monday February 28, Judge James Watson presiding.

We have learned that both the suspect, Doug Hart, and the victim, Kristen Smith, are going back to UT to pick up their classes where they left off. It will be much more difficult for Miss Smith than for Mr. Hart, she has missed almost a month of classes and he has just missed a week. Hopefully they will not be in any of the same classes at the same time.

Ace scanned the rest of the paper and settled back in his recliner to take a nap before watching the Tennessee Volunteers take on the Kentucky Wildcats in basketball.

Chapter 47

Sunday

After a breakfast of hotcakes and sausage, Ace settled in the den to read the five pound Sunday newspaper when Lisa walked into the room. (Lisa is Paula's twenty year old daughter whom Ace adopted shortly after marrying her mother. She attends Vanderbilt University in Nashville where she is studying PreMed). Paula walked in at about the same time.

"What's up, Big Daddy?" asked Lisa.

"Not much, Lisa; how is everything at school?"

"I am doing real well; I have a 3.82 GPA (Grade Point Average) and Sean's is about the same.

"It looks like I taught you well, Lisa," kidded Ace.

"You really helped me more than you will ever know, Ace, by giving me all those difficult problems over the years. Some of the problems I get in school are child's play compared to some of the ones you made me work." (Ace was always giving Lisa tough problems to work when she was in High School. He would have her derive equations and proofs that she would be using in college but would never be asked to derive them. One of the problems was to prove the Pythagorean Theory and another was to derive the Quadratic Equation; students would never be asked to do this in college. They memorized and used these two equations frequently in their studies to help in solving problems but just took them for granted.)

"Have you heard much about the rape of the UT coed in Nashville, Lisa?" asked Paula.

"We did at first but I haven't heard much lately. I understand that Denise's husband has been charged for the crime. I have never met him; what's he like?"

"He is one of the finest young men that I have ever met, Lisa, and I believe that he is completely innocent, in fact, Brad and I are working on the case and I may need your help before it's over."

"I would be glad to help, Ace; what do you want me to do?"

"I may need for you to do some computer work for me in a few weeks." (Lisa is very good at finding information about individuals on the computer. She was very helpful in a couple of civil lawsuits and in finding the kidnapper of five year old Trisha Parker three years ago.)

"Do you have any plans for this afternoon, Lisa?" asked Paula.

"I have a couple of hours; what do you have in mind?"

"I would like to go to West Town Mall and look around and do a little shopping; would you like to go with me?"

"I'd love to, Mom."

After Paula and Lisa had left, Ace picked up the Sunday paper to see how Al Jameson's investigative report on nuclear power was coming along.

Chapter 48

INVESTIGATIVE REPORT ON
NUCLEAR POWER
BY AL JAMESON

For this segment of my report I visited TVA's Watts Bar Nuclear plant near Spring City, Tennessee. I was greeted by the plant manager, Mr. Ralph Reynolds who practically gave me the key to the plant. One of the things that impressed me most with the Watts Bar Plant was the cleanliness of the plant and especially the Turbine Room; the floor in there looks clean enough to eat off of.

As I did in my previous report on the Kingston fossil plan, I am going to present it in dialogue form with permission from the plant manager, Mr. Ralph Reynolds. That dialogue follows:

"Is it OK if I call you Ralph?"

"Only if you let me call you, Al."

"It's a deal, Ralph. What can you tell me about Watts Bar Nuclear Plant; what's unique about it?"

"It probably took almost as much time to build this plant as it did to build the Great Wall of China." he kidded.

"How long did it take and why?"

"From the start of design in 1970 it wasn't until 1996 that it came on line."

"Is twenty six years considered a long time to bring a nuclear plant on line?"

"Both Units at Sequoyah Nuclear Plant a few miles down the road on the same river was built in one third that time and we only have one unit operating here at Watts Bar."

"Why do you think it took so long, Ralph?"

"There are two reasons, road blocks because of politics, and the NRC."

"What is the NRC?"

"It is the Nuclear Regulatory Commission and because of them and their policies there has not been another commercial nuclear plant to come on line in this country since Watts Bar in 1996; Watts Bar was the last one."

"What do you think is the reason for no more nuclear plants?"

"It's the cost; nobody can afford the cost. The original cost estimate for both units at Watts Bar was in the neighborhood of five hundred million dollars but unit one alone ended up costing seven billion dollars, an increase over the original estimate of fourteen hundred percent. They could have built twenty World Trade Centers in New York City for that money."

"What was the cost of the two units at the Sequoyah Plant and why was it built in one third of the time for the one Watts Bar unit?"

"I believe that the cost for the two Sequoyah units was about one billion dollars or one seventh of the Watts Bar Unit one cost. The main reason for the huge cost and delay of the Watts Bar Plant was because of the Three Mile Island Nuclear Plant accident on March 28, 1979 in Pennsylvania. Although there were no deaths or injuries in that incident, the NRC clamped down on all nuclear plant design and construction and the electrical utilities were forced to go back and look at anything and everything that the NRC could dream up. It added years and tremendous costs overruns in the industry and caused it to practically die out. Many companies shut down construction and abandoned plants that were well along in construction. TVA was forced to stop design and construction on four mammoth nuclear plants. They completely abandoned three which they sold for scrap for just pennies on the dollar and put a fourth one in moth balls."

"Do you think that what NRC was doing was wrong?"

"I think that NRC overreacted. We had the Watts Bar design almost completed when the Three Mile Island accident happened and had made it as much like the Sequoyah plant as possible. We were waiting for an operating license from NRC when the Three Mile Island accident happened. At that time the Sequoyah plant was sitting there quietly and safely producing electricity, and Watts Bar, which was almost identical to Sequoyah with many more bells and whistles, would not be granted an operating permit from the NRC. In my opinion the NRC was directly responsible for adding six billion dollars to the Watts Bar cost. If their purpose was to save lives then that six billion would have been better spent to provide enough money to construct concrete barriers between every mile of interstate highways in the Southeastern United States which would certainly save lives. If automobiles were built to the same safety standards as nuclear plants then every car would have two engines, four spare tires, two starters, and a back-up braking system and cost over a million dollars each. When I think about it, it might not be a bad idea to make our cars like this; after all, there are about 40,000 people a year killed in automobile accidents in this country. That's 40,000 more than are killed in nuclear plant accidents. If all the restrictions placed on nuclear plants is to save lives and protect the public then the money would be better spent to protect us from deer."

"Are you talking about the four legged deer?"

"That's exactly what I'm talking about, Al. Every year in this country, there are on average, 1,500,000 collisions between vehicles and deer that result in 150 deaths and thousands of injuries causing $1,100,000,000 in vehicle damage alone. The hospital and Doctor costs are considerably more. If we could thin the deer population by 50% we could cut all this carnage by half. We didn't have this deer problem fifty years ago until the government started releasing deer all over the country. My Father who lived in East Tennessee all of his life told me that he had never seen a deer when he was growing up. I think an environmental impact statement would have been in order before this insane policy went into effect. We have to prepare an environmental statement for almost everything we build in this country because of the extreme environmentalists. I think we should require them to file one also showing what would happen if we didn't build that nuclear plant. People would freeze from the cold and the electrical power might go off in the operating room.

We need to get rid of our nuclear hysteria and inject some common sense into our citizens. You can tell your readers that deer are much more dangerous than Nuclear Plants, Al."

"You just did, Ralph; I am recording our conversation and I am going to publish it word for word in Sunday's paper."

"How does TVA compare with other utilities in their design and construction, Ralph?'

"I think we have the best design and construction because we have our own design and construction people who work closely with one another. One example was the design and construction of Douglas Dam in East Tennessee in 1942during World War Two. By working day and night TVA was able to complete the Dam in one year. This is amazing when you think about what all is required to accomplish this feat. First there were coffer dams that had to be built and pumped out before the dam construction could begin. Then there were the turbines and generators that had to be ordered, built, delivered, and installed. There were thousands of cubic yards of concrete that had to be poured and left to set up before more was poured on top of it. In my opinion this was one of the most remarkable pieces of construction in the history of the United States."

"How does TVA's design and construction compare with the rest of the industry?"

"I can give you a good example."

"In 1950 the Atomic Energy Commission (AEC) requested TVA to submit a plan to supply one million kilowatts of power for a new gaseous diffusion plant the AEC planned to build in Paducah, Kentucky. TVA submitted a plan which the AEC accepted in November 1950. Shortly thereafter the AEC appeared before the House Appropriations Committee to request funds for the project. In December before the Committee had approved the funds, the AEC announced that it had accepted a proposal from a private utility to provide half of the needed power and TVA could provide the other half. It was decided that two new coal-burning plants would be built, one on one side of the Ohio River, and one on the other side with both plants in sight of each other. It became a contest between public and private enterprise. Many people thought that private enterprise could do it for half the cost. TVA's steam plant was named Shawnee and the private company's was called Joppa.

Both TVA and the private company had delivery and labor problems and both missed the original scheduled completion dates. Both had labor problems with work stoppages but the Joppa plant seemed to have many more than TVA's Shawnee Plant. Both plants drew from the same labor unions and paid about the same wages, but the comparisons stopped there; the first unit at TVA's Shawnee plant went into commercial operation in April 1953 while there was no indication of plant operation from the Joppa Plant. TVA's second unit went into operation on June 21, 1953 and there was still no operation at all from Joppa across the river. Several weeks later Joppa's first unit went into operation. TVA's third unit was placed in operation in October of 1953 and it's fourth in January of 1954. Two of the four Joppa units were in operation at this time.

To sum it all up cost wise, it cost the Private Company $184 per kilowatt of capacity, forty five percent above their cost estimate of $126 and it cost TVA $122 per kilowatt of capacity, which was below their cost estimate of $147.50. Based on these figures it means that the private company will have to charge the AEC more per kilowatt hour than TVA would in order to recover their higher construction costs."

"Was TVA subsidized by the government in building the Shawnee Plant?"

"Not in any way; TVA has never been subsidized by the government in the building of any fossil or nuclear plants."

"I wish that all government agencies were as efficient, Ralph."

"Don't we all, Al?"

"What is the capacity of Watts Bar, Ralph?'

"Watts Bar unit one has a capacity of 1167 megawatts."

"Just what does that mean to an average person like me, Ralph?"

"This one unit supplies enough electricity to power 650,000 average homes."

"How long can the unit run before you have to shut it down for refueling?'

"Watts bar holds the record in this country for continuous days of operation; it operated for 512 consecutive days in 2000."

"Do you consider this plant to be safe?"

"Absolutely; I wouldn't be working in here if I felt otherwise."

"What is the worst postulated accident that could happen?"

"It is a loss of coolant accident (ALOCA) that would probably be the worst."

"Would you mind explaining to me the exact sequence of events that follow that loss?"

"First let me explain just how the system operates. In the reactor building we have a pressurized water reactor where the coolant water is heated in the reactor and pumped by four reactor coolant pumps through the tubes of four large steam generators. In the shell side of these steam generators is the condensate from the steam that has been exhausted in the turbines that are on the same shaft that turn the generators that produce the electricity. The returning condensate, which we call feedwater at this point, goes through the shell side of the steam generator and picks up enough heat from flowing over the tubes, which contain reactor coolant, to convert it back to steam. The steam then goes back to the turbines and the process is continuously repeated.

A loss of coolant accident is highly unlikely because a pipe will leak before it breaks. All of our critical piping is certified and can be traced back to the heat number of the metal used to make the piping. In addition all of our welded pipe joints are radio graphed to insure the integrity of the welds. If a loss of coolant accident occurred the extremely hot water in the reactor and the pipes would immediately flash to steam and if it wasn't contained it could cause a very high pressure spike in the reactor containment vessel. About the only way one of our reactor coolant pipes could break and cause a loss of coolant would be the result of a massive earthquake."

"I thought all of TVA's nuclear were designed for earthquakes."

"If my memory serves me correctly, I believe that Watts Bar is designed to withstand an earthquake level of around 7.0 on the Richter scale. That's the same magnitude as the one that struck Haiti on January, 12 of last year. That earthquake practically wiped out the capital city of Port-au-Prince and killed almost a quarter of a million people. If that magnitude earthquake happened in this area our nuclear plants would still be capable of operating, but we might not have many customers with so many buildings destroyed. There would be wide spread damage to buildings and underground piping all around the area. We might have to cut back on our electrical output because of downed buildings and downed power lines. This design level of an earthquake of 7.0 has been agreed on as adequate by The NRC and earthquake experts all over the country. All of our plants could still operate or be safely shut down if one of these extremely large 7.0 rare earthquakes occurred. However if an earthquake was as large as the Great Alaska earthquake of 9.2 on the Richter scale in 1964, the entire country would probably be in bad shape. The earthquake was centered near Anchorage and at a magnitude of 9.2 on the Richter scale it was the largest earthquake ever recorded in North America and the second largest ever recorded on a seismograph. It created tsunamis (Waves) up to seventy feet high that occurred hundreds of miles from the epicenter of the quake. Some residents of Crescent City, California had gathered near the pacific to await the huge tidal wave that had been predicted for that area. Unfortunately twelve of those people who were evidently too close to the ocean when the tidal wave came ashore were swept back out with it and were killed. The entire earth vibrated, and as a result, minor effects were felt worldwide. It was reported that several fishing boats were sunk in Louisiana and water sloshed in wells in Africa. An earthquake of this magnitude could possibly cause a rupture of our reactor cooling pipes but then the least of our problems in the Tennessee Valley would be nuclear radiation; there would be wide spread damage such as high rise buildings and bridges collapsing all around us. Water piping underground would probably break also. There would probably be several thousand people killed and injured in the process and I still believe that we could still safely shut down the plant with all of our safety systems and contain the radioactivity.

The Reactor Building is not the only structure that is designed for a 7.0 earthquake; the Diesel Generator building which provides backup electricity in case of loss of our transformer station, the Control Building which houses the Control Room, and the Auxiliary Building which contains our safety systems are all designed for a 7.0 earthquake. As far as I know very few of our bridges and buildings in the private sector are designed to withstand an earthquake of the magnitude as the one postulated for Watts Bar"

"You mentioned a pressure spike associated with a loss of coolant accident; how do you control the pressure spike?"

"There are several ways. One of the first things that happen in an ALOCA is that the borated control rods will fall by gravity down between the fuel rods to absorb the neutrons that are causing all the heat to be generated in the reactor vessel. This action essentially stops the nuclear reaction but we still have to deal with all the heat that still exists in the containment vessel. We have many tons of borated ice inside the containment vessel that would absorb most of the heat and thereby reduce the pressure. The boron is added to the ice to help retard any further nuclear reaction in the coolant. The containment vessel is a steel dome about one inch thick and there is about a three foot separation between it and the concrete reactor building. It is designed to withstand fifteen pounds of pressure per square inch. Ice is much better able to reduce the pressure in the Containment Vessel than water because it takes 144 BTU's just to melt one pound of ice while remaining at the same temperature. After the ice has been melted, the water would still be available to provide further cooling to the atmosphere until its temperature reached equilibrium with the atmosphere inside the Containment Vessel."

"What is a BTU, Ralph?"

"A BTU, British Thermal Unit, is the amount of heat required to raise the temperature of one pound of water one degree Fahrenheit. It takes a thousand BTU's to condense one pound of steam; that means that it would take seven pounds of ice to condense one pound of steam back to water. This is the reason we use ice rather than water to condense the steam; if we used water it would take 144 times more water than ice. As a result of using ice here at our Watts Bar and Sequoyah plants we were able to have a much smaller reactor and containment buildings than at our Brown's Ferry units which do not use ice.

"What would happen here at Watts Bar in A 9.2 earthquake, Ralph?"

If we did have a 9.2 earthquake we would still have the ice to cool the containment vessel."

Besides the ice we have a containment spray system that will automatically come on and its pumps will pump water to a series of spray headers and nozzles inside the top of the containment vessel to further reduce the temperature and pressure of the reactor coolant water. We also have residual heat removal pumps that recirculate the leaked coolant water from a sump inside the containment and pass it through a heat exchanger where it gives up some of its heat to river water which flows back down stream to the river. Both of these pumps will operate continuously as long as they are needed because we have a backup for each pump in both systems."

"What is residual heat, Ralph?"

"Residual heat is heat that resides inside the reactor Building after a loss of coolant accident. This heat is in all the equipment inside; there is a tremendous amount of heat in the thick shell of the reactor vessel, the four huge steam generators, the Pressurizer, and the four large reactor coolant pumps and their piping. There is even heat in the walls of the reactor building; all this heat must be removed to lower the temperature and pressure down to an acceptable level. That is the job of the heat residual pumps and heat exchangers."

"How do you heat the water in the reactor, Ralph?"

"I'm surprised that you asked me that question, Al. First we fill the reactor and all the reactor coolant piping and pumps with pure distilled water; would you like to take a guess as to how we heat the water?"

"My best guess would be that you place a teakettle on the stove and pour the hot water into the reactor vessel.

"Very funny, Al; actually we heat the water by spinning the reactor coolant pumps. If we run them long enough we can heat the water as hot as we wish. Much of the electrical energy going to operate the pumps goes to heat the water through friction in the piping and equipment.

Here at Watts Bar we have four separate reactor coolant loops; each loop consists of a reactor coolant pump, the piping, and a steam generator. Unlike TVA's Browns Ferry Nuclear Plant, we don't want any steam inside our reactor vessel. It is kept under a very high pressure and temperature by a large vertical pressure vessel called a Pressurizer. When we start heating the reactor coolant after we have heated it to a certain level with the reactor coolant pumps, we heat it further with nuclear power. We position the control rods a little to start the nuclear reaction and keep heating the water until we reach the desired pressure and temperature in the Pressurizer. When that happens there will be a cushion of steam in the top of the Pressurizer. The temperature of the water in the reactor vessel must be kept much higher than the temperature of the steam leaving the steam generator. The Pressurizer takes care of this problem for us."

"You mentioned that you did not want steam in the reactor like Browns Ferry plant does; what did you mean by that statement?"

"The Browns Ferry three unit plant is a boiling water reactor type where the steam is actually made in the reactor vessel. This causes their reactor vessels to be much larger than the one at Watts Bar because the vessels have to contain both water and steam. As a result of making the steam in the reactor vessel, the steam that goes to the turbines is slightly radioactive and its piping must be shielded. The steam here at Watts Bar is not radioactive. There are advantages and disadvantages of both systems."

"What would happen if you lost electrical power at the same time as the loss of coolant accident?" asked Al.

"We have diesel generators that are sized to supply all the power we need in an accident. We even have a back up in case one of them goes out."

"How do you start them if there is no electricity?"

"We have compressed air to the diesels to start them immediately upon loss of electricity and we periodically test the diesel generators do ensure that they will work as required."

"It sounds like you have all your bases covered, Ralph; how many people do you think would be killed in a loss of coolant accident?"

"None; but we would have a big mess to clean up."

"If there are none, what is all the negative stuff I hear about nuclear power being unsafe?"

"In my opinion it is nothing more than fear mongering by people who know absolutely nothing about nuclear power. The reason I say nobody would be killed or even over exposed to radiation is because there is no one inside the lower compartment of the Reactor Building while the unit is operating."

"Is there any danger at all from radiation from working or living near this plant?"

"There is no danger for people working here if they follow procedures. The amount of radiation to an individual allowed by the NRC is set at extremely low levels; the human body could probably safely absorb much more, but I'm glad that it's that way. As far as radiation exposure to people living nearby is concerned, they could receive more radiation from standing atop Lookout Mountain in Chattanooga than they would by leaning against the reactor building because they would be nearer the sun which emits radiation. If you're worried about radiation yourself, don't be. The radiation dosimeter badge we gave you will be checked for over exposure when you leave here.

It amazes me, Al, that, so many otherwise intelligent people in this country are scared to death of nuclear power when we have had people voluntarily living just a few feet from nuclear reactors in the same structure for more than fifty years."

"Are you sure about that, Ralph, and why have I not heard about it?"

"It's absolutely true, and to my knowledge, there has not been a single death or over exposure to nuclear radiation to these people. I'm sure that you have heard of our nuclear submarines; they have the same type of pressurized water reactor that we have here at Watts bar except it is much smaller."

"Yes, but you said that the people who are there, are there voluntarily; how is this possible in the Navy?"

"Submarine duty is voluntary duty; it does however pay a little more, but not because of the nuclear part, but because it has always been voluntary; even before we had nuclear submarines. Submarine duty is not for everyone; some people could not tolerate being locked in a sealed container for weeks and months on end and I would probably be one of them."

"You are right, Ralph; a submarine is not very large compared to other navel vessels and those sailors couldn't be very far from the reactor."

"That's correct, Al, but there is adequate shielding provided just as there is here at Watts bar. Before you go I would like to share an amusing story that happened right here at Watts Bar during construction. When nuclear piping is installed in the plant, all the pipe joints are welded together. This includes elbows, tees, flanges, and the welding of lengths of pipe together. To insure the integrity of the welded joints, each weld is radio graphed.

One day the weld of a pipe joint at the intersection of two lengths of piping was being radio graphed. This requires that a small hole be drilled in the piping near the joint so that a small probe can be inserted inside the piping; it's sort of like your dentist placing an x-ray film behind your tooth. By the way, the small hole is welded shut after the x-ray is taken. If any defects are found in the weld joint it is properly repaired.

On this particular day, unbeknown to the workers performing the x-ray, there was a man sleeping on duty inside of the thirty six inch diameter pipe about ten feet down the pipe from the x-ray joint. The other end of the pipe was open and that is where he had crawled in. All the commotion and activity at the x-ray joint must have awakened him from his goofing off because he sheepishly crawled out pipe for everyone to see. When he discovered that the workers were performing an x-ray just ten feet from him he hired a lawyer to sue TVA for over exposure to harmful radiation."

"Did he win his lawsuit, Ralph?"

"I don't know; I never heard anymore about it; I doubt very seriously if he could have received enough radiation to even register on his dosimeter. I think he would have been very lucky just to have kept his job."

"Thanks a lot for sharing with me Ralph; I have really been enlightened about nuclear energy; I don't have any more questions at this time. Is it Okay if I come back next week to finish my report?"

"I will be looking forward to it, Al; it has been my pleasure."

This concludes my report for this segment; next week I will conclude my Watts Bar Nuclear Plant portion of my investigative report on TVA Power.

Al Jameson.

Chapter 49

Monday

Brad, Ace, and Denise were all back at work Monday morning and were having their traditional coffee and donuts. Doug was back in class at UT and had managed to get into an English Class that didn't include Kristen Smith.

"I think we need to face the fact there is going to be a jury trial for Doug and it may be the best thing for all those involved. We need to clear Doug's name once and for all and the only way to do that is to have him found not guilty by a jury of his peers. If he were to be let off now without a trial there would always be doubt in most people's minds about his guilt," said Brad.

"I agree with you, Brad," replied Ace. I know down deep in my heart that Doug is innocent but the two girl's identification of him is very strong; they both believe that he is the rapist. My problem is; if it wasn't Doug that they saw, it had to be someone who looked a whole lot like him. That leaves me with just one conclusion."

"What are you getting at, Ace?" asked Brad.

"We know that Doug was adopted and who could look more like him than an identical twin?"

"I think you're just day dreaming, Ace; they would never separate identical twins, and even if they did, the odds of that other twin raping a girl that goes to the same university as Doug are astronomical."

"Never say never, Brad anything is possible. Denise, Could you get me a copy of Doug's birth certificate?"

"Yes, we have one at home. I'll make you a copy and bring it in tomorrow."

"We need to be thinking about the trial, Ace, not some far-fetched theory without any facts to back it up," said Brad.

"You're probably right, Brad, but what are we going to do to clear Doug's name?"

"We're going to prepare for the trial that we all know is coming and we need to start right now. I will be asking for a speedy trial as guaranteed by amendment V1 of the Constitution."

"How long a duration from the time of arrest until the trial starts does the constitution allow?" asked Ace.

"It doesn't specify the precise amount of time, but I am going to insist that it be no longer than three months."

"That doesn't give us much time, Brad," said Ace.

"You're right about that, Ace; I am going to need Paula's help on the jury evaluation. She can work out of her home if she prefers."

"She would be happy to help, Brad; she has already indicated that to me."

"We need to prepare for the Preliminary hearing that is coming up in just one week from today on Monday February 28. We don't need to do much preparation for that because I am not going to fight it too hard."

"What about the Grand Jury, Brad?" asked Ace; are you going to do anything about it?"

"As far as I'm concerned, Ace, the Grand Jury is nothing more than a rubber stamp for the preliminary hearing; they will vote to send this case on to a jury trial and I will not fight it. If there is nothing else to discuss we will adjourn for now. It's time for everybody to get back to work."

Chapter 50

Tuesday

As promised, Denise brought Ace a copy of Doug's birth certificate; he picked it up as he was heading back to his desk. He grabbed a doughnut and a cup of coffee and took a look at the birth certificate.

In block 1, the child's name on the certificate was listed as Douglas Lee Hart born on June 10, 1985 in Nashville in Davidson County, but the name of the hospital in block 5d was left blank. Ace thought this was rather odd. The mother's maiden name shown in block 6a was listed as Elizabeth Ann Jones, and in block 8a the father was listed as Ralph W. Hart. Block 4a was the one that interested Ace the most; its heading read: **'THIS BIRTH-SINGLE, TWIN, TRIPLET, ETC. SPECIFY'**; the block was left blank; Ace found this to be very interesting. He called Denise on the phone; "Do you know the hospital in Nashville in which Doug was born," he asked her.

"He was born in Vanderbilt Hospital, Ace; why do you need to know?"

"I am working on a long shot hunch; I think that Doug may have an identical twin somewhere. I know in my heart that Doug didn't rape that girl, and if he didn't do it, it had to be someone who looked a lot like him."

"I really appreciate the effort that you are making on his behalf; we can never repay you and Brad for all you're doing."

"Proving that Doug is innocent is all the payment I want, Denise."

Ace then called Jennifer Adams, a former nurse at the now defunct Baptist Hospital. (Ace had crossed paths with Jennifer in 2006 when she was working at Baptist and he tried to snow her by claiming that he was a doctor from Vanderbilt Hospital when he was actually working for Brad Adams on a scam lawsuit brought by a patient who had been in Baptist Hospital and with whom Ace had wanted to check up on. Jennifer recognized him right away because about twenty years ago when she was only five years old, her mother had hired Ace to try to locate her ex husband to get to pay the alimony that the court had ordered him to do. She led him on for several weeks and almost drove him crazy because she would do almost anything he asked her to do. It came to a head one day when Jennifer called him on his office phone. He knew then that she knew who he was all along. He introduced her to Brad's son David and they were married in a double wedding ceremony with him and Paula. She quit working at Baptist when their son, David Bradford was born in 2008 on the same day and in the same hospital as Ace and Paula's son, Little Ace.)

She answered the phone on the first ring.

"This is Ace, Jennifer and I need your help."

"You sound a lot like Dr Zachary from Vanderbilt Hospital, Sir."

"It's funny that you should mention Vanderbilt Hospital, Jennifer; that subject is exactly what I'm calling you about."

"How may I help you, Ace?"

He explained to her about what he was doing to bring her up to speed. "Do you know anyone who works at Vanderbilt Hospital?"

"I just happen to know the Head Nurse there; she was my supervisor when I did my nursing internship at Fort Sanders Hospital here in Knoxville."

"I wonder if you could set up an appointment for me to meet her at Vanderbilt Hospital."

"I believe I can; when do you want to meet?"

"The sooner the better; tomorrow afternoon would be a good time for me. What is her Name?"

"Her name is Joan Sanders; let me give her a call and I'll call you back as soon as I talk to her. Are you at the office?"

"Yes, the number is 554-7777; thanks a lot Jennifer"

Jennifer called Ace back in about fifteen minutes.

"You have an appointment with Joan at one p.m. tomorrow afternoon, Ace. Nashville is on Central Standard Time so you will gain an extra hour going. Just go to the desk in the main lobby and inform them that you have an appointment with Joan Sanders and they will direct you to her office."

"I don't know how to thank you, Jennifer; it seems like I am always asking you for help."

"Good luck on your venture, Ace."

After he got off the phone, Ace walked over to Brad's desk. "I need to make a trip to Nashville, Brad."

"Are you still on that wild goose chase with your, 'identical twin', scheme of yours, Ace?"

Ace showed Brad the copy of Doug's birth certificate.

"Take a look at block 4a where the type of birth heading, such as Single. Twin, Triplet etc. is supposed to be listed?"

"Yes I do; I see that it was left blank."

"I find it a little strange that they would leave that blank, Brad, I need to go to Nashville so that I can fill in block 4a. I will pay my own expenses if you can do without me tomorrow."

"Just put it on your expense account, Ace; we've had a pretty good year to date. Do you plan to spend the night?"

"It all depends on what I find out at the hospital."

"Just keep a record of all your expenses, Ace and don't worry about the costs."

"Thanks Brad."

When Ace got home from work he explained to Paula what he was working on and why he needed to go to Nashville.

"Why don't you stop by Vanderbilt University and look up Lisa; The University is next door to the hospital?"

"If I can locate her I will, but she will probably be in class. If I have to spend the night I'll try to take her out to dine."

"What time are you leaving, Ace?"

"I plan to leave about 8:00 a.m. so that I will have time to stop at the Cracker Barrel in West Knoxville and get some breakfast."

"I would be more than glad to fix you breakfast, Ace."

"You can get your beauty sleep. Paula; I've been looking forward to having some country ham and eggs."

Chapter 51

Wednesday morning - Trip to Nashville

Ace left home at eight and got on I-40 West at Papermill-Northshore Drive and headed toward Nashville in his beloved 76 Mustang. He got off about eight miles west on the Lovell Road Exit and crossed back under the Interstate and pulled in to the Pilot gas Station on his right. He looked at another Pilot Station just across the road and a half block south. The only difference between the two stations was that the one at which he stopped did not sell diesel as did the one across the road. (Pilot Corporation was founded by James Haslam who attended the University of Tennessee where he played tackle on the 1951 National Football Championship team. His first station was a four-pump gas station where he also sold soft drinks and cigarettes. As the company grew he added more stations in Tennessee and throughout the Southeast. In 1965 Pilot was bringing in about $2,000,000 per year, and by 1973 it was operating fifty stations and bringing in $30,000,000 a year. By 1981 Pilot had converted most of its locations into convenience stores-gas stations with annual sales of $175,000,000.

Pilot continued to grow and by 1997 it was ranked 99th on Forbes Magazine's list of the largest family held companies in the United States. It is now the largest supplier of diesel fuel for over the road trucks in the United States as well as the twenty fifth largest restaurant franchises in the country. Today Pilot operates more than 300 travel centers in the United States and Canada.

The Federal Trade Commission approved the 1.8 billion merger of The Pilot Corporation and Flying J in June of 2010. The merged company (Pilot Flying J) which will have its headquarters in Knoxville will have a total of 550 travel centers which makes it the largest retail operator of travel centers in North America. Denny's Corporation is planning to incorporate 140 restaurants of The Flying J into their own in the near future.

James Haslam and his wife, Nancy, have given $32,500,000 to the University of Tennessee toward the University's one billion dollar fundraising effort. The new James A. Haslam Business Building on the University Campus was dedicated a couple of years ago.)

Ace gassed up and drove to a nearby Cracker Barrel restaurant to get breakfast. He was immediately seated and shortly his waitress arrived with the menu. He noticed that her name was Gail and he decided to have a little fun at her expense; he said:

"Gail, I would like two fried chicken eggs with country ham."

"I'm sorry; Sir, but we don't serve fried chicken until 11:00 a. m."

"I just want two fried chicken eggs with country Ham."

"I just told you, Sir, that we don't serve fried chicken until eleven."

"Do your cooks back in the kitchen fry eggs, Gail?"

"Of course they do."

"What kind of eggs do they fry, Gail?"

"She thought for a minute and replied; they fry chicken eggs, Sir."

"I thought that was what I ordered, Gail."

"You're exactly right, Sir; my mistake. Would you like to order that from the senior menu?"

"The regular menu would suffice," Ace sheepishly replied.

The bill came to about six dollars; Ace left her a five dollar bill for the tip and paid the bill at the cash register as do all other Cracker Barrel customers. He reasoned that they did it that way to give their restaurants a touch of the days gone by. After eating, Ace continued on his Nashville trip.

Chapter 52

Ace arrived in Nashville around eleven thirty central time and found a parking garage a block from Vanderbilt Hospital; he decided to call Lisa on her cell phone. She answered on the second ring.

"What's up, Ace," she asked.

"I'm in Nashville working on a case and I would like to take you out to lunch if you have time."

"I would love to. I don't have to be in class until one this afternoon; where would you like to eat?"

"Why don't you pick a place; you know Nashville better than I do."

"There's a Ruby Tuesday on Broadway about a block from the University and the hospital."

"I can be there in ten minutes, Lisa."

"I'll meet you there."

Ace arrived at the restaurant ahead of Lisa and when he was seated he discovered a copy of the Nashville Tennessean Newspaper someone had left in the chair. He opened it up and an item caught his eye. It was about an article in the Vatican Newspaper that addressed the Vatican's efforts to be more relevant in today's society. It read in part:

The weekend story was the latest example of the Vatican's paper's efforts to be more relevant in the last few years, and follows stories not only lauding

Harry Potter but even praising the Beatles and waxing philosophical about John Lennon's boast that the British band was more popular than Jesus.

As soon as Ace had finished reading the article Lisa walked in and sat down across the table from him.

"It's good to see you again, Lisa; we have all missed you."

"How is Little Ace doing; I miss that little rascal?"

"He doesn't like to be called Little Ace anymore; he wants to be called Freddy, and he misses you too."

"I like that name; it just fits him."

"I was just reading an article in the Nashville paper when you walked in, Lisa and I would like to get your comments on it."

Lisa took about a minute to scan the article and turned to Ace and said: "Who is John Lennon, and what are the Beatles?"

"Where have you been, Lisa, the Beatles were the most popular band in the sixties and the seventies?"

"I wasn't even born until 1991, Big Daddy, but they must have considered themselves extremely important if John Lennon thought they were more popular than Jesus Christ."

"Do you know what my reply would have been to John Lennon, Lisa?"

"No, but I know that you are going to tell me."

"You are right; my reply would have been: Check back with us in 2000 years, John, and see if you still feel that way and tell me how popular you are then."

'That's a good reply, Ace."

"Thanks, how is school, Lisa; do you have enough money to live on and buy your books?"

"I am doing very well, Ace; as you know I have a full scholarship here that includes room and board and I get lottery money from the state as well."

"Do you need a car?"

"No. my dorm is within walking distance of all my classes; plus Sean has a car and we use that to go out and eat and when we travel back to Knoxville about once a month."

"Paula and I both miss you and Freddy is always asking: 'where is Litha?' It's hard for him to understand why you had to leave home."

"How is Denise holding up, Ace; I can't believe what her and Doug must be going through. Is there any chance that Doug might be guilty?"

"Not a chance in this world, Lisa. The reason I am here today is try to prove his innocence." Ace explained the salient points of the case to Lisa and why he was going to Vanderbilt Hospital.

"If I can help in any way just let me know Ace."

"I will probably need your help before it's over, Lisa."

"If you and Sean come up to Knoxville we will take you out to the restaurant of your choice if you give us enough notice so that we can make reservations."

"I think Sean would love that unless his parents have other plans; I'll let you know as soon as I talk to him."

"How are your studies coming along at Vanderbilt, Lisa?"

"I am doing real well and so is Sean."

"What is the most interesting subject you are taking?"

"Almost any subject would be interesting compared to Anatomy I suppose, but I would have to say that it is Political Science."

"I think that calling it Political Science is quite a stretch, Lisa; what are you studying in it now?"

"We are studying the Communist Manifesto by Karl Marx."

"Didn't he have a co-partner in writing the paper, Lisa?'

"Yes, Friedrich Engels worked with Marx but Marx is considered the father of Communism today"

"Did you know that Marx did not really believe in Communism as we know it today, Lisa?"

"What are you talking about, Ace; I have never heard anything about that?"

"Karl Marx was a very stubborn, conservative, and proud man who did not like to admit mistakes. The Communism we know today is because of one German woman."

"What German woman, Ace?"

"Her name is Frederica Steinhauser."

"Why have I never heard of her, Ace?"

"It is a well kept secret, Lisa, but it is because of Karl Marx's pride that this has been kept secret for over 160 years."

"Who was this woman and what part did she play in the Manifesto?"

"She was Marx's secretary-typist and it was a one letter typo that changed history."

'Tell me more."

"After he and Engles had written the Manifesto, Karl felt that it needed a phrase or slogan to go along with it so he wrote it out on a sheet of paper and gave it to Frederica to type but he didn't notice the typo until the manifesto had been picked up and serialized in a London newspaper and was being written about around the world, especially in Russia."

"What was the typo all about, Ace?"

"The slogan was supposed to read: 'From each according to his abilities, to each according to his deeds'."

"How did it read after it was typed?"

"Frederica made only a single letter typo when she typed an 'n' instead of a 'd'." After she had finished the typing, it read: 'From each according to his abilities, to each according to his needs'."

"I believe that Frederica made more than one typo unless Old Karl was a Male Chauvinist."

"What are you talking about, Lisa; it happened just like I told you. How do you think it was supposed to read?"

"It should have read: 'From each according to their abilities, and to each according to their needs.'"

"I see your point, Lisa; I guess Karl was a Male Chauvinist but that was the way things were done in that era." Ace then removed his recently acquired iPhone from his inside coat pocket and logged on to the internet and pulled up Section Seven of Article 1 of the US Constitution and handed it to Lisa; it read in part:

Every bill which shall have passed the House of Representatives and the Senate, shall, before it becomes a Law, be presented to the President of The

United States; if he approve he shall sign it, but if not he shall return it, with his Objections to that house in which it shall have originated.

"Did you pick up on the word, 'he' in that section, Lisa?"

"I see your point, Ace. When did you get your iPhone?"

"It's a gift from, Brad; he thought it might be helpful in my work."

"You got a nice boss, Ace."

"Yes, I know, Lisa; I think we could use that section of the Constitution to prevent a woman from becoming President of the United States." joked Ace.

"I believe that you are more of a Male Chauvinist than Karl Marx, Ace, and besides that, you're still full of it. Do you ever get serious?"

"You sure know how to hurt a fellow, Lisa, but it's my story and I'm sticking to it. I do have my serious moments you know; in fact, this is a very serious mission that I'm on here in Nashville to clear Doug's name."

Sean and I don't have early classes tomorrow so we are going to a movie tonight, Ace?"

After they had eaten, Ace gave her a big hug and she headed back to her next class and Ace walked the short distance to Vanderbilt Hospital to meet Joan Sanders.

Chapter 53

Filling in block 4a

Ace walked the short distance to the main lobby of Vanderbilt Hospital and Joan sanders was standing at the receptionist's desk waiting; it was one 0'clock exactly according to the big clock on the wall.

"You must be the famous Ace Sleuth," she said as she stuck out her hand which Ace shook vigorously. "I like people who are punctual; let's walk back to my office where we can have some privacy."

"Sounds good," replied Ace; do you mind if I call you Joan?"

"I wouldn't have it any other way. Jennifer seems to think a lot of you, Ace, and I think a lot of her and trust her judgment; she was my best nurse intern at Fort Sanders in Knoxville. She has explained a little of what you are working on; could you please expand on that a little further?"

"I would be happy to, Joan. The husband of Denise Hart who has been working for my boss, Brad Adams for five years has been charged with rape and attempted murder of a University of Tennessee coed and I know that he is not guilty. The only evidence is the eye witness identification by the victim and her roommate. I have come to the conclusion that if it wasn't Doug it had to be someone who looks a whole lot like him. I think that he might have an identical twin."

"How can I help, Ace"

"Doug Hart was born in Vanderbilt Hospital on June 10, 1985 and I have a copy of his birth certificate. In block 4a, where the type of birth, single, twin etc., was supposed to be recorded, it was left blank."

"That does sound a little unusual; let me check my computer records and see what I can pull up. We have just completed the laborious task of installing all of our hospital records in our computer system. There are still a few glitches, but I'll give it a try and see what I can come up with."

She brought up the computer screen and typed in 'Maternity Ward' followed by the year 1985. When the year came up she typed in the date, June 10.

"Let's take a look, Ace and see what we have here; there were six births on that date, three boys and three girls; however one of boys was a still birth. I see the names of the girls but for the boys; they are both listed as John Doe 1 and John Doe 2."

"What does that mean, Joan?"

"It means that both of the boys were adopted; we didn't have the adopted parent's names for our records at that time."

"Does it mean that the two boys were twins?" asked Ace.

"Not necessarily, Ace; however it is possible."

"How can I find out?"

"The records show that a Mrs. Alice Hutchins was the head Maternity Ward nurse at the time, but she no longer works here; she retired about five years ago."

"Do you have her address?"

"I can have my secretary get it for you. (She called her secretary and told her to get the address for Ace.) She'll have it ready for you as you leave, Ace."

"Thanks, Joan; I really appreciate your help. You may have enabled an innocent man to obtain his freedom."

"I certainly hope it works out to your satisfaction, Ace; is there anything else that I can help you with?"

"I can't think of a thing, Joan; thanks again."

Ace picked up the address from Joan's secretary and noticed it was a Nashville address and that she had also included a phone number. He stopped in the hospital gift shop and purchased a map of the city of Nashville.

Chapter 54

Ace walked to the parking garage, and as soon as he got in his old Mustang, he dialed 615-554-9871 on his Knoxville based cell phone; a female voice answered.

"Is this Mrs. Alice Hutchins, he asked?"

"To whom am I speaking," the voice asked.

"My name is Ace Sleuth from Knoxville, and I just left the office of Joan Sanders and she gave me your name. I need to talk to you about a birth in Vanderbilt hospital in 1985."

"Come on over, Ace I could use a little company; my husband died two years ago and I get lonesome here by myself all alone. She gave him directions and Ace was ringing her doorbell twenty minutes later. She opened the door and welcomed him in.

"If I had known you were so handsome, Ace I would have rolled out the red carpet."

"You're too kind, Alice." Alice looked to be about seventy years old and still rather attractive.

"Would you like some tea or coffee, Ace?"

"Yes I would like some coffee with cream."

She went into the kitchen and returned with the coffee and some homemade peanut butter cookies.

"You're going to spoil me, Alice."

"You just enjoy those cookies, Ace, I don't get to bake and cook for anyone but myself these days; how can I be of help?"

Ace explained the entire situation to her and she seemed eager to help.

After Ace had explained the Doug Hart situation, Ace asked Alice for the birth information.

"I am interested in the births at Vanderbilt Hospital on June, 10, 1985. I have a copy of the birth certificate of Doug Hart who was one of the boys who was born on that date. Joan told me that there were three boys and three girls born on that date and one of the boys was a still birth. I am trying to find out if the two boys who survived were twins,"

"Let me look at the birth certificate, Ace."

Ace handed her the document.

"I can't recall if there were twin births on that particular date; did the records list the names of the two boys?"

"No, it only listed them as John Doe 1 and John Doe 2; does that mean that they were twins?"

"Not necessarily; what it means to me is that they were both put up for adoption."

"Do you know who adopted them?"

"The hospital didn't get into that; we just turned the babies over to the Tennessee Department of Welfare in those days."

"Do you remember who you turned them over to?"

"I remember there was one lady from Welfare that we worked mostly with back in those days."

"Do you happen to remember her name?"

"Let me see; she was a sweet and caring Jewish lady named Rose Golden, but she has probably retired by now. She was about my age."

"Do you have a phone number for her, Alice?"

"I can look it up in the phone book, but I don't even know if she's still alive."

"I can look it up, Alice." She handed Ace the phone book and he found only one Rose Golden listed.

"Would you mind calling her for me and breaking the ice?"

"I would be glad to, Ace," she replied as she dialed the number.

"Is this the Rose Golden that worked for the Welfare Department a few years ago?" asked Alice.

"Yes it is; who is calling?"

"My name is Alice Hutchins I was the Head Maternity Nurse at Vanderbilt and I worked with you with the adopted babies."

"Yes, I remember you Alice; how are you doing?"

"I am doing very well, Rose; my husband died two years ago but I am getting by okay."

"I'm in the same boat, Alice, my husband died last year. Why did you decide to call me after all these years?"

"I have a very handsome man sitting here in my living room by the name of Ace Sleuth who needs your help on an adoption that took place several years ago."

"I sure wouldn't mind talking to a handsome man, Alice, and how in the world could I not want to talk to a man named Ace Sleuth? Let me talk to him."

"Hello, Rose; this is Ace and I would like to visit you and pick your brain about an adoption several years ago."

"Well get your tail right on over here and I'll serve you some Bagels with cream cheese and hot tea."

"Just tell me where you live and I'll be there in two shakes of a sheep's tail?"

"I live at 308 Shady Grove Lane in Southwest Nashville just about a mile from I-65 South. Take the first Old Hickory exit, number, '74-West', and go about a mile and you will come to Shady Grove Lane on your right. Go another mile and you will find my house on the right. My house number is on the mail box and my house is a white cottage with green shutters; you can't miss it."

"I'll be there within thirty minutes, Rose."

"I'll be waiting for you Ace."

"Thanks Rose," said Ace as he hung up. "I really hate to go, Alice, but I'm on a tight schedule and I don't want to spend the night in Nashville if I don't have to."

"I understand, Ace; I really enjoyed your visit. I hope that I was able to help you in getting that poor innocent boy acquitted; you come back and see me anytime."

"I sure will, Alice; my wife, Paula and I have a daughter in Vanderbilt and we get to Nashville occasionally. Thanks for the coffee and cookies."

"It was my pleasure, Acc."

Chapter 55

Ace arrived at the home of Rose Golden in just under thirty minutes and pulled into the driveway at the neat small cottage on Shady Grove Lane. Rose was waiting for him by the front door and opened it before he had time to ring the door bell.

"Come into my house, Ace Sleuth; you're even more handsome than I expected you to be."

"If everyone in Nashville is as nice as you and Alice, Rose, I wouldn't mind living here."

"Go sit in the big easy chair in the den and I'll bring you some hot tea and Bagels." Rose returned with the goodies in a couple of minutes.

"I want you to enjoy the bagels, Ace; they are genuine New York bagels that I have shipped to me monthly."

"These are the best bagels that I have ever eaten, Rose."

"I'm glad that you think so, Ace; most people around here don't appreciate them as much as I do. The New York bagels are sort of like the New York hot dogs; no one around here can seem to duplicate them."

"I love New York hot dogs as well, Rose."

"How can I be of help to you Ace?"

"There is a very nice young man in Knoxville who has been mistakenly identified as the person who raped an eighteen year University of Tennessee coed on January 14th of this year. His wife, Denise has been working for our firm for over five years and she and Doug, the accused rapist, have only been married for a few short months. He is an engineering student at UT."

"I don't understand how I fit into the picture, Ace."

"Doug Hart was born in Vanderbilt Hospital on June 10, 1985 and I believe that he may have been a twin."

"At the mention of Doug's name and the word twin, Ace saw a worried expression cross Rosc's face.

"What makes you think that he was a twin, Ace?"

"There are two reasons, Rose; I feel so strongly about Doug's innocence that I think that it must have been an identical twin, or someone who looks a whole lot like him who raped the coed. Secondly I have a copy of Doug's birth certificate and in block 4a the type of birth, single, twin etc. was left blank. I know that Doug was adopted, and after talking to the Head nurse at Vanderbilt, I believe that both of the surviving boys were adopted."

"Why do you believe that, Ace?"

"I believe that because the hospital records list the names of the two boys only as John Doe 1 and John Doe 2."

"How strongly do you feel about the innocence of the young man, Ace?"

"I would bet everything I own on his innocence and give a hundred to one odds on it."

"I have a confession to make, Ace. I did a terrible thing in 1985 which I have regretted ever since; the two baby boys were twins. I was the one in charge of the adoptions at that time and I had to make a hard choice. I had promised two couples each a child. The Hart's were supposed to get the child from the woman who had the twins but the baby who I had promised to the other couple was the still birth. I was in a dilemma and didn't know what to do. I decided it was better to make both couples happy rather than just one of them. The other couple would have been devastated if they had not gotten a child. Neither of the couples ever knew that they had each adopted the twin of the other. I knew that I should not have separated them but I thought it was the best thing to do at the time."

"Then my theory was right all along, Rose; do you know how I can get in touch with the second twin?"

"It won't do you any good, Ace; he has and iron clad alibi and seventeen thousand witnesses who could testify as to his whereabouts on the night of January 14, 2011."

"How can you be so sure about the date, Rose?"

"It's because of the Hat Trick, Ace."

"What Hat Trick are you talking about, Rose?"

"I remember it very well; the twin whose name is, Benjamin, is a Forward for the Nashville Predators and he had the game of his life the night of January 14th; he scored a Hat Trick for the first time in his career. Later that night I saw on the eleven O'clock news about the raped UT coed; that's how I remember the date."

"Do you know Benjamin very well, Rose?"

"Yes, we go to the same Synagogue and I have known his father and mother since before he was adopted."

"Do you think it would be Ok if I called him and talked to him?"

"I would rather you not talk to him about being a twin; I don't know how he would react to that. It might really shock his parents."

"I believe that if I were an identical twin that I would welcome the news of another me," said Ace; "what is his last name?"

"I guess I should go ahead and tell you because you'll find out anyway." Rose pulled a Nashville Tennessean newspaper dated January 15, 2011 out of a drawer and opened it up to the sports page and handed it to Ace. Ace looked at it and saw the article, along with Benjamin's picture and about him scoring three goals (the hat trick) the night before; he was a spitting image of Doug.

"I guess my Nashville trip has done nothing to help in clearing Doug's name but I have met some wonderful people here and you are one of them, Rose."

"I appreciate those kind words, Ace; I have really been worried over the years whether I made the right decision in separating those twin babies twenty five years ago."

"I believe that I would have made the same decision, Rose; we have all had to make some hard choices in our lives and we just have to do what we think is right at the time."

"Thanks for those kind words, Ace; they make me feel better already."

"I guess I had better head back to Knoxville, Rose if I want to get home before my wife Paula goes to bed."

"I understand, Ace; if you're ever in Nashville again, give me a ring."

"I will, Rose and thanks for the tea and Bagels and also your help."

"You're welcome, Ace."

It was almost 5:00 p.m. when Ace left Rose's house and almost six in Knoxville; As soon as he got into his car he called Brad at the office. Denise answered and connected him to Brad.

"It's almost five Nashville time, Brad, and I have decided to spend the night in Nashville because I don't want to be driving home in the dark and possibly waking up Paula and Freddy. I wondered if you wanted me to drive to Dixon and see what I can uncover regarding Kristen and Julie. It's only about forty or fifty miles away, and I could do that in the morning."

"I've had some second thoughts along those lines, Ace, and I don't want to dig up any dirt on those two young women; I don't believe that you would find anything, and even if you did, it would probably backfire on us and make us look like the bad guys in this case."

"I agree with you, Brad, so I'll just find me a nice motel and head on home first thing in the morning; I'll see tomorrow afternoon."

"What did you find out in Nashville, Ace? Did you confirm your theory that Doug has an identical twin?"

"Yes, I was able to fill in block 4a and confirm my theory but the identical twin has an iron clad alibi with seventeen thousand witnesses who could testify as to his whereabouts on the night of January 14; he scored a hat trick for the Nashville Predators that night."

"I'll be darned, Ace; you seem to have ESP. I'll see you tomorrow."

"You don't have to worry, Brad; it's not contagious." Ace hung up and was now on I-40 East heading back in the direction of Knoxville when he noticed a nice new-looking Days Inn at Exit 220; he pulled into the office overhang and walked in to book a room. Just as he was approaching the check-in desk a rather large heavy set woman walked right in front of him and said to the male clerk:

"I want a room on the ground floor facing away from the interstate and I want a wake up call at seven in the morning; not a minute sooner and not a minute later, and by the way, you may want to call a wrecker service, someone has abandoned an old Mustang right in front of your office."

As the woman was paying for her room, Ace saw her name on her credit card and made a mental note of it. He also made a mental note of the large late model sedan that she had parked behind him so that he could find her room number with her Caddy parked in front. He also checked in and got a room on the second level. He set his travel alarm clock at six fifty a.m., and when it woke him up Thursday morning, he dialed room 107. When the fat lady answered, Ace said: "Good morning Mrs. Smith, this is your wake up call; its time to get your big fat butt out of bed." He then hung up, brushed his teeth, shaved, and took a shower. He stopped at the lobby to leave the key card and grab a blueberry muffin and a cup of coffee and got on I-40 East again. Just before he reached Lebanon there was a car coming at him going west in the inside lane of the east bound side. The driver passed Ace and seemed to be driving within the 70 mph speed limit but he was nonchalantly driving along without a care in the world. Ace immediately called 911 on his cell phone and gave them his name told them about the wrong way driver at mile marker 233. Ace never heard anything more about the driver or an accident happening. *"The errant driver must have discovered his mistake, or else the State Highway Patrol may have stopped him,"* thought Ace.

"The remainder of his trip back to K-Town was uneventful. He stopped by his home to see Paula and Freddy before going to the office where he arrived Thursday afternoon.

Chapter 56

Sunday

Sunday afternoon was a restful period for Ace after the three of them had gone to church and then out to eat. He liked to relax in his easy chair, read the Sunday paper, and watch sports on TV. Today the Lady Vols Basketball Team which has already won Eight National Championships was well on the road to a ninth. They were undefeated this season, and if they whipped Vanderbilt today, it would wrap up the Southeastern Conference Championship for the umpteenth time.

"It would be thirty minutes before the game started so Ace decided to look at Al Jameson's latest column on Nuclear Power in the features section of the paper.

INVESTIGATIVE REPORT
ON NUCLEAR POWER
BY AL JAMESON

This is my third installment of my report on nuclear power; I am still reporting on watts Bar Nuclear Plant near Spring City, Tennessee. As I did in my second installment, I am going to present this report in dialogue form between the Watts Bar Plant Manager, Mr. Ralph Reynolds and myself.

I was at the Coal-fired TVA Kingston Steam Plant two weeks ago and talked to the plant manager about

the lack of cooling towers there. The conversation follows:

"Just what is it about Nuclear plants, all of which seem have cooling towers, when none of TVA's fossil plants do, Ralph?"

"We do have a cooling tower at one of our coal-fired plants; it is the Paradise Steam Plant in western Kentucky."

"Why is it the only fossil plant that has one?"

"Paradise was built right on top of a coal bed where all we had to do to get the coal was to remove a few feet of top soil to get to the coal. It was an ideal situation except for one thing. The plant was located on the very low flow, Green River, and there was not enough flow in the river to condense the steam into water so that it could be converted back to steam again."

"How does cooling the water help? It doesn't give you any more water does it?"

"Of course not; the way a cooling tower works is by passing air through the water coming from the condenser tubes causing about one percent of the water to vaporize. It takes about 1000 BTU's to vaporize one pound of steam and guess where that 1000 BTU's comes from?"

"I'm sorry, Ralph; I don't have a clue."

"I really didn't think you would, Al; It comes from the ninety nine percent of the water which didn't condense and cools that ninety nine percent down by ten degrees Fahrenheit; that's why they are called cooling towers."

"Where does the vaporized water go, Ralph?"

"In the natural draft hyperbolic cooling towers which have no fans, such the one we use here at Watts Bar, the surrounding air flows in beneath the 500 foot tall cooling tower which is open several feet around the bottom to let the air flow up by the natural draft chimney effect that is created by the towers. If the flowing air is dry enough then the water that has vaporized will mix with it and flow out the top of the cooling tower."

"What happens if the flowing air is not dry enough?"

"Then we have a problem; if the air is already saturated with water vapor (100% humidity), there is no room for any additional water vapor in the air and we get very little cooling of our cooling water going back to the condenser."

"Let me ask you a stupid question, Ralph; if the water leaving the condenser goes back to the steam generators to be heated up again why do you want to lower the temperature of the condenser water? It seems to me that it would save TVA money by not having to heat the water as much."

"That is not a stupid question, Al; we try to squeeze every extra BTU out of our steam wherever we can. We even pull a vacuum on the condenser shell so that the steam will condense at a lower pressure and temperature. The steam that goes through the turbines contains a vast amount of energy; each pound of steam coming from the Steam generators contains around 1,000 BTU's; even at low temperatures slightly above 100 degrees. We want to get as much of the energy spinning our turbines and generating electricity as possible.

"I sort of got you off the track, Ralph; you were going to tell me what happens when there is 100% relative humidity in the air and the cooling towers are not cooling the condenser water very much."

"The efficiency of our plant goes down significantly. Even when we have dry air, the cooling towers cause our plant efficiency to be around one percent less than it would if we were using raw cooling water from the river and returning it farther downstream as most of our fossil plants do."

"I take it that you don't think much of cooling towers, Ralph."

"I don't believe in anything that wastes our natural resources and serves no useful purpose. Our cooling tower here at Watts Bar in addition to lowering efficiency has two other bad side effects. It wastes water and indirectly causes air pollution."

"How in the world could just putting water vapor into the air cause air pollution?"

"We can produce electricity for about one third of the cost using nuclear fuel as it would be to burn coal based on the fuel costs; therefore we like to use nuclear power whenever we can and cut back on using fossil power. Because of the one percent inefficiency of Watts Bar we have to burn one percent more coal to make up for it."

"That sounds logical to me. Ralph; what all goes into making the cooling towers so inefficient?"

"There are many things, Al; first there is the cost of the cooling tower which I think was about fifty million dollars here at Watts Bar. If you compute the yearly interest on that money you have to deduct it from the money that Watts Bar earns each year. The water that is cooled in the cooling tower that goes back to the condenser is warmer than the river water and that causes the plant to be less efficient. Then there is the extra pumping cost to pump a quarter of a million gallons of water per minute two or three hundred feet up inside the cooling tower where it cools and falls down into the cooling tower basin and is pumped back to the condenser. This costs untold millions of dollars a year. Then on top of all that, there is the extra maintenance that is required on the cooling tower and all its appurtenances. I told you that the cooling towers cause the plant to be one percent less efficient; that is my estimate. It could be more or it could be less; I don't know if TVA ever made the comparison, but I think we should."

"You said that a cooling tower wastes water, Ralph; how much water does it waste?"

"If I remember correctly, I believe that the flow to the cooling tower is around 250,000 gallons a minute. If one percent of that is evaporated that means that 2500 gallons of water a minute is wasted. If my calculations are correct, that is over three and a half a million gallons of water being wasted in a day while I keep hearing about water shortages."

"I'm still not sure I understand why all the nuclear plants have cooling towers and almost all the fossil plants don't have them, Ralph?"

"It's because our fossil plants were built when you didn't have all of these extreme environmental types scaring the bejabbers out of everyone and convincing some of our brain dead politicians that a ten degree water rise is going to kill fish. I would be surprised if a single fish has been killed at any of our fossil plants since their inception. We need to get politics out of the nuclear game. I have heard that the French laugh at us over our paranoia about nuclear power when eighty percent of their electricity comes from nuclear generating plants. A good example of how uninformed the general public is, unfolded right here at Watts Bar a couple of years ago. We had a slight leak in our reactor coolant system which by law we are required to report to the NRC and is in turn picked up by the press and released to the public. When incidents such as this occur, the News media seem to enjoy it and have a field day with it as they did when the Three Mile Island incident took place in Pennsylvania. I actual believe that the extreme environmental nuts took great pleasure in that incident because they believed it would stop nuclear power in its tracks, which it did. I'm sorry but I am getting a little off the beaten path; let me get back to the reactor coolant leak. When one of the nearby school systems heard about the leak, they closed the school and sent all the kids home. I have no idea what their thinking was but some of the kids lived closer to the plant than the school. The leak was inside a sealed one inch thick steel reactor containment vessel surrounded by a three foot thick Reactor building. Those kids would have had a greater chance of being struck by lightning in church during a leap year when February 29 fell on a Sunday. It was nothing more than a hiccup to us; we had it repaired and back to normal in short order. We all got a good laugh out of that."

"I can understand where you're coming from, Ralph; we had something similar that happened in the Knox County about the same time frame as your leak. A bank was robbed a few blocks from one of our High Schools and the school authorities locked down the school."

"For what purpose did they do that, Al?"

"That was my question also, Ralph; I suppose they thought that the bank robber would come to the high school and hold all the thousands of students hostage, when in fact, all the he would have on his mind was to get out of Dodge ASAP. Go figure; I think we need to be educating our school officials along with the students."

"I'll amen that, Al."

"Let me get back to what we were talking about before we got sidetracked, Ralph; how much would you say that it costs TVA customers in dollars from the one percent inefficiency of Watts Bar due the use of the cooling tower?"

"That shouldn't be too hard to calculate. Watts Bar-1 has a capacity of over 1100 mega watts; that's equivalent to 1.1 million kilowatts. Lets say that TVA sells its power to it's distributors for five cents a kilowatt hour which is probably on the low side. TVA could produce 1.1 million kilowatts per hour; if you multiply 0.05 cents per kilowatt hour times the 1,100,000 kilowatts equals $55,000 per hour or $418,180,000 per year. If we take one percent of that we get $4,181,000. That's how much money is wasted every year by the use of cooling towers at Watts Bar alone. If you add in the three units at Browns Ferry and the two at Sequoyah the cost would be around $25,000,000 per year."

"Tell me again why TVA has to use cooling towers."

"TVA was forced to use them to protect the fish in the Tennessee River."

"How many fish do you think would have been killed if the cooling tower had not been used at Watts Bar, Ralph?"

"There would be the same number that have been killed at all of our fossil plants without cooling towers; zero."

"What a waste of resources and TVA customers money; this is almost unbelievable, Ralph. Could you explain to me how a nuclear power plant works?"

"Nuclear fuel comes as pellets placed in small diameter metal fuel rods which are strategically placed around the inside of the reactor vessel. The fuel is highly enriched and we pump borated water around the fuel rods that gets heated before it goes to the steam generators. To control the temperature of the water we lower the control rods down between the fuel rods. The lower we place the control rods the less energy is provided by the fuel rods so we position the rods to give us the exact amount of energy that is needed to heat the water to the temperature at which it needs to be to make steam in the steam generators. If we drop the rods all the way down, we essentially stop production of energy. The control rods contain a poison to absorb the neutrons and do not allow them to keep the limited chain reaction going. In case of a loss of coolant accident, the control rods are automatically lowered all the way down into the reactor."

"How often do you normally have to refuel, Ralph?"

"We refuel about once a year but sometimes we can go almost two years without refueling. When we refuel only one third of the fuel rods are replaced with new ones. The ones that are not replaced are relocated within the reactor based upon the amount of available energy left in each according to our monitor readings. Our computer tells us just where to place the remaining two thirds of the rods."

"How long is the normal shutdown period for refueling?"

"We are usually shut down for about three weeks; it all depends on what other work we have to do. There is a lot more work involved besides replacing the fuel."

"I just have one more subject to ask you about, Ralph, and I'll get out of your hair."

"Fire away, Al."

"Tell me what the problem is with the disposal of the used fuel?"

"We refer to that as spent fuel and that subject is another one of my pet peeves."

"Tell me about it, Ralph."

"Many years, and many studies, and fourteen billion dollars have gone into the planning and building for the storage of spent nuclear waste at The Yuccca Mountain Facility in Nevada where it could be safely stored in dry arid caves for years and years. In 2009, President Obama, in what may have been an illegal action, with one stroke of the pen, wiped out the funding for this nuclear waste facility. Of the fourteen billion dollars already spent a good part of that money was defending lawsuits from environmental groups who apparently seem to oppose anything that has to do with electrical power producing plants. Incidentally Tennesseans have already contributed almost a half a million dollars to the project through taxes on their energy consumption

"Where do you store it now?"

"All nuclear plants are storing spent fuel on site under several feet of water above it for shielding due to the radioactivity. It is really not a big problem because we can continue to store it on site for years to come but it would be more economical and sensible to place all of it at one location. Here in the spent fuel pool at Watts Bar we have to continually pump water through the pool to remove the heat it generates until it calms down a bit."

"Why do I hear so many negative things about storing the spent fuel and the other nuclear waste?"

"It's politics and ignorance along with resistance from environmentalists who don't seem to like energy plants of any kind and nuclear plants in particular; they, along with the willing news media, have even convinced much of the population into believing it's unsafe to transport the spent fuel through their towns. The containers that would be used to transport the spent fuel are shielded to prevent any significant radiation and the containers will withstand an impact from a locomotive and remain intact. There is absolutely no chance of an atomic explosion in a nuclear reactor or with the spent fuel. The resistance to nuclear power reminds me of the time in the early part of the twentieth century when people were afraid of the automobile and enacted laws giving horses the right of way over the cars and even going so far as to have someone out in front of the car at night waving a lantern to warn people that a car was coming, but that attitude only lasted a few years. Nuclear plants have been operating safely for over fifty years in this country yet we still have grown people who seem to think that a nuclear plant is going to blow up like an atomic bomb. My grandfather who has been dead for many years told me an amusing story about the time, when as a young man, he saw his first automobile. In the small community of Alpha in East Tennessee where he lived, they were informed that a motor car would be coming through their area, and most if not all, of the local citizenry had come out to see this contraption. They spotted a cloud of dust about a half a mile up the road and shortly the vehicle appeared traveling at a speed of around fifteen miles per hour along with the cloud of dust when one of the local men was heard to say: 'Look at that damn fool go.'"

"That's an amusing story, Ralph and I get your point; you are suggesting that people get accustomed to the new ideas and improvements to our lives but this has not happened to nuclear power."

"At least not in the United States, Al; it seems to me that a lot of people are still living in the horse and buggy days. When we have to start rationing electricity in this country I think that we should write down the names of the people who have fought nuclear power and all other kinds of energy and cut back on their electricity first; then we would really find out if they are serious about their mistaken notions."

"I really want to thank you, Ralph, for your enlightenment regarding nuclear power; you have answered all of my questions and I agree with you. You have changed my thinking and won me over; I was so stupid and ignorant and fell in lock-step with the liberal spiel and felt that I knew all I needed to know about nuclear power. From now on I am going to question every thing I hear that sounds the least bit political or unfounded. I felt smug and broad minded in my ignorance."

"It is real easy to sit back and do nothing and take every thing you read in the paper as gospel, Al; people need to get off their duffs and find out the truth of things. We now have the internet at the tip of our fingers and there is no excuse for ignorance. Nuclear power is green power and we have had it for over fifty years; maybe your article will wake up America to the truth. Unlike stupidity, ignorance can be fixed."

"I don't have any more questions, Ralph; thanks again for your help."

"Thank you, Al; it's very seldom that we ever get the chance to set the record straight."

There will be one more article which will appear in this paper in my series on TVA power plants; my next article will be about the Raccoon Mountain Pumped storage facility near Chattanooga.

Al Jameson

Ace was well pleased after reading Al's column and made a mental note to call and tell him about the excellent job he was doing in his reports. He laid back in his recliner to watch the Lady Vols win another home game; they seldom lost on their own court. He had become concerned for the past two years about the operation of the scoreboard. He had never mentioned it to anyone but there was a problem with getting the score posted to the scoreboard in a timely manner. Sometimes the score would not be posted until the teams were back on the other end of the court. In fact; he once was watching a game when the score for the previous basket was not posted until the opposing team had already made a basket at the other end of the court. *"If I were operating the scoreboard, I would have those two points up there before the ball hit the floor after going through the basket,"* thought Ace. He didn't know whether the problem was the fault of the person who input the data or whether it was a technical problem; he suspected it was the former. He had also noticed the problem, but to a lesser degree when the Tennessee men played. He had also noticed it in some other televised games around the country. *"It seems strange to me that I have never noticed this scoreboard problem prior to the past two years, and I have watched a lot of them over the years,"* thought Ace.

Chapter 57

Monday Feb, 28 Preliminary hearing

Doug and Ace arrived at the office around 8:00 a.m. to discuss the preliminary hearing with Brad and get their morning cup of coffee and donuts.

"I hope the hearing will not last very long, Doug; you don't need to miss any more classes than you have to," said Brad.

"I only have one class this morning and it started at eight and my next one is at one this afternoon."

"How is it going at UT, Doug; are you being treated well by your fellow students?" asked Ace.

"I am doing well in my studies and I could not be treated any better by my classmates; I think that they all believe in my innocence."

"That is great, Doug," replied Brad. At the hearing today I want you to just sit beside me and look as pleasant as you can without being smug. You won't be called to the stand or asked to testify; I will do all the talking for our side. If there are no questions why don't we walk down to the City-County Building; it's only a couple of blocks; the exercise will do us good?"

They reached the courtroom about ten to nine and passing through the security checks they found that door to courtroom 308 was already open. The three of them walked in and Assistant AG, Jim Satterfield, was right behind them with Kristen and her friend, Julie. There were also the two policemen who had arrested Doug; there were no spectators present. The bailiff walked in and announced the appearance of the honorable Judge, James Watson. After everyone was seated the judge addressed the parties:

"The purpose of this hearing is to listen to the prosecutor and the defendant's attorney to determine if there sufficient evidence to send this case on to the Grand Jury. The prosecutor may now make his case."

"May I speak, Your Honor," spoke up Brad.

"You certainly may, Mr. Adams."

"Thank you, Your Honor. I think that we can save a lot of time here today by hearing what I have to say. The only evidence that the AG has against my client is the eyewitness accounts by the victim and her roommate. He is determined to proceed with only that evidence which I don't believe is sufficient to convince a jury of my client's guilt; based on that, I feel that it would be best to go forward with a jury trial where I can exonerate my client in a court of law by a jury of his peers. We can save a lot of time here today if we all agree on this approach. My client will wave the grand jury hearing which will speed things up and at the same time save the County a lot of money."

"Is the prosecution agreeable to this, Mr. Satterfield?"

"We are your honor," he replied.

"Very well; I would like to say that this is one of the most pleasant preliminary hearings over which I have had the honor of presiding in my twenty years as a judge; is there anything more that we need to discuss?"

"I would like to request a speedy trial for my client as provided by Amendment V1 to the Constitution of the United States, Your Honor. In the best interest to all the parties involved, the victim, and the accused, it would be best to schedule this trial as soon as possible so that all of these young people can get back to a normal life."

"Just how soon do you think the trial should begin, Mr. Adams?"

"I would like for it to be no longer than three months, Your Honor; sooner would be better."

"Is this time frame agreeable to the prosecution?" asked the Judge.

"It is agreeable to us, Your Honor," replied the AAG.

"Very well; I will see what I can do to speed things up. It's all going to depend on the availability of a judge. If there are no other questions this hearing is now concluded,"

Brad and Ace went back to their office and Doug headed back to school.

Chapter 58

Tuesday March, 1

Ace and Brad were enjoying their morning coffee and donuts when Denise came in with the morning paper and handed it to Brad and said; "Look at the headline." It read:

FORMER MARINE, DOUG HART TO BE TRIED IN COED RAPE CASE

At the preliminary hearing yesterday in Criminal Court it was agreed by both the prosecution and the defendant's attorney, Brad Adams, that a trial for former marine, Doug Hart, accused of the rape of University of Tennessee coed, Kristen Smith, will go forward. Both sides requested a speedy trial so that all the young people involved could get back to a normal life which is unlikely for Mr. Hart if he is convicted. No trial date has been set but it is expected to be within three months from now if they can find an available judge.

The only evidence the prosecution appears to have is the eyewitness testimony of Kristen and her roommate Julie Brown, however the AG believes that to be sufficient for conviction.

There seems to be two camps in Knoxville regarding the case. One side believes that Hart is a rapist who has been trained to murder and rape by the military although there does not appear to be any evidence of wrong doing while he was a Marine in Iraq and Afghanistan. The other camp believes him to be a hero who sacrificed several years of his life for his country. His military records are not available but we have discovered that he was honorably discharged a few months ago. We have also discovered that Mr. Hart was an Eagle Scout growing up in Nashville.

We have also learned that both Ms. Smith and Mr. Hart are back in their classes at the University of Tennessee that they attended prior to the unfortunate incident.

Chapter 59

Sunday March sixth

Ace was sitting in his den watching the Tennessee Lady Vols win another Southeastern conference Championship game and warming up for the Big Dance called, "March Madness." He picked up the Sunday paper to read Al Jameson's last installment on TVA's various electrical generating facilities.

INVESTIGATIVE REPORT ON TVA's
ELECTRICAL GENERATING FACILITIES
By Al Jameson

This is my final report on The Tennessee Valley Authority electrical power generating stations. My previous reports have been limited to nuclear power and steam plants, but today I am going to concentrate on TVA's Raccoon Mountain pumped storage facility. The facility is located about twenty miles northwest of Chattanooga, Tennessee. I drove down from Knoxville and took I-24 along the beautiful Tennessee River embayed by Nickajack Dam and got off at the exit to the road that would lead me to the top of Raccoon mountain where the plant Manager, Glen Masters was waiting for me. As with my previous reports, I am going to present this report in dialogue format between Mr. Masters and myself.

"Welcome to Raccoon Mountain. Al"

"Do you mind if I record our conversation, Glen?"

"No, not at all."

"Thanks, Glen; I'm pleased to meet you. It was quite a drive up here. Where is your pumped storage plant located? All I see is a large lake on top of this mountain."

"The generating plant is located several hundred feet beneath us and the only way to get there is by elevator."

"How did a lake this large get on top of the mountain, Al? I don't see any water flowing into it."

"This is a man made lake, Al, and the water is taken from the Nickajack Reservoir and pumped up here by pumps from our plant below. The same pumps also serve as generators when we turn this water loose through a tunnel that TVA drilled through the center of the mountain so that we could get water to our generators and start generating electricity."

"How big is the lake, Glen?"

"The lake covers an area of 528 acres and is held back by a dam that is 230 feet high and 5800 feet long. It takes twenty eight hours to pump the lake full and we can generate 1600 megawatts of electricity continuously for twenty two hours before we have to fill it again."

"Just what is pumped storage all about, Glen?"

"It is really a method to store electricity."

"It doesn't really store electricity does it?"

"Indirectly it does. There is really no way to store large quanties of electricity in the amount we are talking about here. At the rate at which we generate electricity here at Raccoon Mountain we could supply the electrical requirements of almost one million homes for twenty two hours. If you really want to get rich, Al, all you have to do is come up with a method that stores large amounts of electricity directly; similar to what an automobile battery does now. TVA has large quantities of electricity available after midnight every day of the week but there is no way to store it as electricity."

"What about solar and wind generated electricity, Glen; don't they help out? Isn't solar generated electricity generated during the day when it is most needed?"

"That's true, Al, but right now solar energy is a drop in the bucket compared to the other ways that we produce electricity, and to make matters worse, it doesn't work during the daylight hours when it's cloudy or raining. The wind turbines only work in a window of speeds. If the wind speed is too low or too high the turbines are shut down, and when they operate at night, we have plenty of abundant power during that time. Those two sources of electrical power are more expensive than what it costs TVA to generate power here at Raccoon Mountain; they would probably not exist if not for federal subsidies. When you really stop and think about it, wind power and hydroelectric power are both solar power."

"How did you arrive at that conclusion, Glen?"

"Wind power is solar power indirectly. The winds are created by the heat from the sun causing different temperatures within the air causing it to flow. The water in our reservoirs is there because the sun heats up the water on the surface of the earth and causes it to rise as water vapor and fall back to the earth as rain."

"I had never thought of it in that light, Glen, but it makes sense.

"Are you ready to go several feet below and see what makes this plant tick, Al?"

"I have been breathlessly awaiting this moment since I got here, Glen."

"They walked through the Visitor's Center toward the elevator and there was a sign that read:

"NO VISITORS BEYOND THIS POINT"

"Why are no visitors allowed past the sign, Glen?"

"It's because of 9-11. Ever since the World Trade Center was destroyed by terrorists we do not allow visitors to go down below to our plant. A bomb going off down there could cause a lot of damage."

The ride down the elevator took a couple of minutes and they got of in the plant area. Al was surprised at the cleanliness of the entire underground plant.

"These are our generators that produce all the electricity that is generated when all that mass of water comes roaring down the tunnel from the lake on top of the mountain. When we empty the lake and decide when we want to refill it, we reverse the generators and use them as electric motors to pump water from Nickajack reservoir back up to refill the lake. The turbines that were spinning their blades to generate electricity now become pumps to pump the water back up to the mountain top."

"How does the amount of electricity you get out of the generators compare with the amount of electricity it took to pump the water up to the lake?"

"Our facility is around 78% efficient; for every kilowatt hour we use to pump the water up we get only 0.78 kilowatts hours in return, but this is Ok with us because we only pump the water up to the lake in the wee hours of the morning when we have a lot of unused capacity. We only use electricity from this facility when we need more power than all of our other power plants can supply. Essentially we store up electricity for a 'rainy day.'"

Glen then took Al all around the plant and introduced him to some of the workers; Al was most impressed with the control room, with all of its dials and gages. After a couple of hours below, he was ready to leave. Glen rode back up with him in the elevator to the Visitor Center where Al picked up a few of the available brochures to take back to his office.

"I want to thank you for your courtesy and your time, Glen."

"I want to thank you and your paper, Al for finally looking at TVA, and nuclear power in particular, in a truthful light. There has been so much disinformation and untruths concerning it that I'm surprised that we have any nuclear power at all. Hollywood doesn't help any when it comes out with movies such as 'The China Syndrome.' which was nothing more than nonsense and propaganda. Hollywood movies can be very misleading. I saw the Howard Hughes movie a year or two ago and they showed that film clip of him taking off from the water in his giant 'Spruce Goose', the plywood airplane he built for the U.S. Government. The movie gave the impression that the giant monstrosity was a huge success, but the fact of the matter was that this was the first and last time that plane ever flew and it only flew for one mile. Hughes said that it vibrated so badly that he had to land it back in the water after a mile flight. The movie failed to mention that one small fact.

Thanks again, Glen; I feel so much safer knowing that our electrical generating facilities are in safe and competent hands."

"I'm glad that I could be of help, Al; come back any time."

"I would like to sum up my investigative report, especially the nuclear power portion. I suppose that I was like a lot of our population that just goes along with all of the negative things we hear from our news media regarding the dangers of nuclear power. I was amazed to discover that in over fifty years of nuclear power plant operation in this country that I was not able to discover a single instance of anyone being killed or injured from overdoses of radiation. I can't understand what all the negative things we see on television and in our newspapers regarding nuclear power are all about. It almost seems to me to be a conspiracy by people who seem to be opposed to any type of electrical generating plants. I have to admit that I was one of the guilty people by falling in lock step with the dumb masses by failing to do any investigations of my own to arrive at the truth. It is so much easier to sit back fat dumb and happy, and go along with the crowd, and not make waves. I apologize to my readers for my ignorance."

Al Jameson

Chapter 60

Monday march 14th

Brad and Ace were having a discussion in the office when Denise walked in and informed them she had received word from the Criminal Court Clerk that the trial date for Doug's trial date has been set for Monday June 6th, 2011 and the presiding judge would be the Honorable Judge Albert Prince. The judge is a no nonsense man who is jokingly referred to as Prince Albert by the local attorneys; however he rules more like a King in his courtroom than a prince.

At the mention of Judge Prince, Ace recalled a humorous event that occurred in one of the cases that Prince was presiding over a couple of years ago. There was a man testifying on the witness stand when someone in the front of the courtroom broke wind rather loudly and odorously. It took a couple of minutes for the judge to restore order and he seemed visibly upset and looked suspiciously at the man in the witness chair. He was so mad that he stopped the trial right then and there and ordered everyone out of the courtroom. Most of the spectators thought that the judge himself was the culprit and just used the witness as a scapegoat. Ace was surprised that the Judge didn't end up with the nickname of Windy instead of Prince Albert. The morning newspaper the next day carried a column on page two the next day with a headline that read:

IS IT ORDER, OR ODOR IN THE COURT?

"Brad, Do you remember who the judge was in Knoxville that turned the man loose who was found with 600 pounds of marijuana in his pickup truck that was sniffed out by a drug sniffing dog,?" asked Ace.

"I don't remember his name or whether he was a county or federal judge. It wasn't Judge Prince if that's what you're thinking. If I remember correctly, the presiding judge turned him loose because the dog that sniffed out the drugs didn't have a high enough batting average; however the judge didn't specify exactly what the batting average would have to be to convict the accused."

"Do you think they had to return the drugs to the man?" replied Ace.

"If they were taken from him and violated his constitutional rights, I would think they would have to by law," said Brad. What brought this up in that crazy mind of yours, Ace; I can see the wheels turning in your brain?"

"I saw on TV the other day that there are 700 bomb sniffing dogs at US airports and LAX has more than any of them. I was wondering what would happen if one of those LAX dogs sniffed out a bomb on a person going through the airport security line and that person was brought before a like-minded judge in LA and the judge ruled that the dog did not have a high enough batting average. Do you think that they would have to set the would-be bomber free and give him his bomb back?"

"I have seen crazier rulings in this country, Ace; especially by some of the liberal judges with their bizarre rulings."

"When do you expect the jury list will be released, Brad?"

"The jury list will be made available by the end of April, and I expect to see a list of at least a hundred names because of all the publicity regarding the case,"

Denise brought back the morning paper and was almost in tears as she handed it to Brad.

"Take a look at the 'Letters to the Editor' section," she said.

Brad read it aloud:

Our Military is doing nothing more than teaching our young men to rape, plunder, and kill as evidenced by the rape Of Kristen Smith by that former marine, Doug Hart. This rapist should be thrown in prison for the rest of his natural life for what he did to that young coed. The military trains them to kill innocent women and children in Iraq and Afghanistan and they come back home and do the same things here. We need to get all of our forces out of the Middle East and bring them back home. We have enough murderer's and rapists already in this country without our Military training more of them.

Ronald Skidmore, Knoxville

"How can people be so cruel, Brad?" asked Denise.

"I believe it is bias against our Military which some people seem to despise."

"It amazes me that there are some people in this country who hate our Military and our Law Enforcement Agencies, said Ace. Don't they realize that they would not be safe in their own homes if it were not for our Law Enforcement agencies and our prisons which keep the predators off the streets? If it wasn't for our Military, we would all be doing the goose step and calling each other Herr and Frauline and eating Weiner schnitzel and sauerkraut for dinner each night. And by the way, whatever happened to the 'presumed innocence until proven guilty' provision in our laws?"

"I just hope he doesn't get tried in the press," said Denise.

"He is going to be exonerated, Denise, and you can take that to the bank," replied Brad. "Let's all get back to work now and take our mind off these unpleasant thoughts; we have a lot of work ahead of us to clear Doug's name."

Chapter 61

Tuesday, March 15

Ace had the day off and Brad and Denise were the only ones in the office. At about ten a.m., Brad rang Denise.

"What's up Brad?"

"I was wondering what your plans were for lunch today?" "I was planning on eating my baloney and cheese sandwich I brought from home unless you have a better offer."

"How about lunch with me at the Marriott around noon; things are kind of slow here today and I think a change of scenery would do us both good."

"Are you paying?"

"You're beginning to sound a whole like Ace, Denise; can you be ready by noon?"

"I will be looking forward to it, Brad."

Brad drove her the short distance over in his Mercedes S550 and parked in the adjacent parking garage from which they walked the short distance to the Marriott lobby. The lobby was beautiful with the marble floor and the vast open space above it and the beautiful elevators at both end of the lobby that were exposed to the outside and appeared to go right on up through the roof when you were riding in them. They decided to dine in a portion of the dining area that actually extended part way into the lobby; from there they could view everyone who passed by.

A young male waiter, who identified himself as Henry placed their water glasses on the table and announced the daily specials and handed them the menus.

Denise ordered the chicken salad on lettuce leaves with fried green tomatoes along with hot tea.

"Would you like some white wine to go along with that?" asked Brad.

"No, but thanks anyway, Brad; neither Doug nor I drink alcoholic beverages, but don't let me stop you from having a glass."

"Thanks, Denise; I think I'll have a glass of a good red wine, Pinot Noir, to go along with the rib eye steak sandwich I am going to order."

After they had eaten, Brad remarked to Denise;

"Besides the enjoyment of your company, I wanted to talk to you about the upcoming trial and how you are coping with all this, Denise. You sounded real upbeat when I called you to go to lunch."

"I am laughing through my tears, Brad; this all seems like a bad dream to Doug and me. The best thing that has happened to us was the help from you and Ace. You put up the bail money and you and Ace both were instrumental in getting him back in school. If it wasn't for all the homework that he has to do, I think that he would just sit around and mope. I have never had anything affect me like the false accusation against Doug. Has anything like that ever happened to you Brad?"

"Yes, but not like anything that has happened to you and Doug. On a final exam in Finance in college my instructor accused me of copying off the paper from the student sitting on my left since our papers were almost identical. Unlike grammar and high school teachers, college instructors know very little about the academic skills of their students, and for the most part they don't seem to want to know. I knew the student beside me wasn't a very smart student and any copying would have had to come from him. The instructor told me that my test paper was identical to the other student. I told him that my paper wasn't identical to his but that his was identical to mine."

"How did you get it resolved?"

"The professor threatened to flunk me in the course but I came up with a solution to the problem."

"What did you do?"

"I suggested to the instructor that he make up a brand new test and placed me and the other student across the room from each other and let us both take the test and see who scored the highest."

"Did you score the highest, Brad?"

"No; the other student refused to take the test."

"What happened to the other student?"

"He received a failing grade for refusing to take the test and I bet you a dollar to a donut that you know who he was."

"I bet it was Luther Spenser, Brad.

"You're right on the money. I knew that you would know who it was; you were right in the middle of the lawsuit that Luther brought against me that time.

We need to start right away in the trial preparation, Denise, but there is not a whole lot that we can do before we get the jury list; we should have that in a couple of weeks."

"What did Ace find out in Nashville about the possibility of Doug having an identical twin?"

Brad didn't think it would serve any useful purpose for her and Doug to know that there was indeed an identical twin. In the first place he didn't want to intrude on Doug's twin who also didn't know he had a twin; and in the second place he thought that she and Doug might think that the twin was the guilty person.

"We hit a dead-end down in Nashville, Denise; sometimes Ace gets carried away with some of his wild theories. But there was one bright spot in his trip; he got to have lunch with his daughter Lisa. Is there is anything at all that I can help you and Doug with, just let me know."

"Do you think that it would be okay if I sat in on the trial, Brad?"

"I don't have a problem with it; your and Doug's family may also want to attend."

"Thanks Brad; I don't know what we would have done without you."

"I feel like I'm on a crusade for good, Denise, and I'm going to win this thing; are you ready to go back to work?"

"I just hope that I can stay awake from eating all this good food; thanks for asking me, Brad."

"It was my pleasure, Denise."

Chapter 62

Friday, March 18

Ace and Brad were downing their morning cup of coffee and donuts when Denise walked in with the morning paper.

"Take a look at this letter to the editor." She said. "I like it a lot better than the one I read last week." It read:

> **To the Editor**
> **I read the letter to the editor in your paper concerning the alleged rape and brutal beating of a UT coed and I would like to address that article.**
>
> **As a former Marine myself, I take exception to people who want to blame the military every time a military or former military person gets accused of a crime. The Marine Corp does not teach their soldiers to kill and rape. They teach them to fight for and defend their country when we are attacked as we were on 911. We don't like to fight; all the Marines I knew in Iraq and Afghanistan wanted nothing more than to finish the war and get back home to their families. The children in both of those countries love our American soldiers who were always sharing their cookies and candy with them. America is not like Germany, Japan, and Russia, who fought wars to just expand their territories; almost every country that we have fought, has been better off after we have beaten them because**

of America's goodness. We even helped many of them with restoring their infrastructures. There was even a movie made years ago entitled, 'The Mouse that Roared' about a small country that declared war on United States so that they could us get us to come in and help them improve their living conditions after we had whipped them. If I ever wanted to lose a war I would rather lose to the United States than any other country.

It appears to me that the writer of this letter to the editor has already decided that the former marine is guilty. I would advise Mr. Hart's attorney to take down this writer's name and make doubly sure that he never serves on his jury.

We need to give Mr. Hart a fair trial and not try to convict him in the News Media as they almost did to those Lacrosse players a few years at Duke University when they were falsely accused of rape by a black female. It didn't help their cause any when the local DA, who was up for reelection, ignored evidence that would have proved that the Duke students were innocent.

Semper Fi,
Col. Jefferson Millsaps
USMC-Retired
Knoxville

After reading the ex-marine's letter to the editor, Denise informed Ace that he had a call.

"Ace here," he answered.

"Ace, this is Al Jameson and you won't believe what just happened to me."

"I'm all ears, Al."

"The Consolidated Press is going to pick up my report on Nuclear Power and run is as installments; it will be in all the major newspapers in the country."

"I am really happy for you, Al, but I wouldn't count on winning the Pulitzer Prize for investigative reporting just yet."

"Why is that, Ace?"

"It's because you are on the wrong side of the political correctness fence to win that award, even though you deserve it."

Do you know what the majority of the American people who are against nuclear power remind me of, Al?"

"I don't have a clue, Ace."

"They remind me of the 'Three Sillies'."

"Who are the Three Sillies?"

"They are the Characters in a story many, many years ago by an Author named Arthur Rackman that my first grade teacher used to read to us. It went something like this if my memory serves me well and Google does not lie:

> **Once upon a time when folks were not so wise as they are nowadays, there lived a farmer and his wife who had one daughter. And she, being a pretty lass, was courted by the young squire when he came home from his travels.**
>
> **Now every evening he would stroll over to see the daughter and supper in the farm-house and every evening the daughter would go down into the cellar to draw cider for supper.**
>
> **One evening when she had gone down to draw the cider and had turned the tap as usual, she saw a big wooden mallet stuck up in one of the beams in the ceiling. It appeared to have been there for ages because it was all covered with cobwebs; however this was the first time that she had noticed it, and at one began to think how dangerous it was for that mallet to be there.**
>
> **"For," thought she, "supposing him and me was married, and supposing we was to have a son, and**

supposing he were to grow up to be a man, and supposing that he were to come down to draw cider like as I'm doing, and suppose the mallet were to fall on his head kill him, how dreadful it would be!"

And with that she put down the candle she was carrying and, seating herself on a cast, began to cry. And she cried and cried and cried.

Since she had been gone so long her mother came down into the cellar to see what was wrong and found her seated on the cast crying ever so hard, and the cider was running all over the floor.

"Lawks a mercy!" cried her mother, "whatever is the matter?"

When the daughter explained to her mother exactly what she was she crying about, the mother also became upset and she also starting crying as hard as her daughter.

When neither his daughter nor his wife failed to return from the cellar, the farmer went down there to see what was wrong and found them both crying.

"Zounds!" says he, "whatever is the matter?"

"When they explained the mallet in the cellar ceiling and the consequences if it fell, he also began to sob.

After a several minute absence of the three, the young squire came down into the cellar and found them all uncontrollably sobbing.

"Why are you three after, sitting there sobbing like babies, and letting good cider run all over the floor?"

They the explained the danger of the mallet in the ceiling to him and he started laughing and reached up and pulled the mallet out of the ceiling and said:

"I've traveled far and I've traveled fast, but I have never met three such sillies as you three. Now I can't marry one of the three biggest sillies in the world. So I shall start again on my travels, and if I can find three bigger sillies than you three, I'll come back and be married-not otherwise."

So he wished them good-bye and started again on his travels, leaving them all crying: this time because the marriage was off.

The young squire traveled far and wide looking for a bigger silly and finally found one. She was an old woman trying to coax her cow up a ladder to the roof of her house so that the cow could eat the grass that was growing out of the thatch. She finally got the cow to climb the ladder up to the roof and then tied a rope around the neck of the cow, passed the rope down the chimney. She then got off the roof and went inside the house where she fastened the other end of the rope to her wrist so the cow wouldn't fall off the roof without her knowing it. Unfortunately when the cow fell of the roof it pulled her up and wedged her inside the chimney where she was smothered by the soot. *"One down and two to go,"* thought the young man.

He kept traveling until he was tired and when he came to a little inn which was so full that he had share his room with another traveler. When he got up the next morning he noticed that the stranger had hung his breeches on the knobs of the tallboy.

"What are you doing?" he asked his fellow traveler.

"I'm putting on my breeches," says the stranger: and with that he goes to the other end of the room, takes a full jump, and tries to jump into his breeches. The young suitor watched and laughed as the man tried several more times to jump into his breeches without success.

"It's very well laughing," said the stranger, "but breeches are the most awkwardest things to get into that ever were. It takes me the best part of an hour every morning. How do you manage yours?"

Then the young squire showed him as well as he could for all his laughing. The stranger thanked him and said he would never have thought to do it that way.

"Two down and one to go," thought the young squire.

He continued his travels until one bright night when the moon was shining right overhead and he came upon a village. Outside the village was a pond and round about the pond was a great crowd of villagers. And some had got rakes, and some had got pitchforks, and some had got brooms. And they as busy as busy shouting out, and raking, and forking, and sweeping away at the pond.

"What is the matter?" cried the young squire, jumping off his horse to help. Has anyone fallen in?"

"Aye! Matter enough," says they. "Can't 'ee see moon's fallen into the water an' we can't get her out nohow."

The young squire started laughing and said to himself, "There are many more sillies in this world than I thought for: so I'll go back and marry the farmer's daughter. She is no sillier than the rest."

So they were married, and if they didn't live happy ever after, that has nothing to do with the story of the three sillies.

That is a very nice story, Ace, but how do you equate it with the people who oppose nuclear power?"

"The anti-nuke Soothsayers evidently think that there is big wooden mallet wedged in the ceiling of nuclear power and is getting ready to fall, Al; the truth is that there has never been a mallet in the ceiling."

Why do you think that a lot of people feel that way about nuclear power plants, Ace?"

"I think that there are actually three reasons. The first and, and I think the major reason, is because of the two atomic bombs we dropped on Japan. These people don't realize that a nuclear power plant does not have enough critical mass of fuel in the reactor to create a nuclear explosion.

The second reason is that the news media in this country does not check out the facts when some of these anti nukes groups spout out their unfounded propaganda; they just run with it. I have a feeling that your investigative report will put a damper on this type of skullduggery.

The third reason is part paranoia and part ignorance."

"You seem a little paranoid to me at times," joked Al.

"You would be paranoid too, Al, if everybody was out to get you," Ace jokingly replied.

"What is your definition of paranoia, Ace?"

"My definition is someone who has an abnormal fear of someone or something without a logical reason; like the mallet in the ceiling."

"How do you relate that to the people who are against nuclear power, Ace?"

"I think these people are a very good example of paranoia, Ace; just look at the facts which are available on the internet for anybody to look up. All they have to do is go in under 'Google' and type in: 'Deaths and injuries to people from radiation overdoses caused by operating nuclear plants in the United States in the past fifty years or since the inception of nuclear power in this country" I think the answer they will find is zero to both parts. There have been deaths, such as being scalded by steam from burst pipes in U.S. nuclear plants, but not from radiation."

"What about the ignorant part, Ace?"

"Ignorance, unlike stupidly, can be fixed with a little education, but unfortunately the majority of people who are against nuclear power know absolutely nothing about it, but are just spoon fed by the media.

It is much easier to go along with the masses like the people did with the king who wore no clothes.

"I can give you a real-life example of ignorance and how education cured it. My father who grew up in the rural community of Alpha, about forty miles Northeast of Knoxville told me this story;

"When I was about five years old I thought I was the smartest kid in the world; I knew everything there was that was worth knowing. One day I saw these two men hoeing a garden adjacent to ours and walked up to see what they had growing in their garden. I recognized all the vegetables except for some green looking pods that were hanging from a green plant about two feet tall. I pointed to them and asked the men what they were."

"Those are hot peppers," they replied.

"I thought they were pulling my leg and I replied back to them: 'Those are not hot peppers; hot peppers are red."

"Why don't you take a bite of one and see for yourself," one of the men said.

"I pulled one of the green peppers off the plant and popped it in my mouth, took a big bite, and ran home to my mother as fast as I could; my young tender mouth was on fire while the two men were laughing their heads off. That story, Al. is a good example of ignorance and how education can cure it."

"Touché, Ace."

Chapter 63

Monday, March 21

Brad and Ace were discussing the upcoming trial of Doug Hart.

"We should be getting the jury list in a couple of weeks and I was wondering when would be a good time for us to talk to Paula about the jury selection, Ace."

"She is available almost any weekday between ten a.m. and two p.m. when Freddy is in day care," replied Ace.

"Why don't you have her come in tomorrow and we can have a general discussion. The jury selection is probably going to be the most important phase of this trial and we need to get a head start. Do you have any ideas on how we should proceed, Ace?"

"I think that we should get all the former military people seated on the jury that we can, Brad."

"I agree with that approach but I am wondering about placing any liberals on the panel; they always seem to side with the accused."

"I don't think that would be a good idea because I believe that their overriding hatred for the military would come to the surface and poor Doug would be the victim here. I believe that the liberals would consider this trial to be a trial against the military."

"I tend to think you're right, Ace; we just need to get Paula in here tomorrow. She's got more jury savvy than anyone else I know."

"You're right about that, Brad; she will be here tomorrow as soon as she drops off Freddy at Daycare."

Chapter 64

Tuesday, March 22

Paula arrived at Brad's office around ten thirty in the morning.

"How have you been, Paula?" asked Brad; "I haven't seen you since our office Christmas party."

"Ace and Freddy keep me hopping; that boy is just like Ace, he has to know everything that is going on."

"How old is he now, Paula?"

"I'm surprised that you asked me that question, Brad; he was born on the same day in October 2007 as your grandson, David; he's almost four years old."

"You're right of course, Paula; I just wasn't thinking. Do you have any thoughts on the jury selection for Doug's trial?"

"Yes I think that we should include as many former military personal as possible on the jury and have as few females as possible. I am speaking in generalities only and we need to look at each individual separately before we make a decision."

"I agree with that concept, Paula, but how do you plan to go about that?"

"You can find out a lot about almost anybody you want to by Googling them up on the internet. I can usually find out something about them ninety nine times out of a hundred. For that hundredth person, Ace can go digging in that person's garbage can"

"O boy," replied Ace; "that's my favorite pastime."

"Do you have any other thoughts, Paula?" asked Brad.

"We will get some information about each perspective juror from the jury list, such as their name, which should indicate their sex; the list will also list the occupation of each one, but that's about all the list will show. We can probably get their phone numbers from the telephone book which will also list their addresses. We can find out quite a bit about a person from their address alone. We can determine if a person lives in an affluent or a poor neighborhood or if they live in a predominately black neighborhood. People of the same races seem to want to live in the same neighborhood. Greeks seem to want to live close to one another because they have more in common with one another. You can also sometimes determine the nationality of a person just from their name."

"I agree with you about being able to determine the sex of a person from their name, Paula; I've never met a woman named Ralph," said Ace.

"If we have nothing further to discuss now I think we'll close on Ace's comment. I will get you the jury list a soon as I get it Paula. In the meantime let me know if you think of anything else that would help us in our jury selection," said Brad.

"I will," replied Paula.

Chapter 65

Thursday Evening, March 24

It was after eight p.m. and Ace and Paula had rented the movie; 'The Blind Side" from Blockbusters and were looking forward to watching it. Lisa had put Freddy to bed and Ace had popped a bag of 'Cousin Willies' butter popcorn in the microwave.

The movie was excellent and took place in Memphis. It was all about an effluent married couple who lived in Memphis who had become the legal guardians of a large homeless young black man whom they had taken into their home after they had picked him up on the street. The young black man became a terrific high school football player and almost every coach in the Southeastern Conference (SEC) including Tennessee's head coach, Phillip Fulmer who appeared in the movie along with several other SEC coaches who were trying to recruit him. The young football player ended up playing for the Ole Miss Rebels in college and eventually for the Baltimore Colts in Pro Football. They both enjoyed the movie immensely and were discussing it.

"Ace; I'm pleased that Sandra Bullock received the Oscar for her role in the movie; don't you think she deserved it, Ace?"

"I agree with you completely, Paula, but there's one thing that bothers me about this movie and all the other Hollywood movies that involve sports."

"I didn't see anything wrong with it, Ace."

"The problem is that Hollywood does not know how to depict sporting contests in their movies. They need to hire some of the cameramen from ESPN or Sports South to show them how to film sports."

"Just what was wrong with this movie, Ace?"

"When they were showing the football scenes they didn't show enough of the field to even tell what yard line the teams were on. They just seem to zoom in on an individual and the viewer doesn't know who has the ball or which direction they are going or what down it is. It's the same with all the sports I've seen in movies whether it be baseball, pool, tennis, or golf. It seems like the camera is doing all the moving instead of the players. A new image seems to flash upon the screen about every second. It's hard for me to follow the progress of the games. I think the worst sport that Hollywood tries to film is the game of pool. They show the player shooting the cue ball toward an object ball and the object ball going into the pocket but with nothing in between. There is no continuity in the game at all; it's just a bunch of balls randomly rolling around the table. I just hate to see any type of movie that is basically about sports. I don't like horse racing movies, car racing movies, boxing movies, or football and baseball movies. The weak plots of sports movies are bad enough, but the flash filming of the sport events drives me crazy."

"But this movie wasn't really a sports movie, Ace."

"You are right, Paula; this was a heart warming movie which I enjoyed very much in spite of the poor sport filming."

"They can't please everyone, Ace."

"I guess that I'm just too critical, Paula."

Chapter 66

Saturday, March 26

It was Saturday morning and Ace and Paula had decided to make a day of it and drive across the Great Smokey Mountains to Harrah's Casino in Cherokee, North Carolina. It was about a two hour drive from Knoxville, a distance of sixty or seventy miles. They took I-40 East to exit 407 and headed south through Sevierville and Pigeon Forge. They took the bypass around Gatlinburg to save time and mileage but Paula insisted that they stop there on the way back so that she could get some delicious chocolate fudge from one of the many candy shops there. They took US 441 across the mountain into Western North Carolina and US 19 East to the small town of Cherokee. Lisa was home for the weekend from Vanderbilt in and volunteered to baby sit Freddy, but Paula and Ace didn't want to intrude on her time so they made arrangements for Freddy to spend the day and night with his best friend, David Bradford. Ace and Paula planned to spend the night at the beautiful Harrah's Cherokee Hotel at the Casino. The 90,000 square foot hotel contains 576 rooms and twenty one suites alone with five full service restaurants.

The Casino is owned by the Eastern Band of Cherokee Indians and is located on their reservation. The casino is operated by Harrah's which operates many casinos around the world. The casino was initially formed by an agreement with the Cherokee's and the state of North Carolina with the stipulation by the State that all gambling devices would have some element of skill involved by the gamblers, and this included slot machines, of which there are around 3000.

The city of Cherokee, North Carolina is on an Indian Reservation located in the foothills on the southern side of the Great Smokey Mountain National Park. It has a population of around 12,000 inhabitants. In 2009 the tribe received around $14,000 for each tribe member, but half of that amount went to fund the infrastructure and projects of the city. Each tribe member received around $7,000 dollars for their share of profits from the casino. One half of the profits from the Casino go to Harrah's and the other half to the Cherokee's.

Ace and Paula had reserved a Luxury room in what was called the Soco Tower. The room came with a king size bed, upscale furniture, a whirlpool bath, hair dryer, coffee maker, and a 31 inch TV; all for only $86.00 for the one night. They decided that they would dine in the 'Sycamore' which looked to them to be the best restaurant. As it turned out, they were right; they both enjoyed their delicious repast immensely.

Ace and Paula were amazed at the number people who were in the casino; there appeared to be thousands. There were many buses parked in the huge parking lot along with campers and motor homes. It appeared that many of the gamblers had arrived by bus and were only there for the day, because it was very apparent that there was not enough room in the hotel for more than about five percent of them. There were buses parked in the lot from several nearby states such as Tennessee, Kentucky, Virginia, Georgia, South Carolina, and of course, North Carolina.

Ace and Paula did very little gambling and Ace had allocated only $100 dollars which he used to play the poker machines. He milked the machines for about two hours before his C-Note evaporated. Paula was even more frugal; she only ran fifty dollars through the slot machines.

"Do you want to gamble some more, Paula?" asked Ace, how about the poker machines?"

"My beginners luck is gone, Ace; I used it all on our cruise to the Mediterranean in 2009 when I won that $3,000."

After a good night's sleep and an hour for Paula in the whirlpool, she and Ace drove back to Knoxville, but not before picking up some chocolate fudge for Paula in Gatlinburg and stopping for a breakfast of ham and eggs with apple fritters at The Applewood Restaurant in Pigeon Forge.

Chapter 67

Monday, March 28

After working late Ace left the office Monday evening around seven p.m. and had driven a few blocks when he sensed that someone was following him. He purposely made several turns and the car behind him was still following at a distance. With the great acceleration of his 'souped up' 76 Mustang, Ace was able to go several blocks making turns and ended up behind the person who was following him. He was unable to recognize the driver, but he was able to get the license number which he wrote down on the newspaper lying on the passenger seat. He decided to follow the car to see where it was going. He did not know if the driver knew that the pursuee had now become the pursuer. As both cars approached a traffic signal that had just turned amber, the car that Ace was following drove on through the intersection. Ace had decided to follow the car and run the red light until he saw a police car behind him and so he stopped.

Ace waited until Tuesday morning to call Gene White, a Knoxville policeman with whom he had worked on in the kidnapping case of Trisha Parker, a first grader at Sequoyah School in West Knoxville a few years back. He and Gene had become good friends while working the case. Ace dialed Gene's cell phone number.

"What's up Ace?" asked Gene.

"I sense that you have all the bells and whistles on your phone, Gene."

"Nothing but the best for the good old Knoxville KPD," replied Gene; "what can I help you with?"

"I was wondering if you could run a plate number for me, Gene."

"Is this official police business, Ace? You know that we're not allowed to use the system for anything but official police work."

"Of course I do, Gene; that's the only type of work I do."

"In that case I'll see what I can do; what is the plate number?"

"It is a Knox County plate, number CRL-675."

After a minute or so Gene replied: "I don't think I like the looks of this, Ace; why do you want to know"

"The driver of that car was following me last night but I lost him at a traffic light."

"Just remember that you didn't get the owners name from me, but the car is registered to your old nemesis, Rupert Cooper."

"I should have known, Gene. No one will ever know where I got the information; thanks a million."

"Take care and be careful, Ace; I just found out that Rupert has filed for bankruptcy and his home is under foreclosure and I think that he probably blames you and Brad for all of his woes. He might be under a lot of stress and try to cause you bodily harm."

"Thanks, Gene; what you just told me answers a lot of questions that were going on in my head. I will be extremely careful."

"You're welcome, Ace; take care."

"Will do, Gene."

Chapter 68

When Ace got home Tuesday evening and had finished supper he told Paula that he needed to run a small errand. His watch read 6:55 p.m. and it was beginning to get dark outside.

"What time will you be home?" she asked.

"No later than nine."

"Do you want to tell me where you're going, Ace?"

"It is better that you do not know because what I will be doing as is just a little bit shady; I still have my PI license, you know."

"Take your cell phone along in case I need to get in touch with you and also make sure that your 'Last Will and Testament' is up to date."

Ace hopped in his car and drove over to north side of the city to the residence of Rupert Cooper. He still lived in the little three bedroom frame home with a detached one-car garage that he had moved into from his half a million dollar condo in which he resided before he had to pay $250,000 for bringing a baseless lawsuit against one of Brad's clients. Rupert had fallen a long way since then.

Ace drove around the house and noticed that several lights were on and concluded that Rupert must be home. He parked about a block away and walked back to the house. The blinds were drawn and he couldn't see in, but by the same token, Rupert couldn't see out. This suited Ace just fine because he wanted to get into the garage and inspect Rupert's car. He found that the old garage did not have an automatic door opener, but instead a hinged door that did not even have a lock; there was only a metal pin in the hasp where a lock was normally placed.

After donning his rubber gloves, Ace removed the pin, opened the door, walked in and closed the door behind him. There were no windows in the detached garage, so using his flashlight, he found a light switch and turned on the overhead light. There was not much of interest in the garage but Ace was more interested in what was inside the car. He first looked in the trunk of the car where he discovered several feet of sturdy rope and a large roll of duct tape. There was also a large bolo knife with a twenty four inch blade. Besides the usual spare tire and car jack there was nothing else in the trunk.

The inside of the car was very messy with empty soda bottles, candy wrappers, old newspapers, and used coffee cups. Ace looked at the stack of old newspapers and every one of them had a mention of himself or Brad in them. The papers went all the way back to 2008 when Rupert lost the lawsuit to Brad and had to pay out the $250,000. There was even an article about Ace and Paula's wedding and several articles about the time Ace had stirred up a big controversy about tire dust on the interstates being unhealthy and causing black lung disease and deaths. There was also an article about Ace appearing on the Dave Michael's television talk show in Washington.

It appeared to Ace that Rupert had an obsession about him and was planning to get even with him, but in what way, he did not know. He opened the glove compartment and discovered an army style forty five caliber hand gun that was so powerful that it was rumored that its bullet could knock a man to the ground just by hitting his out-stretched hand. Ace felt that he was going to be the target of this handgun unless he could do something about it. He knew that he could just take the gun, but Rupert would just buy another one. There was no way that he could go to the police with just nothing but his suspicions so he had to find another solution to the problem, which he did.

After Ace had taken care of business he put everything back just as he had found it. He then turned off the overhead light, closed the garage door, walked to his car, and drove home to Paula. It was only eight thirty.

"You didn't leave any dead bodies lying around; did you, Ace?"

"You sure know how to put a guy in his place, Paula; I'm just your average everyday Private Eye trying to eke out a living and provide for my wife and child."

"There's a good old Alfred Hitchcock movie coming on TCM (Turner Classic Movies) at nine which I would like to watch; would you like to watch it with me, Ace?"

"What is the movie?"

"It's 'Dial M for Murder.'"

"I would love to; I bet I've seen that move ten times and I never get tired of seeing it."

"Good; I'll put a package of 'Cousin Willie' popcorn in the microwave and nuke it to go along with our cokes."

"Sounds good to me, Paula."

Chapter 69

Friday, April 1

Today was April Fools day and Ace had not played a joke on anyone or had one played on him. He was working a little bit late when he noticed that it was almost seven p.m. and he had forgot to call Paula and tell her that he would be late so he called her and told her that he would be home by around seven thirty.

He finished up his work, locked up, and took the elevator down to sub level two to his normal parking slot. He took the keys out of his pocket and just as he opened the car door, he felt something hard poking him in the back.

"Don't make a move," a voice that Ace recognized as belonging to Rupert Cooper told him. "Give me your keys, spread your legs, and place your hands on top of your car."

Ace did as he was told while Rupert frisked him for a gun and came up empty; Ace very seldom carried a gun although he had a permit to do so.

"Now I want you to walk to the rear of your car and open the trunk and crawl inside."

Ace did as he was told and Rupert slammed the trunk door closed. A minute later, Ace felt the car backing out of the slot and heading out of the garage. Since Ace's car (1976 Mustang) was so old there was no escape mechanism from inside the trunk that now exists in all cars as required by law; he was trapped and had no idea where Rupert was taking him. He reached into his right rear pocket and retrieved his cell phone that Rupert had missed when he frisked him. He tried to call

Paula first but he could not get a signal from inside the trunk. He also tried 911 with no luck.

He found his flashlight that he always kept in the trunk and inserted the two D-cell batteries that he always kept separated from the flashlight to prolong battery life. He looked at his watch and it read 7:10 pm. He intended to time how long it took for Rupert to get where he was going so that it would give him an estimate of how far the car had traveled. At first Rupert was having a hard time getting the feel of a car with a 500 horsepower engine under the hood. After a mile or so and many rapid accelerations followed by the brakes being applied, Rupert seemed to have mastered driving the Mustang. Two minutes later Ace felt that Rupert had gotten on the interstate because the car speed had picked up considerably. He believed that the car stayed on the interstate for about ten minutes and got off and turned right and drove for about a minute and stopped for what Ace believed was a traffic light. It made another stop a couple minutes later and then made a sharp right turn and started going steeply uphill and making a lot of sharp turns. He felt the car going slowly over some bumps on the road which Ace assumed to be railroad tracks. About three minutes after turning on the winding road his car came to a stop. He heard Rupert get out of the car and presently he opened the trunk.

"Happy April Fool's Day, Ace, and you're the biggest fool of all."

Ace crawled out of the trunk and looked out over the lit-up city of Knoxville; it would have been a beautiful sight under different circumstances. Rupert had brought him to the top of Sharp's Ridge and at the dead end turn-around of Ludlow Street that connects the street to Broadway about two miles back down the ridge. There was a single light shining down on the area from a pole that provided enough light for Rupert to see well enough to shoot Ace. Sharps Ridge contains a seldom utilized city park and seemed to be in a state of disrepair. There are around a dozen communication towers on the ridge and one of them extends more than seventeen hundred feet into the sky. Besides the towers there is nothing much else located there. It is uninhabited and is usually a spot where young lovers like to come and park, but unfortunately for, Ace, not tonight.

Ace noticed Rupert's old car parked nearby. He surmised that Rupert drove it up to the top of the ridge and probably called a cab to take him to BB&T Bank Building in which Ace worked. He didn't believe that Rupert was physically in shape to walk the two miles or so back down to Broadway. For what reason Rupert brought him up here, Ace didn't know, but he was soon to find out."What are you up to Rupert; don't you realize that kidnapping is a criminal offense?"

"You are going to wish my crime was only kidnapping, Ace; let me tell you what is going down. You drove your car up here and took this gun in my hand and committed suicide."

Ace recognized it as the gun in Rupert's gloved right hand as the one he found in the glove compartment of his car a few nights ago.

"That won't fly, Rupert."

"And just why is that, Ace?"

"You are not going to make my death look like a suicide because I'm not going to let you get close enough to shoot me so that there would be powder burns on my body."

"I've already thought about that eventuality, Ace, and this is what I did to prepare. I took a round out of the magazine and removed the bullet and took out the powder which I burned. I took the residue and put it in this little zip lock bag here in my pocket, and after I shoot you, I'm going to sprinkle it all around the hole in your heart."

"You're all heart, Rupert, but there is still one fly in the ointment."

"What fly is that, Ace?"

"You're going to have to shoot me from a distance of several feet because I'm not going to stand still and let you shoot me from two feet away."

"When I shoot you with this 45 caliber slug, it will leave such a large hole in you that they won't be able to tell if it came from one foot or thirty feet; it will look like a suicide, Ace."

"Why are you doing this, Rupert?"

"As if you didn't know; you have ruined my life completely."

"You brought it on yourself, Rupert, with your dishonesty and by sending threatening letters through the mail to Brad,"

"I did that to try to make Brad as miserable as he made me; he took almost all of my money when he stacked the jury in the case where his client ran over my client and the dumb jury found me liable for half a million dollars."

"But Brad let you off for $250,000."

"That 250 G's just about wiped out my savings account."

"That's the price you pay when you bring a bogus lawsuit to trial. Brad even warned you in the courtroom that you had better withdraw the suit, but your pride got in the way. Don't blame Brad and me for your poor decision."

"You are not making it any easier on yourself, Ace; I can make your death slow and painful by shooting you in non vital places and let you slowly and painfully die."

"Why don't you just go ahead and shoot now and get it over with," said Ace as he pulled his cell phone out of his pocket and turned it on.

"Give me the cell phone, Ace."

"What are you going to do to me if I don't; you've already said that you were going to shoot me. What else could you do? I would just like to call Paula before I die."

"You can hang on to the phone but if you start to talk to anyone I will shoot you here and now; however I'll shoot when I get good and ready, and I'm not ready. Do you know what you put me through with all your shenanigans, Ace? Let me tell you about it. You had six tons of manure dumped in my front yard for which I was billed on my credit card. You contaminated my entire HVAC system and every nook and cranny of my house; I never did get that entire skunk odor out of my house. Then to add insult to injury there was a charge of over five thousand dollars for a continuous nine hour phone call to a phone toll line. I had to declare bankruptcy to get out from under all those charges. My law practice has dropped off so bad that I can no longer afford an office or a secretary to staff it, and on top of all of that, I have lost my house as well; I have one more month before they put me out on the street."

"You live by the sword and you die by the sword, Rupert."

"You are the one who is going to die, Ace; do you have any last words?"

"I really wish that you would reconsider what you are doing, Rupert; you will live to regret it."

"At least I will live; that's more than I can say for you. Get ready to meet your maker," replied Rupert, as he pointed the Army forty five pistol directly at Ace and pulled the trigger.

As soon as Rupert pulled the trigger the gun exploded in his hand and the force was so great that it knocked him to the ground. (What Rupert didn't know was that the night when Ace was in his garage that he had doctored up the gun. He found a one half diameter round wooden dowel in Rupert's garage, sawed off a one inch length and tapered it with his pocket knife, and drove it half way down the barrel of the gun where it became firmly wedged.

Ace walked over to see about Rupert; he had some powder burns to his face and it appeared that his trigger finger was broken, but the glove that he was wearing prevented his right hand from suffering severe powder burns. When Rupert had fired, the 45 flew out of his hand into two pieces and there were wood splinters all over the ground. Ace picked up what was left of the gun and put it in his jacket pocket.

"When was the last time you cleaned your gun, Rupert; you must have had some rust in the barrel? Do you need to go to emergency?"

"Are you going to take me to the emergency room before you take me to jail?"

"I am not going to take you to jail, Rupert."

"Aren't you afraid that I will try to kill you again?"

"No, Rupert, I have everything you just did and said recorded on my cell phone in a movie with color and sound. I am going to download the movie to my computer and transfer it to a CD and place it in my safety deposit box which will be opened upon my death. No one except you and me will ever know what went down here this evening unless you tell them. You didn't answer my question; do you want to go to emergency?"

"I think that there would be too many questions to answer there, Ace; I'll just go home and try to take care of myself. I don't believe I could have behaved toward you the way you have toward me; I would want revenge. I think I may have misjudged you; you won't have anymore trouble from me."

"Nor you from me, Rupert; do you think that you are able to drive home?"

"I believe so, Ace."

"If you're are not going to the hospital I suggest that you pull that broken trigger finger back into it's socket and place a splint around it. If you don't, you will end up with a crooked finger like my pinkie here. Tape your trigger finger to your middle finger to make it more secure"

"Thanks for the advice, Ace; I'll do just that."

"I'll follow you home Rupert to make sure you get there in one piece."

"Thanks, Ace."

Rupert got into his old car and started down the mountain with Ace right behind; he seemed to be driving okay. Ace pulled out his cell phone and called Paula.

"Paula; I'm going to be coming home a little later than I anticipated, I got held up."

Chapter 70

Saturday, April, 2

Lisa was home from Vanderbilt for Spring Break and would be out of school all of next week. Paula was in the kitchen preparing a delicious standing rib roast which just happened to be Ace's favorite dish.

"What are you going to do on Spring Break, Lisa?"

"Nothing much' Sean and I have plans to drive to Cades Cove in the Smokies (Great Smokey Mountain National Park) and hike to Abrams Falls; they say the falls are at their peak flow this time of year and that it is a sight to behold. We also plan to visit The New Titanic Museum Attraction in Pigeon Forge. (The Titanic Attraction is a 30,000 square foot half scale model of the forward half of the Titanic which sank in 1912. The famous spiral staircase is built to actual size and to the same specifications as the original. Each guest is given a boarding pass in the name of one of the actual passengers who were on the ship when it hit the iceberg and sank. The guests do not know if their passenger survived or went down with the ship until the end of the tour of the ship.) After we leave the Titanic we are going to find us a good restaurant and pig out."

"Let me give you a word of caution, Lisa; Make sure that they have enough lifeboats for all the Passengers before you board."

"That was the first thing we did, Ace."

"Did you ever wonder how many Women Libbers they had on the Titanic when it sank, Lisa?"

"I don't think that you would have to take off your gloves to count them on your fingers."

"You're not going to Florida like all the other students?"

"That's for teenagers, Ace, and I never even wanted to go when I was one of them."

"You are a very unusual girl, Lisa."

"I prefer the term unique to unusual, Ace; there are all sorts of connotations associated with the word, unusual. In fact, that word fits you much better than it does me."

"Okay, your uniqueness; I haven't given you a difficult problem to work in almost two years. I believe that I have finally found a problem that will stop you in your tracks."

"Would you like to make a wager on that, Ace Sleuth?"

"If you get it right I will take you and Sean out to any restaurant in Knoxville of your choosing, and that includes the pricy 'Ruth's Steak house.'"

"What if I don't solve the problem?"

"Then you have to shine my shoes anytime I ask you to."

"That sounds fair to me; what is the problem?"

"Do you know the difference between the two different temperature measuring systems, 'Fahrenheit' and 'Centigrade'?"

"If my physics professor was right, then on the Fahrenheit scale, water freezes at 32 degrees and boils at 212; in this system there are 180 degrees between freezing and boiling. Conversely, in the Centigrade System, water freezes at 0 degrees and boils at 100 degrees. In this system there is 100 degrees between freezing and boiling and if my math serves me right, a Centigrade degree is nine fifths (180/100) larger than a Fahrenheit degree."

"Do you know how to convert the temperature of either system to the other?"

"If I remember correctly the equations go like this: Let 'F' represent the Fahrenheit temperature and 'C' represent the Centigrade temperature; Then:

$$T (C^0) = 5/9[T(F^o)— 32]$$
$$T (F^0) = 9/5 (T(C^0) + 32$$

"You are correct so far, Lisa, but the problem that I want you to solve consists of two parts. At some temperature point the Fahrenheit and Centigrade temperatures will be equal and I want you to find exactly what that temperature is."

"That shouldn't be too hard, Ace; what is the second part of the equation?"

"This is the part where I believe that you will meet your Waterloo. I never did like those two equations with different brackets; they were hard for me to memorize. On the left side of the equations, the first one has brackets around the 'T' and the '32' and the other one only has the bracket around the 'T'. I had a hard time memorizing the equations because I could never remember which equation had the full bracket around it. I want you to come up with two entirely new and different equations that are much simpler to remember and use; I want you do give me two new user-friendly equations; do you think you can do that?"

"You have got to be kidding, Ace; I'm smart but I'm no Einstein."

"I knew that I would finally stump you, Lisa, but I wouldn't give you anything to work that I haven't already worked myself; and you've got a whole lot more smarts than me."

"There goes my whole Spring Break, Big Daddy, "I'll get even with you for this."

"You will thank me for this because you will be so proud of yourself if you work it."

"We'll see about that, Ace."

"Are you two intellectuals ready for a delicious rib roast with roasted small red potatoes in butter along with creamed asparagus?" asked Paula.

"That sounds great, Paula; I always enjoy your low fat-low, low-calorie meals," replied, Ace.

Chapter 71

Monday, April 4

Ace was already at work when Brad arrived; presently Denise brought in the usual coffee and doughnuts along with the morning paper. Brad looked on the front page and remarked:

"There was another bank robbery over the weekend, Ace; there seems to be almost one a week lately, why do you think that is?"

"I think it's because of the economy and some people are desperate because many of them are losing their homes."

"I think that you are right, Ace; what do you suggest that we do about it?"

"I think that we should place a trap door in front of each cashier's window directly over an alligator pit below so that all the cashier has to do is push a button and wave bye-bye to the would-be robber."

"I know that you're only joking, Ace, but let's get serious. I don't think that most bank robbers are career criminals but are desperate men who are doing desperate deeds. There ought to be a way to discourage this sort of thing."

"I know a sure way to do it, but I doubt if the banks would go along with it. All they need to do is to place all of the cashiers behind a partition about six feet high with bulletproof windows in front of their station that will rise up to the top of the their opening at the touch of a foot on a button beneath the station. This would seal the cashier off from the would-be robber who would be just standing there looking stupid."

"But what about the other customers in the bank; wouldn't their lives be in danger?"

"I think not, Brad; bank robbers of today are not like Bonnie and Clyde who killed people. These robbers today would just like to get out of there as fast as possible."

"You may have something there, Ace; and I don't believe that it would be all that expensive to install."

"I think that we could practically eliminate bank robbery attempts if each bank had a sign explaining exactly what would happen in the event of an attempted robbery. I know that I wouldn't want to try to rob a bank with this system in place, and this system would save a lot more money than just the amount the bank would have lost in a successful robbery."

"How do you figure that, ace?"

"It probably costs more money to try a bank robber in a court of law than the amount of money he got in the heist. And another plus for the system is that someone who had decided to become a bank robber would figure that it would not be in his best interest to pursue this line of work with this system in place."

"Do you know what, Ace?"

"No; what?"

"I'm glad that I hired you."

"So am I, Brad; So am I."

"I may need your help on a new lawsuit that I expect will be filed in the next couple of weeks."

"What's it all about, Brad?"

"It's nothing more than a nuisance lawsuit which will never make it to court but we stand to gain $100,000 if we can make it go away. It's been around for awhile and the statute of limitations runs out in three weeks. Both sides have been stalling, the lawyer hoping for an out of court settlement, and the other side hoping that the whole thing will go away."

"What's the basis of the lawsuit, Brad?"

"A pregnant lady in Nashville witnessed a rather severe accident on Old Hickory Road in Nashville and had a miscarriage and blames it on the car accident."

"Which of the drivers is she suing, or which one of the driver's insurance company is she suing?"

"She is suing the insurer of the driver who was at fault."

"It appears to me, Brad, that it would be impossible to prove in a court of law that the accident caused the miscarriage."

"You're exactly right, Ace; that's the reason the lawyer doesn't want to go to court and neither does the insurance company."

"Who is the lawyer, Brad?"

"He is a shyster lawyer in Nashville by the name of Ralph Knell who goes by the nickname, Rusty."

"That name sounds very apropos, Brad; what insurance company is involved and who is the woman?"

"It a relatively small insurance company that goes by the name of 'Commonwealth Auto Insurance Inc'; it's based in Louisville. Kentucky. The woman's name is Wanda Patrick who lives in Nashville."

"Wouldn't it be rather hard to prove that she had a miscarriage just by witnessing an auto accident, Brad?"

"Its not what can be or cannot be proven in a court of law these days, but what some tort attorney can convince a jury of twelve of, and I've seen some of these juries whom I believe could be convinced that the earth is flat."

"It looks like I will be spending about three weeks in Nashville until the statute of limitations expires. I will need to keep Mr. Knell occupied until that time."

"How do you plan to go about doing that, Ace?"

"Mr. Knell doesn't know it yet, but he is due for an IRS Audit Starting Wednesday Morning or sooner. Call Commonwealth Insurance and tell them to stall Knell at least until then; that's when the audit kicks in. I need to get started right now, Brad."

"Go for it Ace," replied Brad.

Ace left Brad and stopped by Denise's desk.

"Do we have an extra phone line coming into our office that we could activate, Denise?"

"We have four active lines at this time but I believe that there is a fifth line that we could get. I have five lights on my master phone line but only four that light up. Just what do you have in mind, Ace?"

"I want you to call AT&T and see if you can get a toll free 800 number for line five. And when you get it I want you to write down what I am about to tell you and to answer the phone in that manner. You are to answer the phone as follows:

"Internal Revenue Service, Memphis Regional Office of Robert Childress, and I would like for you to record the following message on the answering machine:"

"You have reached the office of IRS Agent, Robert Childress; please leave your message after the tone."

"What are you up to this time, Ace?"

"If I told you, Denise, I would have to kill you. I also want you to book me a nice room at the Indigo Hotel on Union Street in downtown Nashville; the number is 877-270-1394. (The hotel is within walking distance to Ralph Knells office in the First Tennessee Bank building on Deadrick Street). Do you have my cell phone number?"

"Yes I do; is that all, Sir? I sure hope that you don't get me in trouble for answering the phone as an IRS employee: that's a federal offense"

"On second thought just let the answering machine go into action and call me after you get the message. If anyone ever asks you about the toll free number just tell them that you had it installed on my instructions. Utilize the phone company's automatic answering service so that your voice will not be on it; then you will not be involved in any way."

"I would sure hate to have you as an enemy, Ace."

"So would I, Denise. Try to get the new phone line activated today; I believe that they can do that remotely without having to send someone to our office. Call me at home and give me the 800 number as soon as you get it. I will need it for some documents that I will be preparing. I plan to leave for Nashville the first thing in the morning and I will call you as soon as I get there."

"Take care, Ace, and don't do anything illegal such as posing as an IRS agent."

"Everything's fair in love and lawsuits, Denise."

Ace walked back to Brad's desk and told him that he needed to go home right now to do some work on the case.

"I will be leaving for Nashville the first thing in the morning and I plan to come home Friday afternoon. I expect I will have to spend three weeks there until the statute of limitations runs out in the case. I will be staying at the Indigo Hotel in downtown Nashville. You can reach me on my cell phone."

"Keep it as legal as possible, Ace; I don't even want to know how you plan to go about this endeavor."

"I'll never tell, Brad."

It was ten a.m. when Ace left the office to go home where he had some preparations to make. It was lucky for Ace that Lisa was still at home until Sunday; he had some work for her to do.

Chapter 72

Ace got home about two thirty Monday afternoon and Lisa was absorbed in a book she was reading.

"What's the name of your book, Lisa?"

"It's 'World Without End' by Ken Follett."

"That's a rather lengthy book, isn't it?"

"It's about 1100 pages but it is easy reading. The setting for the book is in England several hundred years ago which corresponds to the period which we are studying in my world history class; I thought I could get a leg up by reading this book."

"That's a good idea, Lisa, but I was wondering if you could take a few hours off and do some Googleing on the internet for me; I will pay you twenty five dollars an hour."

"What do you want me to do?"

"I want you to find out everything you can about a lawyer in Nashville by the name of Ralph Knell who goes by the nickname of Rusty Knell."

"How cute, Ace; Rusty Nail is quite unusual."

"I guess it's somewhat like Dusty Rhodes."

"Is there anything else that you can tell me about him, Ace?"

"I don't know a whole lot more except that he has an office in the First Tennessee Bank Building in downtown Nashville and he is suing one of Brad's clients."

"When do you need this information?"

"ASAP, Lisa; if you could get it before I leave for Nashville in the morning that would be great."

"I'll get started on it right now, Ace."

"I don't want you to neglect the temperature scale problem I gave you the other day, Lisa."

"That is a real tough one, Ace; you may have finally found a problem I can't solve."

"I'll get out of your hair now and let you get to work, Lisa; I have some work to do of my own."

When Ace went to work for Brad five years ago he closed his PI office and moved all of his forging paraphernalia into his garage. He hadn't needed it up until now. He had everything he needed to forge all kinds of documents and to laminate them so that it would take an expert to tell them from the real thing. He went to work on creating a Tennessee drivers license, an IRS identity card, and several businesses cards with the fictitious name of Robert Childress.

The driver's license and his IRS ID Card were the hardest because they both required his photo on them. He had Lisa take an official-looking close up picture of him on his digital camera which turned out real well. He scanned the picture on his scanner and transferred it to 'My Documents' on his computer and then printed it to the proper size to exactly fit a Tennessee driver's license card. Using his own driver's license as a model, he had pasted the picture on the fake DL with all the other pertinent information and laminated it; he then showed it to Lisa.

"What do you think, Lisa; do you think that this could pass as a valid Tennessee driver's license?"

"It looks as valid as mine, Ace; you are a real artist."

Next Ace needed to make a fake IRS ID card; he had no idea what one looked like, but he suspected that Rusty 'Nail' wouldn't either. (Ace had already formed a dislike for the lawyer by thinking of his name as Nail) When he was finished with the card it contained the following information along with his photo.

**UNITED STATES OF AMERICA
INTERNAL REVENUE SERVICE
MEMPHIS REGION
AGENT- ROBERT CHILDRESS
22 N Front St, Memphis, TN 38103
Ph- 1-800- 426-2209**

Denise had called Ace and given him the bogus toll-free number which he added to the bottom of the card. Except for the toll-free number, and the name Robert Childress, everything else on the card was accurate including the Memphis address for the IRS. Ace just hoped that if Rusty decided to call the IRS in Memphis that he would use the number on the card and not look up the number on the internet or in the phone book.

Ace had just one more fake document to create and that was a business card; he could hardly go wrong on that because they came in all shape and sizes. He made one and printed twenty copies to pass around in Nashville if the need arose.

He was rather pleased with his forgeries as he looked at them with an air of confidence. He had never had one of his fake ID's discovered in all the years he had manufactured them. He was now ready to head to Nashville in the morning and he hoped that Lisa would have some information about Rusty before he left.

Chapter 73

Tuesday Morning, April. 5

It was around eight a.m. and Ace was getting ready to head off to Nashville in his 76 Mustang when Lisa walked into the room.

"I wasn't able to dig up much dirt on Ralph Knell, Ace; there were quite a few articles in the Nashville Tennessean about him and all the lawsuits he has filed and settled. It appears that practically all of them were settled out of court. I found that he is forty five years old and has been married to a woman named Doris for fifteen years and it appears to be the first for both of them; they have ten year old son named Anthony. He has been accused of being unethical by some other attorneys but I couldn't find anything to show that the accusations ever amounted to anything. I gathered that he is not overly popular in Nashville. It appeared to me that he is the 'Rupert Spenser' of Nashville."

"I suspected as much, Lisa; if you come up with any additional information just call me on my cell phone."

"I'm going to miss you, Ace," said Paula; we haven't been apart for this long since we were married."

"I'll be back home Friday evening around seven, Paula, and we can go out to dine at the restaurant of your choice and you and Sean can come along too, Lisa."

"I'd like to go back to the Copper Cellar if they would let us after the way you treated our waitress the last time we were there," replied Paula.

"I think that the twenty dollar bill I left under my plate more than made up for my little indiscretion," said Ace.

"I'll be working on the Fahrenheit-Centigrade problem you gave me, Ace, but I haven't figured out how to approach it yet."

"I believe that I've finally got you stumped, Lisa."

"Don't you be picking up any of those pretty women in Nashville, Ace," chimed in Paula.

"I promise that I won't take out more than one of them, Paula."

"Well if its only one I suppose I could live with it, but I just couldn't live it with you."

"I better be on my way if I want to get to Nashville by noon; I will gain an hour going because Nashville is on Central Time, but I will lose that hour coming back home. I'll call you as soon as I get there."

"Take care and drive carefully," said Paula.

"I will, Love Bird."

Chapter 74

It was nine a.m. Tuesday as Ace headed to Nashville; he stopped at the Krystal Restaurant in West Knoxville on Kingston Pike and grabbed a quick breakfast of sausage and eggs along with coffee, and grits, which he liked occasionally.

The drive was uneventful and three hours later Ace pulled into the parking garage of the Indigo Hotel on Union Street in downtown Nashville. It was only 11:00 a.m. Nashville time; he took the elevator up to the lobby and checked in. He had plenty of time before he planned to make his surprise visit to Knell's office, but first he had to make sure that Rusty would be there so he called his office.

"This is the Law Office of Ralph Knell; how may I help you?"

"This is Robert Childress of The IRS Regional Office in Memphis and it is of the utmost importance that I see Mr. Knell as soon as possible. If it's convenient I could drop in at one this afternoon. If you wish to call me back, you can reach me here at the Indigo Hotel just a few blocks from your office; I'm in room 609. Their toll free number is: 1-877-270- 1394, I don't know what their local number is."

"That's alright, Mr. Childress, I have the number. I'll call you right back as soon as Mr. Knell gets finished talking to a client."

"Thanks; I'll be awaiting your call."

Thirty minutes later the phone rang.

"This is Shirley from Mr. Knell's office, and he can see you at one this afternoon, Mr. Childress."

"Thanks, Shirley; I'll be there on time."

Chapter 75

Tuesday afternoon

Ace walked the three blocks to the First Tennessee Bank Building and walked into the lobby and saw that Knell's office was on the seventh floor; he was dressed in the $700 suit he had purchased back in 2006 which he used to impersonate a Medicare Official concerning a case in which he was working on. He took the elevator up to seven and strutted into Knells office as if he owned the place. He walked to the receptionist desk that had a plaque that read: "Shirley Jones." She appeared to be in her early thirties with shoulder length blond hair, straight teeth, large brown eyes, and a contagious smile. Ace thought that she must be an asset to Knell if her work was as good as her appearance.

"Good afternoon Shirley," said Ace, I'm Robert Childress and I'm here to see Mr. Knell."

"He's been waiting for you, Mr. Childress; I'll take you right back."

"Thanks, Shirley' you can call me Bob if you wish."

"Thanks, Bob"

"Mr. Childress is here to see you, Mr. Knell," said Shirley as she ushered him into Knell's office.

"Please close the door behind you, Shirley," said Knell. "Have a seat Mr. Childress; what is the purpose of your visit?"

Knell appeared to be pretty much as Lisa had described him. He was wearing a wedding ring and had a picture of an attractive woman on his desk that looked to be in her middle thirties whom Ace assumed to be his wife.

"That's a picture of my wife, Doris," spoke up Knell, as he noticed Ace looking at it; she's the love of my life."

"She's a beautiful woman, Ralph," replied Ace.

"Thanks, Mr. Childress."

"Just call me Bob," said Ace as he showed him his driver's license, his IRS ID card, and gave him one of his business cards, and I'll call you Ralph if that's OK with you?"

"If we want to get personal, I would rather that you call me by my nickname, Rusty."

"Ok, Rusty; I wish that I was here under more pleasant circumstances but it's a requirement of my job. I have come to audit your 2009 income tax return."

"I feared as much, but why did they choose me; I've always paid my due taxes on time?"

"I realize that, Rusty; I have checked your returns for the past five years and found no problems, but for some reason, our computer found something in your 2009 return and kicked it out, and that requires us to do an audit. I don't like it anymore than you do, but it's my job."

"Why wasn't I called and notified that you were coming?"

"We have found when we do call ahead that it gives the person whom we are auditing ample time to cover up their tracks, hide documents, and forewarn others to keep quiet and not cooperate with us. We have found we do better when our audit is a complete surprise."

"How long is it going to take, and exactly what do you want from me?"

"It will take about two weeks, three tops, and I will need a copy of your 2009 return with all you supporting documents. I will also need a copy of all your bank transactions for 2009 along with copies of all your credit card statements for the same period."

"I can get you the copies of the bank statements but I don't know if I have copies of my credit card statements."

"We can get all that information from the computer, Rusty; that won't be a problem."

"It seems to be a little late to be auditing the 2009 income taxes when the 2010 taxes are due in a week."

"We take the audits in order, Rusty; yours was on my desk a few days ago with instructions for me to perform an audit. Sometimes we will perform an audit for a return that is several years old."

"What is the next step, Bob? I'm a very busy man and I can't neglect my work very long."

"I realize that Rusty, and I want to get this audit over with as quickly as you do. The audit will require quite a bit of your time because I will need you to work closely with me on this. It would speed things up tremendously if you could find me a cubbyhole here in your office from which I could work. If not I will have to work from my hotel room and I would be walking back and forth between here and there and that would probably add two or three more weeks to my task."

"I have a spare desk that you can use, Bob and I have an extra phone that you can use also."

"Your helpfulness in this audit will go a long way with me, Rusty; most people I audit seem to resent me, and truthfully, I would also if I were in their place. I really don't believe that I will find a smoking gun. Your whole attitude leads me to believe that you have nothing to hide. I will speed things up as much as possible if you are here to answer my questions as they arise. I had to spend three months on one audit I did because it was like pulling teeth to get any help from the man. He was always calling my boss in Memphis and was trying to exert political pressure on them to call off the dogs, so to speak. I think his congressman was a personal friend and the IRS doesn't take too kindly to that type of action."

"How did that audit turn out, Bob?"

"The man is spending three years in Federal Prison at the Government's expense. He was stalling for a good reason; he had something to hide."

"What do you need from me first, Bob?"

"What time do you open your office in the morning?"

"We open at nine."

"Could you possibly have a copy of your 2009 tax return on my desk along with all your bank statements for the same year?"

"That won't be a problem at all, Bob; they will be on your desk when you come in the morning. I am going to have Shirley show you where you will be working. We will have your telephone there working also."

"I couldn't ask for anything more, Rusty."

Shirley took him to a corner window room that Ace guessed was normally used as a small conference room.

"Thanks, Shirley; I'll see you at nine in the morning. You are fortunate to be working for such a nice gentleman."

"Thanks Bob." *"He must not be talking about the boss I know,"* thought Shirley.

Ace walked back to his hotel room to make a local phone call to a number he had programmed into his cell phone data base. He dialed the number.

"Hello Rose; (Rose Golden is a retired welfare worker about seventy years old whom Ace met a few weeks ago while working on a case) I bet you can't guess who this is."

"As I live and breathe, Ace; it's good to hear from you. I recognized your masculine voice; where are you?"

"I'm working on a case and I'm staying at the Indigo Hotel in downtown Nashville."

"How long are you going to be here; I would like to fix you a nice Jewish dinner if you have time."

"Do you remember your last words to me when I left your home a few weeks ago, Rose?"

"I think I told you to give me a ring the next time you were in Nashville."

"That's exactly what you said, and I'm here and I would like to take you out tonight."

"I would be honored, Ace; where do you want to take me."

"I would like for you to accompany me to the Sommet Center to see the Predators play the Philadelphia Flyers in hockey tomorrow night; I was fortunate enough to get two seats in the fifth row."

"I bet you want to see Benjamin who plays forward for the Predators don't you, Ace?"

"That did cross my mind, Rose, but I believe your presence would be just as important."

"I must correct you on a couple of things, Ace. One is the pronunciation of the word, Sommet; we have become quite cosmopolitan here in Nashville lately and it is not pronounced like 'The Summit' which is painted on the floor of the University of Tennessee's basketball Arena in honor of Pat Summit, the Lady Vols Basketball Coach. Our Sommet is pronounced "Soh May', and let me tell you, I would be honored to go with you."

"You only corrected me on one thing, Rose; you said you had two."

"The arena no longer goes by the name, 'Sommet Arena'; it is now called 'The Bridgestone Arena.'"

"It looks like Bridgestone threw some money at The Sommet and knocked it down, Rose."

"You are right about that, Ace."

"Nashville has come a long way, Rose; you Nashvillians are so cosmopolitan and us Knoxvillians are just a bunch of Hillbillies. You have the Parthenon and we have the Sunsphere; you have the beautiful Opryland Hotel and we have Motel six. We are so far behind Nashville that we still pronounce Vanderbilt as two words instead of running them together as you do here. I knew a young lady once from a small burg in Kentucky that was so impressed with the way Nashvillians pronounced Vanderbilt that she started pronouncing her home town in Kentucky as Horscuve rather than Horse Cave, and a friend of mine who lives in a small East Tennessee community started pronouncing his burg as Bullsgup instead of Bulls Gap. Your cosmopolitanism is catching, Rose, but you Nashvillians still have a long way to go to catch up with Massachusetts and New Hampshire."

"How is that, Ace?"

"You have a Peabody College here in Nashville don't you?"

"Yes we do."

"How do you pronounce the name of it?"

"We pronounce it as if it were two words, Pea Body; but what does that have to do with Massachusetts?"

"There is a town of around 50,000 named Peabody up there and you would never guess how the natives pronounce it. They refer to the town as Pibbidy."

"We do have a little catching up to reach them, Ace; thanks for the geography lesson, but what about New Hampshire?"

"I believe that New Hampshire takes the cake with their pronunciation of their Capital City, Concord."

"How could anyone possibly mispronounce Concord, Ace?"

"They pronounce it as 'Conquered'; believe it or not, Rose."

"I guess we learn something new every day, Ace."

"I'm always glad to help, Rose; I do whatever I can."

"What time do you want me to be ready tomorrow evening?"

"Why don't I come by about seven; the game starts at eight?"

"I will be eagerly awaiting, Ace."

"See you then, Rose."

Chapter 76

Wednesday morning

Ace arrived at Rusty's office at nine a.m. sharp. Shirley was at her station and Rusty was in his office.

"Good morning, Shirley; you look wide-eyed and bushy-tailed this morning."

"Would you like a cup of coffee and a donut, Ace?"

"I certainly would, thanks."

Ace walked by the open door to Rusty's office and stuck his head in and said hello.

"All the documents that you requested are on your desk, Ace; if you need anything else just let me know."

"Thanks a lot, Rusty; I better get to work because the harder I work the sooner I get out of your hair."

"Don't rush on my account, Ace."

There were two large piles of paperwork on his desk when Ace walked into his office; the first thing he looked at was the 2009 tax return which was a joint return with his wife Doris. Rusty's taxable income was $855,000 for the year. He took in almost two million in 2009 but he had a lot of expenses. His rent for his suite of offices was $7,000 a month and he paid Shirley $40,000 annually. Ace felt a little guilty about snooping through the paperwork but he rationalized that it was for the greater good.

He didn't see anything unusual with the 1040 form itself; he decided to check later to see if there were receipts in the pile of papers to back up all the deductions. Next he looked at the monthly bank statements, There were weekly checks to Shirley and monthly checks for the office rent and a monthly check for $1,000 to a company called The Davidson Group. He looked at all twelve months and they also showed the $1,000 check; he was curious so he looked up The Davidson Group in the phone book and dialed the number. A female voice answered.

"You have reached the Davidson Group. This is Mary; how may I be of help?"

"My name is Robert Childress from the IRS, Mary, but don't panic; I'm not here to audit your company. Would it be alright if I come over to your office? I had rather talk to you in person because of the confidentiality of the subject matter. Would it be okay if I walked over to your office; I can be there in fifteen minutes? You don't need to worry; I'm not going to audit you either."

"Sure, come right on over, Mr. Childress; my office is on the first floor on the left as you enter the front door."

Ace walked the three blocks to the Davison Group Building and had no trouble locating Mary's office. Mary looked to be around forty with blond hair and blue eyes and would probably be about five-six standing up. He introduced himself.

"What I need to talk to you about, Mary is very sensitive. I need some information from you regarding an audit that I'm working on which I suggest that you keep top secret even from the rest of the people at your company. If the name of the person that I'm auditing ever leaked out it could adversely affect his business even if I find nothing wrong in my audit. Can I assume that you will be discreet in this matter before I ask you the question?"

"Yes; I certainly want to cooperate 100 percent with the IRS; what is the question?"

"I have been going over the 2009 income tax return for Mr. Ralph Knell and I see that a monthly check for $1,000 from his office has been going to your company. I need to determine if this is a legitimate income tax deduction; can you tell me the purpose of the checks?"

"Let me look on my computer, Robert; it will take me a few minutes." After a short wait Mary replied, "Our Company is quite diversified and one of our fields is handling rental properties for some our clients. The checks in question were for the monthly rental of an apartment in the Commodore Towers on Broadway in West Nashville about a mile west of the Parthenon."

"Thanks a lot for your help; Mary, and remember, 'mums the word'."

"You can trust me, Robert; I'm honored that you took me into your confidence."

"I could tell from the moment that I first met you, Mary, that you were a person of integrity who could be trusted."

"Thank you for those kind words. Mr. Childress."

"You are quite welcome, Mary, and you may call me Bob if we ever meet again."

"I hope if that ever happens, Bob, I hope that you will not be auditing me."

"You can bet your bottom dollar that I won't be, Mary"

When Ace he got back to the office it was almost lunch time and he decided to take a visit to The Commodore Towers. On the way out he stuck his head in Rusty's office and informed him that he was going to lunch and might be a few minutes late returning.

"Take your time, Bob; I'll be here when you get back."

Chapter 77

Ace decided to take a city bus the short distance to the Commodore Towers. There was a bus stop right in front of the twelve story towers. He walked into the lobby and saw the rental office on his right. He knocked on the closed door and a female voice answered telling him to come in, which he did.

"My name is Alicia; how may I help you sir?"

She was an attractive woman with a bright smile and blond hair and appeared to be around thirty five years old.

"My name is Robert Childress from The IRS regional office in Memphis, but don't be alarmed, I'm not here to audit you."

"You can audit me any time you want to, Robert," she said.

"I didn't expect such a nice reception, Alicia; I'll make you my next audit victim."

"How can I help you, Bob?" (Ace picked up on her calling him Bob).

"You have been receiving a $1,000 monthly check from the Davidson Group for an apartment here and I would like to know who resides in that apartment."

"Let me look on my computer and see what I can find out; we get several monthly checks from them and there may be more than one for a $1,000. I see that we get two monthly checks in that amount."

"Can you tell me who lives in each?"

"Yes; a Mr. Charles Sanders lives in 109 and Megan McGuire in 707."

"Can you describe each one to me?"

"Let me see what I have on my computer, Mr. Sander's age is listed at 73 and Megan is listed as 34."

"Do you know either of them?"

"I only know Megan when I see her, but she is a looker and dresses to the nines."

"Do you know if she lives alone or if she is married?"

"I know that she is not married and lives alone; I have never seen her leave the towers with a man."

"Do you think that some man, maybe a married man, could be visiting her in her apartment?"

"That's highly possible, but he would have to have a card key to get access to the elevators or I would have to buzz him in."

"Would a man be able to have a card key to the elevators?" asked Ace.

"Not unless he lives in one of the apartments."

"Can the residents buzz people in from their apartments?"

"Not anymore; we had some problems with that. Some people who were trying to get in would claim to be maintenance workers or cable guys to get inside and walk off with anything that they could get their hands on. Now everyone has to be buzzed in by this office. We have to keep someone here twenty-four-seven, and no one gets in who doesn't have a reason for being here."

"Do you see everyone who wants to get in to the apartments?"

"Yes; they all have to check in with this office."

"Thanks a bunch, Alicia; you said that Megan lives in 707, didn't you?"

"That's right, Bob; is there anything else that I can do for you?"

"If I show you a picture of a man, is there any possible way that you could tell me if that man visits her?"

"I possibly can; do you have a picture of the man in question?"

"No, but I will have one a little later this afternoon."

"What is the man's name, Bob?"

"I had rather not say until I determine if he has been visiting the woman. What time do you get off work today?"

"I get off at six p.m.; are you planning to take me out to dinner?"

"I am a happily married man, Alicia; otherwise it would be my pleasure. I'll be back around five with his picture."

"I can hardly wait, Bob."

"Would you mind giving me your phone number here in case I need to call you, Alicia?"

"I will if you give me yours." They both exchanged their numbers. Ace gave her his cell phone number and got hers in return.

"Call me any time, Bob; even at home."

"I really appreciate your help, Alicia."

"It's been my pleasure, Bob."

Ace left and took the bus and got off at the Indigo Hotel where he was staying and picked up his car and drove to the First Tennessee bank Building. He parked in their parking garage hoping that he would not run into Rusty or Shirley; he didn't want them to see his car with Knox County tags on it when he had told them that he had flown in from Memphis. He needed the car to get back to Commodore Towers with Rusty's picture before Alicia left for the night.

Chapter 78

Ace got back to the office about one thirty and walked into Rusty's office with his cell phone nonchalantly in his hand and took a couple of pictures of him as he spoke. He pretended to hang up the phone as he placed it in his shirt pocket.

"What can I help you with, Bob?"

"It's really not all that important but I need for you to see if you can round up some supporting paperwork concerning your tax return."

"I will if I can; what do you need?"

"I found some of your deductions for miscellaneous expenses amounting to $5200 and I cannot find any receipts to back them up."

"I don't know if I can find all the supporting paperwork, Bob; it might be easier if you just disallowed the deductions."

"I could do that, Rusty, but I don't work that way; I want to be as fair to you as possible. You just take a few hours and do a reasonable search and if you don't find anything I will go ahead and let it stand."

"I couldn't ask for anything more, Bob; I'll get right on it. Do I need to call my tax attorney for help?"

"I'm afraid that would prolong the audit period by at least two weeks, Rusty, and besides, wouldn't you have to pay him about $200 an hour? I have found that it is much quicker if I work directly with the taxpayer in situations like this. I will, however, say this: from what I have seen so far of your paperwork, I really don't see a major problem for you. If both of us work closely together on this, I believe that I can give you a clean bill of health. I'm impressed with the neat order in which I found all your income tax records; most people that I have audited seem to just throw everything in a cardboard box and I have to spend countless hours sorting it out."

"Thanks for your kind words, Bob; how much longer do you think it will take to complete the audit?"

"Two more weeks, tops, Rusty; I'm as anxious to finish up as you are. My wife and I are scheduled to take a Mediterranean Cruise the first of May."

"I couldn't ask for anything more, Bob; I appreciate it."

"I'm going back to my office now to go over some of the other paperwork, Rusty; as soon as you find something let me know. I will be here until around five. I still need to go through all of your bank statements and look at your checks to verify your deductions."

"I'll get right on that, Bob; is that all?"

"There is one more thing, Rusty. I noticed a monthly check for a thousand dollars going to a firm called The Davidson Group and I can't find any backup documentation in any of the paperwork that you gave me. Do you remember for what purpose the checks serve, Rusty?"

"Yes it's for the rent on our Hospitality Suite at The Commodore Towers here in Nashville. I have found that my clients are more comfortable staying in a nice small apartment where they can better relax and watch television on a fifty two inch HD screen and cook their own meals and pop their popcorn in a microwave. It's also cheaper than putting them up in an expensive hotel. That unit only costs me fifty dollars a day versus two hundred a day in a downtown hotel."

"That's good thinking, Rusty," replied Ace.

Rusty felt that he was on a roll when he said: "I would have liked to have put you in the unit, Bob, but someone else beat you to it."

"And I bet I know who that someone is," thought, Ace. "I appreciate the consideration, Rusty, but the good old US of A is paying for my stay at the Indigo. I will be going back to Memphis for the weekend and I will be back in town Monday about nine in the morning."

"Would you like for me to drive you to the Airport, Bob?"

"I appreciate the offer but I have to return my rental car back there anyway." *"I am as big a liar as Rusty"*, thought, Ace.

"Take care, Bob"

"Thanks; I will, Rusty."

It was about two p.m. when Ace walked back into his little office and dug into more of the paperwork until five. He then took the elevator down to his car and drove back to the Commodore Towers; Alicia was still in her office when he walked in.

"I have the Picture, Alicia."

"Let me see it."

"Why didn't you say something, Bob; I know this man, this is a picture of Rusty Knell."

"Does he come in here often?" asked Ace.

"At least twice a week; he comes in to see his mother who lives here."

"Have you ever met her?"

"No, I never have."

"How do you know that he comes to see his mother?"

"Because that's what he told me."

"What floor does his mother live on?'

"I think that she lives on the eighth floor; Once or twice I have noticed that was the floor at which the elevator floor indicator lit up when he got off."

"Could you check your computer and see if there is a person named Knell on the eighth floor," asked Ace.

"I know for a fact that we don't have anyone named Knell living here; for all I know his mother could have remarried."

"I hadn't thought of that possibility," replied Ace. Would you do me a big favor, Alicia?"

"I will if you promise me to let me be your next auditee?"

"You got it, Alicia; call me the next time Rusty comes in; does he have a pattern of any sort with his visits?"

"I don't know exactly how often or what other days he comes in except that he comes like clockwork every Friday when I work the evening shift until eleven. He usually comes in around seven. I will call you if he comes in this coming Friday."

Ace thanked her and drove back to his hotel to rest up an hour or so before he picked up Rose Golden to take her to the Predator's Hockey game.

Chapter 79

Thursday evening

Ace left about six thirty to pick up Rose Golden to take her to the hockey game. He remembered where she lived off Old Hickory Road on Shady Grove Lane. He arrived at six fifty five and Rose saw him drive up and met him at the door. Ace could sense that she was very excited about going out.

"Come in, Ace; you have really brought some excitement into my life."

Rose was dressed and ready to go. Ace felt a little awkward about driving her in his old Mustang but she seemed to enjoy it.

Ace had paid good money to get the good seats that he had because he wanted to be close enough to get a good look at Benjamin. They went in and were seated about fifteen minutes before the opening square off. Rose seemed very excited.

The game got under way and Rose was yelling for all she was worth. After the Philadelphia Flyers scored the first goal, and near the end of the first period, one of the Fliers shot the puck all the way to the other end of the ice and if wasn't clear if it crossed the goal line at the other end of the arena; Rose screamed at the top of her voice; "that was icing, you blind Refs; didn't you think it was icing, Ace?"

"I really didn't see it all that well, Rose." (Ace really didn't know that much about hockey; all he knew about icing was that it belonged on top of a cake. Icing occurs when player shoots the puck across two red lines, the opposing team's goal being the last and the puck remains untouched. The reason for the rule is to prevent the team ahead from killing time and prolonging the game to enable them to hang on to their lead. Another reason for icing is because tired teams would repeatedly shoot the puck to the other end of the rink to rest a little; this became so boring to the fans and was one of the reasons that the icing rule was put in place.)

At halftime the score was all even at one apiece and Benjamin had yet to score.

"Would you like to meet Benjamin, Ace?"

"I would love to, Rose."

"We can wait until he comes out of the locker room after the game and talk to him; I've done it before."

The predators won the game five to three and Rose screamed her head off when Benjamin scored a goal in the second period. They walked down to the locker room area and Rose knew the guard who let them pass. After about fifteen minutes the players started coming out of the locker room and shortly Benjamin appeared. He was a spitting image of Doug Hart and had the same mannerisms and walk. He walked up and hugged Rose. She introduced him to Ace.

"I would like for you to meet a dear friend of mine, Benjamin; this is, Ace Sleuth, from Knoxville."

"Anybody who is a friend of Rose is a friend; I have known her since I was in my crib. She found a wonderful home for me and I will forever be in her debt."

"She has talked a lot about you Benjamin; did you know that she still has the Nashville Tennessean Newspaper with your picture when you did the hat trick back in January?"

"No I didn't, but I'm glad she has it. Your name sounds familiar to me, Ace, what line of work are you in?"

"He's a big investigator in Knoxville who assists Brad Adams in defending baseless lawsuits," spoke up Rose.

"I believe I read something in the paper about you a few years ago, Ace."

"He's real famous, Benjamin; he was on the Dave Michael's Television show two years ago."

"Well; I'm certainly glad to meet a big celebrity, Ace."

"How you do go on, Rose, but don't let me stop you," said Ace. "I know that you are probably busy, Benjamin, so we'll get out of your hair."

"If you would like to go out and eat sometime, Ace; I would be amenable to it. I bet you would have some good tales to tell. Here's my card; call me any time."

"Thanks Benjamin; I'll do just that," said Ace as he handed Benjamin one of his.

Ace took Rose home and drove back to the Indigo. He was asleep as soon as his head hit the pillow.

Chapter 80

Friday morning.

Ace walked the three blocks to Rusty's office and picked up a cup of coffee and a donut and stuck his head in the door of his office and said good morning. Rusty was hard at work trying to locate all the back up documents that Ace had requested from him; Ace had plans to request a lot more. He had to keep him busy for two more weeks. He looked over some more of the income tax paperwork and by quitting time he had given Rusty enough work to keep him busy all of next week.

Ace left the office and walked the three blocks back to the Indigo. He stopped at the gift shop in the lobby and purchased a black cap with gold letters that spelled; 'Commodores' which is Vanderbilt's nickname. He then went up to his room and opened up one of his suitcases. He couldn't decide whether to wear the coveralls with the Comcast logo on the back and 'The Cable Guy' on the front or the one that read 'Maintenance" on the front and back. In any event he would be wearing the black cap with the Commodore logo. It would not look out of place in the Commodore Towers. He then glued on his false mustache and donned his dark glasses and dialed Paula; he told her what he was up to and that it would be too late to drive home after he finished his work today.

"I won't be able to finish up here until eight p.m. and that's nine Knoxville time; I wouldn't get home until after midnight. I'll stay here tonight and will be home about noon tomorrow Knoxville time," he told her.

Ace arrived at the Commodore Towers around six forty five and Alicia was in her office. He walked in wearing the maintenance coveralls with the Commodore cap and carrying a tool box in his hand; she didn't recognize him at first with the mustache and dark glasses; his own mother could not have recognized him in that get-up.

"We didn't call Maintenance," she said.

"There a leaky commode in 804 and I'm your handy man."

"What in the world are you doing in that get-up, Bob?"

"I need to ask you a tremendous favor, Alicia."

"Just name it, Big Man."

"I need for you to buzz me into the elevators so that I can see where Rusty goes when he comes in."

"You must swear to me that no one will ever know about it, Bob."

"I will never tell a living soul."

"Well you had better get cracking because it is almost time for him to get here."

She let him into the elevators and noticed that he got off at the eighth floor.

Ace stood in front of the bank of elevators on the eighth floor with his cell phone in his hand as if he was waiting on one. Presently Rusty showed up and got off; he didn't pay much attention to Ace as he got a couple of good shots of him with his cell phone.

Rusty walked down to the end of the hallway and opened the door to the stairs. Ace was right behind him as he descended the stairs. He exited the stairwell at the Seventh floor and the door closed behind him. Ace opened it up and spotted Rusty unlocking the door to room 707 with his own key. Ace also got two good shots of him doing that. *Maybe his girl friend hadn't gotten home yet,"* thought Ace. He now had all the information he needed to stop the lawsuit in its tracks. Even if he was discovered to not be what he claimed to be, Rusty would not dare expose him at the expense of exposing himself ala Tiger Woods. Ace was not adverse to a little blackmail himself but he hoped that it would not come to that.

Ace walked the stairwell all the way down to the lobby and stuck his head into Alicia's office.

"Mission accomplished, Alicia."

"Did he walk down to room 707 as you suspected he would?"

"Yes, and he had his own key to the place."

"You're a conniving man, Bob, and I'm glad that I'm on your side. Just who are you?"

"If I told you, Alicia, I would have to kill you."

"Come back and see me any time, Bob, just don't bring your gun."

"I may just take you up on that, Alicia."

Chapter 81

Saturday Morning

Ace had requested a wake up call at seven a.m. and got ready to leave for Knoxville by seven thirty. He thought about grabbing a free muffin and a cup of coffee in the hotel but he decided that he would stop at the Waffle house at I-40 Exit-215 that he had passed on his way into Nashville. He had an appetite for hot waffles and sausage, and since he was on an expense account, why not.

He got off at the exit and drove to the Waffle house; it was now about eight but there was only one car parked in front of the restaurant. He got out of the car and was about to walk inside when he noticed a man with a gun pointed at the girl at the cash register. Ace retreated back to his car and took a valve stem remover from the center console of the Mustang and walked to the hidden side of what he assumed was the Robber's car and removed the valve cap from the right front tire and unscrewed the valve stem just enough so that he could hear the air slowly escaping from the tire. He then placed the valve stem remover along with the valve cap in his pocket and got into his car and drove a short distance and parked where he could see the Robber come out and get into his car. He then dialed 911.

"There has been an armed robbery of the Waffle House Restaurant just off I-40 at Exit-215. The license number of the Robber's car is DCX-432 Davidson County and he will be driving on a flat right front tire."

Ace, who always seems to be where the action is, watched as the robber got no more than three blocks before the Metro police stopped him. The remainder of the drive back to Knoxville was uneventful.

Chapter 82

Ace got back home to Knoxville around 12:30 p.m. Saturday and pulled into his garage. When he walked into the kitchen, Freddy came running up to him and threw his arms around him.

"Daddy, Daddy; where have you been so long. I missed you a lot."

Ace felt somewhat guilty about being away from home and family. He knew that a week seemed like a month to a little boy who wasn't quite four years old. He picked Freddy up and carried him into the den where Paula and Lisa were waiting.

"Welcome home, you big lug," said Paula; "I missed the heck out of you."

"I missed you too, Love Bird."

"How about you, Lisa; did you miss me too?"

"I missed you but I'm going to kill you; I worked my tail off on that temperature scale problem that you gave me."

"Did you get it worked?"

"Yes, but I'm still going to kill you for putting me through pure torture."

"You will be a better person for it, Lisa. Did you keep all your calculations?"

"Yes, and do you remember what you promised me if I solved the problem?"

"Yes I do, and I intend to keep that promise. I will not only take you and Sean out to a restaurant of your choice; I'll throw in Paula and Freddy."

"I'm not sure I like your choice of words," said Paula. "I'll go with you if you promise not to embarrass me and everyone else at the table like you did when we dined at The Copper Cellar a few weeks ago."

"I promise that I will be a good boy, Paula. You get to choose the restaurant, Lisa; where do you want to eat?"

"Sean and I agreed on the Crown Plaza Hotel on Summit Hill Drive."

"Would you mind making us reservations there, Lisa?"

"I'm way ahead of you, Big Daddy; I have already done that. How does seven p.m. sound?"

"That sounds fine to me," replied Ace; that will give me time to rest and watch the Atlanta Braves baseball home opener."

"Are you hungry, Ace?" asked Paula.

Ace was starving; he had completely forgotten to eat after the robbery at the Waffle house. "I am really hungry, Paula."

"How about some good country sausage and some waffles with real maple syrup?"

"Paula knows me too well," thought Ace. "I can't think of anything else that I would rather have, Paula."

After his delicious brunch, Ace went to sleep watching the Braves Game. Paula let him sleep until six when she woke him up and told him to get ready.

Sean arrived about six thirty and they all got into Paula's crossover and drove uptown to the Crown Plaza, parked in the parking garage, and took the elevator up to the beautiful Mahogany's restaurant on level two. Paula held her breath as they walked up to the receptionist.

"We are the Sleuth's and we have a party of five," said Ace.

"Welcome to Mahogany's, Mr. Sleuth; do you have reservations?"

Paula almost had a stroke when Ace replied: "Yes we do but we would like to eat here anyway."

Other than Ace's faux pas, they all enjoyed a delicious dinner. When they had all returned home and settled in, and Sean had gone home, Lisa said:

"Ace I was just pulling your leg about how hard it was solving that temperature problem; I solved it in just over an hour."

"You're getting too smart for me, Lisa; you didn't deserve that delicious dinner tonight. You still owe me some time so you're going to have to solve another problem for me."

"I knew that deal was too good to be true; what is the problem this time?"

"It's really very simple, Lisa; which weighs more, a pound of gold or a pound of feathers?"

"I know you too well to not know that is a trick problem, Ace; I will try to have an answer for you tomorrow."

Chapter 83

Sunday

After Church, Ace, Paula, Freddy and Lisa decided to dine at the Red Lobster Restaurant on Kingston Pike. After eating they returned home.

Ace decided he would leave around five p.m. to go back to Nashville and Sean was supposed to pick up Lisa and head back to Vanderbilt around the same time. He and Paula talked in the den while Freddy played with his Legos. Paula decided that she would take a nap if Ace watched Freddy. Ace agreed and turned on the TV and scrolled until he came to a tennis match. He settled back in his easy chair to watch when Lisa walked into the den.

"I've got my calculations to back up my work on the temperature problem and also for the gold-feather weight problem, Ace."

"Before we get into that, Lisa, I wish that you would explain to me exactly how the inventers came up with their scoring system for tennis; it makes absolutely no sense to me."

"Just what is your problem with it, Ace?"

"There are several problems; the first one is why they call the score love when a player has no points. The scoring starts out at 15 when a player scores the first point and when the second point is scored the score jumps to thirty. When the third point is scored I would expect the score to jump to 45, but that's not the case."

"I don't follow tennis, Ace but I agree with your logic; what is the score when the third point is made?"

"Believe it or not, the score jumps to 40; that misses the mark by five points by all the logic that I can muster up."

"I agree with you, Ace; that is a strange way to score. I wonder why they just don't go numerically with one, two, three, and four."

"I think that would be too simple, Lisa; I not sure, but I believe that the English devised the game just as they devised some of our weights and measures. There have been some brilliant British scientists, such as Sir Isaac Newton and lots of others, but I believe that they dropped the ball on weights and measures."

"In what way, Ace?"

"In many ways, Lisa; in the English system there are twelve inches in a foot and three feet in a yard. It would have made things a lot simpler if they had used the decimal system based on the number ten. There are also sixteen ounces to the pound and fourteen pounds to the stone."

"What in the world is a stone, Ace?"

"A stone is defined as fourteen pounds and is what the English once used to weigh people and things; I believe they still refer to a person's weight by the number of stones. They must have used a balance where they placed a person on one side and found out how many fourteen pound stones it took to balance the weight. It appears to me that they would have to use some pebbles along with the stones to arrive at a reasonable weight. My Father was in England in the 1950's and he was talking to a fellow serviceman about a blind date he had."

"How did your blind date turn out?" my Dad asked him.

"It was horrible; she must have weighed fifteen stones," he replied. If some of our serviceman were using the term stone it must have been in common usage at the time. It hasn't been too many years ago (prior to 1971) that the English didn't have their currency keyed into the decimal system. To total up a sum of money they had to have three columns, one each for, pounds, shillings, and pennies; sort of what we do here in America with our archaic system of feet, inches, and fractions. We need to change over to the metric system as they do in the rest of the world. And to further complicate things each pound

285

contains twenty shillings and each shilling contains twelve pennies; there's the number twelve again. I believe that the British were hung up on the number twelve."

"Why do you think that, Ace?"

"I think that there was so much inner marriage and in-breeding between Royalty back in history that some of the kings may have been born with twelve fingers and twelve toes," joked," Ace.

"You set me up for that, Ace"

"Let's get back to your problem solving abilities, Lisa."

"Alright; first I want to address the problem about which weighs the most, a pound of gold or a pound of feathers."

"What is your answer?"

"My answer is yes."

"That's not an answer."

"Yes it is; a pound of gold is heavier than a pound of feathers and a pound of feathers is heavier than a pound of gold."

"Just how did you arrive at that conclusion?"

"It's really very simple; an ounce of gold is measured in Troy Ounces which equals 31.103 grams and there are twelve ounces in a Troy pound. So a Troy pound weighs 373.326 grams.

Conversely, an ounce in the conventional weight system we use in the United States, an avoirdupois ounce is equivalent to 28.349 grams and there are sixteen ounces to the pound. So a pound of feathers would weigh 453.584 grams; this proves that a pound of feathers is heavier than a pound of gold."

"I agree with that logic, Lisa, but you also said that a pound of gold is heavier than a pound of feathers."

"Yes I did, Ace, and I also have proof of that. Although the Troy Ounce is still used for the weight of gold, the Troy Pound is no longer used. If the pound of gold today is defined as sixteen ounces then a pound of gold with each of those Troy ounces weighing 31.103 would weigh 496.208 grams which is greater than the weight of the pound of feathers which weighs 453.584 grams."

"You're too smart for me, Lisa; what did you come up with for two different temperature measuring systems?"

"There were two parts to that; you wanted me to find at what temperatures Centigrade and Fahrenheit were equal. We know that at the freezing point of water that the Centigrade temperature is zero and Fahrenheit temperature is 32. We also know that at the boiling point of water that Centigrade is 100 degrees and Fahrenheit temperature is 212 degrees. You can see that if we raise the temperature that Old Man Fahrenheit is going to run off and leave Mr. Centigrade so that means we are going to have to lower the temperature to somewhere below freezing; my job was to find that point. Take a look at my sketch."

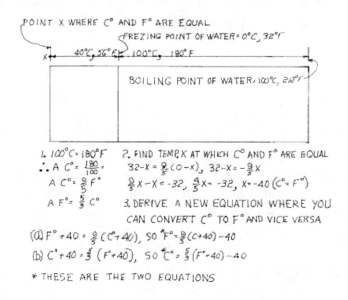

"I let 'X' be equal to the point below freezing at which both the Centigrade and Fahrenheit are equal and solved for 'X'. Starting at freezing where C = 0 and F = 32, it can be seen that 32 — X = 9/5 (0-X). I multiplied out the right side of the equation and got; 32 — X = -9/5X; further simplifying the equation and combining the X's, I got; 9/5X - X = -32; therefore 4/5X = -32, and X= -40. The temperature at which both C and F are equal is minus 40 degrees."

"You are exactly right, Lisa; did you find two simpler equations for converting from one system to the other?"

"Yes I did; look at my sketch again. I pictured both Mr. C and Mr. F on a football field forty yards back of the goal line on one end of the field. I picked a point 'P' at some point on the field between that goal line and the goal line on the far end of the field. Mr. C takes one yard steps and Mr. F takes 5/9 of a yard steps. It can be seen from the sketch that $F + 40 = 9/5(C + 40)$, therefore $F = 9/5(C + 40) - 40$. Further simplifying the equation yields:

$C + 40 = 5/9(F + 40)$ and $C = 5/9(F + 40) - 40$. So the two new equations to replace the ones commonly used in today's text books are:

1.$F^0 = 9/5(C^0 + 40) - 40$
2.$C^0 = 5/9(T^0 + 40) - 40$

The old equations are;
$T(F^0) = 9/5T(C^0) + 32$
$T(C^0) = 5/9[T(F^0) - 32]$

"That is excellent work, Lisa; those two equations are identical in format except one of them uses 9/5 and the other uses 5/9 and we know that the equation for finding Fahrenheit is the one where the 5/9 belongs. These two equations will be much easier to remember. They may revise all the physics books in the country because of your work."

"Now that we have a user-friendly equation for converting the two different temperature measurements, and it's easier for you to remember, maybe you can help me remember a math problem we have in school, Ace."

"Just what is the problem, Lisa?"

"I know that it may sound simple to you, Ace, but we are given problems where we have to do the math in a certain order and I am having trouble remembering the order."

"Tell me more."

"For this particular procedure we have to do the math by adding, multiplying, and subtracting, in that order. Is there some simple way that I can remember the order?"

"There are two ways; the first one is to simply remember to do the steps in alphabetical order, and the second way is to get yourself a memory system."

"What sort of memory system, Ace?"

"**A Memory System**, Lisa."

"You tried to sneak that one past me, didn't you, Ace?"

"You will never forget that system, Lisa."

Chapter 84

Ace left Knoxville on Sunday April 10, around four p.m. for the drive back to Nashville. The week was uneventful for him except for one thing; Rose had him over for dinner Tuesday evening where she served him up a delicious Jewish meal. The meal consisted of a homemade Caesar salad, an entrée of golden lemon chicken breast with a delicious peach sauce along with buglur & vermicilla pilaf. For desert there was a nectarine Tart with whipped cream.

"I couldn't eat like this every day, Rose, or I would blow up like a balloon; that was one of the most delicious meals that I have ever eaten."

"Thank you for the kind words, Ace; you can come back and dine with me any time you wish."

"I may be back sooner than you think, Rose."

Ace stayed for a couple of hours and talked to Rose and told her all about Paula, Freddy, and Lisa; he also informed her that Lisa was enrolled at Vanderbilt.

When Ace he got back to his hotel room he decided to call Doug Hart's identical twin, Benjamin and see if he was interested in dining with him one day this week. They agreed to meet Wednesday evening at the pricey Ristorante Volare Restaurant at the Opryland Hotel off Briley Parkway about a dozen miles from the Indio Hotel where Ace was staying. Ace wanted to get to know him a little better to determine if it would be a good idea to inform him that he had an identical twin brother living in Knoxville. *"I think that I would want to know if I had an identical twin,"* thought Ace.

The dinner went well and Ace felt like he knew Benjamin a lot better, but he still hadn't decided to tell him about his brother just yet.

Ace spent all week at Rusty Knell's office making sure that the Lawyer was so busy with the audit that he had no time for anything else. He was sure that Rusty had not filed the lawsuit up to this point and he was going to make sure that he would not have time this week. The statute of limitations would run out at the end of the day on Friday April 22. Ace found it a little amusing and coincidental that this coming Friday was the last day for filing income taxes; he kept Rusty's nose to the grindstone all week. *"I've got one more week to go and the ball game will be over"*, thought Ace as he recalled the song: 'The Party's Over' that Former Monday Night Football Announcer Don Meredith used to sing when it appeared that one team had the game locked up and put to bed. *"I hope that I will be able to sing that song next Friday,"* he thought.

Everything went well in Nashville all week and Ace was able to return to Knoxville Friday evening, arriving home around 9:00 p.m. Eastern time.

Chapter 85

Sunday, April 18

Ace left Knoxville around four p.m. and arrived in Nashville three hours later; it was six p.m. in Nashville when he arrived. He hoped that this would be his last week here. He arrived at Rusty's office Monday morning at nine a.m. sharp. He grabbed some donuts and coffee, and after speaking to Shirley and Rusty, he went to his desk and made up a list of things he needed from Rusty that would keep him busy all week, which they did.

Everything went as planned all week. About three in the afternoon and the statute of limitations had expired on the lawsuit, Ace walked into Rusty's office.

"I've got some good news and some good news, Rusty," said Ace.

"Don't you mean some good news and some bad news, Bob," replied, Rusty?"

"No; I've got two good news items. I am giving you a clean bill of health as far as the audit is concerned and I will be getting out of your hair after today."

"That is fantastic, news, Bob, except for you getting out of my hair; I have enjoyed working with you."

"Just like you would enjoy a root canal, Rusty; I have just about worn out my welcome here."

"I appreciate the way that you have handled this audit and I am going to call your superior and tell him what an excellent job you did."

"Are you trying to get me fired, Rusty? My superior is expecting me to return back to the office with a big bundle of cash to send off to Washington. We are graded on how much money we find in the audits. I found Uncle Sam a little over a hundred grand in my last audit and I could have found a few thousand here if I had wanted to nit pick, but that's not my style. I can get by this time because of my big haul on the last one. I don't want my superior to think that I was bribed by you to give you a clean bill of health; he is always suspicious when I can't find a single penny. We have actually had a couple of agents fired for accepting bribes. You would be surprised at some of the bribes that were offered to me in such subtle ways that I would not be able to prove that they were bribes in a court of law. I was offered a two week stay with my family at Sea Island, Georgia with free golf privileges at the best golf course there. Another time I was offered a first class plane trip for me and my family and put up in a four star hotel along with box seats to the Kentucky Derby. I turned them both down."

"What happened to the persons whom you were auditing, Bob?"

"They didn't fare too well, Rusty; I went over their tax forms with a fine tooth comb and they probably ended up paying more new taxes than the costs of the bribes they offered. A bribe equal to an agent's yearly salary can be quite tempting to a lowly paid IRS agent who could probably be making several times that much as a CPA with his own business."

"I had never thought about it in that light, Bob."

"It's all because of your cooperative attitude, Rusty. If you had called in your tax attorney at around $200 and hour it would have probably added two more weeks to the audit and have cost you around $20,000 for his fee alone, and on top of that, it would have made me feel that you had something to hide. I'm sure that I could have found five or ten thousand dollars if I had dug deep enough. If your tax attorney ever found out that you were audited and didn't call him, I believe that he would be very upset about not being able to participate at two hundred bucks an hour."

"He will never be the wiser, Bob."

"Thanks, Rusty; I'm going to get all my things together and get out of your hair. I have to go check out of the Indigo, drive my rental car back to Enterprise, and catch a Delta flight back to Memphis; working with you has been my pleasure. I hope that the next time I see you that it will be under more pleasant circumstances."

"I hope so too, Bob; you take care now."

"I will, Rusty; you take care also. Oh, by the way, I don't think that you need to worry about another audit for at least ten years."

"I should be retired by then, Bob."

"So long, Rusty, I am going to stop by Shirley's desk to tell her goodbye. When he reached her desk she walked around from behind her desk and gave him a big hug.

"You sure do make it hard on a guy to leave, Shirley."

"I've sort of gotten used to you being around, Bob; it was quite boring working here until you arrived."

"Maybe I can come back next year and audit you, Shirley."

"I'm afraid that I don't make enough money for the IRS to want to fool with me, Bob."

"You hang in there and take good care of yourself, Shirley. You never know; our paths may cross again some day."

"I sure hope so, Bob; goodbye."

"Goodbye, Shirley."

Ace had one more place to go before he headed back to Knoxville; he walked back to the Indigo Hotel and got in his car and drove the couple of miles to The Commodore Towers, parked his car, and walked into the office. Alicia was sitting at her desk.

"What a pleasant surprise, Bob; I didn't expect to ever see you again. What brings you here?"

"I felt that I owed you an explanation, Alicia; I am not the person that I seem to be."

"I am not surprised, Bob; I expected as much."

"In the first place my name is not Bob Childress; my real name, believe it or not, is Ace Sleuth."

"Are you some kind of detective, Ace?"

"You are exactly right; I have been working on a case where a baseless lawsuit was about to be filed and I had to keep Rusty Knell busy until the statute of limitations expired which it just did today."

"So what is your next step, Ace?"

"I will be heading home to Knoxville in an hour or so and I will be glad to get back home to my wife, Paula and my three and a half year-old son, Freddy."

"I envy both of them, Ace; it's been a pleasure to meet you."

"The pleasure has been all mine, Alicia; without your help it would not have been possible for me do my job. I just wouldn't feel right going home without stopping by and thanking you for your help."

"Well I'm certainly glad that you did; you have made my day, Ace. If you're ever back down this way drop in and see me."

"I certainly will, Alicia, and you do the same if you're ever in Knoxville."

"I don't think that Paula would take too kindly to that, Ace."

"You have a good point there, Alicia; I better get going if I want to get back to K-Town before dark."

"You're not going anywhere until you hug my neck, Ace."

Ace gave her a big hug and he noticed tears in her eyes as he walked out of the office; he felt a little like tearing up himself.

The trip back to Knoxville was very uneventful by his standards and he arrived back home in time to play with Freddy a few minutes before his bedtime.

"I missed you Daddy; please don't go away anymore."

"That goes for me too; said Paula."

"I'll try not to if I can help it. Did Lisa come home for the weekend?"

"Yes she did but Sean and her have gone out for the evening," replied Paula.

Ace was so exhausted that he plopped into his recliner and went to sleep. Paula came over and removed his shoes and said to herself: *"I love you, you Big Hunk; I miss you when you're not here."*

Chapter 86

Monday April, 25

Ace arrived in his office at nine a.m. and was welcomed back by Denise.

"We missed you around here, Ace; it's just not the same around here without you."

"I'm glad to be back, Denise; it seems that I have been away for more than three weeks."

Ace grabbed a cup of coffee and a donut and walked back to Brad's office. Brad was smiling from ear to ear.

"Sit down, Ace; I want to congratulate you on a job well done. Here is a little something for you," said Brad as he handed him a check.

"What do you mean, 'a little something', Brad, this is a check for $5,000?"

"You earned every penny of it, Ace; I would like to pay you more but we are going to need quite a bit of money in preparing for Doug's trial and then more money for the trial itself. I am going to pay Paula $50 an hour for her work on the jury evaluation and we need to make up for some work that I have had to turn down, but this is the most important case that I have ever worked on, and I intend to give it my best effort."

"I am with you a hundred percent, Brad."

"We got the jury pool list at the end of the day Friday and I haven't had a chance to get a good look at it; I do know that it contains fifty names. I had Denise make two extra copies, one for you, and one for

Paula. We will be selecting jurors in just six weeks so we had better get started right away."

"Good; I'll take Paula's copy home tonight and she can get started on it."

"I think that she can do most of her work from home, Ace, and come in about once a week for a few hours so we can find out where we stand."

"I had dinner one evening with Doug's identical twin, Benjamin while I was in Nashville last week."

"Did you mention anything to him about Doug?"

"No, but I believe that he would be receptive to the news. I think that if we decide to tell him that it would be better to wait until the end of Doug's trial."

"I agree with you on that, Ace; it would only be a distraction to both Benjamin and Doug, not to mention, Denise. I don't see how Benjamin could help us in any way with the trial."

"The only way he could help us is if he confessed to the crime," joked Ace.

"I almost forgot, Ace; I saw in the paper where Rupert Cooper's home was foreclosed on. I don't have any use for that rascal but I hate to see him lose his home."

"I have a feeling that Rupert just may change his crooked ways, Brad; I think that all of his bad luck may be a wakeup call for him."

"That day, will be the day when pigs fly, Ace."

"I have seen a horse fly, Brad."

"I've even seen a house fly, Ace, but I have never seen a leopard change its spots."

"We'll just have to wait and see, but I don't believe that Rupert will ever bother you again."

"I think that you may have had something to do with that, Ace."

"I'll never tell, Brad."

"If we have nothing else to discuss, Ace, I'll get back to work and you can do the same."

Ace went back to his office and studied the jury list for the rest of the day and looked up each of their names in the phone book. He knew that Paula would do a complete Google search on each of the fifty names. *"Not many people are aware that their names can be found on the internet along with their phone number, their address, and sometimes their occupation"*, thought Ace. *It seemed to him that there was no such thing as privacy in this country anymore. However he could see both good and bad in it; it was a good tool for enabling law enforcement authorities to apprehend criminals and also in the jury work, but he could see that some of the information could be misused by some dishonest people.*

As soon as Ace had left and went back to his office, Denise rang Brad and said that Roland Newhart from Commonwealth Auto Insurance was on line one; Brad picked up.

"What can I do for you, Roland?"

"I just wanted to congratulate you in the handling of our case in Nashville?"

"I appreciate that, Roland, but I sense that that is not the only reason that you called me."

"You are absolutely right, Brad, but what I want talk to you about would be better face to face. Do you have a vacant spot in your schedule tomorrow for us to get together?"

"Any time tomorrow afternoon would suit me, Roland."

"Good I'll hop a flight from Louisville to Knoxville in the morning."

"Would you like for someone to pick you up at McGhee-Tyson?"

"That's Okay, Brad; I'll just take the Limo. Where is your office located?"

"Just tell your Limo Driver to drop you off in front of the BB&T Bank Building on Gay Street. Take the elevator to the twenty fourth floor and my door is the first door to the left after you get off the elevator."

"Good I'll be there at 1:00 p.m."

"Just stop at Denise's desk and she'll bring you back to my office."

Chapter 87

Tuesday afternoon, Brad's office

It was one p.m. when Denise brought Roland Newhart back where Brad and Ace were waiting on him; Brad wanted Ace to sit in on the conversation.

"Did you have a good flight down here, Roland?" asked Brad.

"I certainly did, Brad, and I didn't even have to go through Atlanta." joked, Roland.

"Roland, I would like for you to meet my right hand man, Ace Sleuth; he is the person who is responsible for making your lawsuit go away."

"I'm certainly glad to meet you, Ace; just how did you manage to pull it off?"

"If I told you; Roland, I would just have to kill you," laughed Ace.

"I don't even know exactly how he did it, Roland but he mentioned to me before he left for Nashville that Rusty Knell didn't know it, but he was due for an IRS audit."

"I have something for you Brad," said Roland has he handed him a $100,000 check.

"This is quite a bit of money, Roland; didn't you know that you could probably have settled out if court for around $25,000."

"We could have settled this case for a mere $10,000 but we did not want to set an example that would let it be known to all the tort lawyers that we were an insurance company that was an easy mark. As we saw it, we had three choices. We could go to court and fight it, but that was like playing Russian roulette with some of the under educated people they put on juries these days. Sometimes it seems that most of them don't know the difference between a million and a billion dollars, and some of the awards they hand out boggle the mind. The tort lawyers like to present the insurance companies as fat cats with no regard for the so-called 'Little People', and for all we know there could have been a million dollar judgment against us.

We could have settled out of court, but as I said before, we don't want the reputation as a company who does not want to fight. We have sent a message to all the tort lawyers in this region that we are not going to be paying off on frivolous or phony tort lawsuits. We will willingly pay off all legitimate injury claims, but we will fight tooth and toenail against the unjust ones.

We decided to take the third option and that's why we hired you. We consider the $100,000 money well spent."

"How do you know that the other tort lawyers will get the word that you are an insurance that doesn't give in easily." asked Ace.

"We sent a short article to several newspapers in the Southeast that stated that the case in Nashville concerning the woman who was suing us for the miscarriage she claimed was caused by one of our customers, was allowed to lapse. The tort lawyers got the word alright. We are not a large insurance company but we are growing pretty rapidly and we want to be super competitive and keep our rates a little lower than the rest of the insurance companies. We have quite a bit of money in our reserves and are financially secure. We also believe that the general public will pick up on our determination to keep our rates low and still provide excellent coverage."

"Did you fly all the way down here to deliver that check, Roland?" asked Brad.

"No. I wanted to meet you and talk to you in person about placing you on a retainer so that you can handle cases of this sort for us in the future, but there is one condition that we insist upon if you decide to accept our offer."

"What is the condition, Roland?"

"The condition is that you allow us to let it be known that you will be handling our lawsuits in the future; we believe the mention of your name would do more to prevent these senseless lawsuits than anything else that we could come up with."

"What type of retainer are we talking about, Roland?" asked Brad.

"I have an exact twin of the check I just gave you already filled out in your name if you decide to accept our offer."

"Since you put it that way, Roland, I don't see how I can refuse your offer."

"You might want to take look at this contract that our accounting department drew up before you decide, Brad."

Brad took a look at the contract and found it satisfactory so he signed it and gave it back to Roland for his signature. He called Denise in to stamp it with her Notary Public Stamp and make a couple of copies and then he gave the original back to Roland.

"It has been a pleasure working with you, Brad. And personally I hope that we never have to use your services. We consider this contract to be 'our' insurance policy."

"It has also been our pleasure, Roland. I am assigning Ace to drive you back to McGhee-Tyson whenever you're ready. I am sure he would like to show you his souped-up, 500 horsepower, 76 Mustang."

"I would be honored, Ace."

Chapter 88

Friday Evening, April 29

It was five in the afternoon and Ace had just left work and was driving home when his cell phone rang.

"City morgue," he answered as he saw on the two inch screen that it was Alicia calling from Nashville.

"I must have the wrong number, Ace, unless you have gone into the embalming business."

"No, Ma'am; we don't do embalming here, we open them up, but we don't close them up. I also do audits and lube jobs on the side."

"Speaking of audits; guess who just left my office fuming and went up to the seventh floor to see his girlfriend."

"Isn't it a little early for Rusty Nail, Alicia; I thought he normally came in at seven?"

"He was very upset; I have never in my entire life seen a man that mad. I think he came early to get a little TLC."

"What was his problem?" asked Ace.

"He said that he was being audited by the IRS for the second time this month."

"What are the odds of that, Alicia?"

"Those are the exact same words I said to him, Ace; what are the odds?"

"As we travel down this road called life's highway, Alicia, there are many twists and turns; there are left turns, right turns, wrong turns, U-turns, upturns, and downturns; and I believe that Old Rusty may have taken a wrong turn along the way."

"I didn't know that you could wax philosophically, Ace."

"I didn't know that you could use wax in a sentence that didn't also contain car wash in it."

"You sure know how to hurt a poor defenseless girl, Ace, but I think Good Old Rusty's problems began and took a downturn the day you walked into his office with that phony IRS ID card."

"You also know how to hurt a guy, Alicia, but I'm glad that you called me, and just to show my appreciation, I am going to grant you ten years of immunity from an IRS audit."

"Rusty said that was the same guarantee that you gave him; your guarantee is not worth the paper it's written on."

"I didn't say that I was going to put it in writing, Alicia."

'Do you know what, Ace?"

"No; what?"

"You're full of it."

"That's the same thing Paula tells me; and speaking of Paula, I'm almost home and I had better get off the phone before I walk into the house. Paula doesn't like me talking to strange women."

"Just tell her that I'm not strange, Ace; I don't have a strange bone in my body."

"Here she is now, Alicia; I'll let you tell her."

"Bye, Ace; It's been great talking to you."

"That works two ways, Alicia; bye, bye."

Chapter 89

Monday, May 2

Ace and Brad were having their usual coffee and donuts when Denise brought in the morning paper.

"There's an article in the paper this morning stating that June the sixth is the day for Doug's trial to began," she said.

"That's when the jury selection phase kicks in, Denise; that may take a week just to select the jury," replied Brad. "How is Paula coming along with the jury Evaluation, Ace?"

"She's been working real hard on it; I've been trying to stay out of her hair as much as possible. She said that she will be able to give us some recommendations by the first of next week."

"That gives us plenty of time for us to prepare, Ace; I have a feeling that no matter how good a job that Paula does in her jury evaluation that the trial is going to end up in a hung jury and I don't want that to happen. I want nothing less than an acquittal for Doug."

"That's easier said that done, Brad"

"You're right about that, Ace, but I am going to stop at nothing to try to get him found not guilty. If there is a hung jury this case could go on for another year or two."

"I may have to do background checks on some of the prospective jurors, Brad, as Paula gets farther along in her evaluation."

"Do whatever it takes, Ace; this is this most important case that I will ever have to pursue."

(As soon as the article about the start of the trial came out in the Knoxville paper it was picked up by the Consolidated Press and appeared in newspapers across the country. People started taking sides and many 'Letters to the Editor' began appearing in the Knoxville paper. It appeared that this trial might gain as much attention as the 'Zoo Man' Killer Case a few years back. There seemed to be a new letter in the paper every day.)

Chapter 90

Ace left the office and when he arrived home around five thirty Monday evening, Paula was on the computer working on the jury list and Freddy was watching the Cartoon Channel. When he saw Ace he ran up and leaped into his arms.

"I'm glad that you are home, Daddy."

"I'm glad too, Freddy, but if you keep growing I won't be able to catch you when you jump into my arms like that."

"I'm already a big boy, Daddy; I'm almost four."

While Freddy continued watching TV, Ace talked with Paula about the jury list.

"What have you found out so far, Paula?"

"The best that I can determine the fifty person jury pool makeup looks like this:"

Women — 23

Men — 27

Black women — 4

Black men — 2

Veterans — 6 men

Ages range from 35 to 70 and there are five engineers of which two are retired. There is one retired college female professor. In addition, there are:

Eleven stay-at-home housewives

One male postal worker

Two small business owners

This is about as far I have gotten but by the end of the week I expect to have all fifty rated on a scale from one to fifty as to their suitability to offer a fair and favorable verdict for Doug."

"It appears that you are doing a bang-up job on the jury selection, Paula, but I don't believe that Brad can win an outright acquittal for Doug."

"I feel the same way, Ace, but on the other hand I don't believe that the AG can get a guilty verdict; I believe that we are going to have a hung jury and a mistrial will be declared by the judge and we will probably be standing around for a year waiting on a second trial."

"I concur, Paula; I wish we could come up with something so that Doug, Denise, and Kristen Smith, could get on with their lives. I know that Doug Hart is not guilty but the only way that he can be exonerated is to find the real culprit and I have no idea how to go about doing that. There are no leads whatsoever."

"Let's change the subject, Ace; where would you like to go on vacation his year?"

"That's a good question, Paula, that reminds me of the woman who was talking to a friend about vacations; the conversation went some like this:

"Where are you going on vacation this year", the first woman asked the other one?

"My husband and I haven't decided yet," she replied.

"Where did you go on vacation last year?" her friend asked.

"We went around the world last year but we would like to go some place else this year."

"I wouldn't mind going on the same Mediterranean cruise again, Paula because I was so busy looking for Roger Bridges that I missed the best part of the cruise, the French Rivera."

"Maybe we could take that cruise again, Ace, but my biggest concern right now is food; what do you want for supper tonight?"

"How about fixing some ghetti for Freddy and me, Paula?"

"You are a poet and don't know it, Ace, with your 'ghetti for Freddy' rhyme.

"I'm a poet and I know it, Paula."

"Whatever. The only thing I know is that you're full of it, Ace; you can watch the news while I prepare the ghetti."

"What did that first word, 'whatever' of your last remark mean, Paula?"

"Nothing, Ace; I was just thinking aloud."

"No thinking aloud, allowed, Paula."

"That sounds redundant to me, Ace."

"I almost forgot to tell you, Paula that I entered a contest at the office and came in second place and won us a two-week all expense paid vacation. We can take it after the first of the year."

"Where does it take us?"

"My second place won us two weeks in Venezuela, Paula."

"What did the first place winner receive, Ace"

"A one week vacation in Venezuela, Paula."

"Ace, I've said it many times and I'll say it again, you are just full of it. I never know when you're joking or when you're serious."

"There is one sure way to tell, Paula; I'm never serious."

Chapter 91

Monday, May 9

Ace arrived at the office around nine a.m. and Brad was already there. He grabbed a couple of donuts and a cup of coffee and walked into Brad's office.

"Good morning, Ace; what's on your mind?" asked Brad.

"It's a little less than a month before Doug's trial gets under way and there are a few things I feel we need to discuss."

"Fire away, Ace."

"Paula will be through with the jury evaluation in about a week and we both feel that no matter how good a job that she does that we will never be able to get Doug an acquittal, but by the same token, she doesn't believe that the AG can get a conviction."

"I have arrived at the same conclusion, Ace, but I don't know of anything else that we can do but go forward with the trial. I can't request a later trial date when it was me that asked for a speedy trial in the first place.

I have been thinking about the trial for some time and trying to decide which way to go. The only evidence against Doug is the testimony of Kristen Smith and her roommate, Julie Brown. I can try to shake their testimony, but if I'm too hard on them on the witness stand that could backfire and get the entire jury on their side.

Let me tell you what I would like for you do, Ace. Talk to Doug and see if you can come up with a couple of character witnesses who could testify in his behalf. He was an Eagle Scout; maybe you could get his scoutmaster to testify. I don't know if that would help very much but it wouldn't hurt."

"When I talk to Doug I will also like to see if we could get one of his Marine buddies to testify as to his good character." replied Ace.

"I think that is a good idea, Ace. Go ahead and get on that, we don't have too much time left. Tell Paula to get me the jury evaluation ASAP. Have her bring it to me personally. I would also like her to attend the Jury Selection portion of the trial to help me in the jury selection."

"I will pass that along to her, Brad. I have noticed that as the trial date nears, the letters to the editor of the Knoxville paper have picked up considerably."

"I have noticed that also, Ace, but a few of them have been fair and not tried to convict Doug in the paper. I have a feeling that things are going to get hot and heavy the closer we get to the trial. I expect all the national news media to come into Knoxville for the trial; it will be similar to how the news media reacted to the Duke University Lacrosse players who were falsely accused of raping the black girl a few years ago."

"It seemed to me that the news media just assumed that the players were guilty, Brad."

"It seemed that way to me also, Ace; I don't understand how the news media decides why some cases are more news worthy than others. I expect to see, ABC, CBS, CNN, NBC, Fox News, and the Associated and Consolidated Presses to show up near the trial date,"

"You may be right, Brad. If it's OK with you I am going to talk with Denise to see when would be a good time to talk to Doug."

"Go ahead, Ace, but keep me in the loop."

"I will, Brad."

As soon as Ace got back to his desk, Denise informed him that he had a phone call on line two; he picked up.

"This is Ace; how may I be of help?"

"You don't sound like the Ace I know," the voice replied.

"What's up Rose?"

"I got a phone call from Benjamin a little while ago, Ace."

"It must have been important, Rose, for you to call me about it."

"It was, Ace; he saw Doug Hart's picture in the Nashville newspaper regarding the upcoming trial and saw the resemblance to himself."

"How did he react, Rose?"

"Benjamin is no fool. Ace; he knew that I was the one who arranged for him to be adopted and he knew right away that he and Doug were identical twins."

"Was he upset about it, Rose?'

"No; it was just the contrary, he said he has always felt that a part of him was missing. I explained the whole scenario to him and he believes in Doug's innocence and wants to meet him. I also explained to him your involvement and why you were in Nashville."

"I think that it would be a good idea for them to meet, Rose, but I think that it should not take place until after the trial is over."

"You may be right, Ace, but Benjamin is hard-headed and he may decide to meet him anyway."

"There is nothing that we can do to stop him if that is what he decides to do. I am not going to say anything to Doug or Denise about this matter because neither knows that Doug has an identical twin. This would distract him from his studies and the upcoming trial, but I will pass the information along to Brad, my boss, who is Doug's Attorney."

"I concur, Ace; I'll keep you informed of anything else I find."

"Thanks for calling me, Rose; you have made my day just by hearing your voice. I believe that everything will work out for the better."

"I certainly hope that you are right, Ace; keep me in the loop from your end and I'll keep you in it from this end."

"Take care, Rose."

"You too, Ace."

Chapter 92

Monday afternoon

Ace had just returned from lunch and settled back in his chair when Denise informed him that he had a call on line one.

Ace was much more careful about the manner in which he answered the phone at the office than he did at home; no 'city morgue' answers here.

"Ace Sleuth here; how may I help you?"

"You don't have to be so formal to me," a familiar voice replied.

"You are the second surprising phone call that I have received today Lamont." (Lamont Brown is the Head of Security for the MGM Grand Hotel in Las Vegas. Ace met him back in 2007 when he was working on a bogus lawsuit that had been filed against Brad. The two of them had so much in common that they became good friends. Lamont flew into Knoxville for Ace and Paula's wedding and put them up for a week in the MGM Hotel for their honeymoon.)

"What's going on out there in Vegas, Lamont?"

"Everything is great out here except for a lack of tourists; I called you to find out what is going on down in Knoxville."

"Do you want to know about anything in particular or just in general?"

"I saw in the Las Vegas paper that Brad was defending a man named Doug Hart for rape and I was wondering if Doug could be Denise's brother." (Lamont had met Denise at Ace and Paula's wedding)

"Believe it or not, Lamont; Doug is Denise's husband. They both have the same last name."

"How long have they been married, Ace?'

"For just a few short months, Lamont." (Ace then went into all the details about Doug being in military in Iraq and Afghanistan and getting discharged and married. He also explained how Doug was identified and arrested) "Brad and I are convinced that he is completely innocent. The only evidence against him is the eyewitness recognition by the girl who was raped and her roommate."

"Is there no forensic evidence?"

"Not a bit, but both girls are convinced that Doug is the person that they both clearly saw."

"How do you and Brad think the trial will go, Ace?"

"We both think that the trial will end up in a hung jury and there will be a second trial down the road. Brad does not want that; he wants a total acquittal for Doug. I got the idea that if Doug didn't rape the girl that it had to be someone who looked a lot like him. Knowing that Doug was adopted, I got the notion that maybe he had an identical twin somewhere so I followed up on that."

"How did that work out?"

"Believe it or not, Lamont, I found that he did have an identical twin living in Nashville, but he had an iron clad alibi."

"It sounds to me like you and Brad need to come up with a plan, B."

"We don't even have a good Plan A, Lamont; we don't know what to do. Maybe we could bring in a bus load of California jurors to Knoxville," kidded, Ace.

"If I were you, Ace, I would think a little bit more about the twin; you don't think that there could have been triplets, do you?"

"There's no chance of that, Lamont, in the first place I doubt that identical triplets are possible, and in the second place, I talked to the former welfare agent that placed the twins. (Ace discovered later that identical triplets are possible but extremely rare.) In fact, she was the first surprising phone call I received today."

"I wish that there was some way I could help out, Ace, short of bumping off the two eyewitnesses."

"The two girls are first class, Lamont; they are sincere but sincerely wrong in their identification of Doug. The rape victim has been put through pure torture and so have Doug and Denise. There are no winners here on either side; just losers. Even if by some miracle, Doug was acquitted, he would still be guilty in the eyes of many people around Knoxville."

"I wish that there was some way to help, Ace; let me know if you think of anything."

"I certainly will, Lamont; thanks for calling."

"Let me know how everything turns out, Ace."

"Will do, Lamont."

Chapter 93

As soon as Ace hung up the phone, Denise informed him that he had a couple of visitors

"Who are they?" he asked.

"It is Alex Parker and a beautiful young lady."

"Bring them on back, Denise."

Ace looked to see Alex and his nine year old daughter, Trisha standing before his desk.

"Have a seat, Alex and you too, Trisha. I believe that you are getting too old to sit on my lap as you did the last time you were here when you were only five years old."

"I remember that visit very well Mr. Ace" replied, Trisha; that was when Daddy brought me to work but it wasn't really the official 'bring your daughter to work day.'" (Trisha Parker is the nine year old girl that Ace had rescued from a kidnapper over three years ago.)

"I would like to thank you, Ace, for the behind the scenes scheming by you to get Brittany and me together; I have never been happier than the day we met." said Alex.

"I have been just as happy as you have because you married Brittany, Daddy, and I want to confess that I was in on the scheme with Ace."

"I suspected as much, Trisha; I am going to leave the two of you alone, Ace, Trisha wanted to come by and see you," said Alex as he walked away.

"It seems like a long time since we have spoken, Mr. Ace. I just wanted to tell you how much I appreciate you for getting my father and Brittany together; she seems like my real mother." (Trisha's natural mother, Amanda was killed by a drunken driver back in 2007 and Ace had arranged for Trisha's Dad, Alex and Brittany to meet and they eventually got married. He and Paula had met Brittany on a cruise where her husband had tried to fake his own death so that she could collect on a ten million dollar double indemnity insurance policy. There was just one problem, however; Brittany was not in on the scam and divorced her husband, Roger Bridges, as soon as she found out about it.)

"I'm real proud of you, Trisha; I read in the paper that you won the Sequoyah spelling bee for the third grade. Why aren't you in school today?"

"We are on Spring break this week, Mr. Ace. I don't like to toot my own horn, but I won the spelling bee for the whole school."

"I didn't know that, Trisha; that proves that you are smarter than a fifth grader."

"Would you like to hear a joke, Mr. Ace?"

"Fire away, Trisha."

"What did the snail say when he climbed on the back of a turtle?"

"I don't know, Trisha; what did the snail say?"

"He said: "Wheeeeeee.""

"That's really funny, Trisha. Now it's my turn to tell you a joke."

"I like jokes, Mr. Ace."

"OK, here goes: A duck walked into a bar and asked the bartender him if he had any nuts. "No, we don't have any nuts," he replied. So the duck comes in the next night and again asks for nuts. The bartender again told the duck that he didn't have any nuts. The duck returned again the third night an asked for nuts; the bartender replied: "I have told you two times before that we don't have any nuts, and if you come in here again asking for nuts, I am going to take my hammer and nail your bill to the bar." The duck returned the fourth night and asked the bartender: "Do you have any nails." When the bartender replied no, the duck then asked him: "Do you have any nuts?"

"That's a cute joke, Mr. Ace; I like it."

"How are you doing in math at school, Trisha?"

"I always make a hundred on all my tests."

"You told me that you knew your multiplication tables up through twelve's. That is far enough but it would be helpful if you memorized the squares of all the numbers through twenty five."

"I already know that 15 times 15 equals 225 and that 25 times 25 equals 625 but I don't know the other numbers between 13 and 25."

"If you promise to memorize the squares of those numbers I will give you a simple way to multiply certain numbers in your head."

"I promise, Mr. Ace."

"Take any two digit numbers, such as 27 time 23, which you want to multiply together where the last two digits of the two numbers add up to ten and the first two digits are equal; you simply multiply the two numbers that add up to ten, and in this case, you get 21. Now multiply one of the two's on the left by one number higher and get two times three which is equal to six. Place this six in front of the twenty one and you have the answer which is 621."

"That looks pretty easy, Mr. Ace; why don't you let me try one on my own?"

"Try to multiply 86 times 84?"

"OK; 4 times six equals 24 so the last two numbers will be 24 and 8 times 9 (one more than eight) equals 72. My answer is 7224. How did I do?"

"You did great, Trisha and you did it all in your head. Take my calculator to make sure that you got the correct answer."

Trisha checked the answer on the calculator and came up with 7224. "The answer is correct, Mr. Ace."

"Now I am going toss you a little exception to the rules I just gave you. Multiply in your head, 71 times 79."

"OK; 9 times 1 is 9, so 9 will be the last number in my answer. Now I multiply 7 times 8 and get 56 and my answer 569, but that's not big enough is it?"

"No it isn't, Trisha, so you have to do a little trick in this problem; I don't know exactly why, but you have to place a zero in front of the nine so that it reads 09. Now you have 09 as the last two digits of your answer. After you place the 0 in front of the 9 proceed the same way you did with the other problem and multiply one of the sevens by one number higher which is 8 and you get 7 times 8 equals 56. Your answer is 5609."

"Trisha checked the answer on the calculator and found that it was right. "That is fantastic, Mr. Ace; what makes you so smart?"

"I take smart pills, Trisha; would you like some?"

"I don't need them Mr. Ace."

"Touché, Trisha; the one thing I like about you the most, is your modesty and humility."

"I got that from you Mr. Ace."

"You have a birthday coming up in a few weeks, Trisha; do you plan to have a big party like you do every year?"

"Since my birthday falls on July 4th, Daddy has decided to add fireworks to this year's party. It will be at the same place, Sequoyah Park near Mr. Brad Adams house."

"Speaking of the Fourth of July, Trisha, do they have the fourth of July in England?"

"Yes they do, Mr. Ace, and they also have the fifth and the sixth."

"You were right, Trisha, you don't need any smart pills. I am going to do some experimenting to see if I can come up with a method to multiply two, two-digit numbers in your head when the first numbers of the double digit numbers are not equal."

"Give me an example of what type of numbers you are talking about, Mr. Ace."

"Two examples would be 48 times 52 and 63 times 97. In the first example the first two digits vary by one number and in the second example they vary by three. In both cases the last digits add up to ten. I want to be able to multiply these numbers when the first two digits vary by as much as 8. It looks like I have my work cut out for me."

"Good luck, Mr. Ace. I don't see how you are going to do this; has it ever been done before?"

"Not to my knowledge, Trisha; wish me luck."

"I will because you're going to need it."

Ace and Trisha enjoyed each other's company for about an hour before he took her back to her father, Alex, on the other side of the floor.

Chapter 94

Tuesday Evening, May, 10

When Ace arrived home from work Paula and Lisa, who was on spring break from Vanderbilt, were in the den watching the ten thousandth and one rerun of the Andy Griffith Show.

"Don't you two have anything better to do than watch a show that you have seen at least twenty times before?" he asked.

"You are the one who got us started on this in the first place," replied Lisa.

"I've invited Brittany and Trisha to dine with us next Monday evening, Ace," said Paula.

"That's great, Paula; she came by to see me at work yesterday and we talked for about an hour. Is Alex coming?"

"No, Brittany told me that he was going to be out of town for a couple of days next week."

"What did you and Trisha talk about for over an hour, Ace? Knowing you, I bet you gave her some math problems to work." said Lisa.

"You are right, Lisa; since you will no longer accept my problems, I have to work with what I have."

"What kind of problems were you giving her?"

"It would probably be over your head, Lisa."

"Get serious, Ace; you haven't given me any problems since the temperature and weight problems several weeks ago. I'm ready to work one right now."

"If you two are going to talk math, I am going into the kitchen and rustle up some grub; you two cowpokes can go at it," Said Paula.

"What kind of problem are you going to give me, Big Daddy?'

"I am going to give you a problem that I want you to work entirely in your head and there is a five minute deadline to work it."

"You sure know how to challenge a girl, Ace, but fire away."

"I want you to calculate how long it takes for a ray of sunlight to reach the earth's surface."

"Are there any givens?"

"There are two factors that you will need to know solve the problem, Lisa."

"Yes; and those two factors are the speed of light and the distance between the Earth and the Sun. I know that the speed of light is 186,000 miles per second but I don't know the distance between the two bodies."

"The distance is 93,000,000 miles and the clock starts ticking right now, Lisa."

"It seems that all I have to do is divide the distance by the speed of light and that will give me the number of seconds that it takes the light from the sun to reach the earth."

"That is correct."

"93,000,000 miles is equal to 93×10^6 miles and 186,000 miles per second is equal to 18.6×10^4 miles per second, so all I have to do is divide 93 by 18.6 and it looks to me to be about five. So when I subtract the 10^4 in the denominator from the 10^6 in the numerator and I get 5×10^2, which is equal to 500 seconds or about eight minutes. How did I do, Ace?"

"You solved that problem in less than a minute, Lisa, and believe it or not 93 divided by 18.6 is exactly equal to 5. So the answer is 500 seconds which is equivalent to eight and one third minutes or eight minutes and twenty seconds. I will give you an A+ plus on that. You are almost as smart as I am and you don't even take smart pills. While we are on the subject of the sun and the earth did you know that the sun has a diameter just about one hundred times greater than that of the earth, and the earth has a diameter four times as great as the moon?'

"No, I didn't, but I'll remember that tidbit of information if I'm ever on 'Are you smarter than a Fifth Grader' TV show and they ask the question."

"It's funny that you mentioned that game show, Lisa; I saw the show a while back and there was a true or false question concerning a solar eclipse."

"What was the question?"

"I don't recall the exact wording, but it went something like this: 'Is it true that a solar eclipse occurs when the sun passes between the earth and the moon?'"

"Did the contestant get it right?"

"Yes he did and so did I; it would be awfully hard for the sun with a diameter of over 800,000 miles to pass between the earth and the moon when there is only 240,000 miles between them. The Emcee, Jeff Foxworthy remarked that he wouldn't want to be around when it happened. The fact is that he wouldn't be around if it happened."

"You're full of it, Ace."

"I know, Lisa."

Chapter 95

Tuesday evening. May 17

Brittany and Trisha arrived about seven and landed in the den.

"It's so good to see both of you again," said Brittany; "has Lisa already returned to Vanderbilt after spring break?"

"She and Sean went back last Friday," replied Paula.

"Are you still working, Brittany?" asked Ace.

"Yes I am; the hospital needs me, and besides, I would not have much to do sitting at home all alone every day while Alex is at work and Trisha is at school. By the way, where is Little Ace?"

"He's in his bedroom watching the Disney channel, but I must warn you, he doesn't want to be called Little Ace anymore; he is now called Freddy. Paula then informed Freddy that he had company: "Trisha is here to see you, Freddy"

Freddy came running into the den and gave Trisha a big hug followed up by a hug for Brittany. "I love you, Trisha" he said.

"And I love you too, Freddy," replied Trisha as she hugged him back.

"I had a test in school yesterday on multiplication Mr. Ace."

"How did you do, Trisha?"

"I made a hundred but when I got my paper back there was a note from the teacher to see her after class."

"What did she want to see you about?"

"There were two problems on the test like the ones you showed me how to work in my head, and I just wrote the answers down below the numbers to be multiplied without showing my work. She told me that she knew that I had not copied off someone else's paper or used a calculator but she didn't know how I knew the answer."

"What did you tell her?"

"I explained to her how to work the problem just as you showed me, and she was really impressed at how easy it was."

"Good for you, Trisha; I have figured out how to work out these types of problems when the two numbers to be multiplied do not have identical first digits, such as 47 times 43. I believe that I can also work it when the first digits vary by as much as eight."

"Are you saying that you can work a problem such as 47 times 63 or 96 times 14?" asked Trisha.

"I believe that I can but the last two digits of the numbers still have to add up to ten."

"Do you have time to show me now?"

"If Paula and Brittany will excuse us we can go to the kitchen table and go math crazy."

"Not before we eat," said, Paula. "Does everyone like chicken stir-fry with brown rice and a Caesar salad?"

"I like that a lot," replied Trisha and Freddy replied likewise.

"That goes for me also," chimed in Brittany.

"Count me in," said Ace. "We can work our math problems after we eat, Trisha."

After they had eaten, Ace got his calculator and he and Trisha sat down at the kitchen table while Paula and Brittany sank back into the den to catch up on the latest gossip.

"Let's try to multiply two, two-digit numbers together when one of the left hand digits is one number higher than the other. You pick the numbers, Trisha."

"Let's try 48 x 52."

"Ok, Trisha, now when I multiply 2x8 I get 16; I then multiply the last digit of the smallest number by the difference between the first two digits, (8 x 1) and place the result, which is 8, under the 1 of the 16 and add them together and get 96. 96 will be the last two digits of our answer. Now multiply the first digit of the smallest number by the first digit of the larger number plus 1. In other words, multiply 4x (5 +

1) = 24. Now place the 24 in front of the 96 and get 2496. Check that on my calculator and see if that's right."

"That's right, Mr. Ace; can I try one by myself?"

"Sure, go ahead; you're on your own."

"My two numbers are 83 and 67; 7x 3 = 21 and when I multiply the last digit of the smallest number by the difference between the first two digits of the numbers, 7 x 2, I get 14 which I place 4 of the 14 under 2 of the 21 and add them together and I get 161. Now I multiply the first digit of the smallest number, 6, times one number higher than the largest number, 9, and get 54. I place the 4 of the 54 below 1 of 161 and add to get 5561." Is that right?"

"You're right unless my calculator is wrong, Trisha."

"This is a lot of fun, Mr. Ace, and you can do it all in your head."

"It may get a little hairy to do some of these in your head but this method has the advantage of not having to carry numbers over to the next column. Let's see if we can work one where the first two digits vary by eight digits. You pick the numbers, Trisha."

"I choose 92 x 18; the first two numbers vary by (9- 1) = 8

"Let's see if this works, Trisha. By the way, it might be a good idea if we wrote all of this down. I've got some paper and a pen so go ahead; you write it down and I will work the problem.

This method works for all two digit numbers whose last two digits add up to 10."

"Here is the gist of this method, Trisha;

Multiply the last two digits together and place them under the two numbers in your head. Next subtract the smaller first digit from the larger first digit and multiple it by the last digit of the smaller number. Place the result under the other numbers making sure that the last number is directly under the number above it. Now multiply the first digit of the smaller number by the larger first digit plus 1. Place this under the other two numbers and align them similar to the way you did in the ones we just did. Now try the two numbers that you chose where the first two numbers vary by 8. I will write every thing down as you work it."

"OK; I am going to multiply 92 x 18."

$$\begin{array}{r} 8 \\ \underline{\times\,2} \\ 16 \end{array}$$

"Now I am going to multiply the difference between the first two digits. 9- 1= 8, and multiply the 8 times the last digit of the smallest number, which is also 8, and I get 64. So now I have:

$$\begin{array}{r} 16 \\ \underline{+64} \\ 656 \end{array}$$

Now when I multiply the first digit of the smallest number times one larger than the first digit of the larger number plus 1, I get 1 x 10 = 10. Now when I place the 10 under the 656, I get:

$$\begin{array}{r} 656 \\ \underline{+10} \\ 1656 \end{array}$$

"Is that is the correct answer, Mr. Ace?

"That is the correct number, Trisha. Do you remember that day in my office and you worked the problem, 71 x 79 and I told you to add a zero in front of the nine but I didn't know why? I finally figured out why and it's in the ground rules I just laid out for you. Let's go through the problem and I'll show you what I mean. You go ahead and work the problem until we come to the zero part of it."

"OK; you write it down as I go."

$$\begin{array}{r} 1 \\ \underline{\times\,9} \\ 9 \end{array}$$

"Now is the step where you told me to place a zero in front of the nine."

"That right, Trisha; now I want you to multiply the difference between the first two digits of the two numbers by the last digit of the smallest number."

"There is no difference between the two numbers because they are both sevens."

"Yes there is a difference; what is the difference, Trisha?"

"It's nothing; there is zero difference."

"You are right; the difference is zero. Now multiply the last digit of the smallest number by zero and what do you get?"

"When I multiply the last digit of 71 times zero I get 1 x 0 = 0."

"Isn't that the number I told you to place in front of the nine last week?"

"Now I see, Mr. Ace; write down the rest of the problem for me. I already have the nine and we need to place the zero in front of it and a place 7 x 8 = 56 in front of the 09."

5609

"By Jove; I believe you've got it, Trisha. I believe that you and I are the first two people to ever use the method we just used; I have never seen this done before; I'm going to call it 'Sleuth Math'."

"Why don't we have to multiply by zero when we multiply two numbers whose last two digits aren't 1 and 9, Mr. Ace?"

"According to my rules you do, but when you multiply two numbers whose first digits are the same by zero you end up placing a zero which does not affect the answer."

"Could you show me an example?"

"Let's multiply 72 x 78 and see what happens. I am going to multiply 2 x 8 = 16. Now I am going to multiply the difference between the first two digits times the last digit of the smallest number (0 x 2) = 0 and place it under the 1 of 16. Now I am going to multiply one of the 7's by one number higher, 8, and get 56. I now add this number in front of the 16 and get 5616. The zero adds nothing and can be ignored unless the last two digits of the numbers to be multiplied are nine and one. See my equation."

$$
\begin{array}{r}
8 \\
\underline{\times 2} \\
16 \\
\underline{560} \\
5616
\end{array}
$$

"How do you come up with these things, Mr. Ace?"

"I have to confess, Trisha. I have been taking two smart pills every day for the past week."

"Tell me the real truth."

"I could, Trisha, but I would have to kill you and I just couldn't do that to you after having rescued you three years ago."

"I love you more than any other man besides my daddy, Mr. Ace; you make me use my mind."

"I love you too Trisha, just as much as I love Lisa. I am so glad that you have a new mother."

"It's all because of you and Paula, Mr. Ace; Brittany is going to adopt me in a few weeks. She will be my real mother then."

"I am really happy for you, Trisha; you will have two important days every year, your birthday and your adoption day. We better get back in the den and see what Paula and Brittany are up to."

Chapter 96

Friday, May 20

Today was Friday and Brad was in the office contemplating the upcoming trial in just about two weeks when he had a thought concerning the trial, so he dialed his old friend, Mel Crosby, the Knox County Attorney General. Mel was shortly on the phone,

"What can I do for you, Brad," asked Mel.

"As a favor to me I was wondering if you would just drop the rape case against my client, Doug Hart," joked, Brad.

"If you will guarantee my reelection coming up next August, I will, Brad."

"Don't forget what happened to the Prosecutor, Mike Nifong, in the Duke Lacrosse players rape case who was disbarred; I would hate for the same thing to happen to you as happened to him."

"But the Duke Lacrosse players were not guilty and he evidently withheld evidence that would have cleared them."

"You are right, Mel, but my client is also innocent."

"We'll let a jury of his peers decide that matter, Brad; why did you really call me?"

"I was wondering if you are going to have a forensic expert available to testify at the trial."

"We don't have any forensic evidence to present, Brad, all we have is the testimony of the two eye witnesses."

"I know that, Mel, but I want you to have one ready for me to call to the stand."

"Why do you need to question him when we have nothing that would help your case?"

"I want you to have someone I can question about the ski mask that the rapist was wearing."

"I will make sure that we have him ready for you, Brad."

"Do you plan on calling anyone to the stand such as character witnesses on Doug's bchalf?"

"I could do that, but I don't think it would do much good, Mel. You know, of course, that you are not going to get a conviction nor am I going to get an acquittal; we are going to have a hung jury. My question to you is: if the trial does end up in a hung jury, are you going to demand a retrial?"

"I don't really know at this point exactly what I would do; I would probably go along with whatever my Prosecuting Attorney, Jim Satterfield, suggests."

"Do you plan to attend the trial, Mel?"

"I may sit in on parts of it; it all depends on my schedule."

"Thanks for you help, Mel; I don't want our friendship to be affected whatever the outcome of the trial is."

"I agree completely, Brad and I think it would be a good idea if you and I don't have anymore private discussions until the trial is over. You can talk to Satterfield about discovery and other aspects of the trial."

"I agree with you Mel' I wouldn't want to place you in a compromising position' I'll play by the rules."

"That's all I could ask for, Brad; we'll talk after the trial. Maybe we could go to lunch one day."

"I would like that, Mel; I'll call you after the trial."

Chapter 97

Monday May, 23

Paula had dropped off Freddy at day care and had come to the office to discuss the upcoming jury selection phase of Doug Hart's rape trial with Brad which was scheduled for Monday June, 6.

"The jury selection is only two weeks away, Paula, and we need to get prepared this week."

"I have gone just about as far as I can with the fifty names on the list, Brad; here is a copy of my latest rendering with the most favorable jurors listed in descending order. The first name on the list would be my first pick and the last name on the list would be my last pick."

"Who might the last name on the list be, Paula?"

"He is a seventy- year old white male who has served on four previous juries in criminal court in Knox County during the past ten years."

"Is serving on all those juries reason enough to exclude him form ours?"

"I believe that the odds of him being called to jury duty for four times in ten years are not accidental, Brad"

"Then how do you account for it?"

"I believe that he has volunteered for jury duty and has informed the court that he is available and someone in charge of the jury list has placed him on the lists. I believe that for some reason he likes to get on the juries of high profile cases such as ours."

"What is his name and occupation, Paula?"

"His name is Homer Paul and he is retired from the telephone company."

"I may question him if I have to go that deep into the jury pool, Paula; I may question him anyway just to see where he stands. I want you to be at my side during the jury selection. You don't have to say a word if you don't want to, just nod you head one way or the other if you agree or disagree with my selection."

"That shouldn't be a problem, Brad, but I don't think that we will be able to get an acquittal even if we end up with the top twelve people on the list."

"I concur, Paula; there is no way in the world that we are going to get a jury with all twelve voting him innocent. On the other hand, I don't believe it would be too hard to select a jury of twelve where there would not be at least one juror who would hold out for acquittal. We have got to be sure that we have at least one juror like that and hopefully several more."

"I believe that we can get a jury like that, Brad."

Brad and Paula spent the rest of the day, with a short lunch sandwiched in between, going over every prospective juror on the list. Paula had put together a thumbnail list of each juror listing everything about each that she could find. The list contained the name, age, race, gender, martial status, and, occupation along with anything else Paula could come up with.

"This list looks very comprehensive, Paula; I will go over it in a little more detail during the next few days and I will call you if I need you help. The jury selection phase will start at nine a.m. in Criminal Courtroom 209 in the City-County Building on Monday June 6th. Why don't you come by here around eight thirty and we can walk the block or two to the CCB."

"I'll see you then, Brad."

Chapter 98

Monday June, 6-Jury Selection

Paula and Ace had met Brad at the office at eight thirty Monday morning as planned and they all walked over to the CCB and through the security line and waited outside Courtroom 209 until the doors were opened a couple of minutes before nine.

Not very many people were there besides the fifty prospective jurors who filled up about half the seats in the Courtroom. The Assistant AG, Jim Satterfield was there with a young looking Assistant or Aide who looked like he had just graduated from law school.

Brad and Paula took their seats and the judge, Albert Prince, walked in from his chambers; he spoke:

"We are here to select a jury of twelve and as soon as we get that done we can get on with the trial. If there is anyone here who has a legitimate reason why they cannot serve, let them speak up now because it will take a death in the family to do so later."

The bailiff called the role from the jury list and found that only forty eight of the fifty were present. One man was excused because his wife was sick and needed his care and a business man was excused because he had an important meeting with an out of town visitor. Paula marked them off her list; neither of them was in the top twelve of her list.

Brad was given the nod to start the questioning of the jurors when he noticed that one of the men in the jury looked familiar to him, a Mr. Robert Allen. "You look familiar to me, Mr. Allen," said Brad; "have we met before?"

"I was in the jury pool for your trial back in 2007, Sir."

'Did you get selected for the jury?"

"No, Sir; I had a hearing problem back then and the judge excused me from jury duty."

Brad then recalled the amusing incident. The judge had asked if anyone in the jury pool could not serve on the jury for one reason or another and Mr. Allen held up his hand.

"What is your problem that would preclude you from serving on the jury, Mr. Allen?" asked the Judge.

"I have a hearing problem, Your Honor," he replied.

"Very well, Mr. Allen; you are excused and free to leave."

Mr. Allen cupped his left hand behind his ear and replied;"How's that Your Honor?" The judge repeated himself in a louder voice as the courtroom broke out in laughter and so did the judge.

"With your hearing problem would you be able to serve on this jury?" asked Brad.

"Yes Sir, Mr. Adams; I have since purchased a new state of the art hearing aid about a year ago and now my hearing is better than it was forty years ago. I hear perfectly now, and I ought to; it cost me $10,000."

"That sounds great, Mr. Allen, but where is the hearing aid; I don't see it in either of your ears?"

"That is another great feature of the gadget, Mr. Adams; the device is no larger than a pea and is almost invisible to the naked eye."

"That is fantastic, Mr. Allen; what kind is it?"

"Let me see," he said as he looked at his watch; "it's coming up on nine fifteen." (The courtroom broke out in laughter much louder than it had in 2007).

"This juror is acceptable to me, Your Honor," said Brad as Paula nodded her head in agreement.

"Chalk one juror up for Brad if the prosecution doesn't reject him", thought, Ace.

Brad didn't have anything to worry about because Mr. Allen was also acceptable to the prosecution; *one down and eleven plus two or three alternates to go;* thought, Ace.

Brad and Jim Satterfield parried the rest of the day like two knights in a duel, but only five jurors were selected. There were only twenty seven prospective jurors left. Brad had rejected six of them for cause and two by using two of his four peremptory challenges. These are challenges whereby the attorney can dismiss up to four prospective jurors for any reason; even if he doesn't like the side on which their hair is parted. The prosecutor had acted similarly in getting rid of the ones he did not want on the jury.

It was around three thirty in the afternoon when the judge called a halt to the proceedings.

"We are going to recess for the day and I want everyone back here at nine in the morning. I would like to finalize this jury by the end of the day tomorrow even if it goes to nine p.m. You are all now dismissed."

Brad turned to Ace and Paula and asked them how they thought it went.

"I believe that we have at least one juror seated who will vote for acquittal." replied Paula.

Chapter 99

Tuesday, Second day of jury selection

Ace, Brad, and Paula were in front of Courtroom 209 waiting for the doors to open. There were also the twenty seven remaining prospective jurors waiting; the jurors who were already selected were allowed to go home until the start of the trial after being admonished by the judge to not watch TV or read anything in the papers concerning the case at hand. The doors opened at nine sharp and the judge entered just a couple of minutes later. Brad was up first and decided to question Mr. Homer Paul who had served on four different juries in criminal court and was at the bottom of Paula's list.

"How are you today, Mr. Paul?" asked Brad.

"I'm doing well, thanks."

"How you ever served on a jury before, Mr. Paul?"

"Yes, Sir, I have,"

"Have you served more than once?"

"Yes, Sir; I have served on four previous juries."

"Were they all in Criminal Court?"

"Yes Sir."

"How do you account for being selected for jury duty four times when some people are never called?"

"I let it be known that I am available when called."

"Why do you want to serve on juries?"

'I can tell you one thing for sure; it's not for the money. I can make more money working for two hours at minimum wages than the eleven dollars a day that Knox County pays me."

"Then why do you want to serve?"

"I want to serve because I believe in justice."

"What is your definition of justice?"

"I see too many people getting off Scot free when some slick attorney finds a loophole in the law and convinces some gullible jurors that the defendant is the victim. A case in point is the California murder trial of the Menendez brothers who killed both their parents in cold blood."

"Do you think that our Attorney General would bring charges against an innocent man?"

"I don't believe that he would do it intentionally; however I do believe that in most cases that the charges are valid."

"Do you think that the charges are valid in the case of my client?"

"I do not know but I don't believe that a person is innocent until proven guilty."

"I agree with you 100% on that statement, Mr. Paul, but that's not what the law says. The law states that a person is presumed innocent until proven guilty. What that means is that it is up to the state to prove a person is guilty with a jury of his or her peers. The law does not want the jury to form an opinion of a case until they have all the facts in the case. Take a look at what happened in Durham County, North Carolina; it seemed that the news media and everyone else had already decided that the Duke University Lacrosse players were guilty, when in fact, they were all innocent. I would have hated to have been their defense attorney if that case had gone to trial."

"I concur with you on that case, Mr. Adams but that is a rare exception."

"Fortunately you are right, Mr. Paul. In that case the Durham District Attorney who was up for reelection over stepped his boundaries and was disbarred. Our case here is entirely different. Here my client, whom I believe is an innocent man, is being charged for a crime by a fair minded Attorney General who believes him to be guilty. I just want you to have an open mind going into this case and not take it for granted that the AG is infallible. Do you think that you could render a fair verdict in this case?"

"Yes, Sir, I believe that I can."

"This juror is acceptable to me your Honor," said Brad; Paula just stared in disbelief.

"This juror is also acceptable to me, your Honor," replied Assistant AG, Jim Satterfield.

Brad and Jim were able to agree on twelve jurors plus three alternates to close out the jury selection phase of the trial by five p.m.

"I would like to congratulate both sides in handling the jury selection in a timely manner," said Judge Prince. "We will take a day off and meet back here at nine a.m. Thursday. I want all of the twelve jurors here along with the three alternates who will sit in the front row of the courtroom; three seats will be reserved for you. I would like for each juror to bring a note pad and write down any pertinent points that you might not be able to recall in the jury room. I would suggest that none of you jurors or alternates watch the news or read anything in the paper about this case until the conclusion of the trial. If for some reason one of you cannot make it, I want you to call the court clerk as soon as possible. Are there any questions? If not, this court is adjourned."

Chapter 100

Thursday morning

There had been many letters to the Editor in the Knoxville newspaper, and the vast majority of them were critical of Doug Hart in particular and the Military in general. Not many letter writers were even slightly interested in seeing him get a fair trial; they seemed to have already convicted him in their minds.

"The local hotels were beginning to see an increase in occupancy, mainly from the influx of reporters. An overflow crowd was expected at the courtroom Thursday. It was obvious that the relatively small courtroom would not hold all who wished to attend. As a result, there were more people standing in line at the door to Courtroom 209 at eight a.m., than there were seats in the room. There was already a guard in front of the doors who made sure that nobody broke into the line improperly.

The doors opened at nine a.m. sharp and the judge allowed a maximum of six reporters, one each from the major news services and one from the Knoxville newspaper, in the courtroom but they would have to stand up in the back.

"No cameras of any kind were allowed inside the Courtroom and the judge was very adamant about that. "There is not going to be a three ring circus in my courtroom," he said.

Brad, Ace, Paula, Doug, and Denise arrived at ten to nine and were let in as soon as the doors opened; Brad had reserved a seat for both Ace and Paula. Doug Hart was sitting to the left of Brad at the defense table and Denise was seated in one of the seats that had been reserved for family members on both sides of the trial. Shortly thereafter the guard let as many of the rest of the crowd in until all the seats were filled. Once everyone was in the courtroom the bailiff announced the presence of His Honor, Judge Albert Prince, who took his seat followed by the rest of the people.

"You people are in a court of law and I expect you to behave as such. I am not going to ban cell phones in my courtroom, but heaven help you if your phone goes off, because I am not going to. If your phone rings, beeps, or vibrates so that I can hear it, the bailiff will take it from you and I will hold it for ransom to the tune of $100. How many phones would you say that we have confiscated in my courtroom to date?" he asked the Bailiff.

"My last count was thirty three, Your Honor."

"You can retrieve your phones each day at the end of the proceedings. No credits cards or checks will be accepted; cash only."

There will be no outbursts or applause during this trial. Anyone so doing will be escorted from the courtroom and will not be allowed back in for the remainder of the trial.

I want each member of the jury to sit up straight in their chair and if I see any of you starting to doze off, I will also find you in contempt of court and replace you with an alternate. I want each of you to listen to the evidence with an open mind and to ask questions if there is something that you don't understand.

This could be a lengthy trial, but I hope not. I want both the prosecution and defense to stick to the facts and not go off on some tangent that has nothing to do with the case as some attorneys are prone to do. I want no surprises in my courtroom; is that clear?" Both Brad and Jim Satterfield nodded their heads.

It looks like we are ready to get this trial underway. The jury is seated and the defendant is sitting at the defense table with his attorney. Will all the witnesses be available when we call them?"

"All of my witnesses are waiting outside the courtroom to be called when needed," replied Jim Satterfield.

"How about yours, Mr. Adams?"

"I have no witnesses to call at this time, Your Honor."

"Very well; we will now begin with the trial. You may both make your opening statements to the jury. You may go first, Mr. Satterfield?"

"I would like for this jury to know that a young woman in the prime of her life was raped, brutally beaten, and left for dead. We need to make our streets and campus areas safe for our students. When you have seen and heard all the evidence I am sure that you will bring in a guilty verdict and convict this rapist and put him behind bars where he will never be able to molest a young woman again. That is all I have to say, Your Honor."

"You may now give your opening statement, Mr. Adams."

"I would like to say that I agree that a heinous crime has been committed against the person of Miss Smith and I would personally like nothing better than to see the perpetrator go to jail for the rest of his natural life; however that person is not my client, Doug Hart. He and his wife and family are victims just as much as Kristin, her family, and her roommate Julie Brown are.

Can you imagine the shock an innocent man would have felt, when out of the blue, he was mistakenly identified as the rapist? I know that both Kristin and Julie believe that Doug is the man but somewhere out there is the real rapist who must look an awful lot like Doug. My associates and I have spent a lot of time and effort to locate that man but we have drawn a blank.

Doug's wife Denise has worked for me for over five years; although I have only known Doug for a few months, I have come to trust him and would be proud to have a son just like him. He and Denise had only been married for a couple of months when this crime occurred and I can personally tell you that both of them were completely shocked and surprised when he was arrested. When Kristin walked into her UT English Class that day and spotted Doug whom she thought had raped her, what would a guilty person have done? I can tell you exactly what that person would have done. He would have run, got out of Dodge, fled. What did Doug do? He waited around with the rest of his class to see what all he commotion was about. He did not run because he had no reason to; does that sound like a guilty person to you?

Doug has served his country faithfully to protect us from the evil ones who do not value human life and who would like nothing better than to blow us all to kingdom Come. He was also an Eagle Scout back in his teenage years and I have never known a bad Eagle Scout. Doug is an All-American in my book and I intend to prove to this jury that he is innocent of all charges. That is all I have to say, Your Honor."

"You may call your first witness, Mr. Prosecutor," said the Judge.

"I call Knoxville City Detective, Ralph Miller to the stand, Your Honor."

"The witness will take the stand, place his hand on the Bible, and be sworn in by the Bailiff." said the Judge.

"Do you promise to tell the truth, the whole truth, and nothing but the truth, so help you God?"

"I do."

"You may be seated." said the judge

"Would you relate to this court the events that occurred on Friday January 14th of this year?" asked the Prosecutor.

"I received a call shortly after nine p.m. of an attack on a young woman who lived in an apartment in the Fort Sanders area near the University of Tennessee."

"Were you by yourself?"

"Yes, I was just getting ready to go home when I received the call so I rushed right on over."

"What did you find when you arrived?"

"I got there right after the ambulance from Fort Sanders Hospital. The victim, Kristin Smith, was still lying on the floor and I couldn't tell if she was alive or dead. She appeared to have a death grip on a blue ski mask."

"Did you notice any bruises or marks on her?"

"Yes, her face was black and blue and she appeared to be missing some front upper teeth."

"Was there anyone else there in addition to you, the responders, and Miss Smith?"

"Yes, her roommate, Julie Brown and a local TV news reporter from Channel 3 and Miss Brown appeared to be in a state of shock."

"Did you observe any evidence other than the ski mask?"

"I saw nothing else even though I made a thorough search of the crime scene."

"What happened next?"

"The medical crew stabilized Miss Smith and placed her in the ambulance to take her to Fort Sanders."

"What happened to Miss Brown?"

"They also took her to the hospital in the ambulance."

"What did you do next, Officer, Miller?"

"I secured and taped off the crime scene and called forensics to come and search for more evidence. I stayed until they arrived and then returned to the station to write up my report."

"Thank you Officer, Miller; I have no further questions from this witness, Your Honor."

"You may now cross examine the witness, Mr. Adams," said the Judge.

"I have just one question of this witness, Your Honor. What did you do with the ski mask that the victim was holding in her hand, Officer Miller?"

"One of the responders removed the mask from her hand and gave it to me; I, in turn, handed it over to Forensics when they arrived."

"I have no further questions, Your Honor."

"You may call your next witness, Mr. Satterfield."

"I call Dr. James Draper to the stand, Your Honor."

The doctor took the stand and was sworn in.

"I understand that you were the ER doctor who first saw Miss Smith when she arrived at Fort Sanders. Can you tell us what happened after she arrived?" asked the PA.

"She was brought into emergency about nine thirty the evening she was attacked. She had a very faint pulse and her face was badly bruised. I gave her a sedative to make her breathing somewhat easier and also looked into her mouth to make sure her air passage was clear. I then removed portions of two teeth from her mouth, and when I was sure that she was out of immediate danger, I examined her to see if there was any injury to her genital area."

"What did you discover there?"

"She definitely had been raped but there was no evidence of semen; it appeared that the rapist used a prophylactic."

"Did you discover any hairs that did not belong to the victim?"

"I am not a forensic expert but we did find some loose hairs which we bagged and gave to your forensic department."

"Is there anything else that you can add to what you have already told us, Dr. Draper?"

"I would just like to say that this was one of the most brutal rape cases that I have ever encountered except one in which the victim was actually murdered. I believe that Miss Smith would have died if her roommate had not returned when she did."

"Objection, Your Honor; this statement is highly speculative and inflammatory and is based solely on the doctor's opinion rather than the facts," said Brad.

"I concur, Mr. Adams; the objection is sustained. Instruct your witness to stick to the facts, Mr. Satterfield."

"I apologize, Your Honor; I can assure you that it won't happen again. I have no further questions of this witness, Your Honor."

"Your witness, Mr. Adams."

"I have no questions of this witness, Your Honor but I would like to call a witness at this time if I may?"

"I thought you said that you had no witnesses, Mr. Adams."

"This is really not my witness but I would like to call the State's Forensic expert in this case unless the PA intends to call him, Your Honor."

"Do you intend to call this witness, Mr. Satterfield?" asked the Judge.

"I had not planned on doing so, Your Honor because we came up short on any forensic evidence in this case."

"Is your forensic expert available to testify at this point?"

"Yes, he is waiting outside the courtroom because I assumed that the defense might want to question him."

"Bailiff, would you please bring in the witness?" asked the Judge. The bailiff brought in the witness.

"Please state your name, Sir," instructed the bailiff.

"My name is Dr. Wilson Cooper, Chief of Forensics for the Knoxville Police Department." He was sworn in and seated and Brad began the questioning.

"Did you handle all the forensic work associated with this rape case of my client, Mr. Doug Hart?"

"Yes, Sir; I handled what there was of it; we didn't have very much evidence to work with in this case."

"I understand that there was a ski mask that the rapist was wearing; what can you tell me about that?"

"We found two hairs inside the mask but none of them matched the hair of Mr. Hart."

"Didn't you find it somewhat unusual that if my client was the rapist that you didn't find any of his hair in the mask?"

"Not necessarily; the mask could have been a used one with someone else's hair in it. Hair does not always come off in a close fitting head covering of that sort."

"Did the hairs that you found in the mask all belong to the same person?"

"All of the hairs matched and probably came from the same person's head."

"And that someone was someone other than my client; is that not right?"

"Objection, Your Honor," spoke up the PA. "Mr. Cooper has already testified that the hairs did not match Mr. Hart's hair."

"Your objection is over ruled, Mr. Satterfield; Mr. Adams is just trying to stress that point, and I will allow it. Answer the question, Mr. Cooper.

"Yes, the three hairs belonged to someone other than your client, Mr. Hart."

"I understand that there were also some hairs that were taken from the victim in the hospital," said Brad. "Did these turn out to be someone else's also?"

"Yes Sir, all of those hairs belonged to the victim."

"So you ended up without one iota of any forensic evidence against my client whatsoever; is that correct?"

"I would have to say that is correct, Sir."

"What did the DNA of the hair show? Did it match up with the DNA of my client?"

"We didn't think that there was any point in having a DNA analysis of the hairs; if the hair samples didn't match we knew that the DNA wouldn't match either."

"I cannot believe what you are telling me, Doctor; did it ever occur to you to do a DNA analysis on the hair sample and match it against your data base to see if you could get a match, or had you already decided that my client was guilty and that it would be just a waste of time? Were you only looking for evidence that would help to convict my client rather than exonerate him?"

Dr. Cooper was becoming very uncomfortable and was squirming and fidgeting in his chair by now because he had been caught in a big faux pas; in other words he had just stepped in it.

"We have a very small DNA data base in our system at this time," the Doctor replied.

'You did not answer my question, Dr. Cooper; I asked you if you were only looking for evidence that would help to convict my client."

"I may have been, but I didn't do it purposely. I suppose that I may have unconsciously been in that mind set. I will try to avoid that type of thinking in the future,"

"Your Honor; I request that this entire case against my client be thrown out for the sloppy and unprofessional manner in which this forensic evidence has been handled," insisted Brad. "I would like to see my client get a fair trial as guaranteed by the United States Constitution."

"I tend to agree with you, Mr. Adams, but here is what I want the AG's office to do. I want the forensic expert to go back to his lab and get a DNA analysis performed on those afore mentioned hair samples and match them against the data base of all the DNA samples in the State of Tennessee's data base and have the results ready and presentable to this court this coming Monday morning or I will throw out this case entirely; does the Prosecution see any problems with this?"

"We will do our best to comply with your ruling, but it may not be possible in that short time frame." replied the PA.

"If the DNA verification is not possible, then this trial is not possible. Do I make myself clear, Mr. Satterfield?"

"Very clear, Your Honor; and I would like to apologize to the court at this time; I had no idea how the forensic part of this case was being handled."

"Your apology is accepted, Mr. Satterfield. I assume that appropriate actions will be taken to prevent anything like this from occurring in the future. I take it very seriously when our system of justice in this country is compromised, and I will not see it trampled upon in any way."

"I can assure you, Your Honor that appropriate steps will be taken to prevent something like from happening in the future."

"I have just about had all I can stand here today. I want everyone back here in the courtroom at nine a.m. Monday to see if we still have a trial to conduct," said the Judge.

It was almost twelve noon when Brad, Ace, Paula, Doug, and Denise walked the two blocks back to the office where Brad held a short meeting.

"How do all of you think it went today?" asked Brad.

"I say we chalk one up for the defense," replied Ace. The others all concurred.

"We are not out of the woods just yet," said Brad. "We struck out the other side today but we still have eight more innings to go. We must not relax our guard; we still have a long way to go. I doubt very seriously if they will find a DNA match for those hairs, and if they don't, we're back to square one. Is anybody up to driving over to the Crown Plaza for a good lunch?"

"Are you buying, Brad?" asked Ace.

"I will buy; we need to celebrate our small victory today and get back to work this afternoon."

"I will drive us all over in my Crossover," said Paula.

Chapter 101

Friday morning

Brad and Denise were already at the office when Ace arrived and got his traditional cup of coffee when Denise brought in the morning paper. She pointed out the Consolidated Press article on page one which went out to papers all over the country. It read:

CHALK ONE UP FOR THE DEFENSE
By The Consolidated Press
In the trial of former Marine, Douglas Hart in Knoxville, Tennessee for the rape and brutal beating of University of Tennessee coed, Kristen Smith, the defense attorney, Brad Adams caught the prosecution acting in a callous and slipshod manner in which they dealt with forensic evidence, mainly the DNA analyses.
The forensic expert, Dr. Wilson Cooper, who testified in the trial, admitted that he had not had a DNA analysis performed on the hairs that were found in the Ski mask that the victim ripped off the head of the rapist. He claimed that since the hairs found in the mask did not match the hair of the defendant, Douglas Hart, that he saw no reason to get a DNA analysis of the hair because the DNA would not match either. The defense attorney, Mr. Brad Adams jumped all over that bit of testimony and accused Dr. Cooper of having already convicted his client in his mind and

was only looking for evidence that would help convict but not any evidence that would help exonerate his client. The Judge, Albert Prince, agreed and gave the prosecution until Monday of next week to perform a DNA analysis of the hairs and check them against all the DNA's in the State Of Tennessee's data Base. The prosecutor, Mr. Jim Satterfield replied to the Judge that it might not be possible to get that done in such a short time frame and the Judge said if that was not possible, neither would the trial be possible. As of today, the trial is in limbo.

"I think the article in the paper is very fair, Brad." said Ace.

"I agree, Ace. Right now I have a lot of work to do to get ready for Monday; I have a feeling that the trial will go on."

"I'll be there for moral support if you need any, Brad."

"I'll see you there, Ace."

Chapter 102

Monday morning

After the judge had arrived and everyone was seated, he started the proceedings.

"Did you get the DNA analysis performed as I ordered, Mr. Satterfield?"

"Yes Your Honor."

"And what were your findings?"

"We could find no matches at all in any of Tennessee's DNA data base."

"Very well; we will now continue with the trial. You may call your next witness, Mr. Satterfield."

"I call Miss Julie Brown to the stand, Your Honor."

She was sworn in by the Bailiff and was seated.

"I understand that you and the victim, Miss Kristin Smith were roommates; is that correct?" asked the PA.

"Yes sir."

"Would you please tell this court what took place at your and Kristin's apartment on the night of January 14, 2011?"

"I got to my apartment around nine p.m. and just as I took out my key and opened the door a man came running out and almost knocked me over. I ran into the apartment and locked the door behind me and that was when I saw Kristin lying on the floor looking all black and blue and bloody; I did not know if she was alive or dead."

"What did you do next?"

"I saw that she was breathing and I dialed 911on my cell phone and then looked to see what I could do for her while waiting for the responders."

"About how long was it before they arrived?"

"It seemed like an eternity to me but it was probably about ten minutes, about the same time as the reporter from the television station.

"What all did you notice about Kristin while you were waiting?"

"I noticed that she seemed to have had some teeth knocked out and she was grasping a blue ski mask in her right hand."

"What happened next?"

"The responders arrived and gave her some kind of shot and were getting ready to load her into the ambulance when Detective Miller arrived."

"What happened next?"

"One of the responders took the ski mask from Kristin's hand and gave it to Detective Miller and they then placed her in the ambulance to be taken to emergency. I was in such a state of shock that the responders insisted that I go to the emergency room also. They placed me in the ambulance along with Kristen and gave me a sedative at the hospital; that was the last I saw of Kristin that night."

"Did you get a good look at the man you saw running out of your apartment building?"

"Yes and I will never forget that evil face." *Brad thought about objecting about the evil face part, but he thought better of it; he didn't want to enflame the jury.*

"Do you see that man in the courtroom her today, Julie?"

"Yes Sir, I do."

"Would you please point him out to the court?"

"That is him sitting at the table to the left of Mr. Adams."

"Are you sure?"

"I am positive."

"I have no more questions of this witness, Your Honor."

"Your witness, Mr. Adams." said the Judge.

"I am truly sorry for what happened to Kristin and for what you had to witness, Julie. I will be brief in my questioning. You testified that you were in a state of shock and also had to be taken to the ER. Don't you think that you could have been mistaken in your identification of my client as the rapist when you glimpsed him for just a second as he was running past you in the dark?"

"I have made no mistake, Sir; I picked Mr. Hart out of a police lineup which included several similar looking people."

"I want you to make sure that the person you pointed out sitting next to me is the same person you saw running out of your apartment. I want you to take a good look around this courtroom to see if there is anyone else here who you might have seen that night."

"I see no one else in this courtroom who could have been the attacker other than the man sitting beside you. He is definitely the man I saw running out of our apartment."

"Thank you for your testimony. I have no further questions of this witness, Your Honor.)" *The PA was well pleased with the way in which Julie handled Brad's cross examination.*

"Very well; you may call your next witness. Mr. Satterfield."

"I call Kristin Smith to the stand, Your Honor."

Kristin was sworn in and seated.

"I am going to be as brief as possible, Kristin; I don't want you to have to relive any more of your horrifying experience than is necessary. We have already gone over much of what happened on that night and all I really want from you is the identification of your attacker. Do you see that man in the courtroom?"

"Yes I do; he is sitting at the table on the left hand of Mr. Adams."

"Are you certain that he is the man.?"

"Yes, I am certain."

"I have no further questions of this witness, Your Honor."

"Your witness, Mr. Adams."

"I just want to say that I am truly sorry for what happened to you Kristin and I want to make sure that we don't send an innocent man to prison. I am going to ask you some questions that you may think to be odd or strange, but I want to be sure that you correctly identify the person who attacked you.

I want you to look very carefully all around this courtroom and see if you can pick him out. Take your time and let me know when you are ready. Take as long as you like."

After a few minutes Kristin said that she was ready.

"Did you look all around the courtroom, Kristin?"

"Yes I did, but it was a complete waste of time when the guilty man is sitting right beside you."

"Let's not be hasty, Kristin. Look at all the male jurors; could it be one of them?"

"Of course not."

"Could it be one of the spectators in the front row?"

"No."

"Could it be one of the spectators in the last row?"

"I object to all this foolish questioning, Your Honor," spoke up the PA.

"Where are you going with this, Mr. Adams?" asked the Judge.

"Please bear with me Your Honor; I will need just a few more minutes."

"Proceed," said the Judge.

"You have looked at everyone in this courtroom to identify your attacker; would you please point him out to the court now."

"As I said before, he is the man sitting on your left hand."

Brad gave her the most incredulous look he could muster and said: "Are you stating that this man sitting beside me is the man who raped you and your identification of him excludes everyone else in this courtroom?"

"Yes, that is what I am saying."

"Would you please stand and let Kristin take a good look at you?" asked Brad of the accused; the accused stood up.

"Do you still insist that this man was your attacker?" asked Brad.

"There is no doubt that he is the one," replied Kristin."

"I would like to call the accused to the stand Your Honor," said Brad. Jim Satterfield thought that Brad had lost his mind. *"Just wait until I get him on the stand,"* he thought.

"Very well; swear him in and get him seated." the judge said to the bailiff.

"Do you swear to tell the truth, the whole truth, and nothing but the truth so help you God?"

"I do."

"Brad then began his questioning. "Are you guilty of raping this young woman who just accused you?" asked Brad.

"No sir; I have never see this young lady in my life before today." There was an unbelievable buzz in the courtroom.

"Do you have an alibi for the time on the evening of January 14th this year when the rape took place?"

"Yes sir."

"Do you have any eye witnesses as to your whereabouts the night and time in question?"

"Yes Sir I do."

"Could you name the eye witnesses that you claim to have?"

"No Sir; I don't know very many of them, and they are too numerous to name." One could have heard a pin drop.

"Just how many eye witnesses do you have?"

"There were approximately 17,000, Sir."

"I object," shouted the PA; "just what is going on here, Your Honor?"

"I would like an answer to that question myself," replied the judge. "Would you be so kind as to elaborate on what is happening in my courtroom, Mr. Adams?"

"I would be glad to clear this whole thing up if you will give me a little more time to question my witness."

"Carry on, Mr. Adams."

"Would tell the court your name, Sir," Brad asked the witness.

"My name is Benny Goldberg." He replied. The entire courtroom broke out in a clamor and a couple of reporters rushed out of the room, probably to call their news agencies.

"May I continue questioning the witness, Your Honor?"

"I can hardly wait, Mr. Adams."

"What is you relationship with my client, Doug Hart?"

"He and I are brothers."

"How do you account for your different last names?"

"I just found out a few weeks ago that I had an identical twin brother and that we were separated at birth and adopted by different parents, who also didn't know that we came in a set. I have always had a funny feeling that a part of me was missing and when I recently discovered that I had a twin brother, I immediately got in touch with him and we became fast friends. When I found out that he was charged with rape I knew that he was innocent and I told him that I would do anything legally within my power to help him in this case. That is why I am here today."

"What kind of work do you do and who are all of those 17,000 witnesses that you mentioned?"

"Those 17,000 are actually eye witnesses; there are probably a couple million more who only saw me on TV. I am a forward on The Nashville Predators Hockey team and we were playing a hockey game while the rape was going on."

"Was there anything exceptional or different about that game that would enable the witnesses to remember the exact date of that game?"

"That was the game in which I scored the only hat trick of my career."

"Would you explain to the court exactly what a hat trick is, Benny?"

"A hat trick is where a player scores three goals in one game."

"Do you have any proof of what you are telling this court?" asked Brad.

"Yes, Sir, I have a CD of the game I bought with me."

"Would the court like the defense to show the CD to the jury, Your Honor?" asked Brad.

"That will not be necessary, Mr. Adams; I saw the game on TV myself. Let's get back to business. Now that Mr. Goldberg has done some explaining, it is now your turn," said the Judge.

"I didn't know that Doug and Benny had gotten together until a few days ago when they both came to my office and asked what they could do to get Doug acquitted. I told them that I would do everything legally that I could. Benny jokingly suggested that he sit in on the trial as the defendant and be mistakenly identified as the rapist. I didn't think much about it at the time but I decided to see if I would be breaking any laws if we did that. I researched all my law books and had Denise, Doug's wife, help me in this. She was not in on the deception; she was only performing a task I had assigned her. I could find nothing in all of my research that indicated that the defendant had to sit at the defense table with me; he only had to be in the courtroom. I would like to state that Doug Hart, Benny Goldberg, and me were the only ones involved in his deception. Denise, Doug's wife, had no idea of what was going on until Doug sat down beside her and she saw Benny sitting beside me at the defense table."

"I didn't see him," said the Judge; where were she and Doug sitting in the courtroom, Mr. Adams?"

"They were both sitting in the back row; that is why I asked Miss. Smith if she could spot her attacker in the back row." (Doug had worn a pair of dark sunglasses into the courtroom to prevent being recognized)

"Your honor, this is the most despicable courtroom fiasco I have ever witnessed, and I think that Mr. Adams should be found in contempt of this court," spoke up the PA.

"I will decide who is, or who is not in contempt of my court, Mr. Satterfield. As I see it right now I have three options. I can find Mr. Adams in contempt, I can declare a mistrial, or I can throw out the whole case because the victim and her roommate both identified the wrong man as her rapist. There has been some misconduct on both sides of the aisle in this case so you don't need to be throwing stones or pointing fingers. What I am going to do is place this trial on hold indefinitely until I have had the time to research this whole fiasco to see if any laws are broken or just badly bent. The jury in this case is hereby dismissed; if we have another trial down the road we will have to select another jury at that time. This court is now adjourned," he said, as he slammed the gavel down so hard that he broke the handle. "I mentioned just three options but I would like to toss out another one; I could just step down from the bench and let someone else handle this entire stinking mess. I should have listened to my Mama when she tried to get me to go into medicine. This court is now dismissed."

All of the reporters scurried out of the courtroom to file a story the likes of which they had never witnessed before.

Chapter 103

Tuesday morning, Brad's Office

Brad and Ace were discussing yesterday's courtroom fiasco when Ace spoke up. "You really blindsided me in the courtroom yesterday; I had no idea that it wasn't Doug Hart sitting beside you during the trial."

"I did that for a very simple reason, Ace; I didn't want involve anymore people than necessary in my deception and have them being charged with being an 'accessory before the fact' in case I was charged with any wrongdoing."

"Thanks, Brad; I guess what they say is right."

"Just what do they say, Ace?'

"They say that blood is thicker than water."

"Much thicker, Ace, much thicker."

"What do you think will happen now, Brad?"

"I don't think anything will happen before fall; I think the Judge will be looking at all the law books that he can get his hands on and calling everyone he can think of to get an opinion on whether I broke any laws in his courtroom yesterday. I think it is about 50-50 whether this case will ever be retried,"

"If it's not retried, Doug will be considered guilty by almost everyone in Knoxville," said Ace.

"I realize that, Ace, but there is nothing we can do about it; it's a lot better than him getting convicted in another trial."

About that time, Denise walked in with the morning paper.

"Would you two like to see what the Consolidated Press has to say about yesterday's court proceedings?" she asked. They looked at the article.

DID BRAD ADAMS OVERSTEP THE LEGAL BOUNDARIES?
BY THE CONSOLIATED PRESS
Knoxville, Tennessee.

There is much discussion among the legal profession as to whether Brad Adams acted illegally or just unprofessionally in the defense of his client, Doug Hart in yesterday's trial in Knoxville. He maneuvered to have Doug Hart's twin brother, Benny Goldberg sit beside him at the defense table instead of the accused. As a result, the victim, Kristin Smith and her roommate, Julie Brown both identified Goldberg, who had an ironclad alibi, as the attacker and rapist. Brad claimed that he only knew that Doug had an identical twin brother a few days before the trial began and that it was Goldberg's idea to sit at the defense table instead of Doug Hart.

The Judge, Albert Prince wasn't all too happy with the proceedings and consequently dismissed the jury and postponed the trial indefinitely so that he can research the law to see if Brad Adams violated any part of it. Judge Prince stated that he had three choices; to find Adams in contempt, declare a mistrial, or throw out the entire case because the two eyewitnesses both identified the wrong man as the culprit. There was no indication as to when and if a new trial will take place.

Chapter 104

Saturday Afternoon, June 25

The trial had ended more than two weeks ago and there had been a lot of speculation as to what affect Benny Goldberg's part in the trial would have on his hockey career. That question was answered when the Nashville Predator fans gave him a standing ovation when he played his first game since the trial. His playing abilities were not affected either as he scored two goals.

Lisa was home for summer vacation and she intended to just relax and enjoy herself. She and Sean, who was also out of school for vacation, had made plans to do some hiking in several of the Great Smokey Mountain National Park's numerous nature trails. Today she was just relaxing and taking it easy. She walked into the den and Ace woke up from his catnap in his easy chair.

"Are you going to sleep all day, Lazy Bones," she asked.

"I had planned to until you woke me up, Lisa."

"I'm bored, Ace; is there anything that you can do to perk me up?"

"I have thought up a new game that will pique your interest and activate your brain."

"I'm game for a new game; how does it work and what is it called?"

"Right now I am calling it 'Word Dueling' for lack of a better name; you pick a word that is a thing and tell me what it is, and I have to give you a word in return that has to be related to that word."

"Give me an example, Ace."

"Suppose that you pick the word house; I could reply with several words; such as wife, cat, hold, etc?"

"What is the purpose of the game?"

"The purpose of the game is for the person who selects the word to get back to that original word by logically following the examples I just gave you. You can also use opposite words such as hot and cold for example. For a person to win there must be a minimum of ten words already used."

"Where does the skill enter into the game, Ace?"

"When the person who gets to go first gives a word, the opponent tries to pick a word that would make it hard for the opponent to get back to that original word. Then the first person tries to pick words that will take him or her back to the original word. In other words, we parry like two duelers with sabers. Why don't you pick a word and see how it works?"

"OK; I pick 'Horse'."

LISA	ACE
Horse	Buggy
Ride	Bus
Stop	Go
Out	Side
Aspect	Ratio
Percentage	Amount
Quantity	Much
Less	Small
Large	Huge
Giant	Midget
Tiny	Wee
They	People
Humans	Man
Woman	Girl
Boy	Scout
Horse	

"How in the world do you come up with horse being related to Scout, Lisa?"

"Scout is the name of the Lone Ranger's trusted sidekick, Tonto's, horse." .

"You don't play fair, Lisa; how did you know that bit of information? The lone ranger was way before your time."

"Freddy told me; 'get um up Scout'"

"Be serious, Lisa; how did you know?"

"We have a TV station in Nashville called 'Retro Westerns', and they show all the old western movies such as Roy Rogers, Gene Autry, and The Lone Ranger." Would you like to pick a word, Ace?"

"Yes, I pick the word, telephone."

ACE	LISA
Telephone	Call
Dial	Up
Down	Stair
Eye	Ball
Game	Show
Time	Out
In	Side
Edge	Mantle
Hearth	Warm
Fire	Place
House	Home
Plate	Kitchen
Door	Bell
Telephone	

"Bingo, Lisa."

"You really got me on that one, Ace; I didn't see it coming."

"I was just paying you back."

Chapter 105

Saturday, August, 27

The summer passed rather slowly for everyone except Lisa and Sean Davis, her boyfriend; September was just around the corner and they had to report back to Vanderbilt to start fall classes, Tuesday the sixth of September. Paula and Lisa were sitting in the den watching the first televised college football game of the season between Iowa and Boise State at the Meadowlands in New Jersey when Ace walked in.

"I didn't know that you two girls were football fans," said Ace.

"We just had it turned on for you, Ace," replied Paula.

"Thanks, Paula; would you and Sean like to go with Paula, Freddy, and me to Boomsday this year, Lisa?"

"When is it?"

"It is Monday September the fifth, Labor Day."

"Sean and I have to be back at Vanderbilt the sixth and it would be too late to drive back that night; we'll have to pass on your offer. Thanks anyway."

"We have tickets to park in the Church Street Methodist Church parking lot right next to the Henley Street Bridge where all the fireworks are located." said Ace.

"Sean and I went with you and Mom last year," said Lisa, "and we really enjoyed it."

"Can we go up in the 'Sunspear', like we did last year, Daddy?" asked Freddy"

"We sure can, Little Man."

"I can't hardly wait, Daddy."
"It's just a week away, Freddy," replied Paula.

Chapter 106

Monday September, 5 - 'Boomsday'

Ace, Paula, and Freddy arrived at the Church around five p.m. and found a good parking space. For only ten dollars each plus five dollars for parking they got to eat a barbeque sandwich along with, slaw, chips, and a drink along with the parking. They took a walk around the area to look at some of the older Victorian Style houses that were very eloquent several decades ago. By the time they got back to the church, people were getting in line to eat. After they had eaten they walked the three blocks to the Sunsphere and took the elevator to the observation deck where they could see almost all of downtown Knoxville. They then went back to the church where there was entertainment for the young folks. Freddy really enjoyed the magician who was performing in one of the church rooms and the puppet show in another room after that. After seeing the shows they all walked to the parking lot to await the fireworks which were still more than two hours away.

Ace had made a gallon of homemade peach ice cream which he took out of Paula's crossover.

"This is good ice cream, Daddy," said Freddy.

"I agree," said Paula; say, isn't that Doug Hart over there, Ace."

"Where, Paula; I don't see him."

"He's over by that black Ford pickup truck."

"I see who you mean, but that's not Doug; Doug doesn't smoke. However he does look a lot like Doug except for the mustache."

"You're right, Ace; from my angle, I didn't notice the mustache at first."

"He could be a dead ringer for Doug if he didn't have that mustache; he even has the same mannerisms as Doug." said Ace. "Hand me the cell phone Paula, I have and idea."

Ace took the cell phone and started walking in the direction of the Doug Hart "look-a-like" holding the phone in his right hand. He pretended to be talking on the cell phone while he took several pictures of the mustached man. Ace saw the man throw his cigarette butt on the pavement so he took out his car keys and was twirling them around when they flew off his index finger and conveniently landed about six inches from the abandoned cigarette. Ace reached down to pick up his keys and in the same motion grabbed the cigarette butt as well. He walked back to Paula's crossover and took a small Ziploc Bag, removed a cookie, and replaced it with the cigarette which he had snuffed out. Paula had been watching him all along.

"You are a sly old Fox, Ace; I know what's going on in that devious mind of yours. I know exactly what you are going to do."

"What do you think I am going to do, Paula?"

"You are going to have the DNA from that cigarette compared with the DNA of the hairs found in the ski mask of Kristin's rapist."

"You know me like a book, Paula, but I bet you didn't know that besides the man's picture that I also got his license plate number."

"Well you had better write it down before you forget it,"

"I don't have to write it down; it's in my cell phone along with his pictures."

"I'm glad that we are on the same side, Ace."

Ace took his cell phone and texted a message to Lisa at Vanderbilt and attached the pictures; the message read: "Lisa; see if you can transfer these pictures to your computer, remove the mustache from them, blow them up as large as possible, and email them back to me."

A couple of minutes later he received a reply from her.

"This guy is a dead ringer for Doug Hart, Ace. I know exactly what you're up to and your pictures will be in your Inbox as soon as you get home. Keep me in the loop. Love, Lisa."

Ace could hardly wait until tomorrow to get the DNA analysis started. He planned to get the pilfered cigarette to the AG first thing in the morning.

The 10,000 fireworks that were set off appeared to outdo the ones last year, but they always did. They seemed to come up with something a little different and better every year. All the colors of the rainbow lit up the night sky with smiling happy faces and heart-shapes formed by the fireworks. The grand finale was the white fireworks that were streaming down from the top of the Henley Street Bridge resembling a waterfall. Freddy had the time of his life and went to sleep in the car before they got him home.

The first thing that Ace did after he put Freddy to bed was to check his email. He found the one he was looking for; it was from Lisa and there was an attachment which he quickly opened. There was an eight by ten color photo of the Doug Hart look-a-like staring back at him that looked almost as much like Doug as Benny Goldberg. The quality of the picture was much better than he had anticipated. He made four copies on photograph paper and thought about framing one of them as a trophy, but he decided to wait to see how everything played out. *"I better not count my chickens before they hatch,"* he thought. Ace now had everything he needed except for a name to go along with the picture; he could hardly sleep because he was so excited.

Chapter 107

Tuesday September 6- The Boomsday Verdict

Ace got to the office an hour earlier than usual and called his friend, Gene White at the Knoxville Police Department.

"What can I do for you, Ace?" asked Gene.

"I wonder if you would run a plate for me like you did last spring."

"Just remember that you didn't get it from me, Ace."

"For the record, I don't even know you."

"What is the plate number?"

"It is Tennessee plate 747 TZL, Cocke County."

"It'll take me a few seconds, Ace. Here it is; the vehicle is registered to a Buford Munson, age 28."

"Thanks a million, Gene; I owe you one."

Brad and Denise both came in around nine a.m. Denise made some coffee and brought some back to Brad and Ace.

"You had both better sit down," said Ace. "I have something to show you that could knock you off your feet and have a lasting affect on all of us."

Ace gave a photo of Buford Munson to each of them and they both looked at it puzzling.

"Where did you get this picture of Doug?" asked Denise; "I've never seen it before."

Ace showed her the picture that was still in his cell phone that showed Munson with a mustache.

"That is what this man looked like before Lisa removed his mustache on her computer last night."

"Where did you take this picture, Ace?" asked Brad.

"I took it in the parking lot of the Church Street Methodist Church as we were waiting for the fireworks to start."

"Do you know who this man is?" asked Denise.

"I had his pickup license plate ran and found out his name is Buford Munson from Cocke County. I expect to find out more about him as soon as I call Lisa at Vanderbilt in a few minutes."

"Do you think that this man is the one who raped Kristin Smith?" asked Denise.

"I am positive that Doug or Benny did not do it, and it had to be someone who looked like them, and I can't think of a better suspect. All I need to do now is place him in Knoxville at the time of the crime and I have a pretty good idea how to go about it."

"What do you plan to do, Ace?" asked Brad.

"You and I need to pay a little visit to Mel Crosby, The AG; I have something I want to show him."

"We will if he's still speaking to me after the stunt I pulled in court back in June. What do you want to show him, Ace?"

"I have a cigarette butt that I would like to get tested for DNA to see if it matches the hairs found in the rapist's ski mask."

"Sometimes you amaze me, Ace," said Brad. Would you get me Mel on the phone as soon as possible, Denise?"

"I'll do it right now, Brad." Said an overly excited, Denise.

Five minutes later Denise had Mel Crosby on the phone.

"What's up, Brad?"

Brad explained the whole scenario to Mel and he told them to come right over to his office.

Brad and Ace decided to walk the short distance to Mel's office in the CCB and were there in ten minutes. They showed Mel the picture and told him who the man was.

"Ace has a cigarette butt that the man threw down and we would like for you to run a DNA and see if matches up with the DNA of the hairs found in the ski mask" said Brad.

"I will put this on the fast track, Brad, and I should have an answer by tomorrow; this looks very promising."

"I couldn't ask for anything more, Mel; I apologize for my courtroom behavior back in June."

"Think nothing of it, Brad; I would have probably done the same thing."

"Thanks for your help, Mel."

"It is my pleasure, Brad; I'm always glad to see justice done even though I'm on the losing side."

"There is no losing side when justice is served, Mel."

"Touché, Brad."

Brad and Ace returned to the office and Ace called Lisa on her cell phone.

"What's up, Big Daddy?"

"I have one more small task for you, Lisa. The name of the man in the picture is Buford Munson form Cocke County, Tennessee and I want you to find out all you can about him, even down to his shoe size,"

"Would you also like to know what brand of tooth paste he uses?"

"Just see if you can place him in Knoxville around January of this year."

"I have a couple of free hours this afternoon that I can work on this; I'll call you about five your time, Ace."

"Thanks, Lisa; this may be the most important thing that I have ever asked you to do."

"I realize the importance of it, Ace, and I will give it my best shot."

Ace got home from work around five thirty and was sitting in his easy chair watching TV when Lisa called. Ace noticed on the caller ID that it was her.

"This is the University Of Tennessee Body Farm; how may I help you?"

"Speaking of burying and digging things up; I think I have dug up the information on Buford Munson that you wanted."

"I'm all ears, Lisa."

"Munson is an electrician helper and has been working on the new Min Kao Engineering Building at the University of Tennessee for the past year and still works there."

"That is fantastic, Lisa; how did you find all of this information?"

"My good friend, Mr. Google has been very kind to me. You can find information on just about anybody with today's technology."

"I have driven past the building on Cumberland Avenue and I bet that Munson has seen Kristin Smith walking past the building on the way to her apartment. I bet he followed her home one day and cased out her apartment before he raped her. There was one problem he hadn't counted on and that was Kristin's roommate coming home to the apartment and finding him there. Julie probably saved Kristin's life that fateful night. Thanks for your help, Lisa."

"You're welcome; let me know how this all plays out, Ace."

"You'll be the first to know."

Chapter 108

Wednesday, Sept 7

Ace and Denise were already at work when Brad arrived around nine. They were enjoying their coffee and doughnuts when the telephone rang; Brad picked it up himself. It was Mel Crosby, The Knox County, AG.

"We have ourselves a match, Brad," said Mel.

"Is it Okay if I put you on the speaker box so that Ace and Denise can get in on the conversation?"

"No problem, Brad; I'll repeat what I just said for their ears. We have a DNA match from the cigarette butt that you gave us with the DNA of the hairs found in the rapist's ski mask."

It was hard to tell who was the most excited, Ace or Denise.

"Does this mean that you can now clear Doug's name?" asked Ace.

"Not exactly; we cannot use the cigarette butt in a court of law because it is just your word that it was smoked by Munson."

"What can you do?" asked, Brad.

"I believe that I can get an arrest warrant for Munson based on the evidence we have and I think I can get a court order to do an official DNA on him. When we have that legitimate DNA in our hands, I will officially announce that we have a new suspect in custody and that Doug Hart is completely innocent."

"Thank God, said Denise."

"When do you plan to make the arrest, Mel?" asked Brad.

"We will arrest him as soon as we can locate him."

"I believe you will find him working at the new Min Kao University of Tennessee Engineering Building right off Cumberland," said Ace.

"It looks like that you have done all the legwork for us, Ace."

"My daughter, Lisa did all of that, Mel."

"Well give her my thanks. I will request that the Knoxville Police Department apprehend Munson as soon as we get the arrest warrant. I expect it will happen before this weekend. I will keep all of you in the loop."

"Thanks, Mel," said Brad.

Denise was so excited that she tried to call Doug on his cell phone but he evidently had it turned off; she could hardly wait to tell him.

Munson was arrested Thursday afternoon and taken to the police station where he was fingerprinted and had a DNA sample taken from him.

Chapter 109

Saturday Sept, 10

Ace was at home Saturday and he had gotten up early to see what the newspaper had to say about the arrest of Buford Munson for the rape of Kristin Smith. He read the article:

**NEW ARREST IN THE RAPE
OF KRISTIN SMITH
BY CONSOLIDATED PRESS
Knoxville, Tennessee**

The Knox County Attorney General, Mel Crosby late yesterday announced that a new suspect had been arrested in the rape of Kristin Smith that occurred on January, 14 of this year. Arrested was twenty eight year old Buford Munson from Cocke County, Tennessee, a small town about forty miles Southeast of Knoxville. He had been working as an Electrician Helper on the new "Min Kao Engineering Building" on the University of Tennessee campus in Knoxville for the past year where Kristin Smith passed each day as she walked home to her apartment.

The Attorney General said that he would like to sincerely apologize to the initial suspect, Doug Hart, an engineering student at the University of Tennessee. He said that Doug is innocent of any wrongdoing whatsoever and that he was sorry for all of the problems

that Doug and his wife, Denise must have been going through for the past several months; "It must have been a nightmare," he stated. "We understand that Kristin Smith and her roommate Julie Brown have both apologized to Doug and Denise."

No date has been set for the trial but we understand that Munson's lawyer is trying to plea bargain. The AG is amenable to this because he does not want to put Kristin Smith through another trial. He knows that she and her roommate, Julie Brown's testimony would not be worth a plug nickel in another trial since they both have already incorrectly identified two innocent men as the rapist in the first trial.

After reading the article, Ace noticed that when the Writer referred to Doug, he did not use the term, 'Former Marine' as he did eight months ago when he evidently assumed that Doug was guilty.

Chapter 110

Monday Sept, 12

Brad, Ace, and Denise were drinking coffee and eating their traditional doughnuts in the small conference room and discussing the recent events leading up to the arrest of a new suspect and the exoneration of Doug Hart in the rape of Kristin Smith.

"Brad, Doug and I cannot begin to express our gratitude for all the effort and expense that you and Ace have incurred for us during the last eight months," said Denise.

"You can thank Ace for finding the real culprit, Denise; if he had not been arrested and charged we would still be hanging in limbo not knowing what to do next," replied Brad.

"I will have to give Paula the credit for pointing Buford Munson out to me, Brad; I might never have spotted him at Boomsday if not for her. And I don't want to overlook all the computer work that our daughter Lisa did in locating Munson," said Ace.

"You are right, Ace; this has been about teamwork from the outset. We have to thank everyone involved and that includes you, Paula, along with Lisa, Benny Goldberg, Doug, and Denise."

"I wonder who is the most relieved with the outcome of this case besides Doug and myself," said Denise.

"Besides you two; I would think that Kristin and her roommate would be grateful that the real rapist has been found and will never be able to molest them or anyone else again," replied Brad.

"Let's don't forget Judge Albert Prince," spoke up Ace; "a heavy load has been lifted from his shoulders, because he probably didn't have a clue of how to dispose of this case."

"I think that it has been a win-win situation for everyone involved with the exception for Buford Munson." Said Brad; what we need to do now is to start mending some fences."

"How do you intend to go about doing that, Brad?" asked Ace.

"I think we need to get everyone together and get to know one another a little better. I would like to get everyone together involved with this case and escort them to the Tennessee-Georgia football game on October 8 at Neyland Stadium. We will probably need two stretch limos to handle all of them. We need to limit the number to twenty four because that's all my Skybox will seat. After the game the limos will pick us up and drop us off at the Crown Plaza Hotel on Summit Hill Drive where we will dine and celebrate.

Let's decide right now exactly who we are going to invite so that Denise can call everyone and make the Crown Plaza reservations. Who wants to start with the list of names?"

"In addition to Paula and me, I would like to see Lisa and her boy friend, Sean. Along with Benny Goldberg on the list," said Ace.

"That's five," said Brad; "I would like to add Kristin, her mother and father along with her roommate, Julie, in addition to my wife, Elizabeth and me."

"The count is now up to eleven said, Denise. "If I could, I would like to add my mother and father along with Doug's Mother in addition to Doug and me."

"We now have sixteen on our list," said Brad; "I will call Mel Crosby, the AG and his assistant, Jim Satterfield to see if they want to come."

"The count is now eighteen," said Ace jokingly; "do you want to invite the judge?"

"I think I'll hold off on that right now, but since we still have six slots left I am going to invite my son David and his wife Jennifer."

"We still have four slots left," said Ace. "Do you mind if I invite Rose Golden from Nashville; she's the one who put me on to Benny Goldberg?"

"Not at all, Ace; we might just as well fill up my skybox so I am going to invite my good friend, Alex Parker, his wife Brittany, and his daughter, Trisha; two dozen is a good round number."

"I will contact everyone we have listed and get them confirmed and I will also make the necessary reservations at the Crown Plaza," said Denise.

"As soon as you get everything in order, Denise, arrange to have two stretch Limos pick us up here at twelve noon on October the eighth," said Brad. Inform them that we will need to rent the two limos for the rest of the day until midnight or later.

That's all I have for now; are there any questions? If not I would like to make a comment; we do not have a perfect legal system in this country, but I believe it is the best one in the world. We sometimes feel that the criminals have more rights than the victims in this country but I was sitting on the other side of the fence in this case and I am glad that most of these safeguards are in place. We still have to give all those persons charged with crimes the presumption of innocence until they have had their day in court. I will no longer assume that a person is guilty just because the Attorney General has charged that person with a crime."

"Well spoken, Brad," said Ace. "Alls well that ends well."

"Who said that?" asked Paula.

"I just did, Paula, Didn't you hear me?"

"You know what I mean, Ace. I've heard that saying before but I never knew who originally said it."

"I don't know if anyone ever said it; it was the title of a Shakespeare play in the early part of the seventeenth century." replied Ace. "In fact, it was just right around 400 years ago."

'Did you know that back in the early years of acting and in Shakespeare's time that, actors and actresses were not very well thought of," asked Paula.

"And just what is your point, Paula," asked Ace.

Paula thought for a minute and replied: "I guess that I don't have one."

"What goes around comes around," said Ace.

Chapter 111

Friday Oct, 7

Lisa got home from Vanderbilt around seven p.m. and Ace was sitting in the den watching 'Wheel of Fortune' when she walked in.

"Where's Mom, Ace?"

"She's cleaning up the kitchen. Are you and Sean ready for the Big UT football game with Georgia tomorrow?"

"We're really looking forward to it."

"How's school?"

"I made a perfect score on my Psychology test this week."

"I remember when I was at UT and I took a psychology course as an elective, Lisa. I had an hour to kill before the final exam so I sat on the curb in front of Ayres Hall and studied from my text book that entire hour. When I went in to take the test I found a question on it that I had just read in my text book. A few days later I got my final paper back and the instructor had counted my answer wrong that I got from the text book. I took my test paper along with my text book to show him so that he could amend my grade and do you know what he told me?"

"I have no idea, Ace."

"He told me that the answer had been changed and my answer was wrong. I asked him just how I was supposed to know that and how could it have been right when the book was published and is wrong now. He had no answer for me but he didn't change my grade. I decided right then I would never again take a course in any other inexact science that had 'ology' tacked on to the end of its name. I like the courses such as math and Physics where two and two is four, F = MA (Force equals Mass times Acceleration) and always will."

"My poor, poor, Ace; did you pass the course?" asked Lisa.

"Yes, but I got a 'C' when I was expecting an 'A'."

"Books are not always right, Ace, after all they are written by humans."

"How right you are, Lisa; did I ever tell you about a man who went by the name of 'By the Book, Bob'?"

"No; tell me about him."

"He didn't believe anything that wasn't written down in a book and believed everything that was written down in one. He didn't believe that a meeting was a real meeting unless it was conducted under 'Robert's Rules of Order.'

He believed that he could become an expert on any subject if he just read all the right books on that subject. He decided one day that he would become an expert in the game of golf. He practically wore out his library card by checking out all the golf books and CD's that he could get his hands on. He did this exclusively for over a year. He knew all the professional golfers and their records. If you gave him the year, he could tell you who won each of the four major golf tournaments, (The Masters, The US open, The PGA, and The British Open) for that year. He even knew of one golf record that would never be broken and who held that record."

"That doesn't seem possible, Ace, surely someone will eventually come along and break that record."

"Not this one, Lisa. Tom Kite holds this record for being the first PGA player to win a million dollars in total tournament winnings."

"What happened to 'By the Book, Bob', as you call him, Ace?"

"He kept at it; he studied how to put backspin and topspin on the golf ball and how to hit the ball to make it hook or slice. He even calculated the ground speed of the golf ball when hit into a headwind or a tail wind. He knew that if he hit a golf ball at a hundred and fifty miles per hour into a headwind of fifty miles per hour, that the ball would only have a ground speed of 100 miles per hour so he knew that the longer the golf ball was in the air the more distance he would lose on his drives. He knew that it was better to hit his drive as low to the ground as possible so that it wouldn't slow down as much.

He learned how to read the greens and researched all the different equipment and the different brands golf balls; he knew which items were the best. He looked at CD's of all the best golfers and studied their golf swings, their stances, backswings, and follow-throughs; even their putting and their sand trap and, 'out of the rough', play. After studying for over a year and spending around $5,000 dollars for equipment, including $3,000 for a set of TaylorMade golf clubs, $200 for a putter, and $300 for a pair of Footjoy golf shoes, he felt that he knew more about golf than anyone in the world. He worshiped books; they were his God."

"What ever happened to him, Ace?"

"He decided that it would be a good idea to play a practice round before he turned Pro."

"How did the Practice round turn out?"

"He shot one hundred and fifty six; he found that you cannot always go by the book."

"Paula's Right, Ace; you are full of it."

"Did you hear about the Golfer, Brian Davis, recently calling a penalty on himself when he accidentally brushed a leaf on his backswing in a hazard, which was against the rules? The club is not allowed to make contact with anything in a hazard before the club hits the ball."

"Did anyone see him hit the blade of grass?"

"No; no one saw him so everyone was praising him for his honesty for reporting it and incurring a two stroke penalty which may have caused him to lose the tournament. The same thing happened to Bobby Jones, a great golfer in the twenties and the thirties. He was also praised for reporting a similar penalty on himself. He was a great golfer who believed in playing by the rules absolutely. When praise was heaped upon for reporting the penalty, he replied: "You might just as well praise me for not robbing a bank.""

"You should be so honest, Ace." said Lisa.

"I'm as honest as the days are long."

"I've noticed that the days are beginning to get shorter, Ace."

"I've said it before; "you sure know how to hurt a guy, Lisa"

"I had a good teacher, Ace."

"Touché, Lisa."

Ace's home phone rang as soon as Lisa left the den; he noticed that the call was from the Law Office of Ralph Knell in Nashville. Ace answered:

"Knoxville Crematorium where we treat your ash with respect."

"Don't you get cute with me, Ace Sleuth; you're in a heap of trouble.

"What can I do for You, Rusty?"

"You're in big trouble, Ace, for impersonating an IRS agent, which is a federal offense."

"How did you find out it was me, Rusty."

"That's neither here nor there, Ace, but suffice it to say; you are not the only private investigator in Tennessee. You may have stopped one lawsuit, but there is a much bigger one coming down the road and you are going to be on the wrong end of it. You are facing two major problems. First I have instigated a $5,000,000 lawsuit against Brad Adam's law firm and I am going to report you to the IRS as soon as they open Monday in Memphis. You will probably be doing some jail time for that caper."

"I have just one question, Rusty."

"What question is that, Ace?"

"Is Megan McGuire onboard with this?"

All of a sudden the phone line went dead.

"Shakespeare was right, thought Ace; *"Alls well that ends well"*

Epilogue

All of the two dozen people enjoyed the football game from Brad's Sky Box and the delicious dinner at The Crowne Plaza afterward.

The football game get-together went a long way toward healing some of the wounds and hurt associated with the crime and the trial. Brad and Mel Crosby were back to their pre-trial friendship and Doug and Denise had a good report with Kristin and her roommate, Julie. Doug held no animosity toward either of the two; he realized that it was just an act of fate and could have happened to anyone.

Buford Munson pled guilty to the rape of Kristin Smith and received a twenty year sentence and will be eligible for parole in ten years. Based on the severity of the crime it is doubtful if he gets out of prison before the twenty years is up and Brad is determined to all he can to keep him locked up.

9 781456 079055